THE REALM

IMAGE COMICS, INC.

ROBERT KIRKMAN — CHIEF OPERATING OFFICER
ERIK LARSEN — CHIEF FINANCIAL OFFICER
TODD MCFARLANE — PRESIDENT
MARC SILVESTRI — CHIEF EXECUTIVE OFFICER
JIM VALENTINO — VICE PRESIDENT

ERIC STEPHENSON — PUBLISHER / CHIEF CREATIVE OFFICER
COREY HART — DIRECTOR OF SALES
JEFF BOISON — DIRECTOR OF PUBLISHING PLANNING
& BOOK TRADE SALES
CHRIS ROSS — DIRECTOR OF DIGITAL SALES
JEFF STANG — DIRECTOR OF SPECIALTY SALES
KAT SALAZAR — DIRECTOR OF PR & MARKETING
DREW GILL — ART DIRECTOR
HEATHER DOORNINK — PRODUCTION DIRECTOR
NICOLE LAPALME — CONTROLLER

IMAGECOMICS.COM

THE REALM, VOL. 2
ISBN: 978-1-5343-0865-7
First Printing. November 2018.

For information regarding the CPSIA on this printed material call: 203-595-3636 and provide reference #RICH–820361.

For international rights, contact: foreignlicensing@imagecomics.com

VOLUME 2

CREATED BY
JEREMY HAUN & SETH M. PECK

COLORS
NICK FILARDI

LETTERING & DESIGN
THOMAS MAUER

EDITOR
JOEL ENOS

PRODUCTION ARTIST
ERIKA SCHNATZ

COVER
JEREMY HAUN
NICK FILARDI

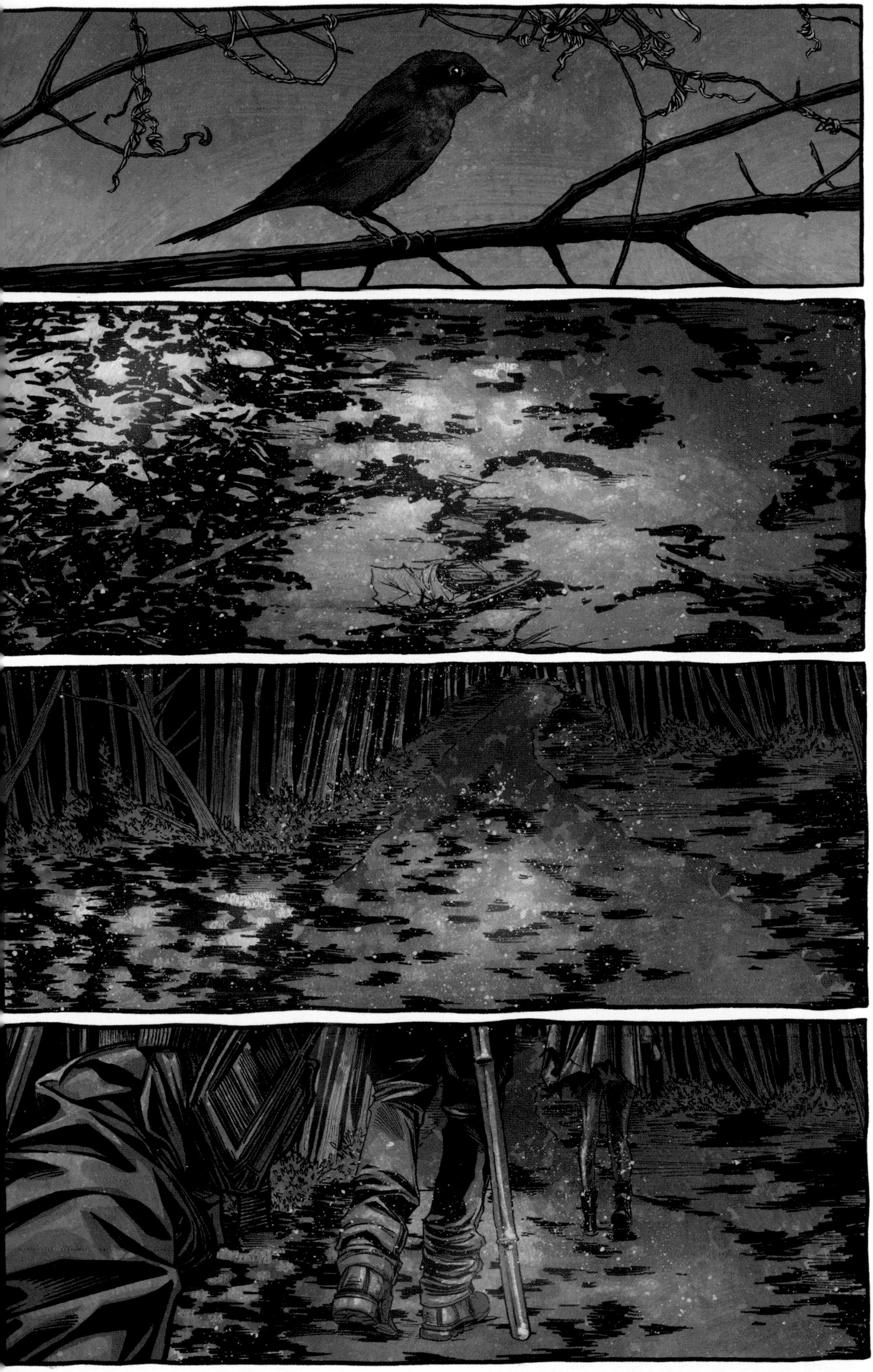

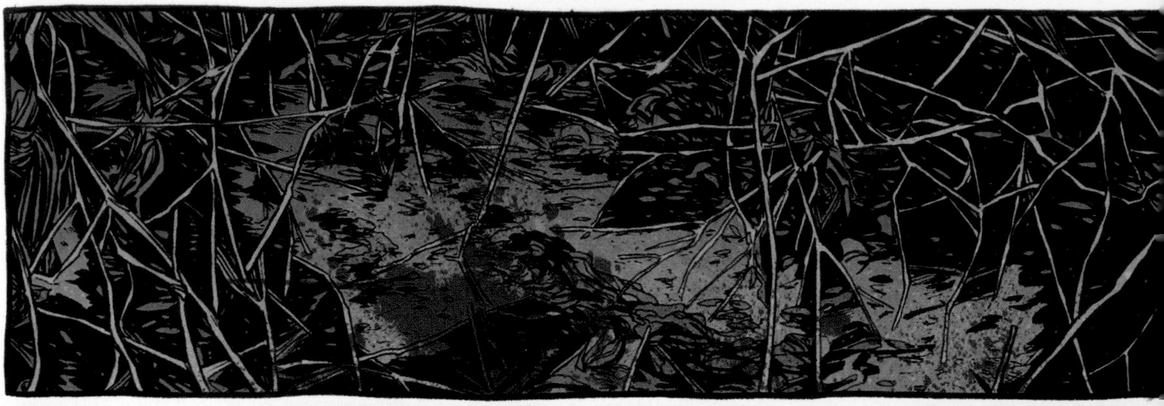

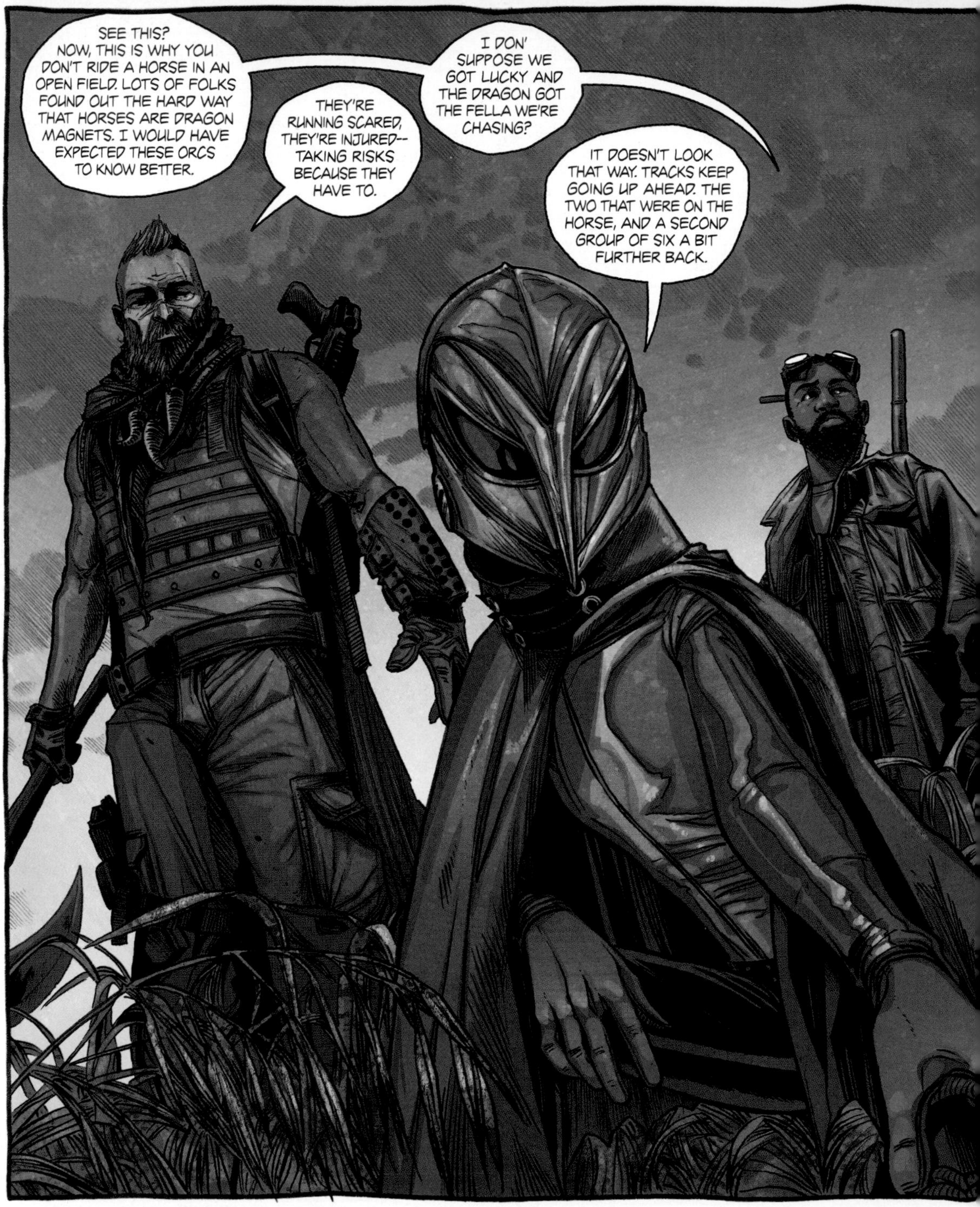
SEE THIS? NOW, THIS IS WHY YOU DON'T RIDE A HORSE IN AN OPEN FIELD. LOTS OF FOLKS FOUND OUT THE HARD WAY THAT HORSES ARE DRAGON MAGNETS. I WOULD HAVE EXPECTED THESE ORCS TO KNOW BETTER.
THEY'RE RUNNING SCARED, THEY'RE INJURED-- TAKING RISKS BECAUSE THEY HAVE TO.
I DON' SUPPOSE WE GOT LUCKY AND THE DRAGON GOT THE FELLA WE'RE CHASING?
IT DOESN'T LOOK THAT WAY. TRACKS KEEP GOING UP AHEAD. THE TWO THAT WERE ON THE HORSE, AND A SECOND GROUP OF SIX A BIT FURTHER BACK.

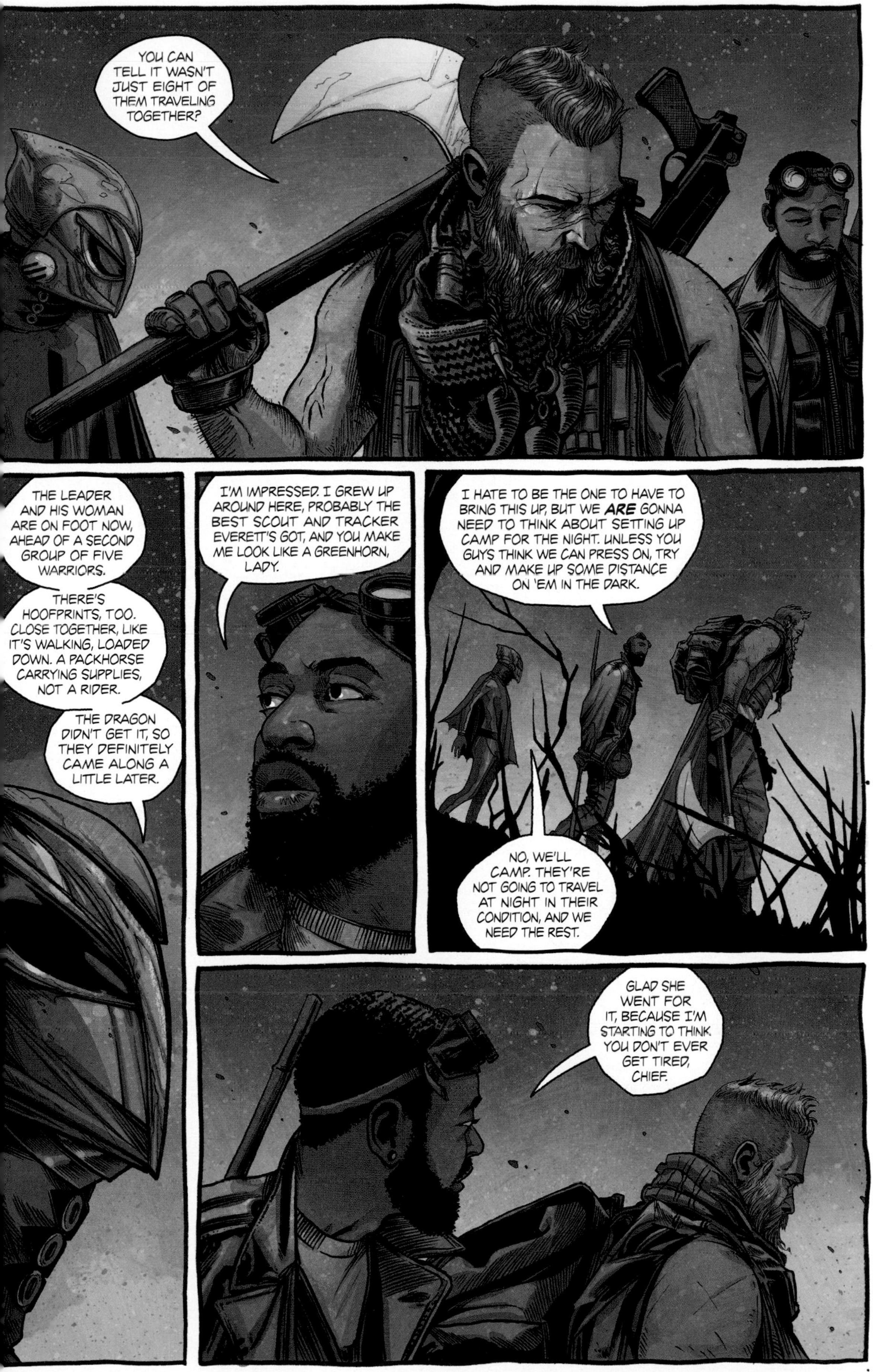
YOU CAN TELL IT WASN'T JUST EIGHT OF THEM TRAVELING TOGETHER?
THE LEADER AND HIS WOMAN ARE ON FOOT NOW, AHEAD OF A SECOND GROUP OF FIVE WARRIORS.
THERE'S HOOFPRINTS, TOO. CLOSE TOGETHER, LIKE IT'S WALKING, LOADED DOWN. A PACKHORSE CARRYING SUPPLIES, NOT A RIDER.
THE DRAGON DIDN'T GET IT, SO THEY DEFINITELY CAME ALONG A LITTLE LATER.
I'M IMPRESSED. I GREW UP AROUND HERE, PROBABLY THE BEST SCOUT AND TRACKER EVERETT'S GOT, AND YOU MAKE ME LOOK LIKE A GREENHORN, LADY.
I HATE TO BE THE ONE TO HAVE TO BRING THIS UP, BUT WE **ARE** GONNA NEED TO THINK ABOUT SETTING UP CAMP FOR THE NIGHT. UNLESS YOU GUYS THINK WE CAN PRESS ON, TRY AND MAKE UP SOME DISTANCE ON 'EM IN THE DARK.
NO, WE'LL CAMP. THEY'RE NOT GOING TO TRAVEL AT NIGHT IN THEIR CONDITION, AND WE NEED THE REST.
GLAD SHE WENT FOR IT, BECAUSE I'M STARTING TO THINK YOU DON'T EVER GET TIRED, CHIEF.

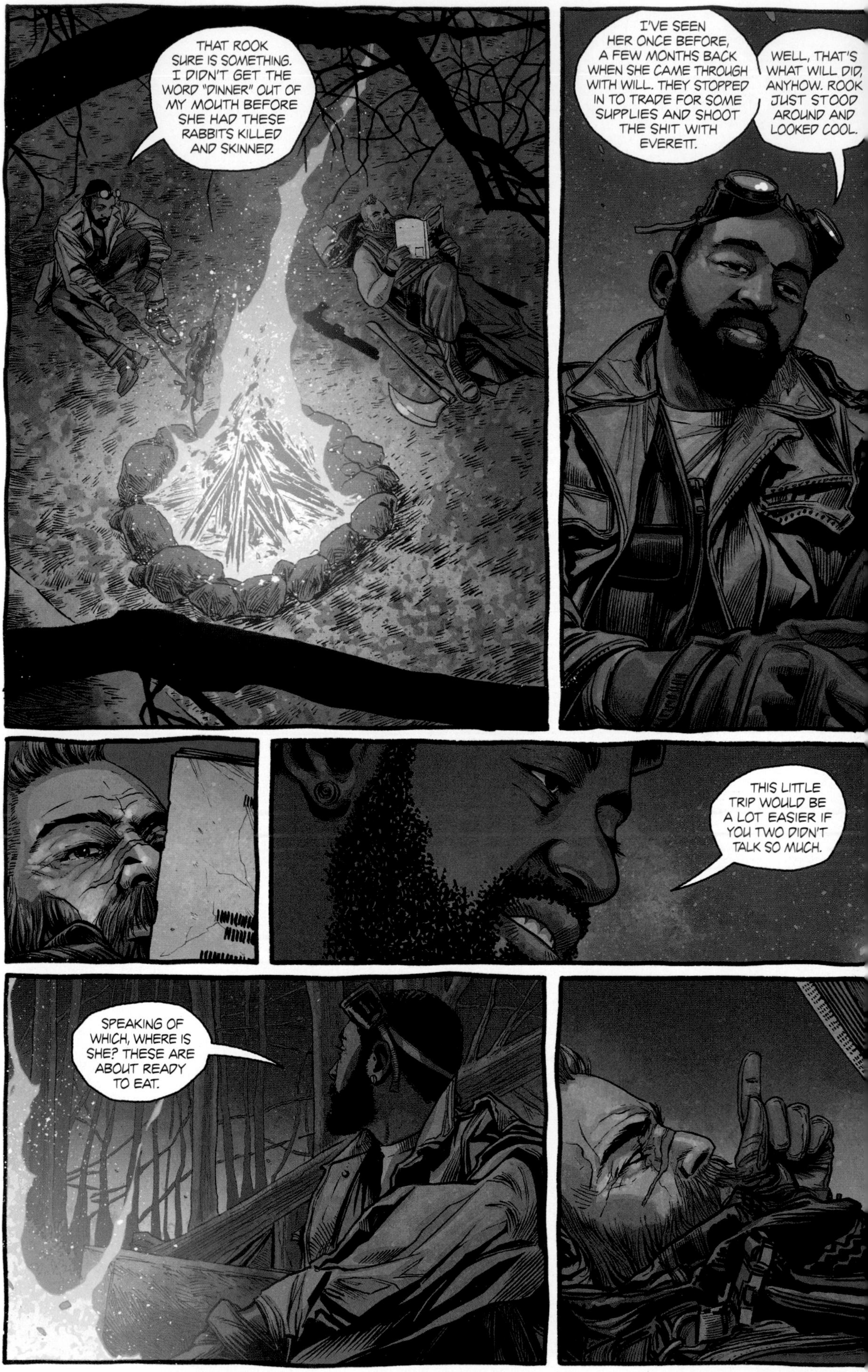
THAT ROOK SURE IS SOMETHING. I DIDN'T GET THE WORD "DINNER" OUT OF MY MOUTH BEFORE SHE HAD THESE RABBITS KILLED AND SKINNED.
I'VE SEEN HER ONCE BEFORE, A FEW MONTHS BACK WHEN SHE CAME THROUGH WITH WILL. THEY STOPPED IN TO TRADE FOR SOME SUPPLIES AND SHOOT THE SHIT WITH EVERETT.
WELL, THAT'S WHAT WILL DID, ANYHOW. ROOK JUST STOOD AROUND AND LOOKED COOL.
THIS LITTLE TRIP WOULD BE A LOT EASIER IF YOU TWO DIDN'T TALK SO MUCH.
SPEAKING OF WHICH, WHERE IS SHE? THESE ARE ABOUT READY TO EAT.

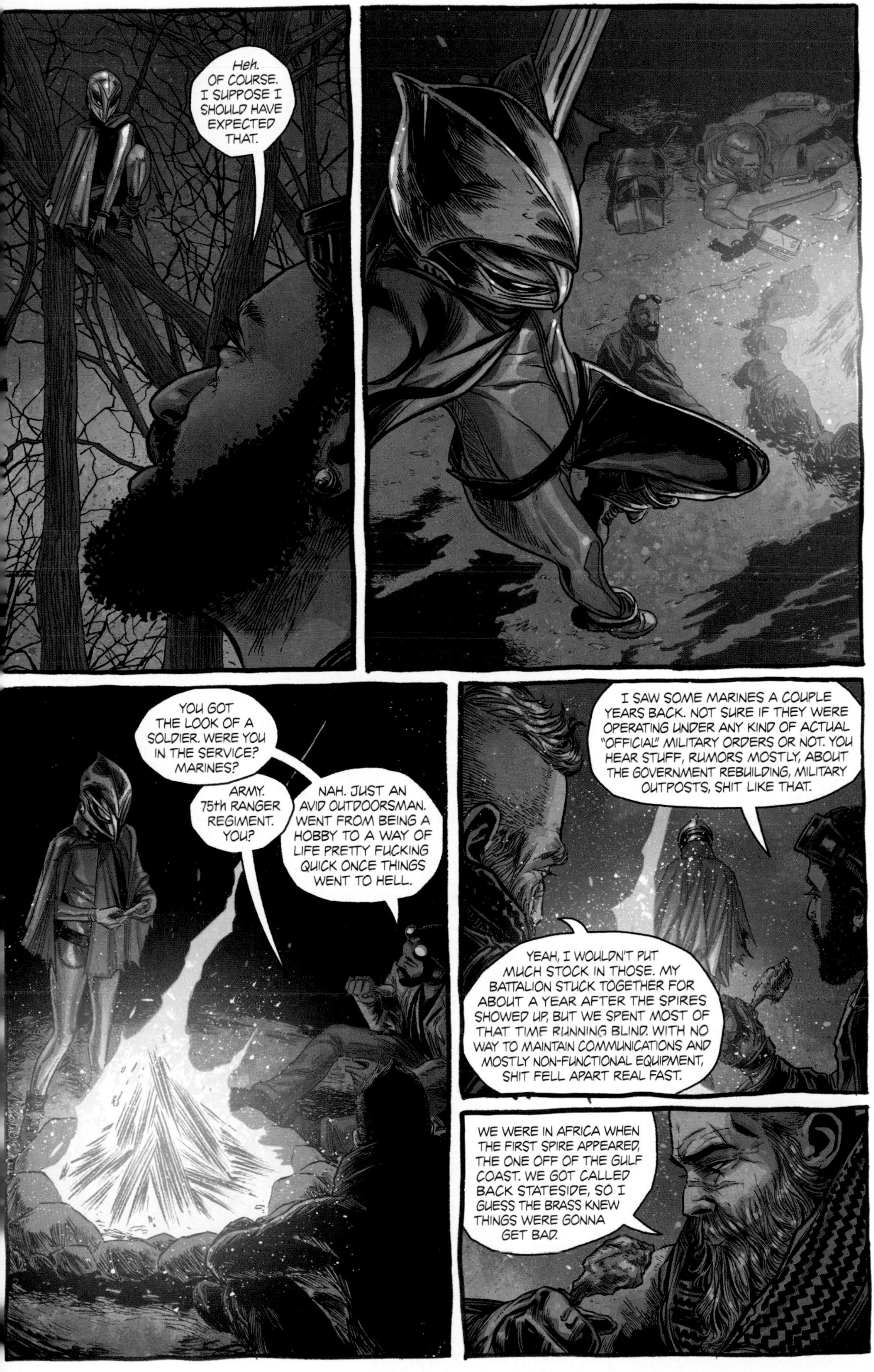

Heh. OF COURSE. I SUPPOSE I SHOULD HAVE EXPECTED THAT.
YOU GOT THE LOOK OF A SOLDIER. WERE YOU IN THE SERVICE? MARINES?
ARMY. 75th RANGER REGIMENT. YOU?
NAH. JUST AN AVID OUTDOORSMAN. WENT FROM BEING A HOBBY TO A WAY OF LIFE PRETTY FUCKING QUICK ONCE THINGS WENT TO HELL.
I SAW SOME MARINES A COUPLE YEARS BACK. NOT SURE IF THEY WERE OPERATING UNDER ANY KIND OF ACTUAL "OFFICIAL" MILITARY ORDERS OR NOT. YOU HEAR STUFF, RUMORS MOSTLY, ABOUT THE GOVERNMENT REBUILDING, MILITARY OUTPOSTS, SHIT LIKE THAT.
YEAH, I WOULDN'T PUT MUCH STOCK IN THOSE. MY BATTALION STUCK TOGETHER FOR ABOUT A YEAR AFTER THE SPIRES SHOWED UP, BUT WE SPENT MOST OF THAT TIME RUNNING BLIND. WITH NO WAY TO MAINTAIN COMMUNICATIONS AND MOSTLY NON-FUNCTIONAL EQUIPMENT, SHIT FELL APART REAL FAST.
WE WERE IN AFRICA WHEN THE FIRST SPIRE APPEARED, THE ONE OFF OF THE GULF COAST. WE GOT CALLED BACK STATESIDE, SO I GUESS THE BRASS KNEW THINGS WERE GONNA GET BAD.

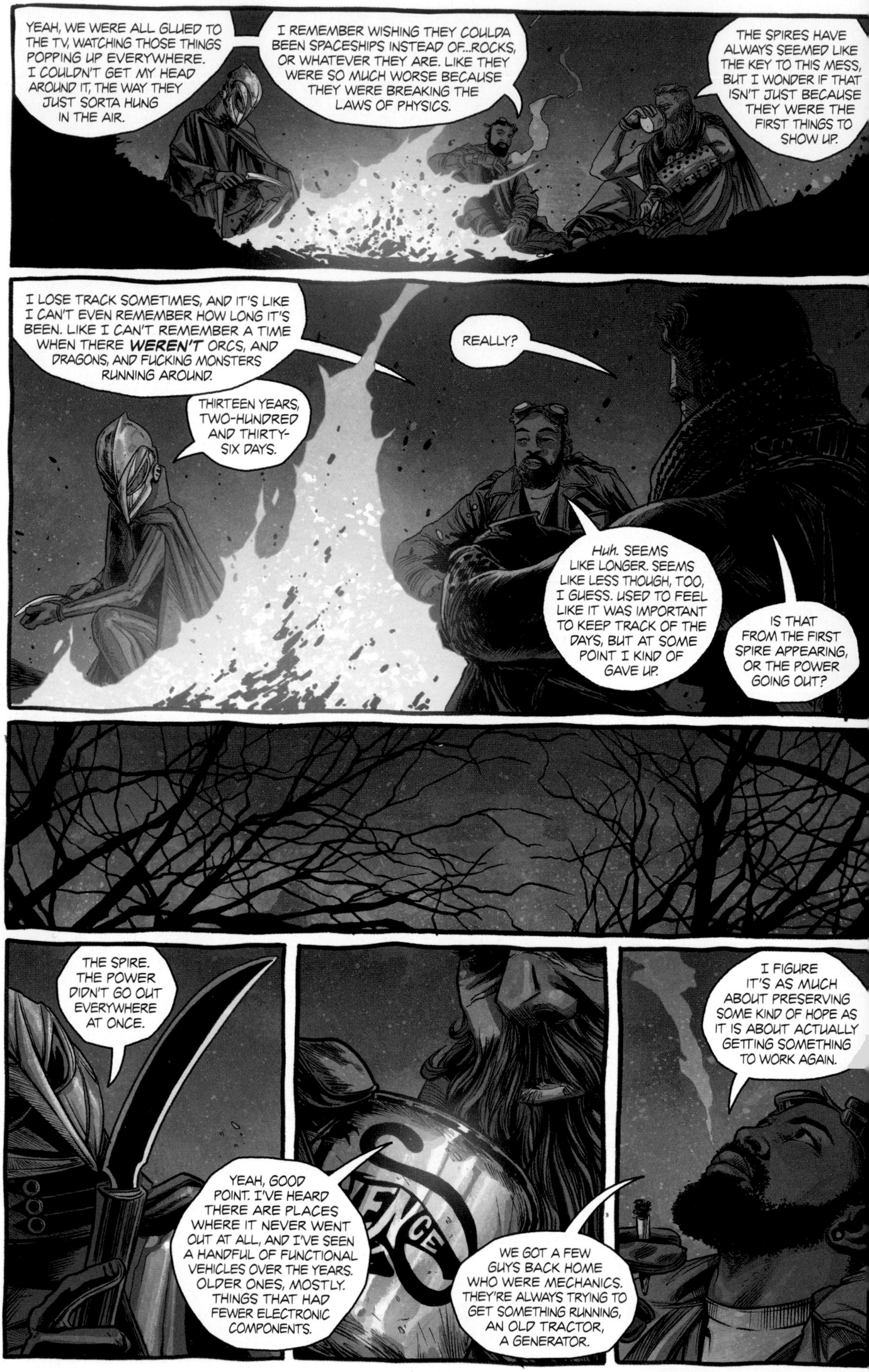
YEAH, WE WERE ALL GLUED TO THE TV, WATCHING THOSE THINGS POPPING UP EVERYWHERE. I COULDN'T GET MY HEAD AROUND IT, THE WAY THEY JUST SORTA HUNG IN THE AIR.
I REMEMBER WISHING THEY COULDA BEEN SPACESHIPS INSTEAD OF...ROCKS, OR WHATEVER THEY ARE. LIKE THEY WERE SO MUCH WORSE BECAUSE THEY WERE BREAKING THE LAWS OF PHYSICS.
THE SPIRES HAVE ALWAYS SEEMED LIKE THE KEY TO THIS MESS, BUT I WONDER IF THAT ISN'T JUST BECAUSE THEY WERE THE FIRST THINGS TO SHOW UP.
I LOSE TRACK SOMETIMES, AND IT'S LIKE I CAN'T EVEN REMEMBER HOW LONG IT'S BEEN. LIKE I CAN'T REMEMBER A TIME WHEN THERE ***WEREN'T*** ORCS, AND DRAGONS, AND FUCKING MONSTERS RUNNING AROUND.
REALLY?
THIRTEEN YEARS, TWO-HUNDRED AND THIRTY-SIX DAYS.
Huh. SEEMS LIKE LONGER. SEEMS LIKE LESS THOUGH, TOO, I GUESS. USED TO FEEL LIKE IT WAS IMPORTANT TO KEEP TRACK OF THE DAYS, BUT AT SOME POINT I KIND OF GAVE UP.
IS THAT FROM THE FIRST SPIRE APPEARING, OR THE POWER GOING OUT?
THE SPIRE. THE POWER DIDN'T GO OUT EVERYWHERE AT ONCE.
YEAH, GOOD POINT. I'VE HEARD THERE ARE PLACES WHERE IT NEVER WENT OUT AT ALL, AND I'VE SEEN A HANDFUL OF FUNCTIONAL VEHICLES OVER THE YEARS. OLDER ONES, MOSTLY. THINGS THAT HAD FEWER ELECTRONIC COMPONENTS.
WE GOT A FEW GUYS BACK HOME WHO WERE MECHANICS. THEY'RE ALWAYS TRYING TO GET SOMETHING RUNNING, AN OLD TRACTOR, A GENERATOR.
I FIGURE IT'S AS MUCH ABOUT PRESERVING SOME KIND OF HOPE AS IT IS ABOUT ACTUALLY GETTING SOMETHING TO WORK AGAIN.

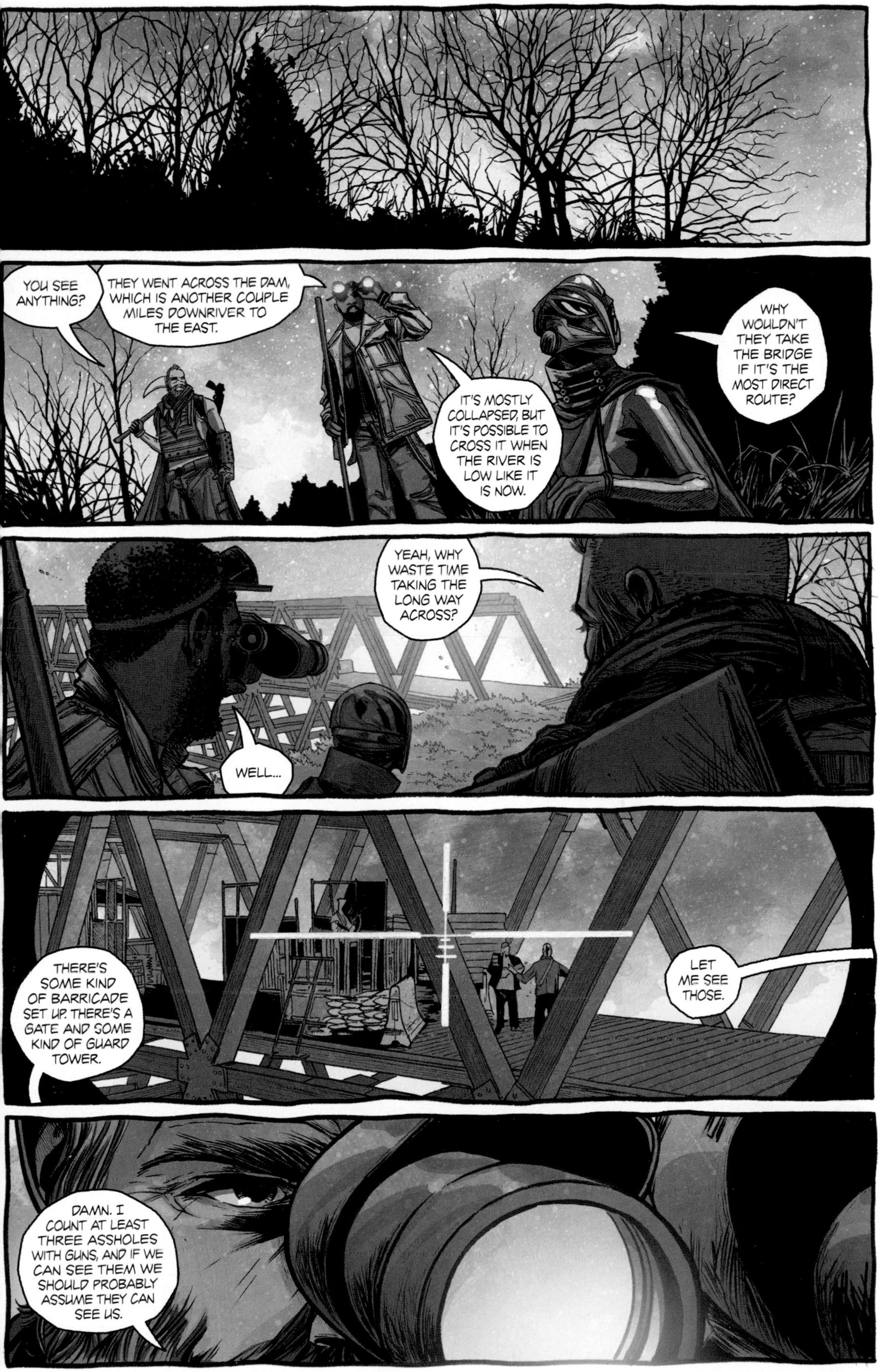
YOU SEE ANYTHING?
THEY WENT ACROSS THE DAM, WHICH IS ANOTHER COUPLE MILES DOWNRIVER TO THE EAST.
WHY WOULDN'T THEY TAKE THE BRIDGE IF IT'S THE MOST DIRECT ROUTE?
IT'S MOSTLY COLLAPSED, BUT IT'S POSSIBLE TO CROSS IT WHEN THE RIVER IS LOW LIKE IT IS NOW.
YEAH, WHY WASTE TIME TAKING THE LONG WAY ACROSS?
WELL...
THERE'S SOME KIND OF BARRICADE SET UP. THERE'S A GATE AND SOME KIND OF GUARD TOWER.
LET ME SEE THOSE.
DAMN. I COUNT AT LEAST THREE ASSHOLES WITH GUNS, AND IF WE CAN SEE THEM WE SHOULD PROBABLY ASSUME THEY CAN SEE US.

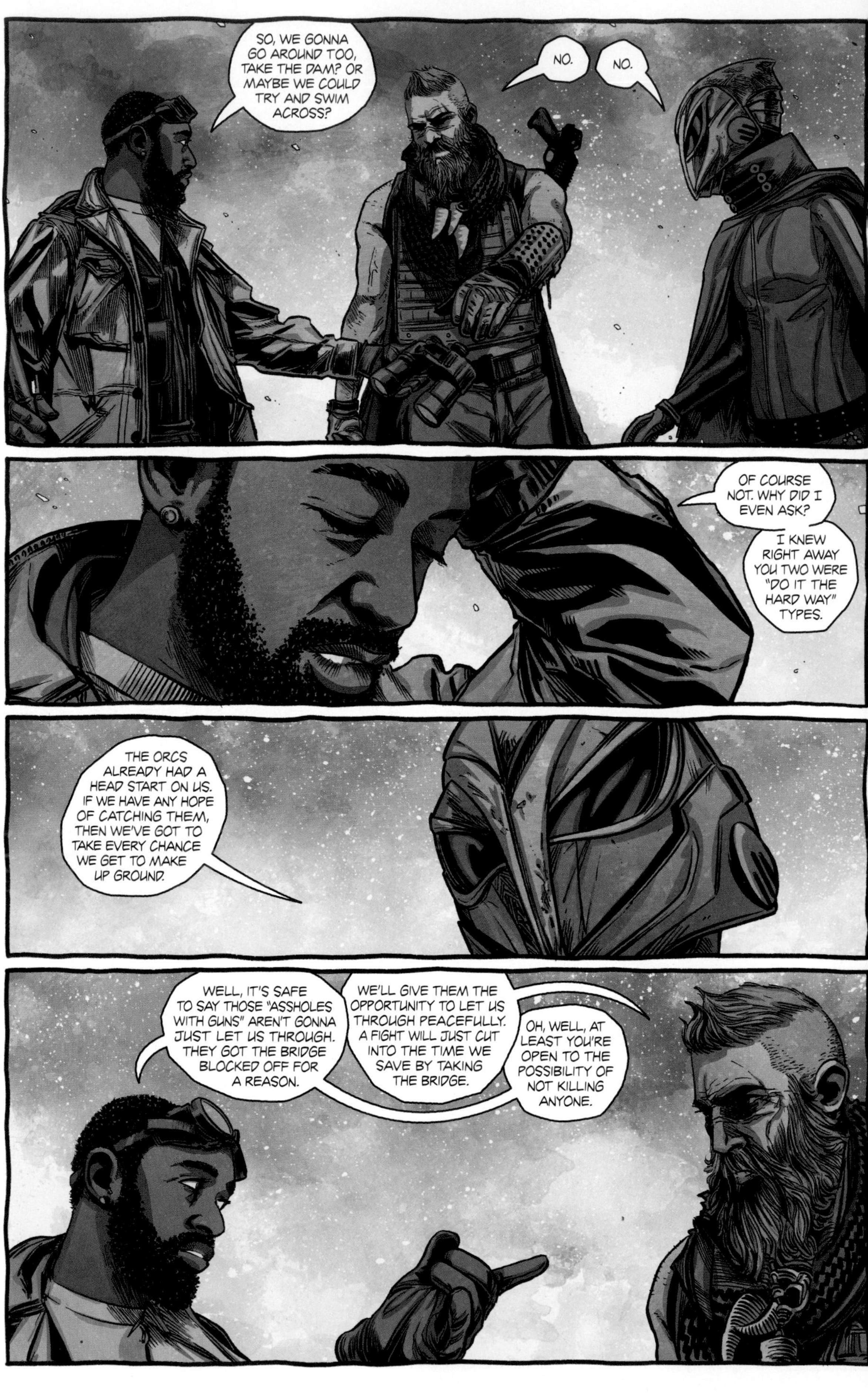
SO, WE GONNA GO AROUND TOO, TAKE THE DAM? OR MAYBE WE COULD TRY AND SWIM ACROSS?
NO.
NO.
OF COURSE NOT. WHY DID I EVEN ASK?
I KNEW RIGHT AWAY YOU TWO WERE "DO IT THE HARD WAY" TYPES.
THE ORCS ALREADY HAD A HEAD START ON US. IF WE HAVE ANY HOPE OF CATCHING THEM, THEN WE'VE GOT TO TAKE EVERY CHANCE WE GET TO MAKE UP GROUND.
WELL, IT'S SAFE TO SAY THOSE "ASSHOLES WITH GUNS" AREN'T GONNA JUST LET US THROUGH. THEY GOT THE BRIDGE BLOCKED OFF FOR A REASON.
WE'LL GIVE THEM THE OPPORTUNITY TO LET US THROUGH PEACEFULLY. A FIGHT WILL JUST CUT INTO THE TIME WE SAVE BY TAKING THE BRIDGE.
OH, WELL, AT LEAST YOU'RE OPEN TO THE POSSIBILITY OF NOT KILLING ANYONE.

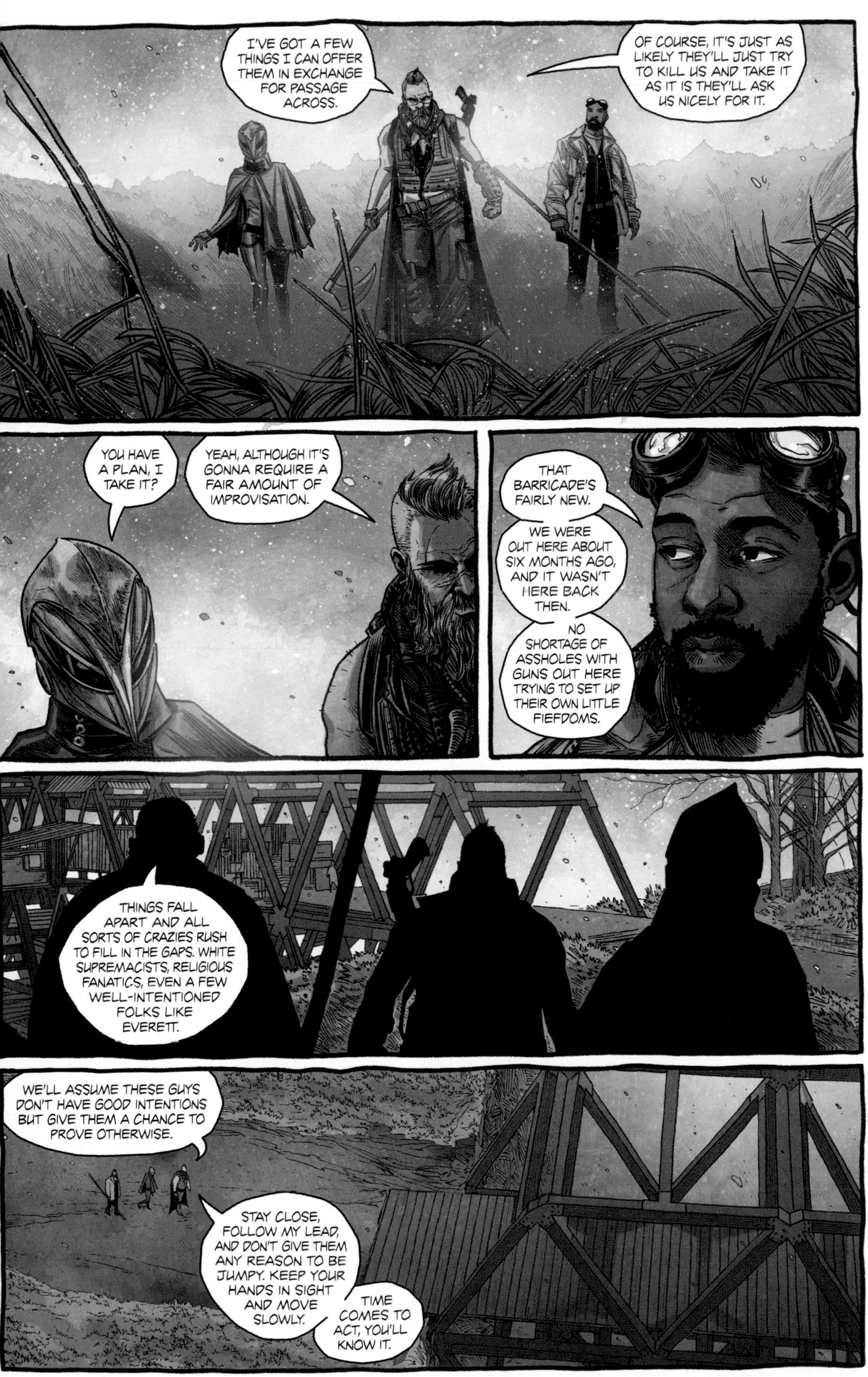
I'VE GOT A FEW THINGS I CAN OFFER THEM IN EXCHANGE FOR PASSAGE ACROSS.
OF COURSE, IT'S JUST AS LIKELY THEY'LL JUST TRY TO KILL US AND TAKE IT AS IT IS THEY'LL ASK US NICELY FOR IT.
YOU HAVE A PLAN, I TAKE IT?
YEAH, ALTHOUGH IT'S GONNA REQUIRE A FAIR AMOUNT OF IMPROVISATION.
THAT BARRICADE'S FAIRLY NEW.
WE WERE OUT HERE ABOUT SIX MONTHS AGO, AND IT WASN'T HERE BACK THEN.
NO SHORTAGE OF ASSHOLES WITH GUNS OUT HERE TRYING TO SET UP THEIR OWN LITTLE FIEFDOMS.
THINGS FALL APART AND ALL SORTS OF CRAZIES RUSH TO FILL IN THE GAPS. WHITE SUPREMACISTS, RELIGIOUS FANATICS, EVEN A FEW WELL-INTENTIONED FOLKS LIKE EVERETT.
WE'LL ASSUME THESE GUYS DON'T HAVE GOOD INTENTIONS BUT GIVE THEM A CHANCE TO PROVE OTHERWISE.
STAY CLOSE, FOLLOW MY LEAD, AND DON'T GIVE THEM ANY REASON TO BE JUMPY. KEEP YOUR HANDS IN SIGHT AND MOVE SLOWLY.
TIME COMES TO ACT, YOU'LL KNOW IT.

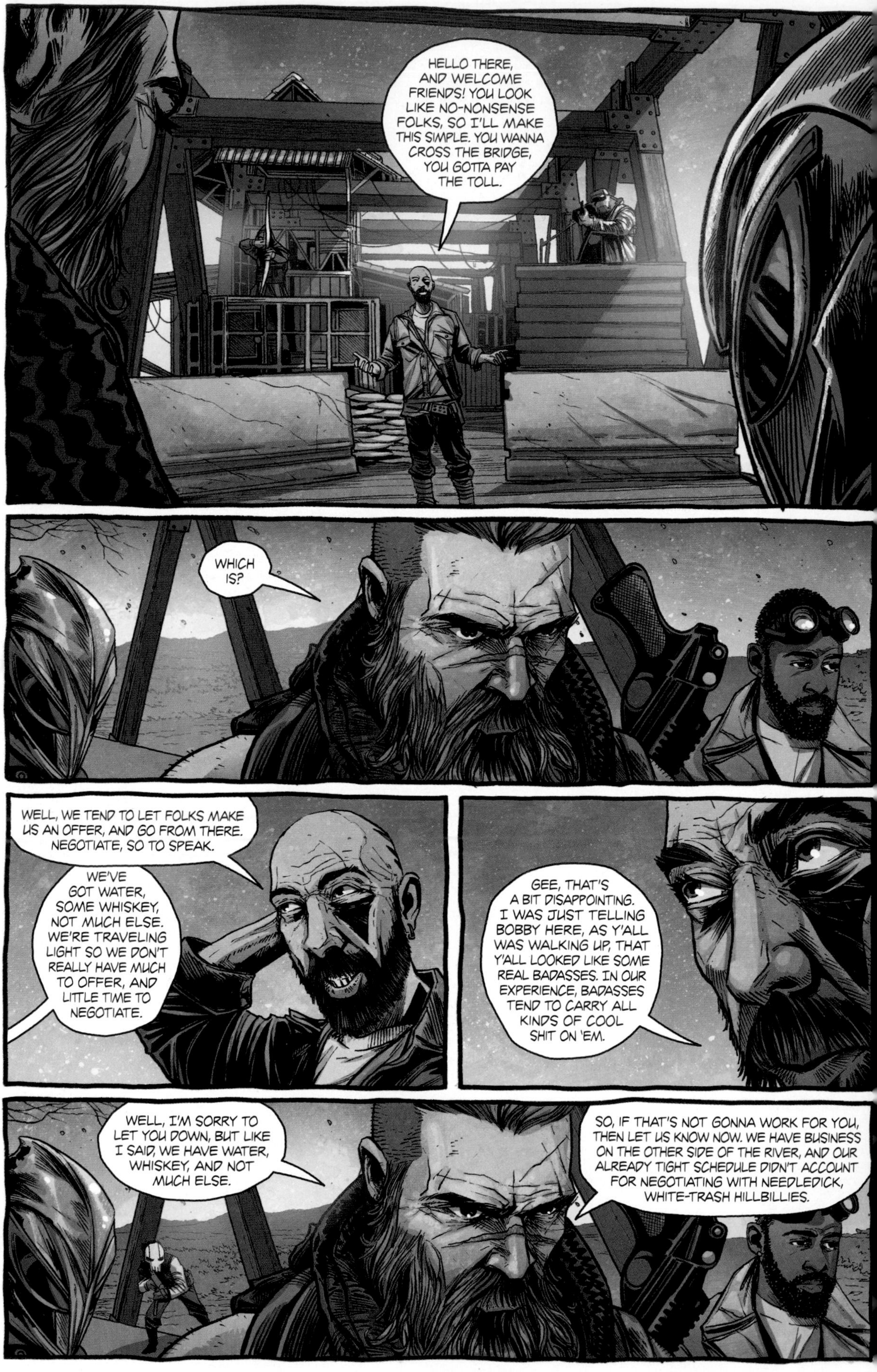
HELLO THERE, AND WELCOME FRIENDS! YOU LOOK LIKE NO-NONSENSE FOLKS, SO I'LL MAKE THIS SIMPLE. YOU WANNA CROSS THE BRIDGE, YOU GOTTA PAY THE TOLL.
WHICH IS?
WELL, WE TEND TO LET FOLKS MAKE US AN OFFER, AND GO FROM THERE. NEGOTIATE, SO TO SPEAK.
WE'VE GOT WATER, SOME WHISKEY, NOT MUCH ELSE. WE'RE TRAVELING LIGHT SO WE DON'T REALLY HAVE MUCH TO OFFER, AND LITTLE TIME TO NEGOTIATE.
GEE, THAT'S A BIT DISAPPOINTING. I WAS JUST TELLING BOBBY HERE, AS Y'ALL WAS WALKING UP, THAT Y'ALL LOOKED LIKE SOME REAL BADASSES. IN OUR EXPERIENCE, BADASSES TEND TO CARRY ALL KINDS OF COOL SHIT ON 'EM.
WELL, I'M SORRY TO LET YOU DOWN, BUT LIKE I SAID, WE HAVE WATER, WHISKEY, AND NOT MUCH ELSE.
SO, IF THAT'S NOT GONNA WORK FOR YOU, THEN LET US KNOW NOW. WE HAVE BUSINESS ON THE OTHER SIDE OF THE RIVER, AND OUR ALREADY TIGHT SCHEDULE DIDN'T ACCOUNT FOR NEGOTIATING WITH NEEDLEDICK, WHITE-TRASH HILLBILLIES.

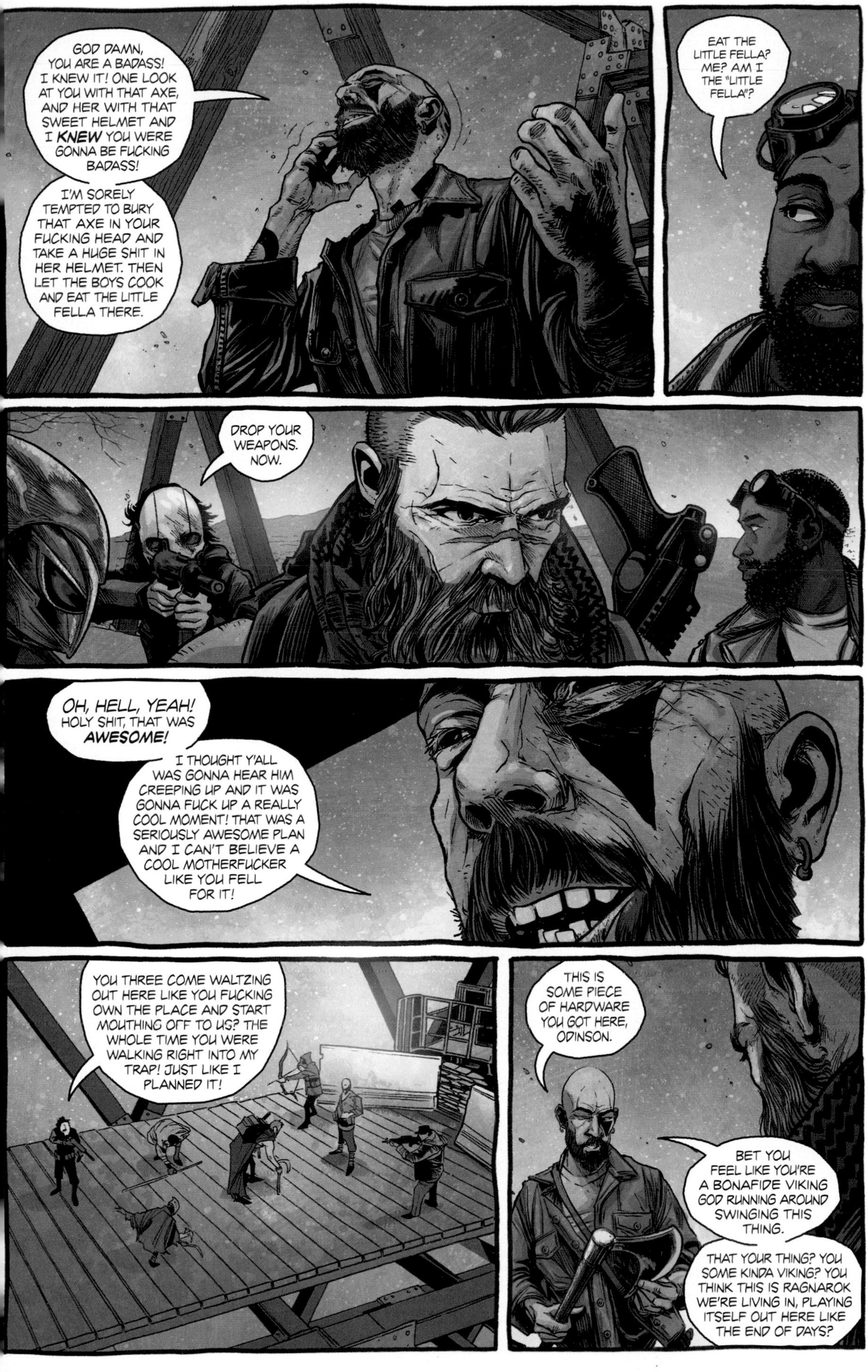
GOD DAMN, YOU ARE A BADASS! I KNEW IT! ONE LOOK AT YOU WITH THAT AXE, AND HER WITH THAT SWEET HELMET AND I KNEW YOU WERE GONNA BE FUCKING BADASS!
I'M SORELY TEMPTED TO BURY THAT AXE IN YOUR FUCKING HEAD AND TAKE A HUGE SHIT IN HER HELMET. THEN LET THE BOYS COOK AND EAT THE LITTLE FELLA THERE.
EAT THE LITTLE FELLA? ME? AM I THE "LITTLE FELLA"?
DROP YOUR WEAPONS. NOW.
OH, HELL, YEAH! HOLY SHIT, THAT WAS AWESOME!
I THOUGHT Y'ALL WAS GONNA HEAR HIM CREEPING UP AND IT WAS GONNA FUCK UP A REALLY COOL MOMENT! THAT WAS A SERIOUSLY AWESOME PLAN AND I CAN'T BELIEVE A COOL MOTHERFUCKER LIKE YOU FELL FOR IT!
YOU THREE COME WALTZING OUT HERE LIKE YOU FUCKING OWN THE PLACE AND START MOUTHING OFF TO US? THE WHOLE TIME YOU WERE WALKING RIGHT INTO MY TRAP! JUST LIKE I PLANNED IT!
THIS IS SOME PIECE OF HARDWARE YOU GOT HERE, ODINSON.
BET YOU FEEL LIKE YOU'RE A BONAFIDE VIKING GOD RUNNING AROUND SWINGING THIS THING.
THAT YOUR THING? YOU SOME KINDA VIKING? YOU THINK THIS IS RAGNAROK WE'RE LIVING IN, PLAYING ITSELF OUT HERE LIKE THE END OF DAYS?

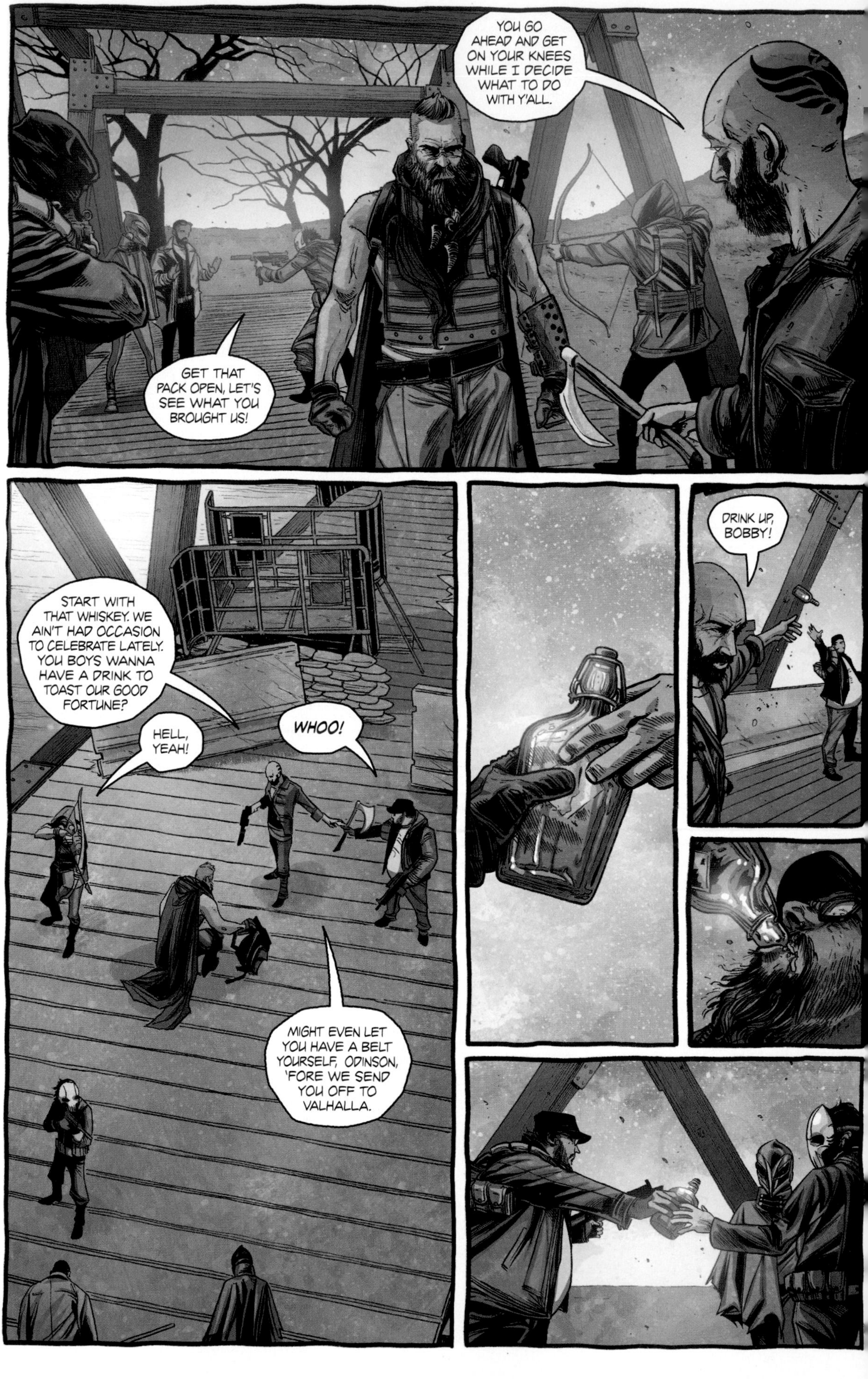
YOU GO AHEAD AND GET ON YOUR KNEES WHILE I DECIDE WHAT TO DO WITH Y'ALL.
GET THAT PACK OPEN, LET'S SEE WHAT YOU BROUGHT US!
START WITH THAT WHISKEY. WE AIN'T HAD OCCASION TO CELEBRATE LATELY. YOU BOYS WANNA HAVE A DRINK TO TOAST OUR GOOD FORTUNE?
HELL, YEAH!
WHOO!
MIGHT EVEN LET YOU HAVE A BELT YOURSELF, ODINSON, 'FORE WE SEND YOU OFF TO VALHALLA.
DRINK UP, BOBBY!

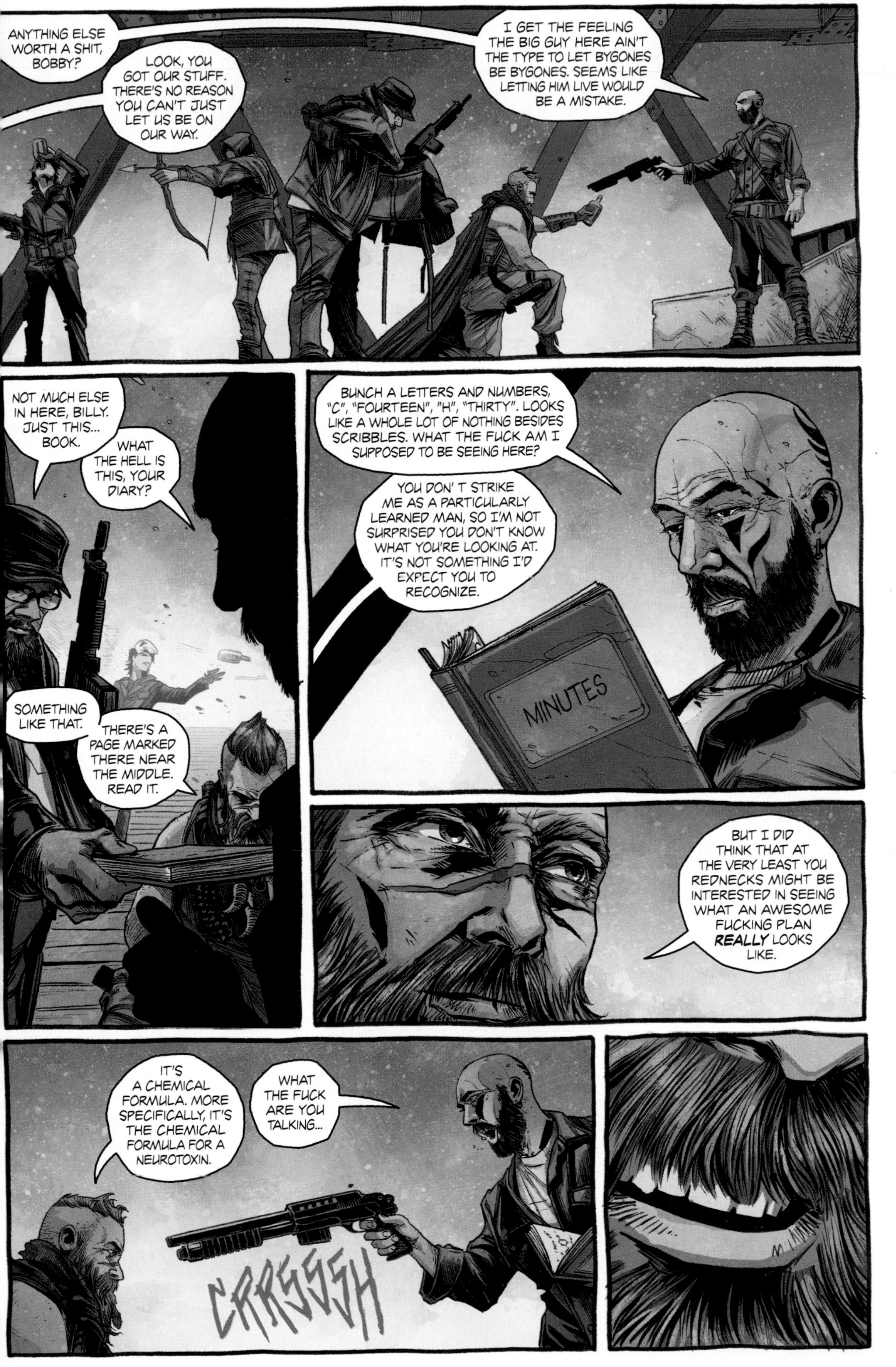
ANYTHING ELSE WORTH A SHIT, BOBBY?
LOOK, YOU GOT OUR STUFF. THERE'S NO REASON YOU CAN'T JUST LET US BE ON OUR WAY.
I GET THE FEELING THE BIG GUY HERE AIN'T THE TYPE TO LET BYGONES BE BYGONES. SEEMS LIKE LETTING HIM LIVE WOULD BE A MISTAKE.
NOT MUCH ELSE IN HERE, BILLY. JUST THIS... BOOK.
WHAT THE HELL IS THIS, YOUR DIARY?
SOMETHING LIKE THAT.
THERE'S A PAGE MARKED THERE NEAR THE MIDDLE. READ IT.
BUNCH A LETTERS AND NUMBERS, "C", "FOURTEEN", "H", "THIRTY". LOOKS LIKE A WHOLE LOT OF NOTHING BESIDES SCRIBBLES. WHAT THE FUCK AM I SUPPOSED TO BE SEEING HERE?
YOU DON' T STRIKE ME AS A PARTICULARLY LEARNED MAN, SO I'M NOT SURPRISED YOU DON'T KNOW WHAT YOU'RE LOOKING AT. IT'S NOT SOMETHING I'D EXPECT YOU TO RECOGNIZE.
MINUTES
BUT I DID THINK THAT AT THE VERY LEAST YOU REDNECKS MIGHT BE INTERESTED IN SEEING WHAT AN AWESOME FUCKING PLAN **REALLY** LOOKS LIKE.
IT'S A CHEMICAL FORMULA. MORE SPECIFICALLY, IT'S THE CHEMICAL FORMULA FOR A NEUROTOXIN.
WHAT THE FUCK ARE YOU TALKING...
CRSSSH

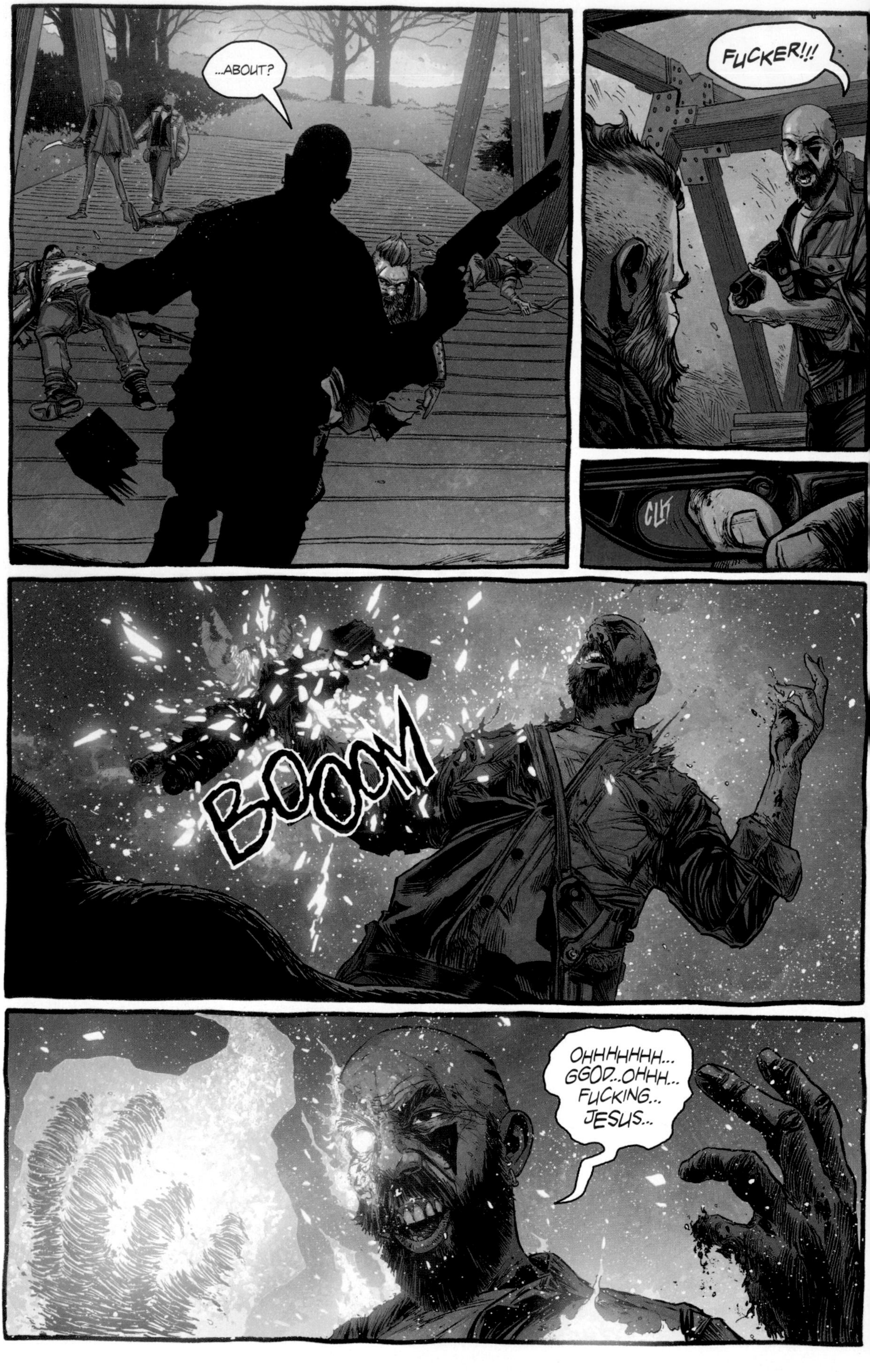
...ABOUT?
FUCKER!!!
CLK
BOOOM
OHHHHHHH...
GGOD...OHHH...
FUCKING...
JESUS...

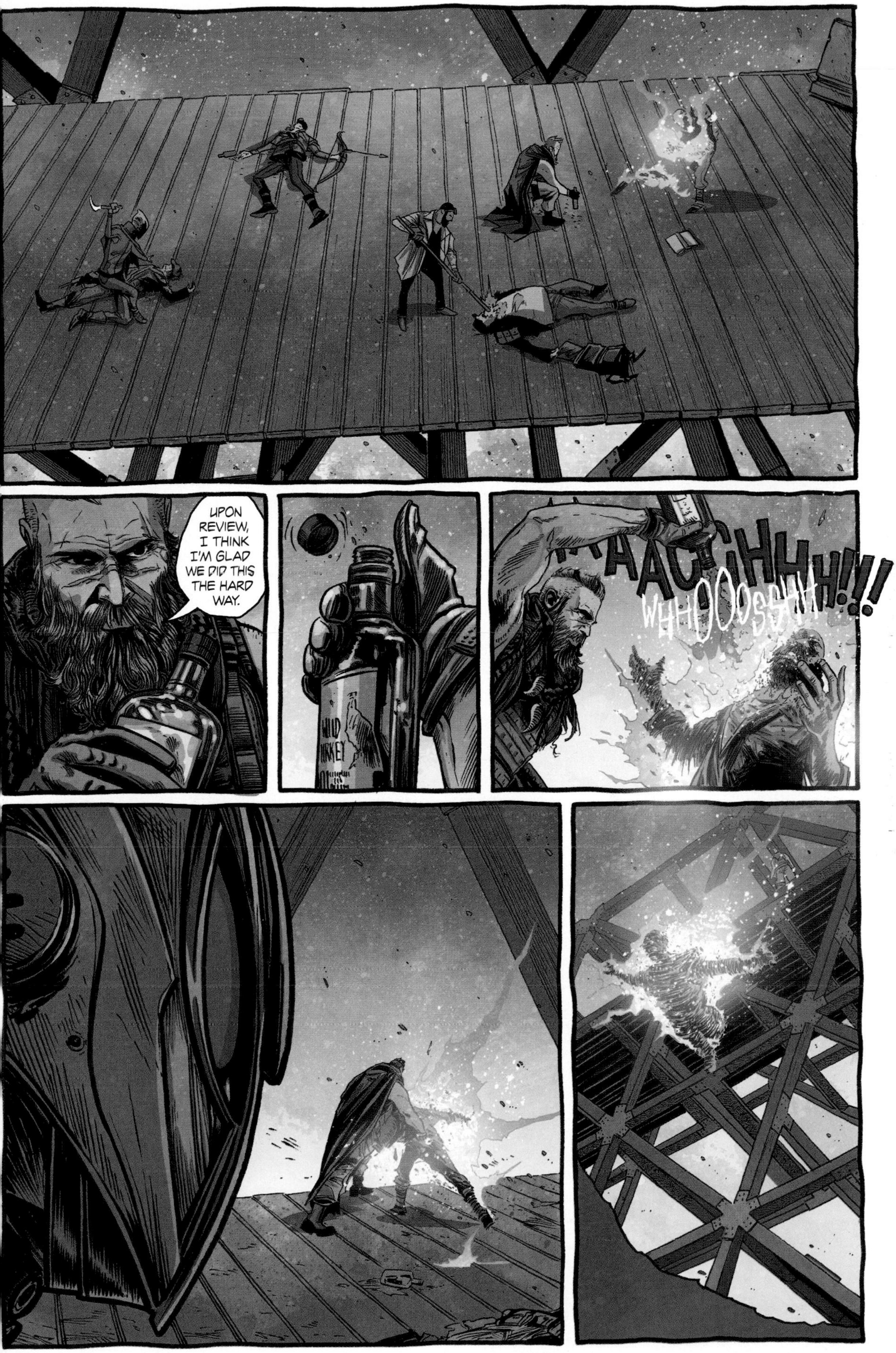
UPON REVIEW, I THINK I'M GLAD WE DID THIS THE HARD WAY.
AACHHHH!!!!
WHHOOOSSHH

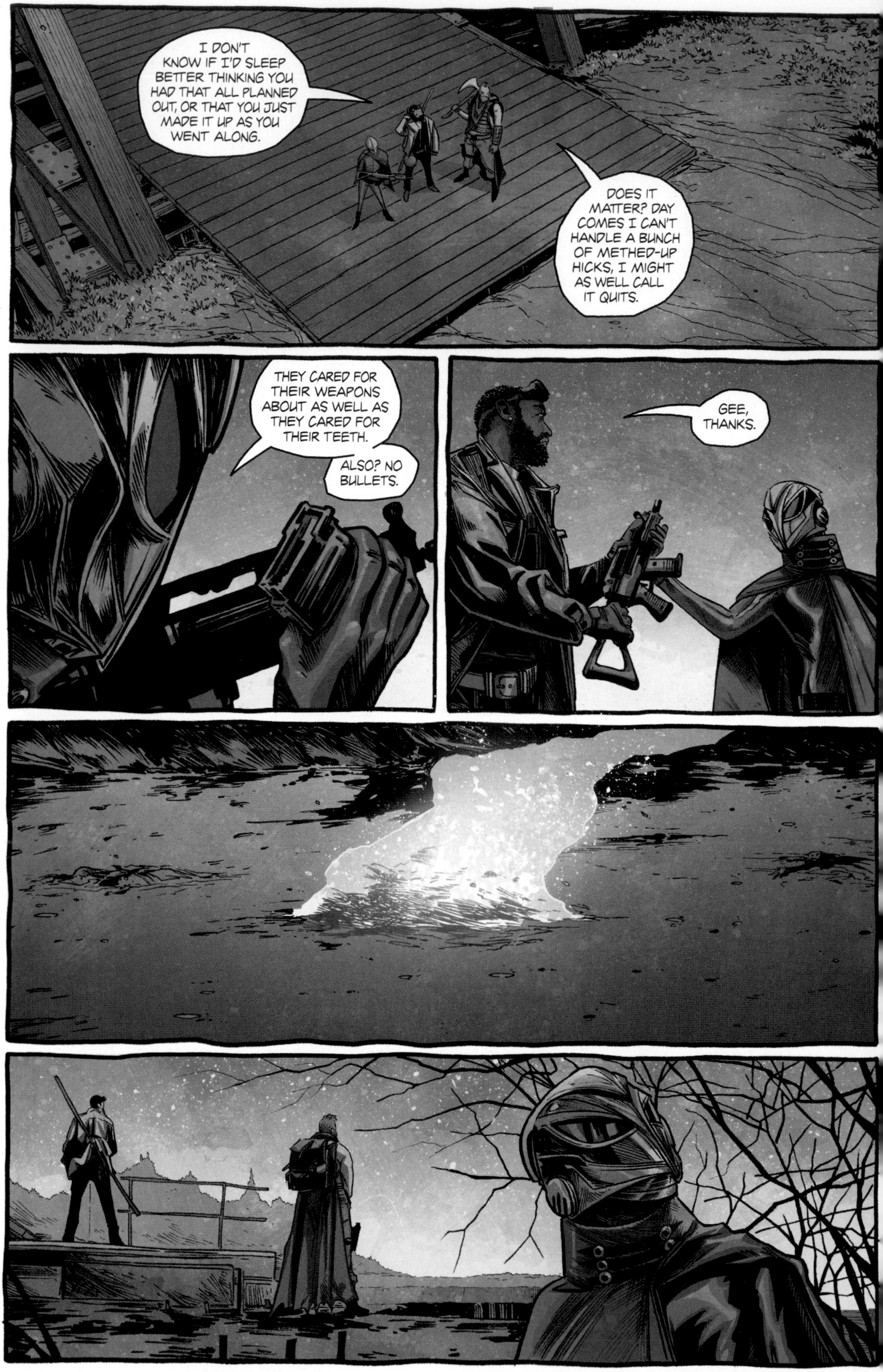
I DON'T KNOW IF I'D SLEEP BETTER THINKING YOU HAD THAT ALL PLANNED OUT, OR THAT YOU JUST MADE IT UP AS YOU WENT ALONG.
DOES IT MATTER? DAY COMES I CAN'T HANDLE A BUNCH OF METHED-UP HICKS, I MIGHT AS WELL CALL IT QUITS.
THEY CARED FOR THEIR WEAPONS ABOUT AS WELL AS THEY CARED FOR THEIR TEETH.
ALSO? NO BULLETS.
GEE, THANKS.

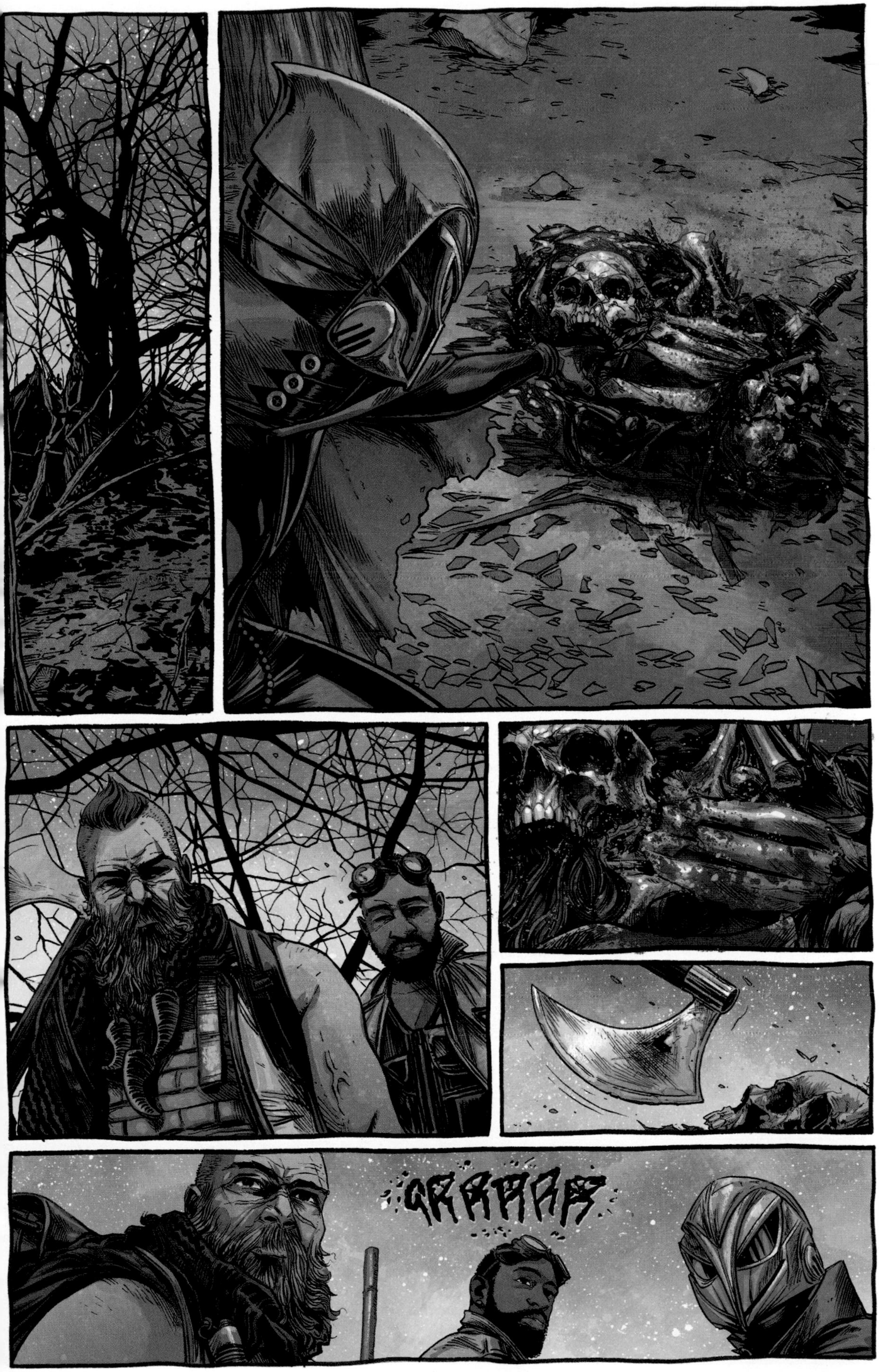
GRRRRR

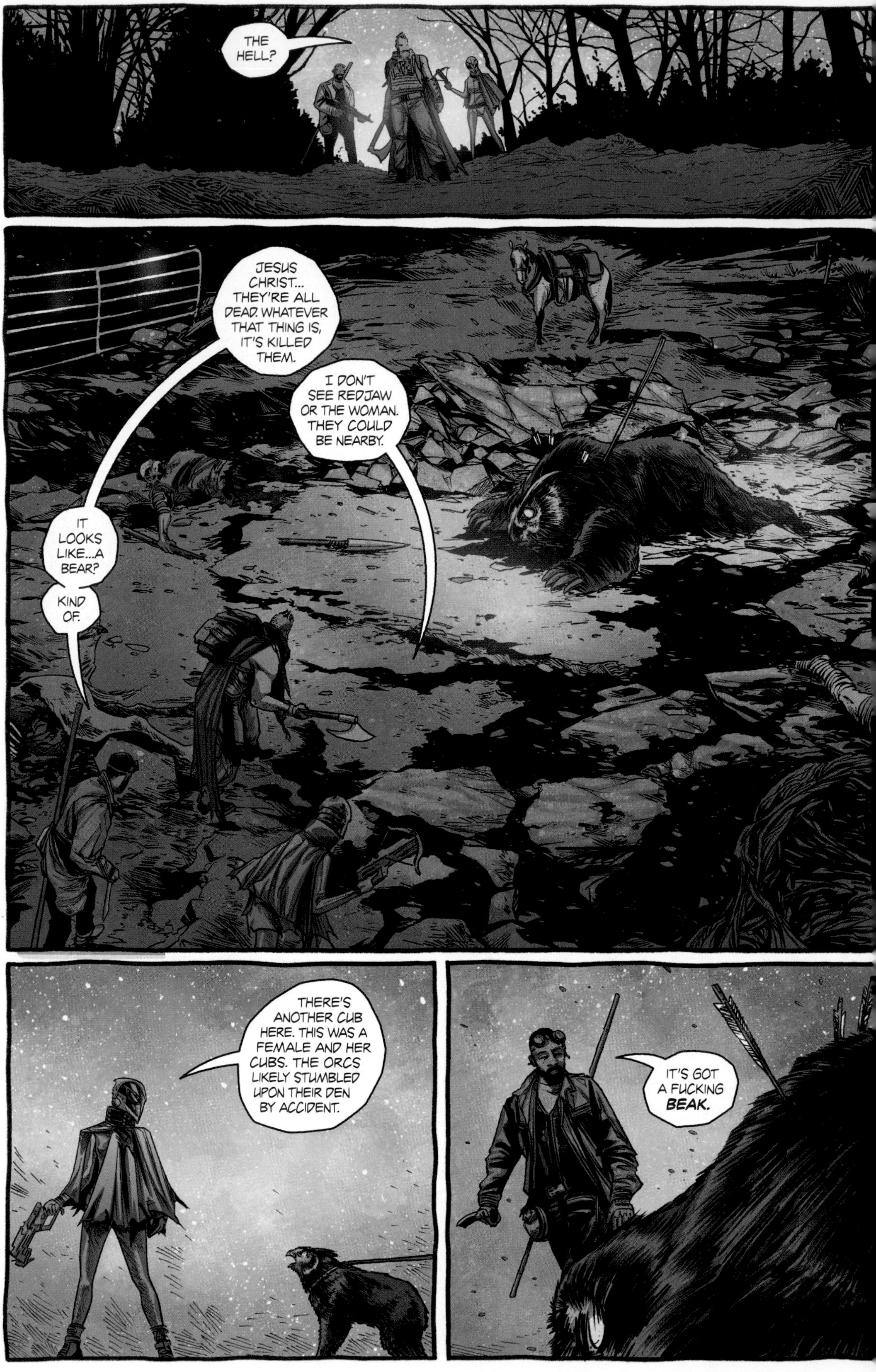
THE HELL?
JESUS CHRIST... THEY'RE ALL DEAD. WHATEVER THAT THING IS, IT'S KILLED THEM.
I DON'T SEE REDJAW OR THE WOMAN. THEY COULD BE NEARBY.
IT LOOKS LIKE...A BEAR?
KIND OF.
THERE'S ANOTHER CUB HERE. THIS WAS A FEMALE AND HER CUBS. THE ORCS LIKELY STUMBLED UPON THEIR DEN BY ACCIDENT.
IT'S GOT A FUCKING **BEAK.**

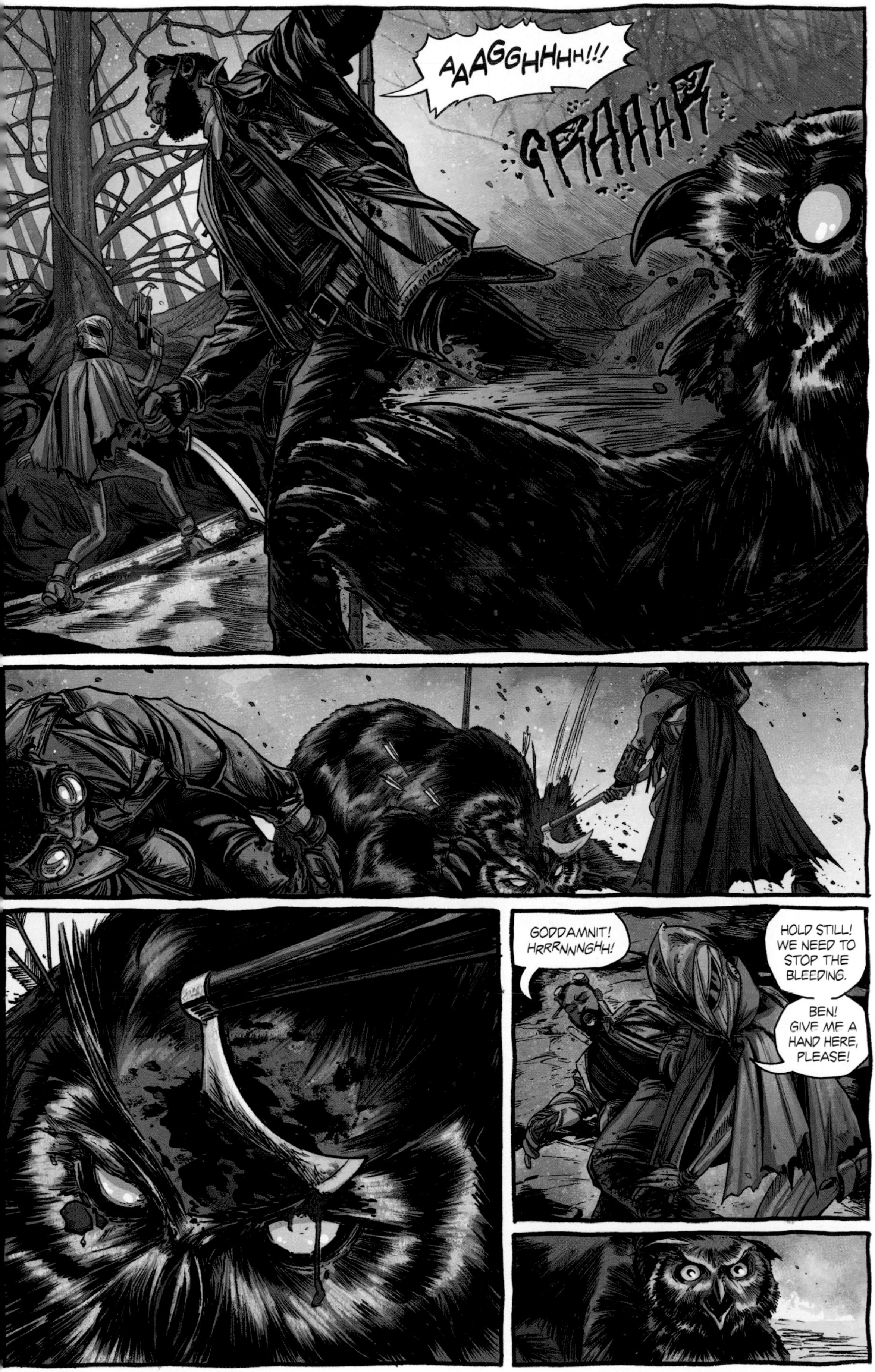
AAAGGHHHH!!!
GRAAAAR
GODDAMNIT! HRRRNNNGHH!
HOLD STILL! WE NEED TO STOP THE BLEEDING.
BEN! GIVE ME A HAND HERE, PLEASE!

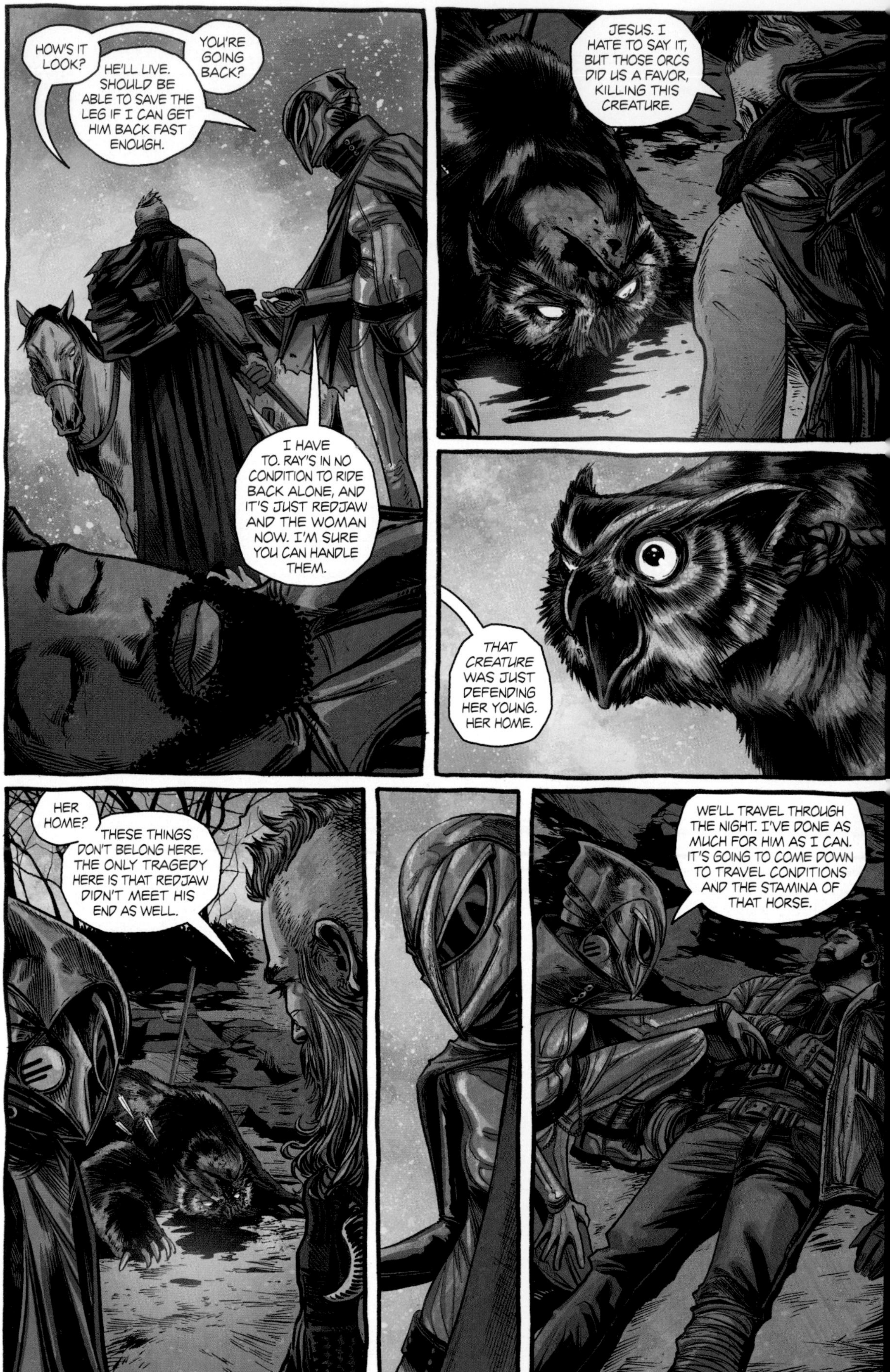
HOW'S IT LOOK?
HE'LL LIVE. SHOULD BE ABLE TO SAVE THE LEG IF I CAN GET HIM BACK FAST ENOUGH.
YOU'RE GOING BACK?
I HAVE TO. RAY'S IN NO CONDITION TO RIDE BACK ALONE, AND IT'S JUST REDJAW AND THE WOMAN NOW. I'M SURE YOU CAN HANDLE THEM.
JESUS. I HATE TO SAY IT, BUT THOSE ORCS DID US A FAVOR, KILLING THIS CREATURE.
THAT CREATURE WAS JUST DEFENDING HER YOUNG. HER HOME.
HER HOME?
THESE THINGS DON'T BELONG HERE. THE ONLY TRAGEDY HERE IS THAT REDJAW DIDN'T MEET HIS END AS WELL.
WE'LL TRAVEL THROUGH THE NIGHT. I'VE DONE AS MUCH FOR HIM AS I CAN. IT'S GOING TO COME DOWN TO TRAVEL CONDITIONS AND THE STAMINA OF THAT HORSE.

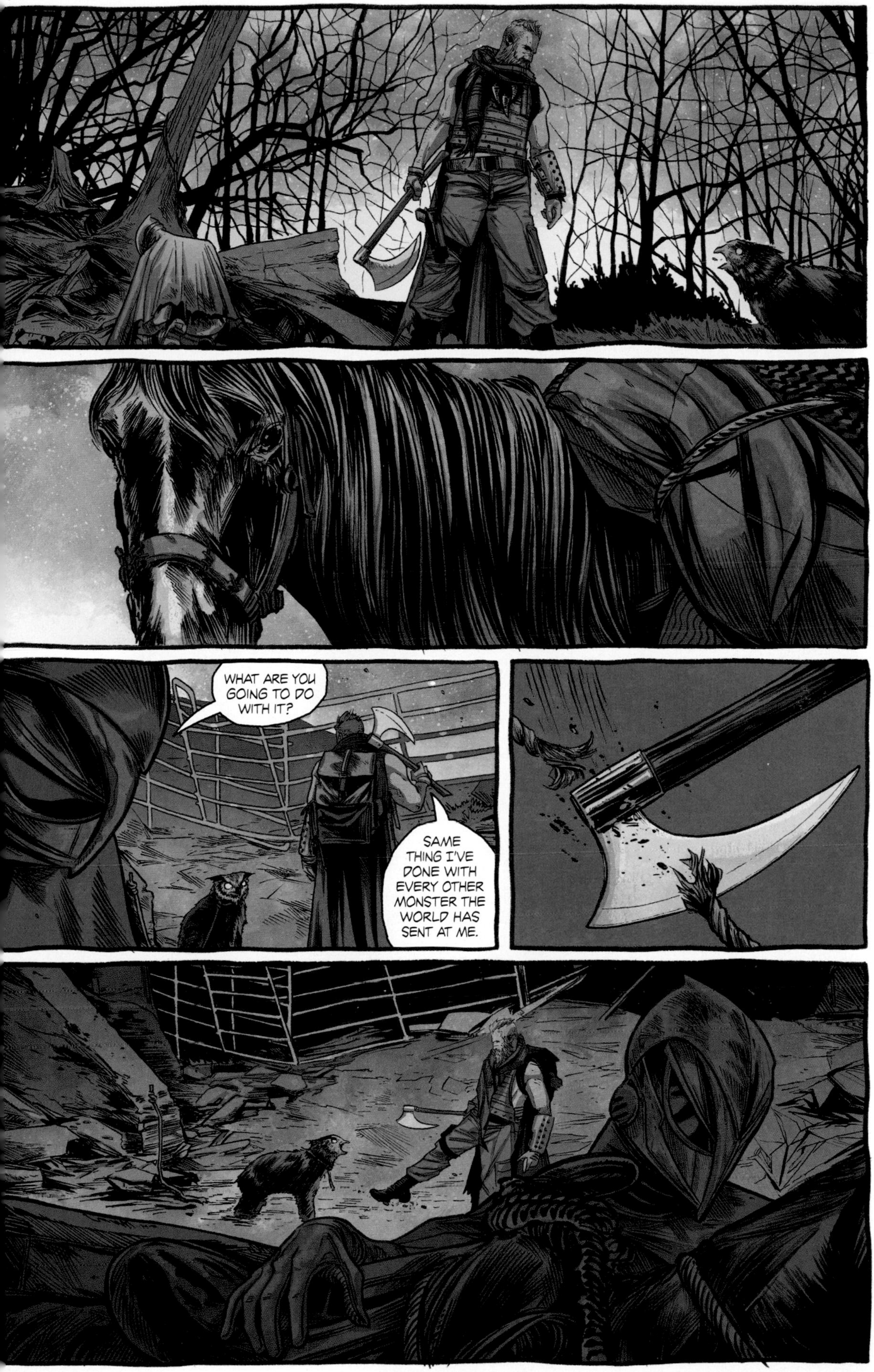
WHAT ARE YOU GOING TO DO WITH IT?
SAME THING I'VE DONE WITH EVERY OTHER MONSTER THE WORLD HAS SENT AT ME.

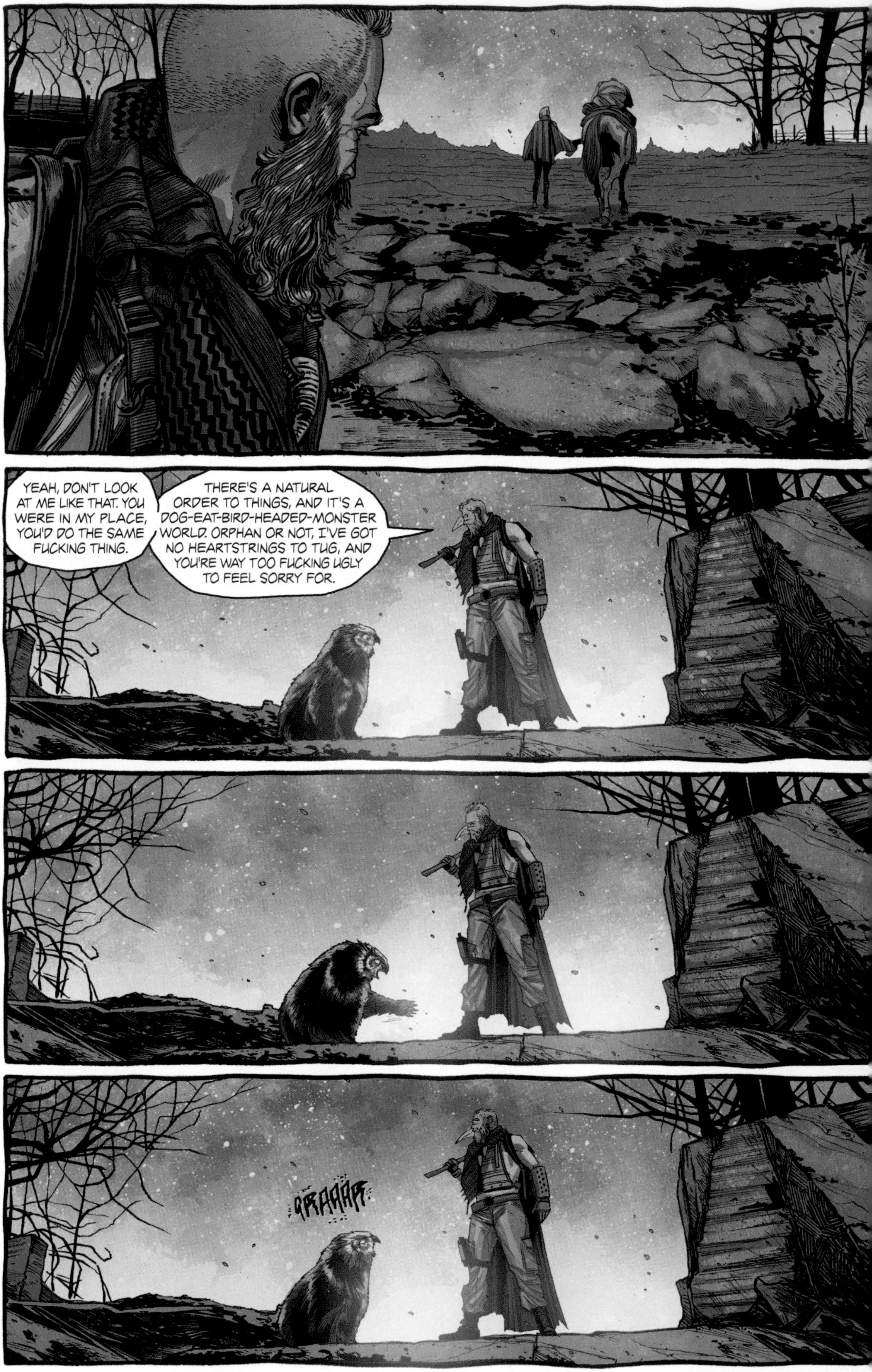
YEAH, DON'T LOOK AT ME LIKE THAT. YOU WERE IN MY PLACE, YOU'D DO THE SAME FUCKING THING.
THERE'S A NATURAL ORDER TO THINGS, AND IT'S A DOG-EAT-BIRD-HEADED-MONSTER WORLD. ORPHAN OR NOT, I'VE GOT NO HEARTSTRINGS TO TUG, AND YOU'RE WAY TOO FUCKING UGLY TO FEEL SORRY FOR.
GRAAAR

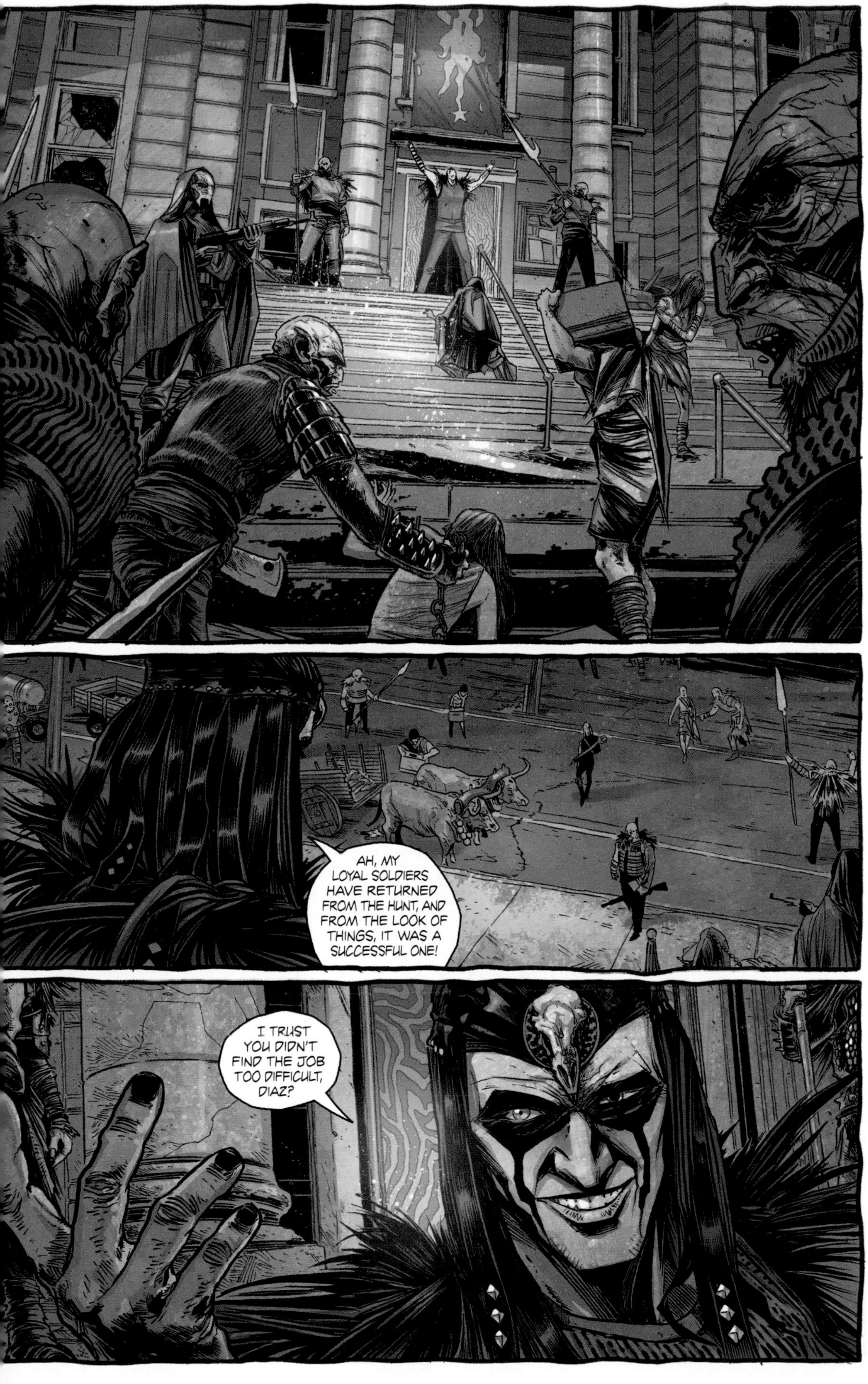
AH, MY LOYAL SOLDIERS HAVE RETURNED FROM THE HUNT, AND FROM THE LOOK OF THINGS, IT WAS A SUCCESSFUL ONE!
I TRUST YOU DIDN'T FIND THE JOB TOO DIFFICULT, DIAZ?

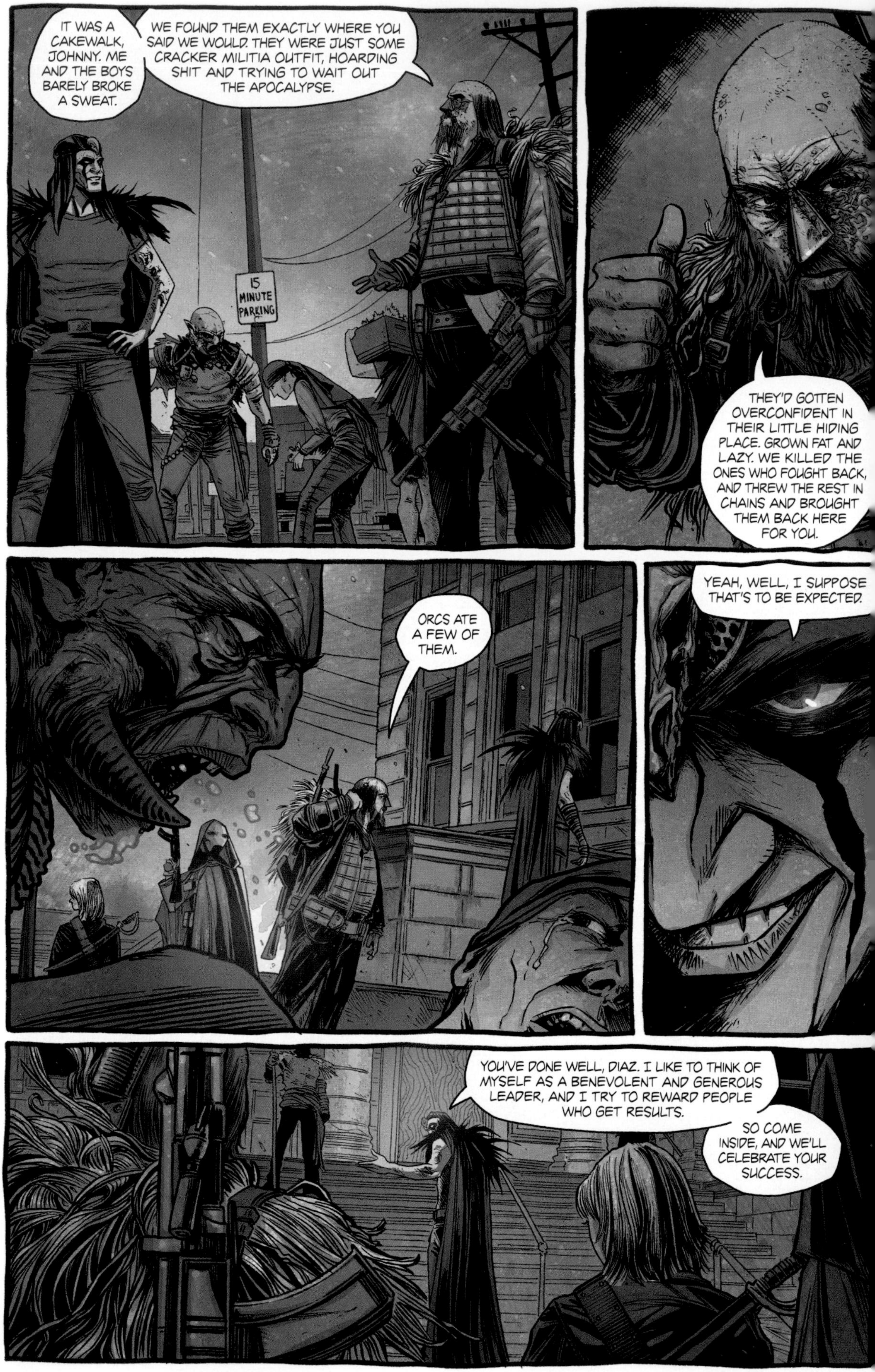
IT WAS A CAKEWALK, JOHNNY. ME AND THE BOYS BARELY BROKE A SWEAT.
WE FOUND THEM EXACTLY WHERE YOU SAID WE WOULD. THEY WERE JUST SOME CRACKER MILITIA OUTFIT, HOARDING SHIT AND TRYING TO WAIT OUT THE APOCALYPSE.
15 MINUTE PARKING
THEY'D GOTTEN OVERCONFIDENT IN THEIR LITTLE HIDING PLACE. GROWN FAT AND LAZY. WE KILLED THE ONES WHO FOUGHT BACK, AND THREW THE REST IN CHAINS AND BROUGHT THEM BACK HERE FOR YOU.
ORCS ATE A FEW OF THEM.
YEAH, WELL, I SUPPOSE THAT'S TO BE EXPECTED.
YOU'VE DONE WELL, DIAZ. I LIKE TO THINK OF MYSELF AS A BENEVOLENT AND GENEROUS LEADER, AND I TRY TO REWARD PEOPLE WHO GET RESULTS.
SO COME INSIDE, AND WE'LL CELEBRATE YOUR SUCCESS.

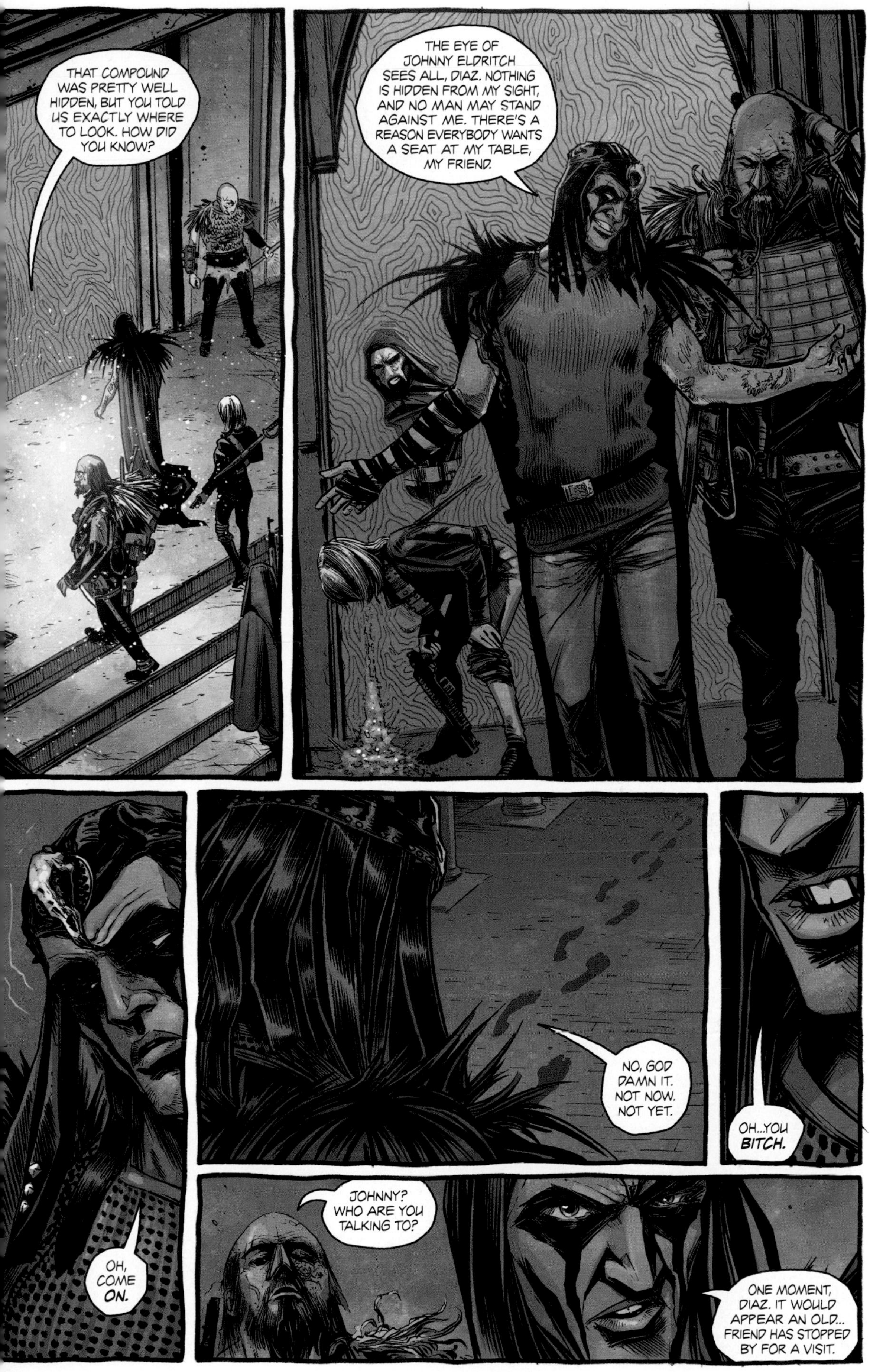
THAT COMPOUND WAS PRETTY WELL HIDDEN, BUT YOU TOLD US EXACTLY WHERE TO LOOK. HOW DID YOU KNOW?
THE EYE OF JOHNNY ELDRITCH SEES ALL, DIAZ. NOTHING IS HIDDEN FROM MY SIGHT, AND NO MAN MAY STAND AGAINST ME. THERE'S A REASON EVERYBODY WANTS A SEAT AT MY TABLE, MY FRIEND.
OH, COME ON.
NO, GOD DAMN IT. NOT NOW. NOT YET.
OH...YOU BITCH.
JOHNNY? WHO ARE YOU TALKING TO?
ONE MOMENT, DIAZ. IT WOULD APPEAR AN OLD... FRIEND HAS STOPPED BY FOR A VISIT.

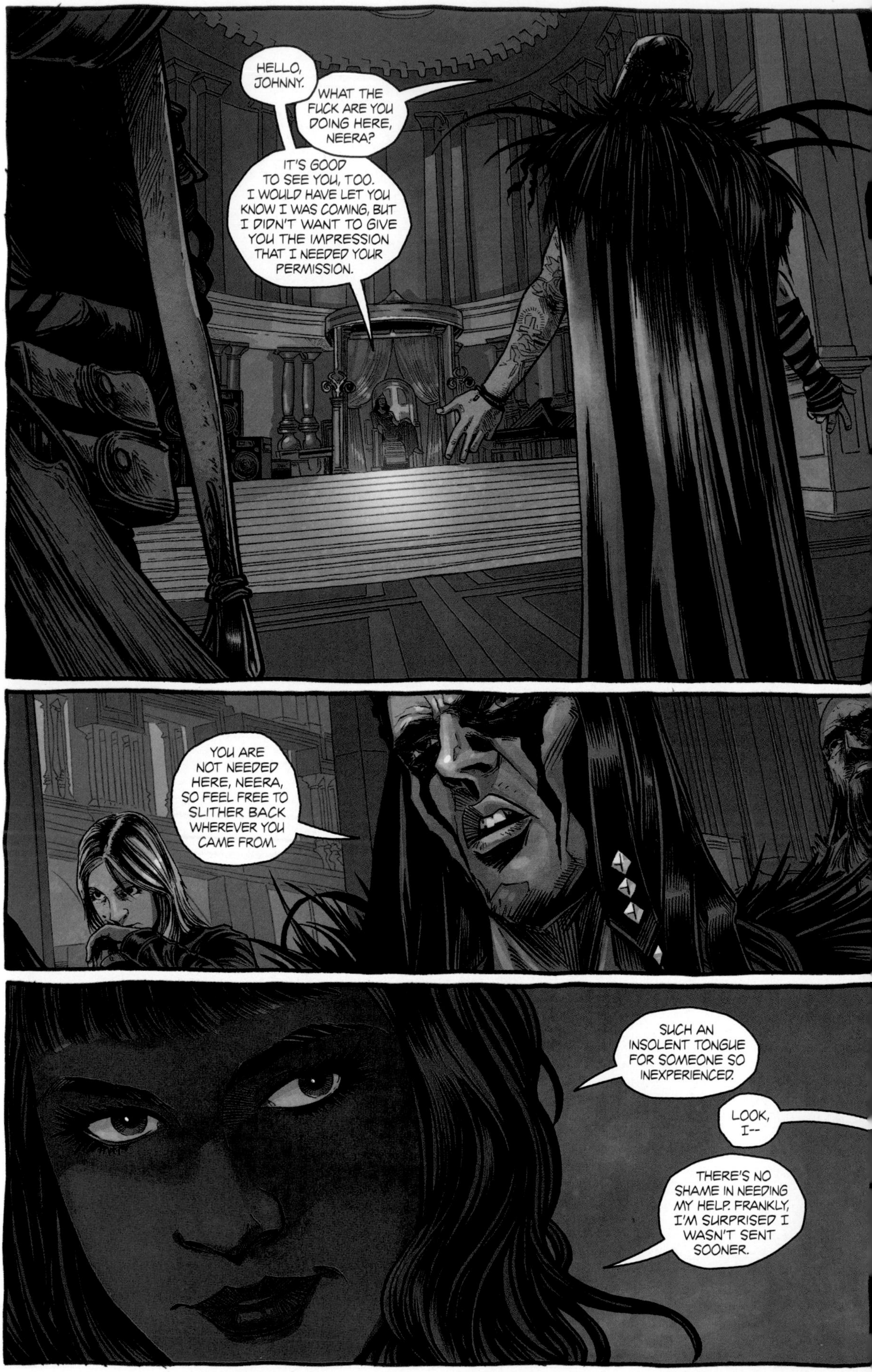
HELLO, JOHNNY.
WHAT THE FUCK ARE YOU DOING HERE, NEERA?
IT'S GOOD TO SEE YOU, TOO. I WOULD HAVE LET YOU KNOW I WAS COMING, BUT I DIDN'T WANT TO GIVE YOU THE IMPRESSION THAT I NEEDED YOUR PERMISSION.
YOU ARE NOT NEEDED HERE, NEERA, SO FEEL FREE TO SLITHER BACK WHEREVER YOU CAME FROM.
SUCH AN INSOLENT TONGUE FOR SOMEONE SO INEXPERIENCED.
LOOK, I--
THERE'S NO SHAME IN NEEDING MY HELP. FRANKLY, I'M SURPRISED I WASN'T SENT SOONER.

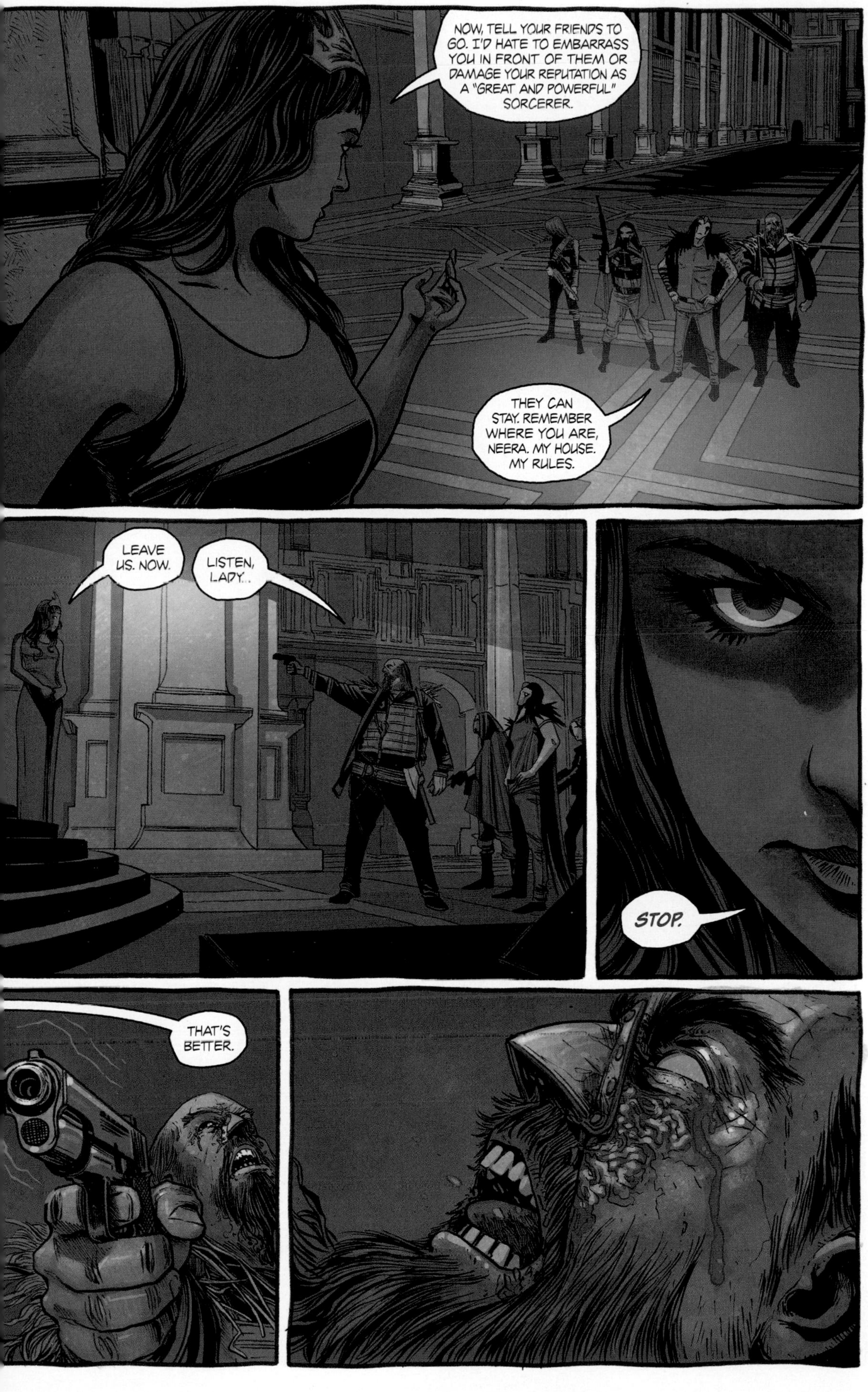
NOW, TELL YOUR FRIENDS TO GO. I'D HATE TO EMBARRASS YOU IN FRONT OF THEM OR DAMAGE YOUR REPUTATION AS A "GREAT AND POWERFUL" SORCERER.
THEY CAN STAY. REMEMBER WHERE YOU ARE, NEERA. MY HOUSE. MY RULES.
LEAVE US. NOW.
LISTEN, LADY...
STOP.
THAT'S BETTER.

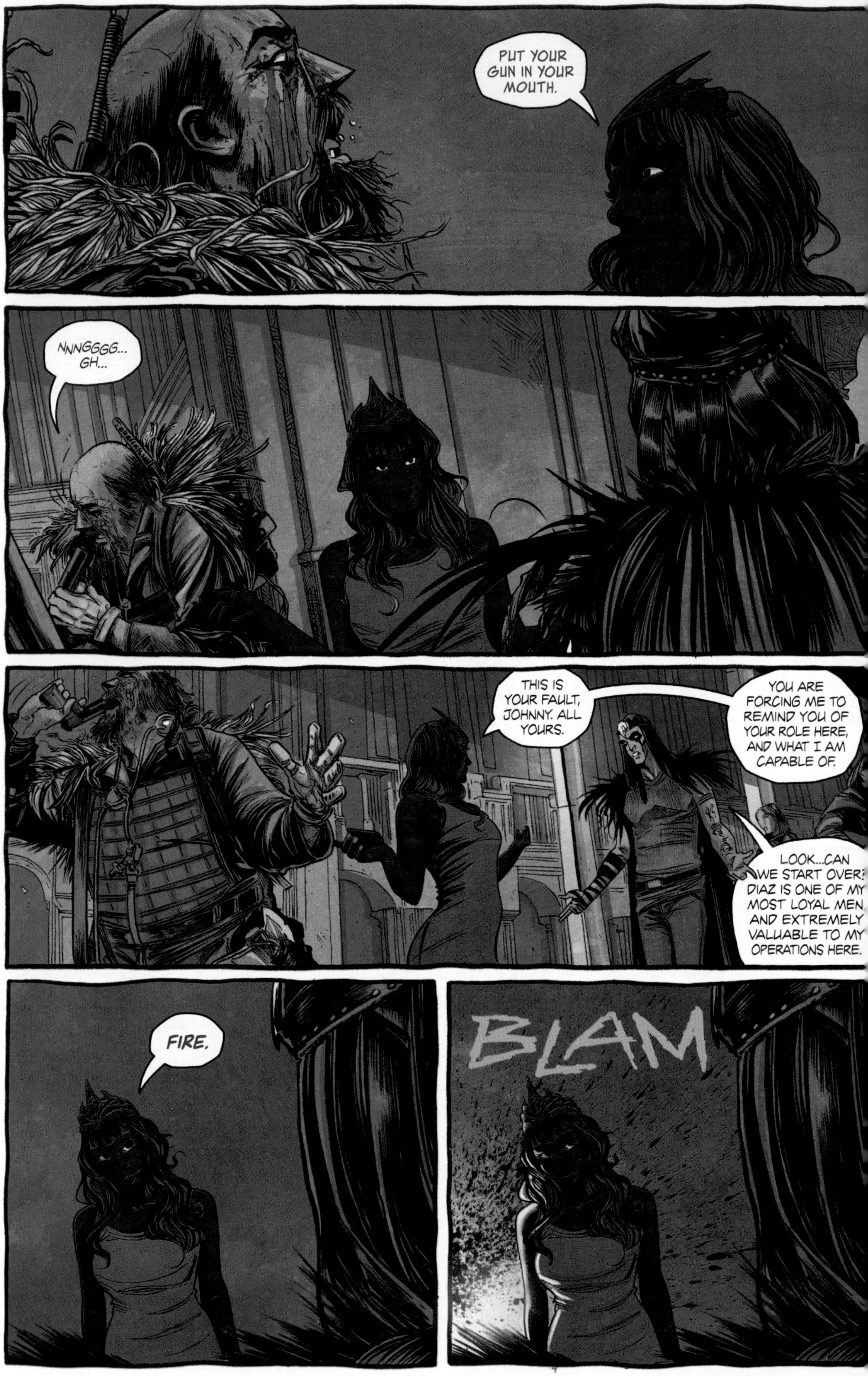
PUT YOUR GUN IN YOUR MOUTH.
NNNGGGG... GH...
THIS IS YOUR FAULT, JOHNNY. ALL YOURS.
YOU ARE FORCING ME TO REMIND YOU OF YOUR ROLE HERE, AND WHAT I AM CAPABLE OF.
LOOK...CAN WE START OVER? DIAZ IS ONE OF MY MOST LOYAL MEN AND EXTREMELY VALUABLE TO MY OPERATIONS HERE.
FIRE.
BLAM

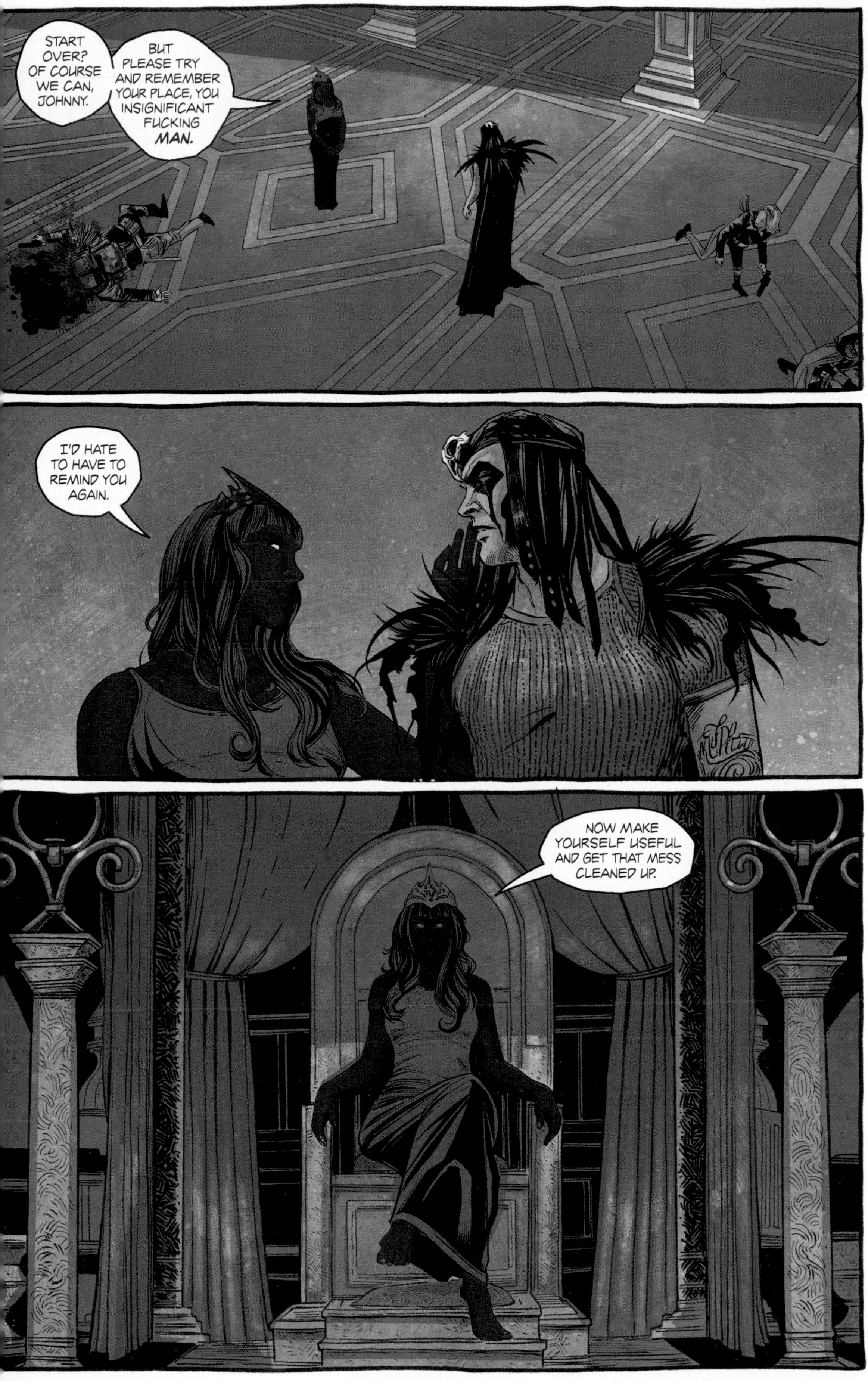
START OVER? OF COURSE WE CAN, JOHNNY.
BUT PLEASE TRY AND REMEMBER YOUR PLACE, YOU INSIGNIFICANT FUCKING MAN.
I'D HATE TO HAVE TO REMIND YOU AGAIN.
NOW MAKE YOURSELF USEFUL AND GET THAT MESS CLEANED UP.

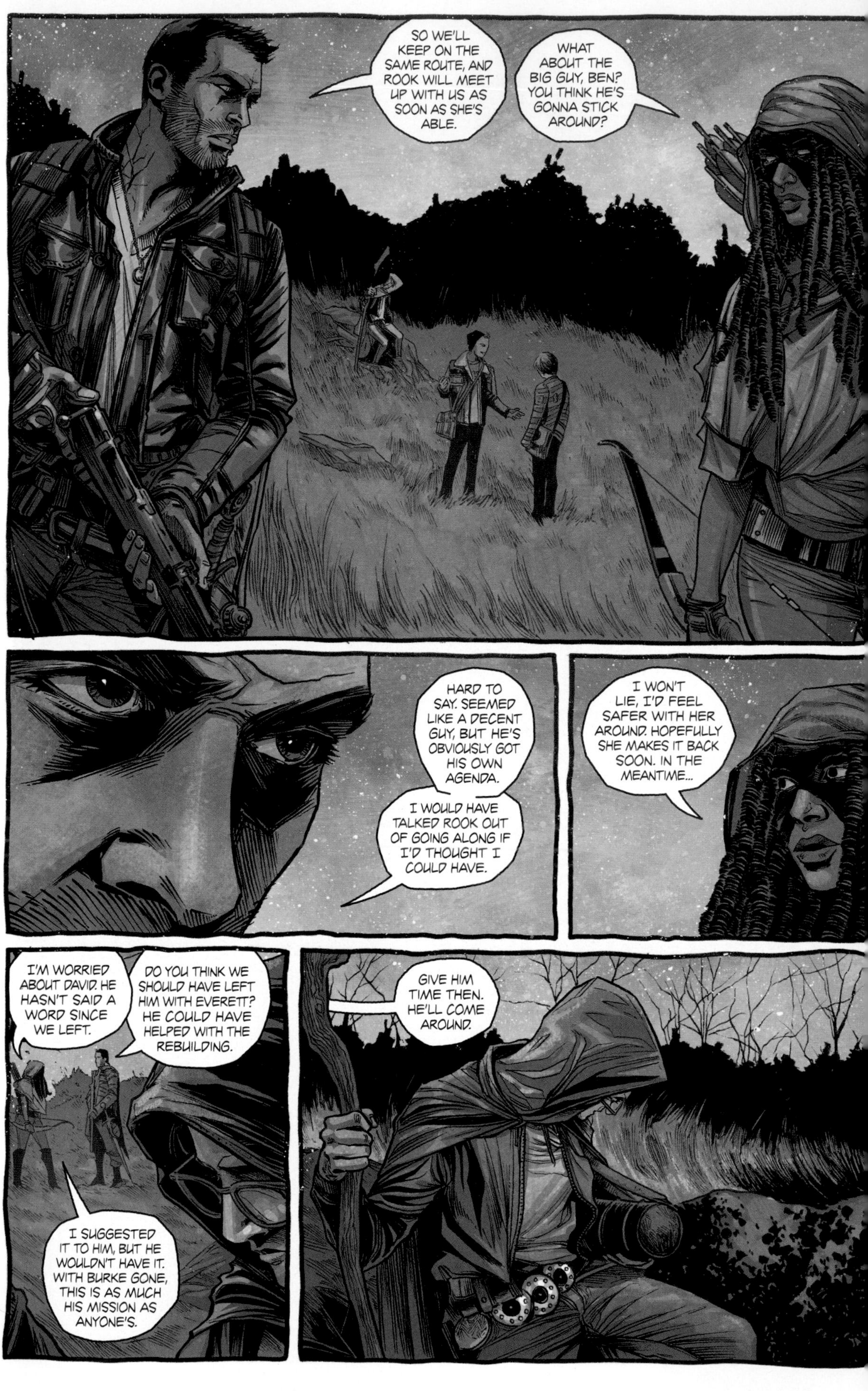
SO WE'LL KEEP ON THE SAME ROUTE, AND ROOK WILL MEET UP WITH US AS SOON AS SHE'S ABLE.
WHAT ABOUT THE BIG GUY, BEN? YOU THINK HE'S GONNA STICK AROUND?
HARD TO SAY. SEEMED LIKE A DECENT GUY, BUT HE'S OBVIOUSLY GOT HIS OWN AGENDA.
I WOULD HAVE TALKED ROOK OUT OF GOING ALONG IF I'D THOUGHT I COULD HAVE.
I WON'T LIE, I'D FEEL SAFER WITH HER AROUND. HOPEFULLY SHE MAKES IT BACK SOON. IN THE MEANTIME...
I'M WORRIED ABOUT DAVID. HE HASN'T SAID A WORD SINCE WE LEFT.
DO YOU THINK WE SHOULD HAVE LEFT HIM WITH EVERETT? HE COULD HAVE HELPED WITH THE REBUILDING.
I SUGGESTED IT TO HIM, BUT HE WOULDN'T HAVE IT. WITH BURKE GONE, THIS IS AS MUCH HIS MISSION AS ANYONE'S.
GIVE HIM TIME THEN. HE'LL COME AROUND.

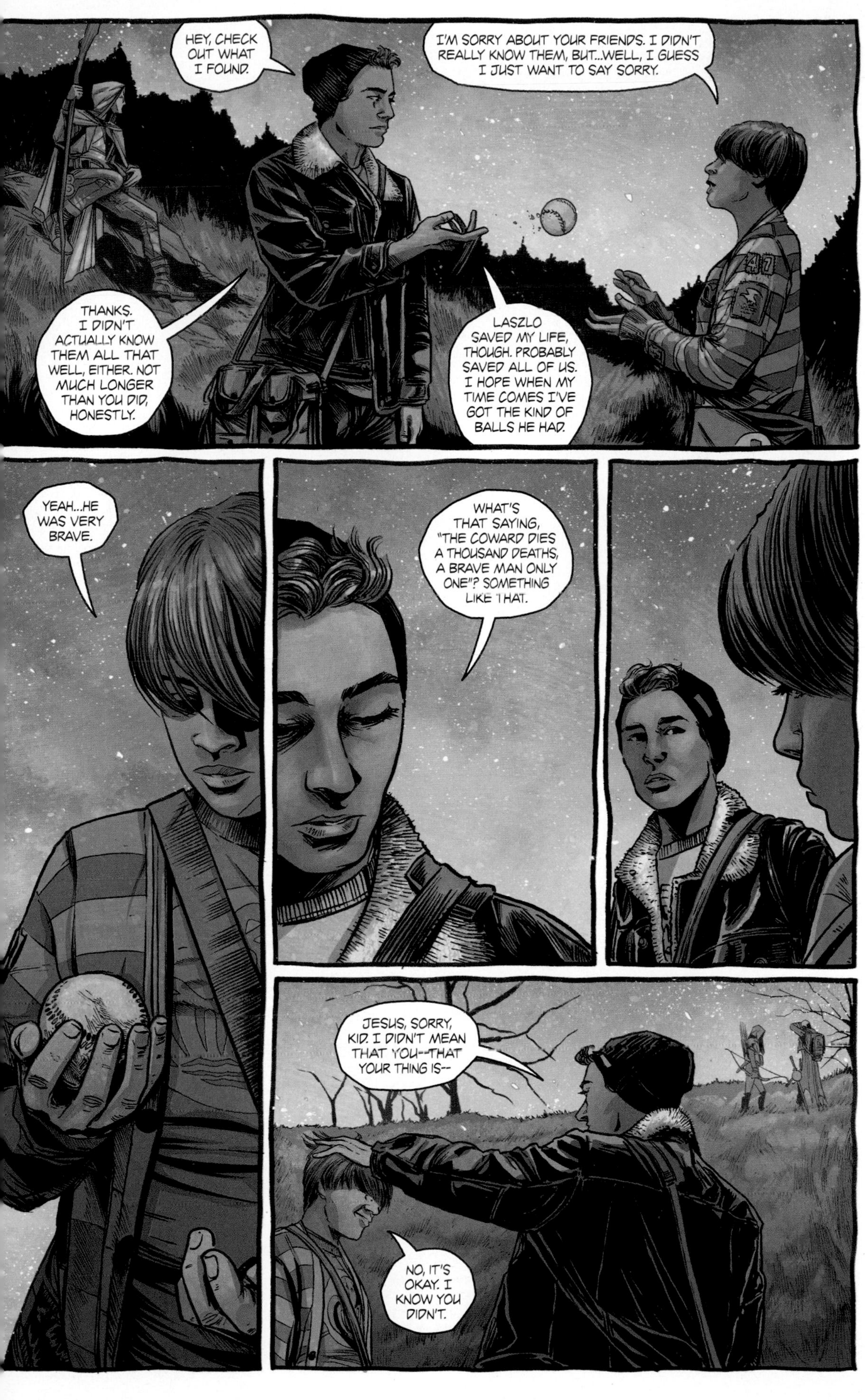
HEY, CHECK OUT WHAT I FOUND.
I'M SORRY ABOUT YOUR FRIENDS. I DIDN'T REALLY KNOW THEM, BUT...WELL, I GUESS I JUST WANT TO SAY SORRY.
THANKS. I DIDN'T ACTUALLY KNOW THEM ALL THAT WELL, EITHER. NOT MUCH LONGER THAN YOU DID, HONESTLY.
LASZLO SAVED MY LIFE, THOUGH. PROBABLY SAVED ALL OF US. I HOPE WHEN MY TIME COMES I'VE GOT THE KIND OF BALLS HE HAD.
YEAH...HE WAS VERY BRAVE.
WHAT'S THAT SAYING, "THE COWARD DIES A THOUSAND DEATHS, A BRAVE MAN ONLY ONE"? SOMETHING LIKE THAT.
JESUS, SORRY, KID. I DIDN'T MEAN THAT YOU--THAT YOUR THING IS--
NO, IT'S OKAY. I KNOW YOU DIDN'T.

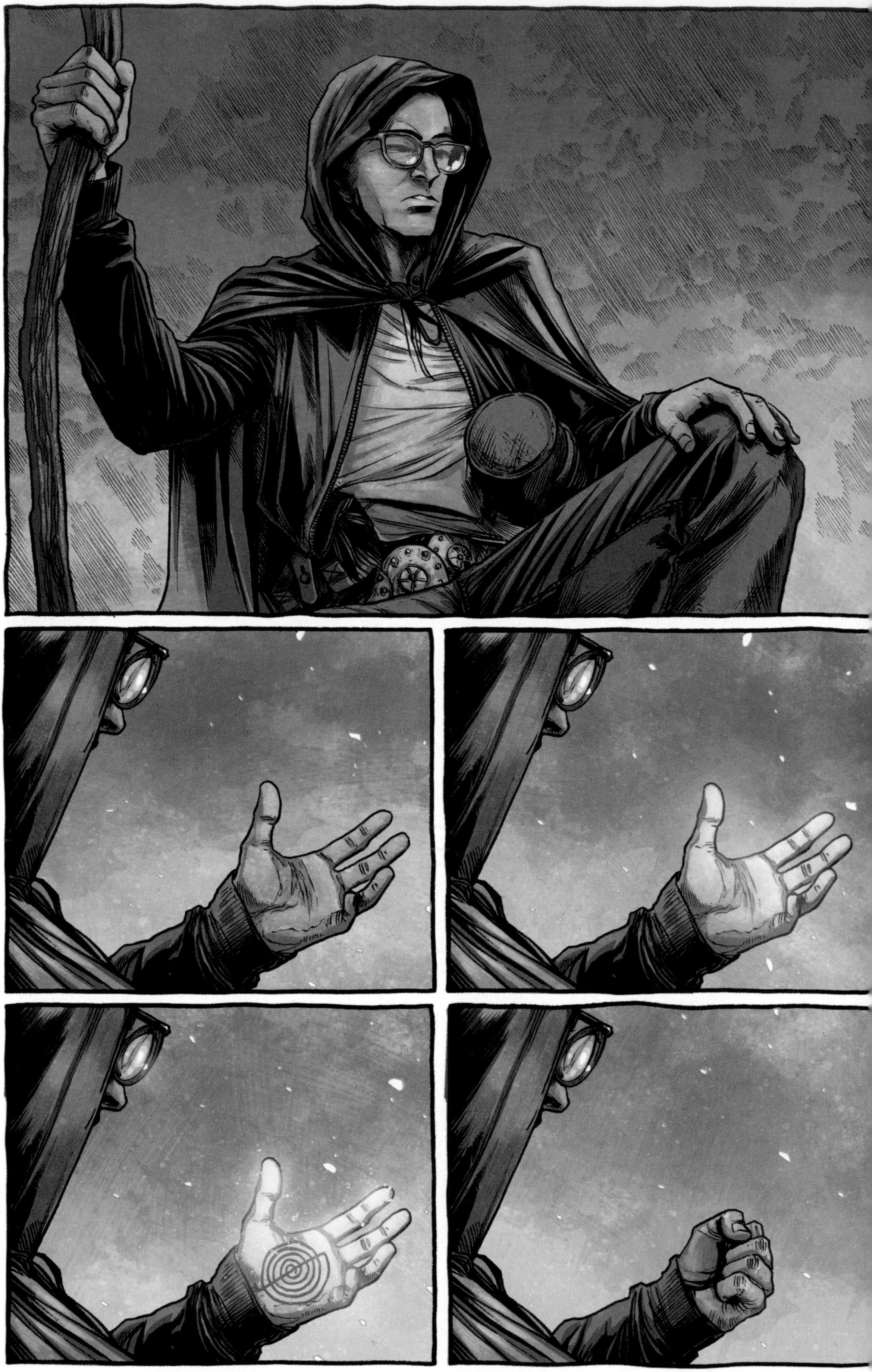

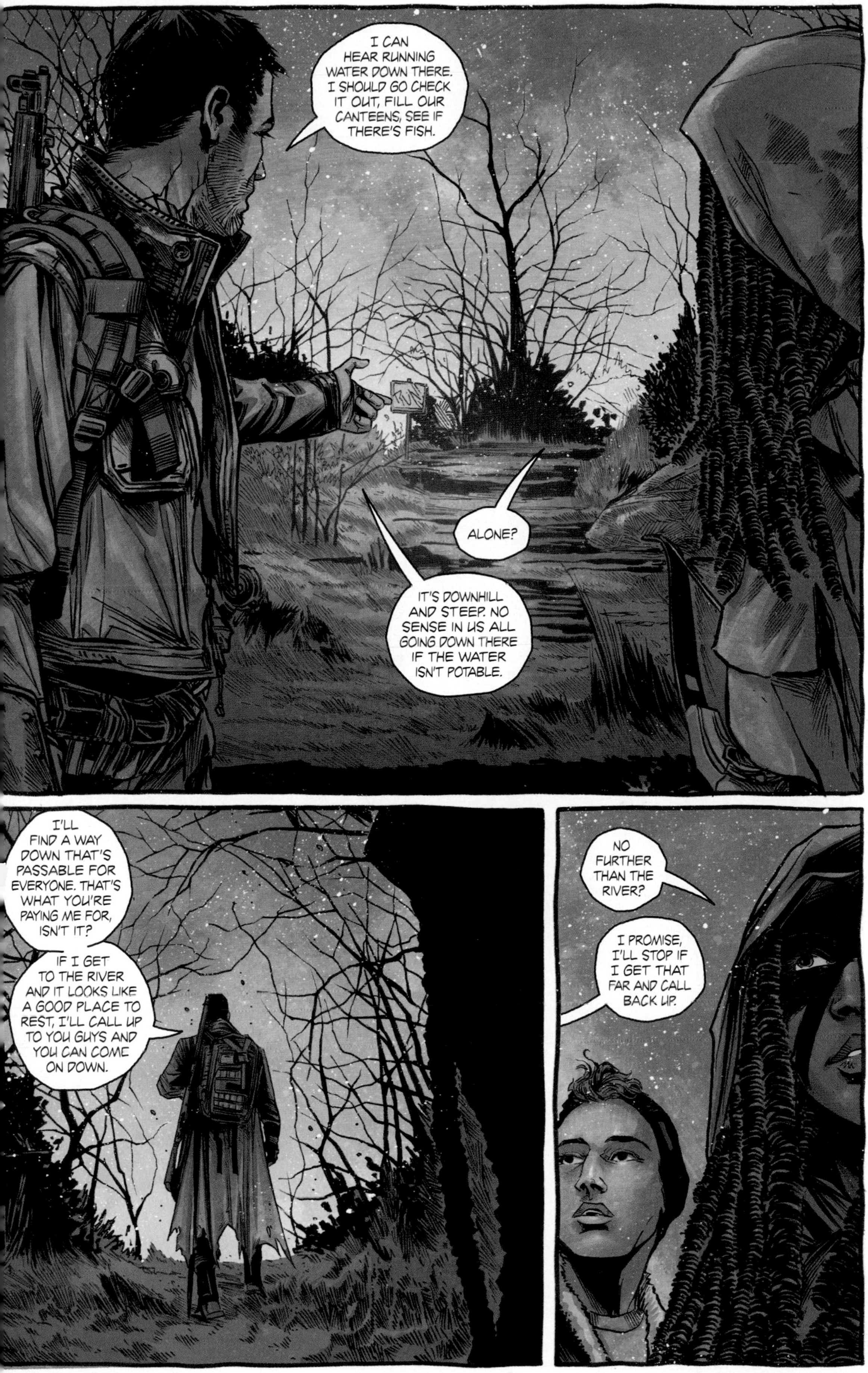
I CAN HEAR RUNNING WATER DOWN THERE. I SHOULD GO CHECK IT OUT, FILL OUR CANTEENS, SEE IF THERE'S FISH.
ALONE?
IT'S DOWNHILL AND STEEP. NO SENSE IN US ALL GOING DOWN THERE IF THE WATER ISN'T POTABLE.
I'LL FIND A WAY DOWN THAT'S PASSABLE FOR EVERYONE. THAT'S WHAT YOU'RE PAYING ME FOR, ISN'T IT?
IF I GET TO THE RIVER AND IT LOOKS LIKE A GOOD PLACE TO REST, I'LL CALL UP TO YOU GUYS AND YOU CAN COME ON DOWN.
NO FURTHER THAN THE RIVER?
I PROMISE, I'LL STOP IF I GET THAT FAR AND CALL BACK UP.

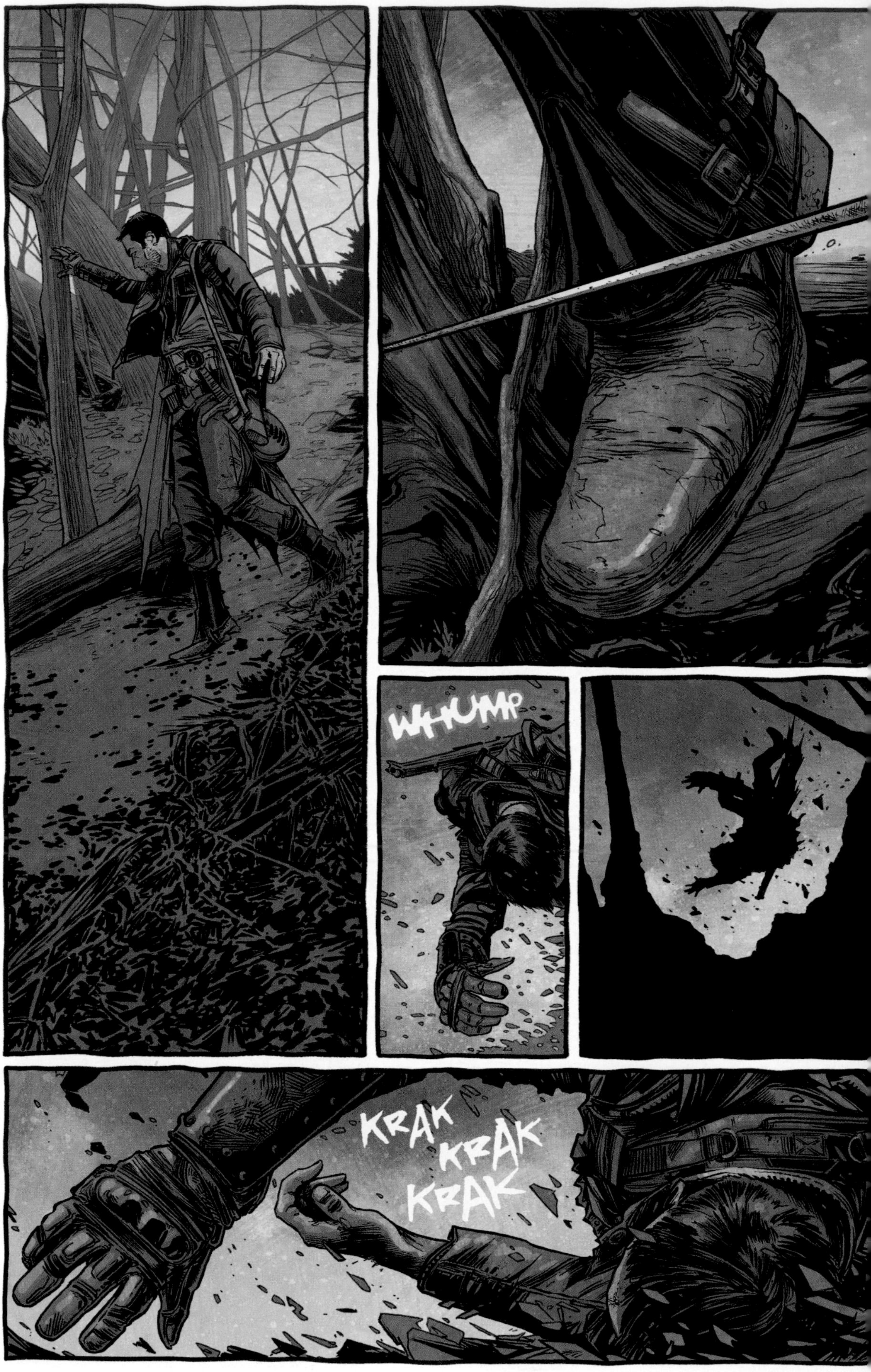
WHUMP
KRAK
KRAK
KRAK

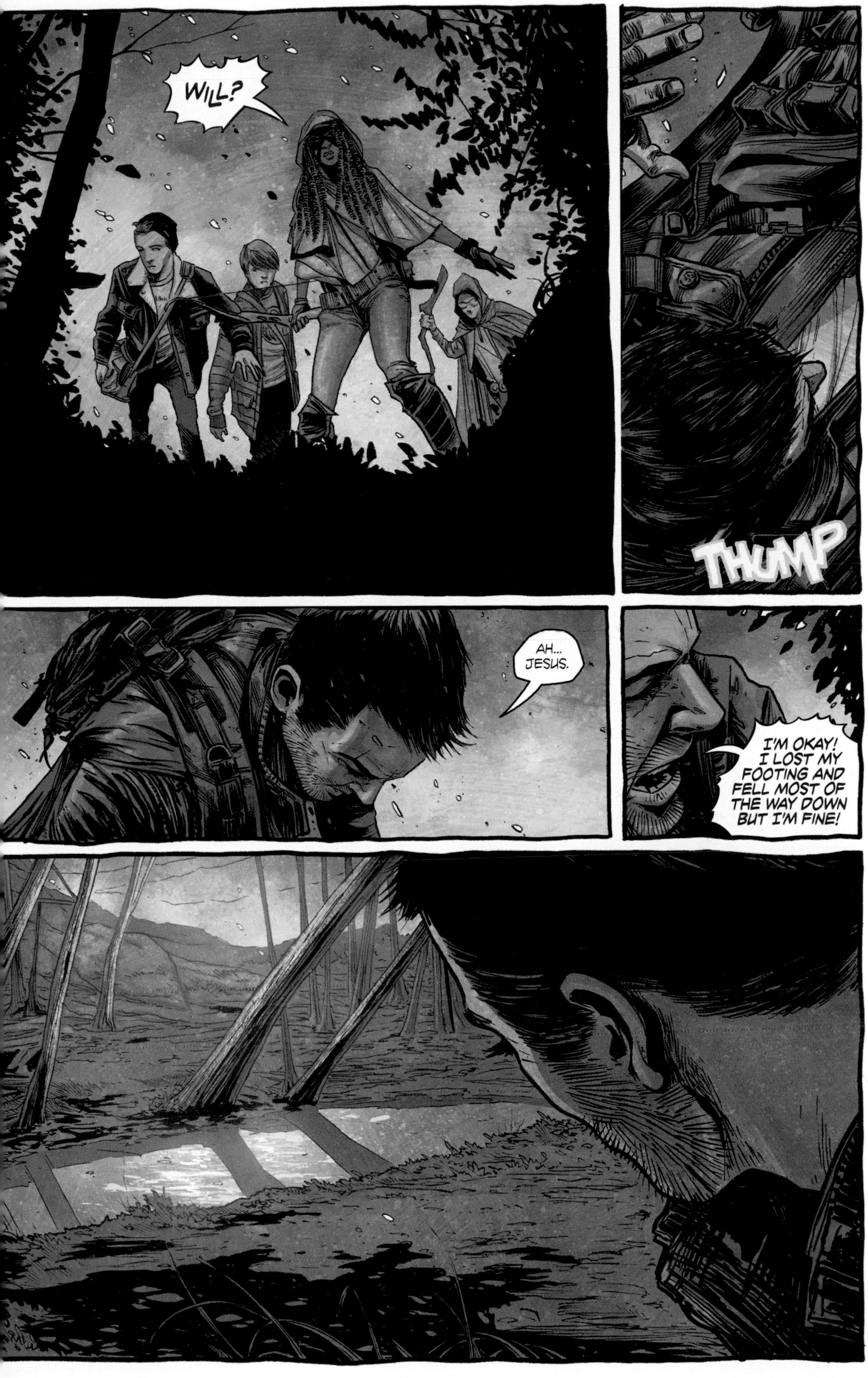
WILL?
THUMP
AH... JESUS.
I'M OKAY! I LOST MY FOOTING AND FELL MOST OF THE WAY DOWN BUT I'M FINE!

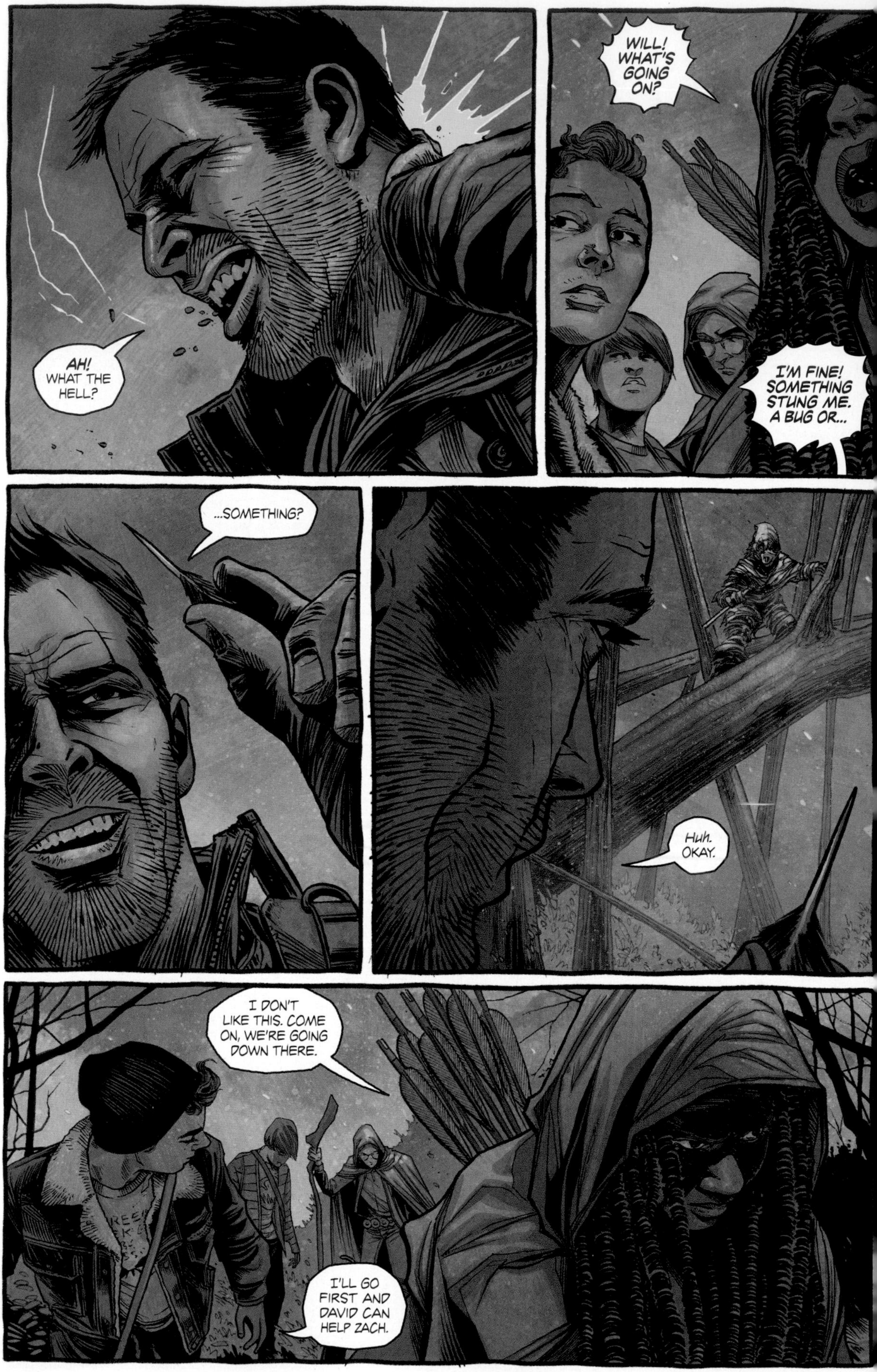
AH! WHAT THE HELL?
WILL! WHAT'S GOING ON?
I'M FINE! SOMETHING STUNG ME. A BUG OR...
...SOMETHING?
Huh. OKAY.
I DON'T LIKE THIS. COME ON, WE'RE GOING DOWN THERE.
I'LL GO FIRST AND DAVID CAN HELP ZACH.

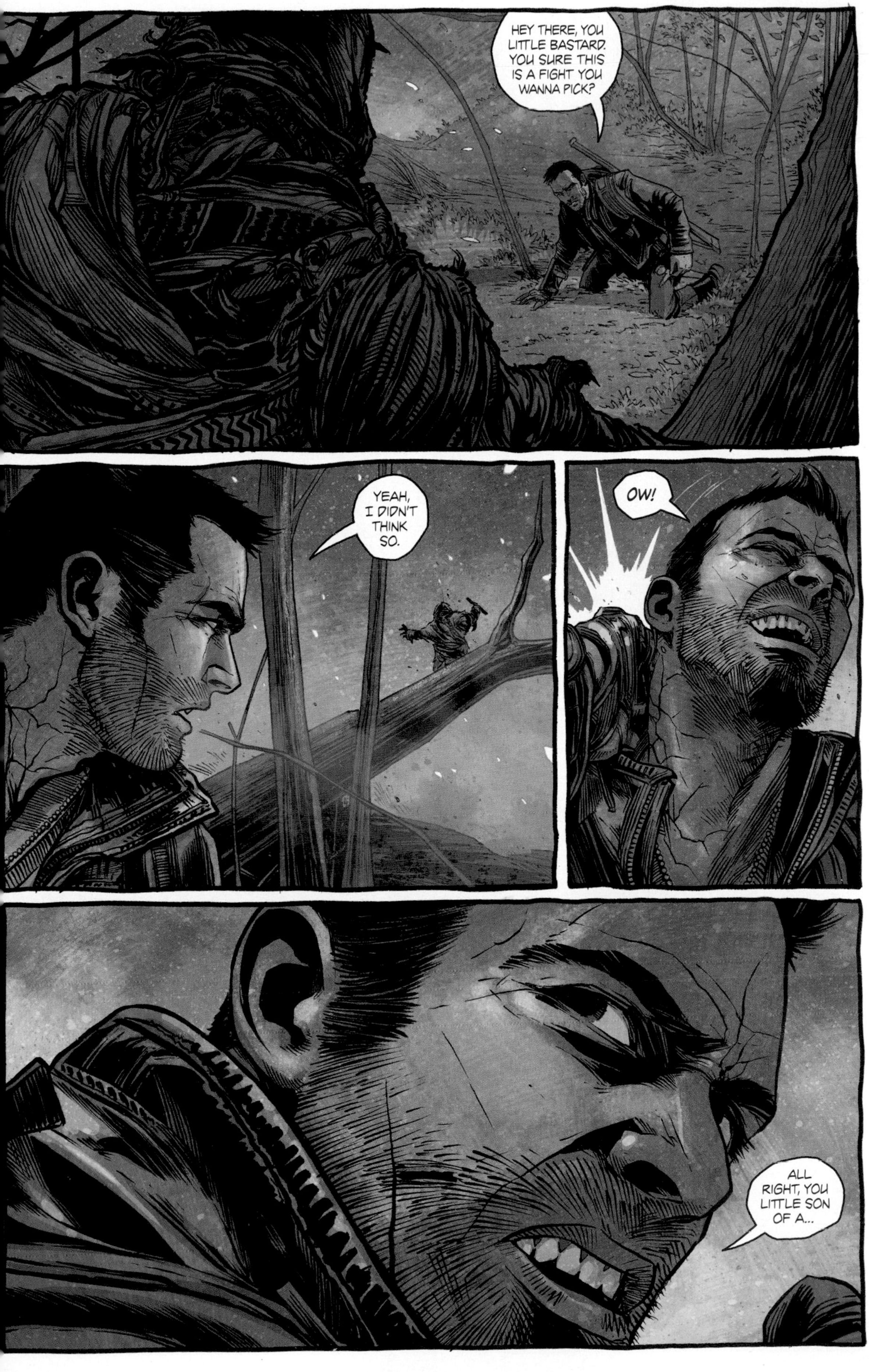
HEY THERE, YOU LITTLE BASTARD. YOU SURE THIS IS A FIGHT YOU WANNA PICK?
YEAH, I DIDN'T THINK SO.
OW!
ALL RIGHT, YOU LITTLE SON OF A...

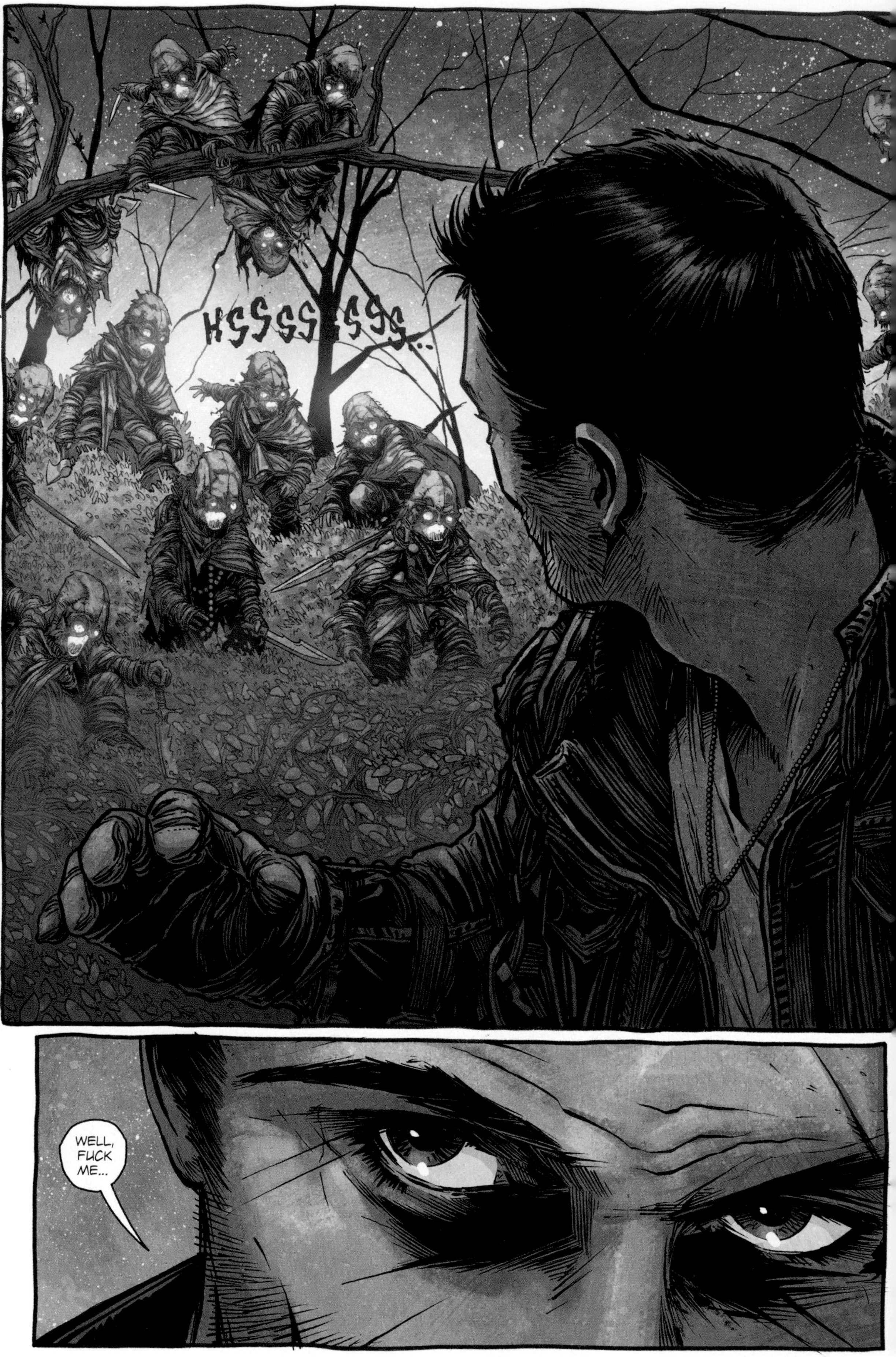
HSSSSSSSS...
WELL, FUCK ME...

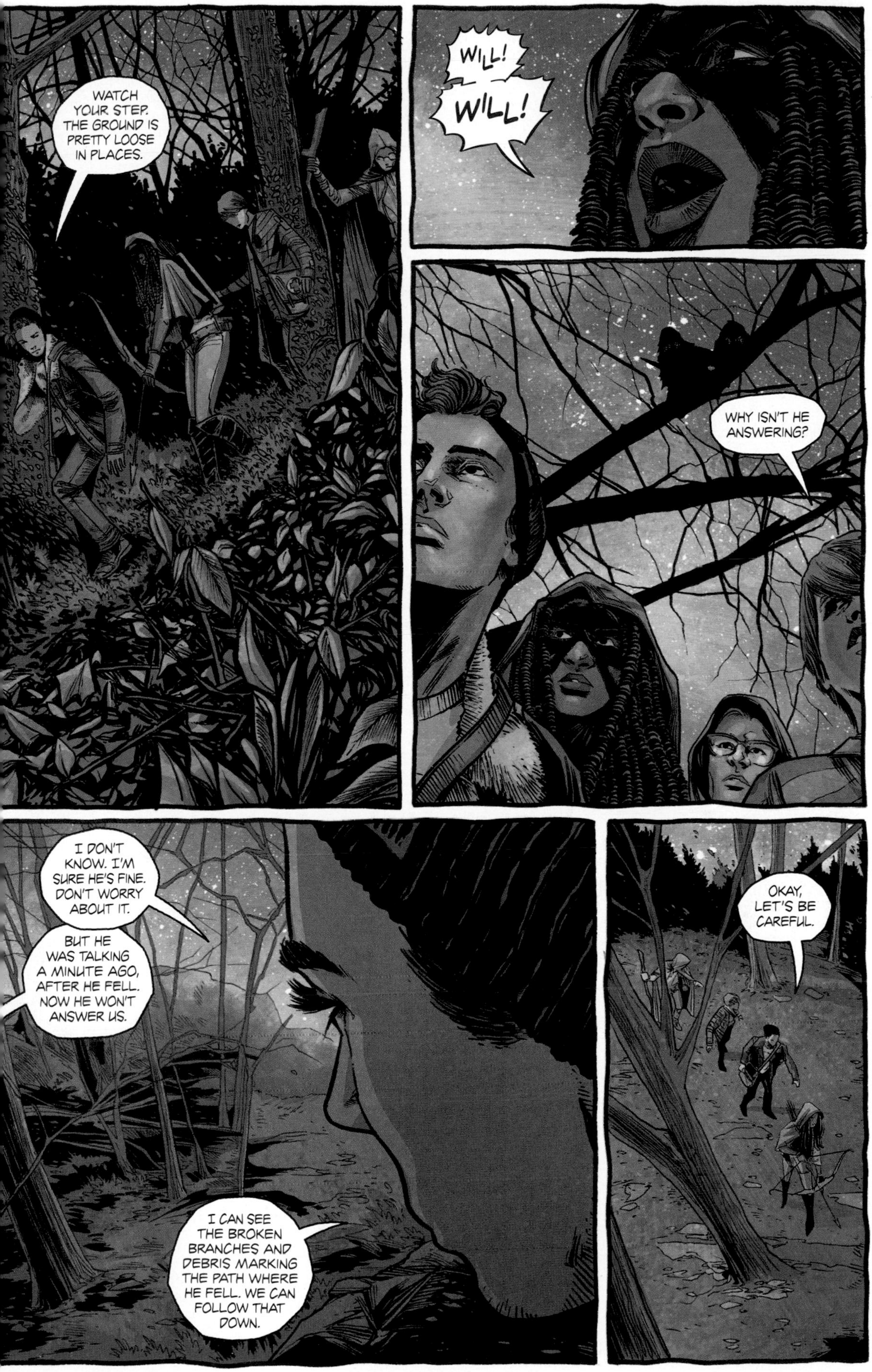
WATCH YOUR STEP. THE GROUND IS PRETTY LOOSE IN PLACES.
WILL!
WILL!
WHY ISN'T HE ANSWERING?
I DON'T KNOW. I'M SURE HE'S FINE. DON'T WORRY ABOUT IT.
BUT HE WAS TALKING A MINUTE AGO, AFTER HE FELL. NOW HE WON'T ANSWER US.
I CAN SEE THE BROKEN BRANCHES AND DEBRIS MARKING THE PATH WHERE HE FELL. WE CAN FOLLOW THAT DOWN.
OKAY, LET'S BE CAREFUL.

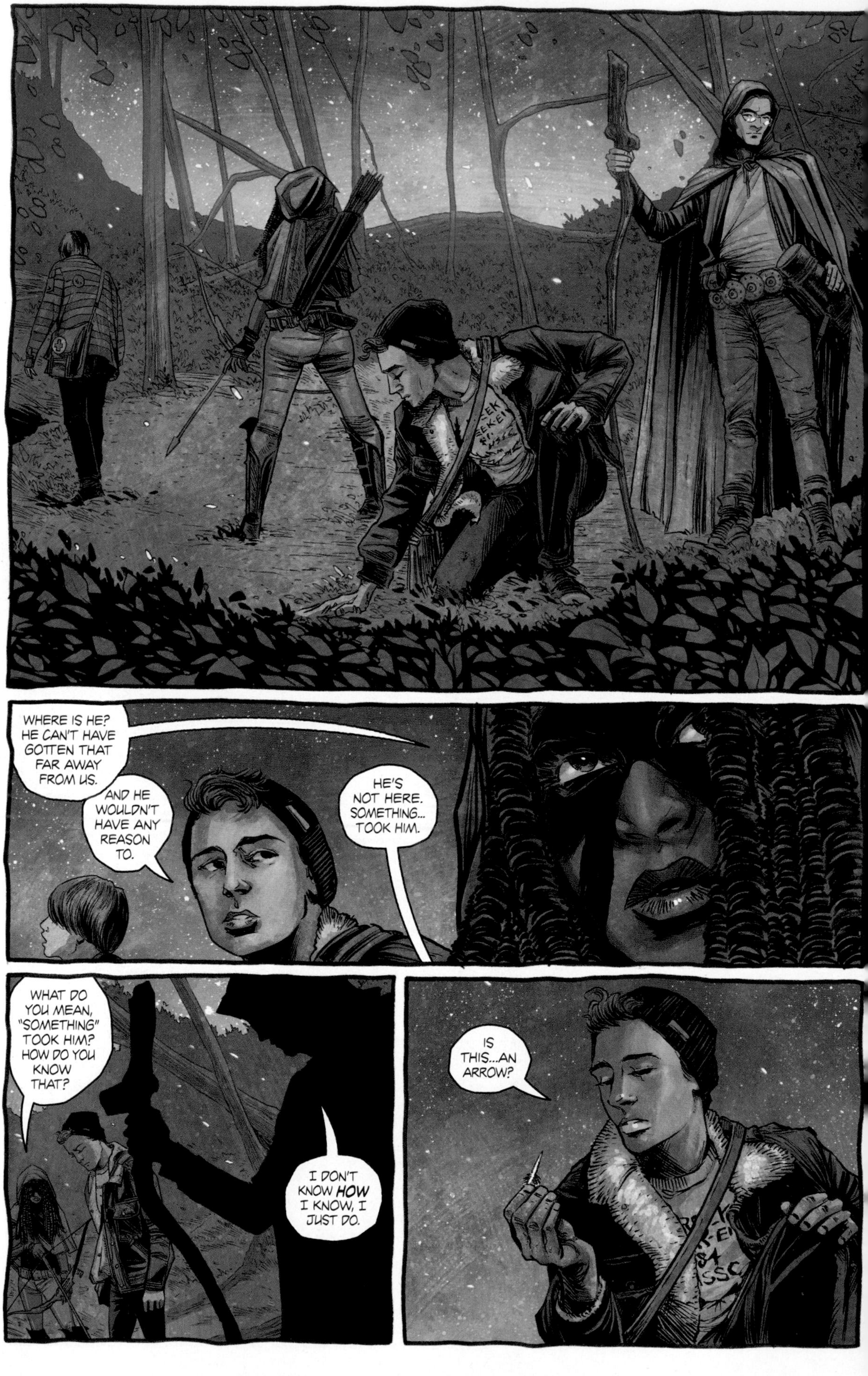
WHERE IS HE? HE CAN'T HAVE GOTTEN THAT FAR AWAY FROM US.
AND HE WOULDN'T HAVE ANY REASON TO.
HE'S NOT HERE. SOMETHING... TOOK HIM.
WHAT DO YOU MEAN, "SOMETHING" TOOK HIM? HOW DO YOU KNOW THAT?
I DON'T KNOW **HOW** I KNOW, I JUST DO.
IS THIS...AN ARROW?

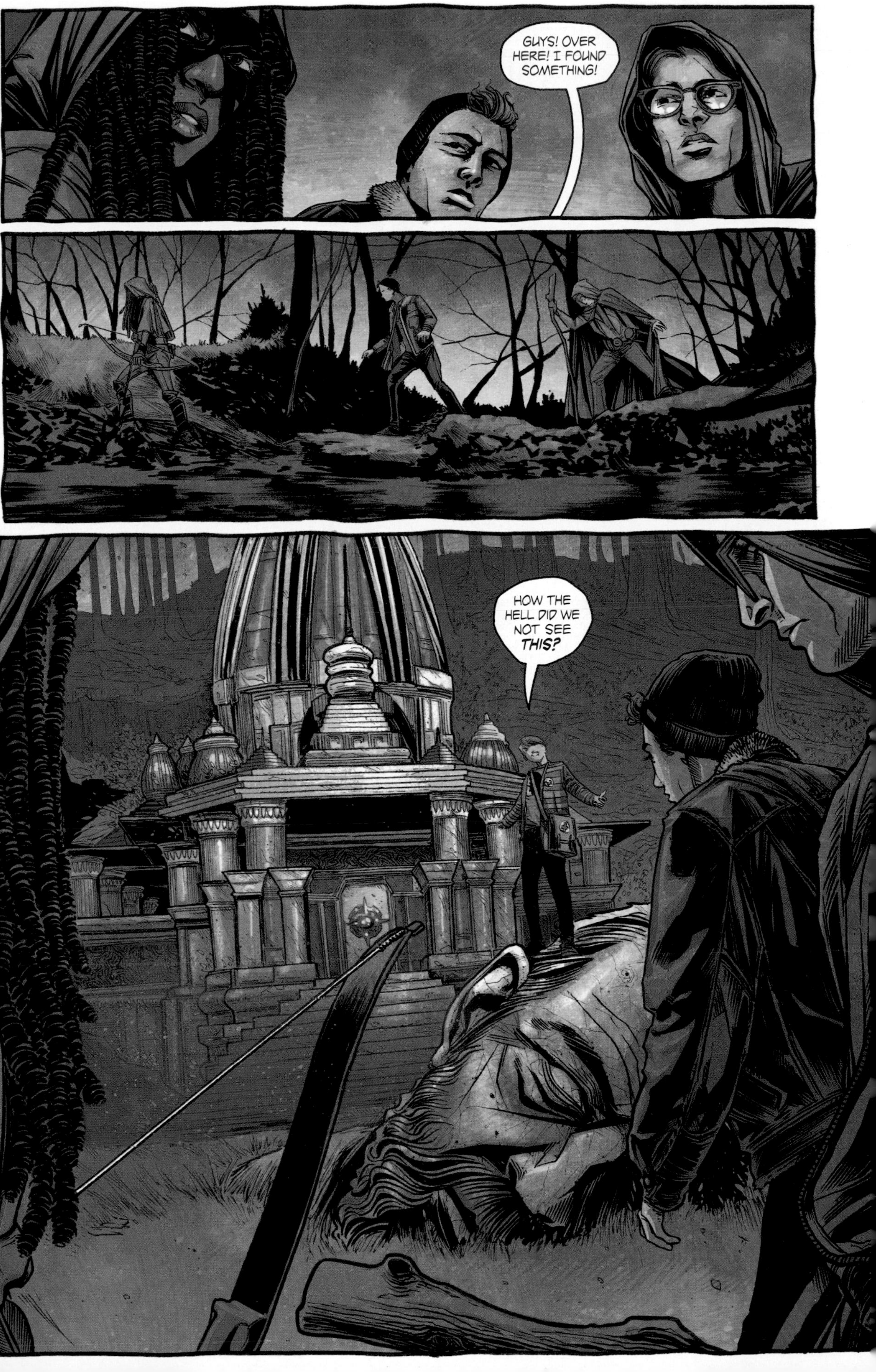
GUYS! OVER HERE! I FOUND SOMETHING!
HOW THE HELL DID WE NOT SEE THIS?

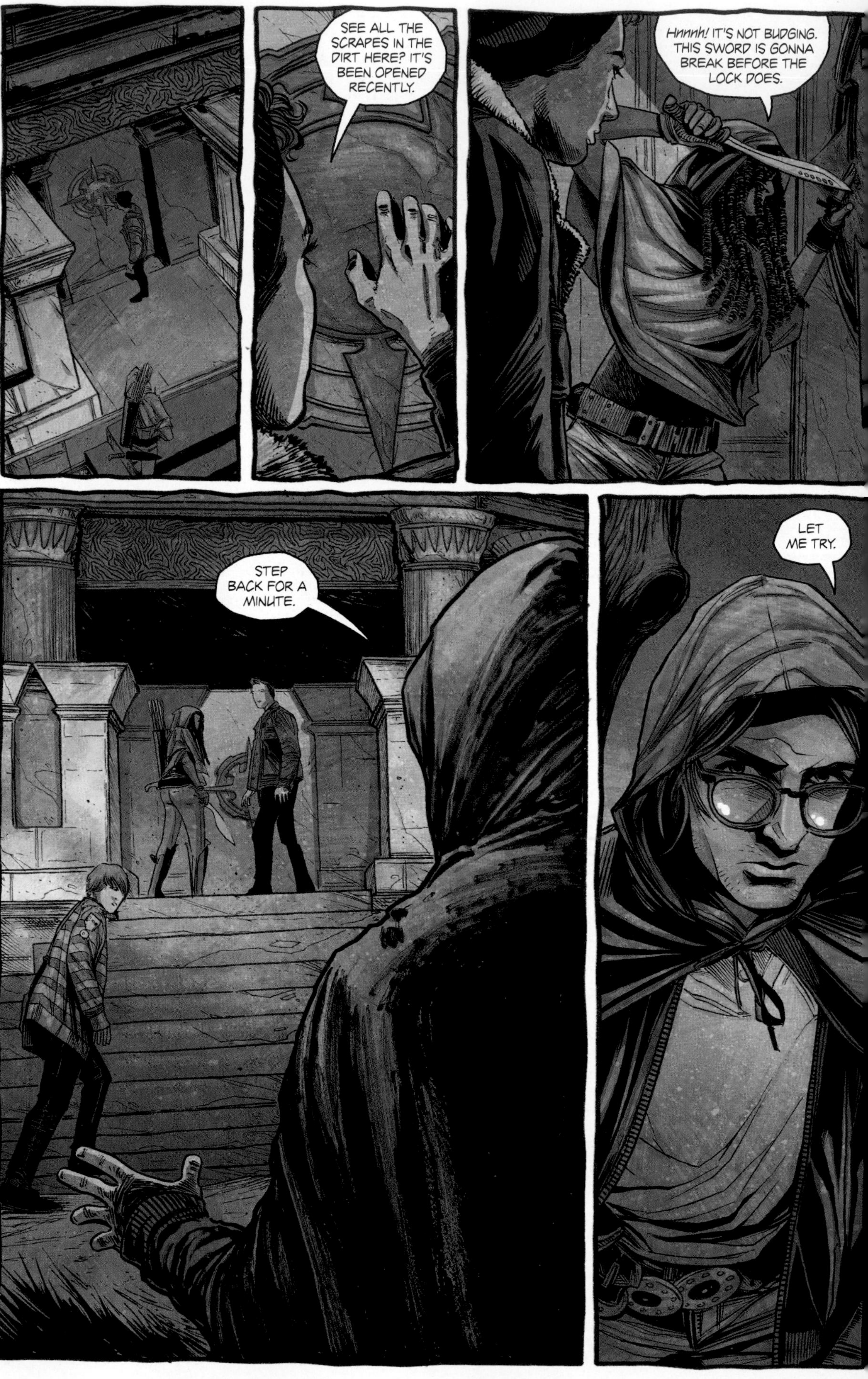
SEE ALL THE SCRAPES IN THE DIRT HERE? IT'S BEEN OPENED RECENTLY.
Hnnnh! IT'S NOT BUDGING. THIS SWORD IS GONNA BREAK BEFORE THE LOCK DOES.
STEP BACK FOR A MINUTE.
LET ME TRY.

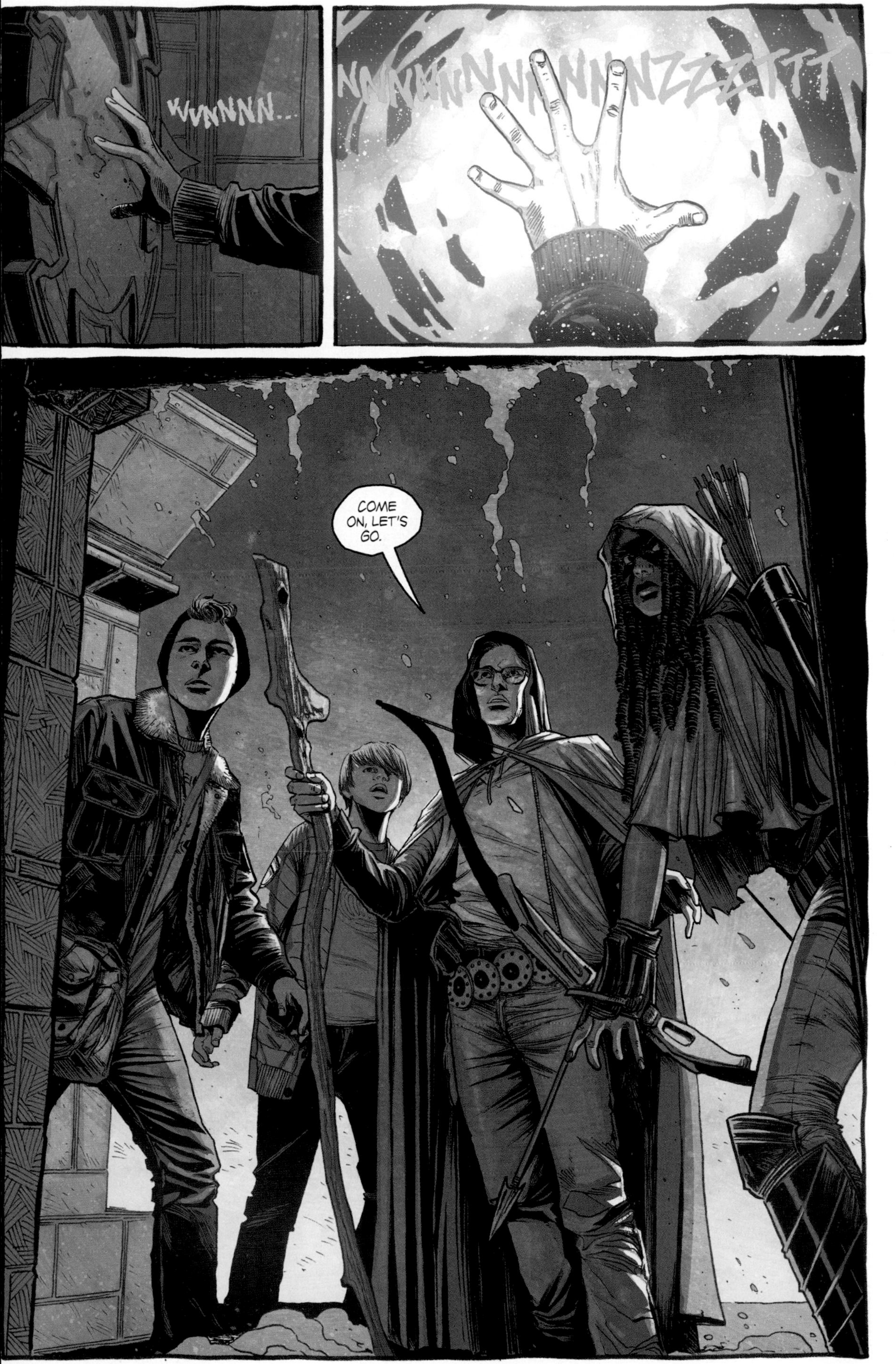
KVVNNNN...
NNNNNNNNNNNNNZZZZTTT
COME ON, LET'S GO.

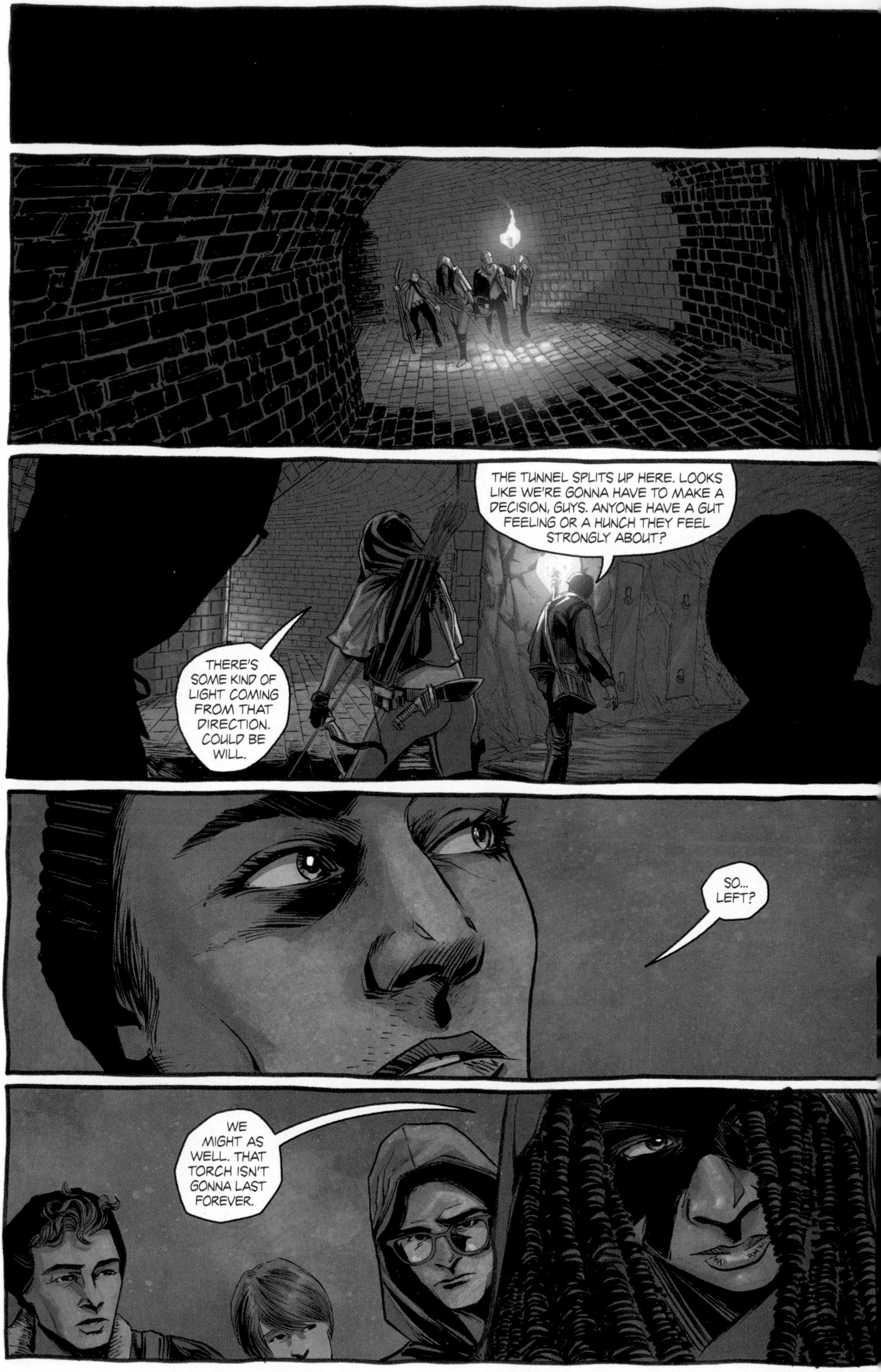
THE TUNNEL SPLITS UP HERE. LOOKS LIKE WE'RE GONNA HAVE TO MAKE A DECISION, GUYS. ANYONE HAVE A GUT FEELING OR A HUNCH THEY FEEL STRONGLY ABOUT?
THERE'S SOME KIND OF LIGHT COMING FROM THAT DIRECTION. COULD BE WILL.
SO... LEFT?
WE MIGHT AS WELL. THAT TORCH ISN'T GONNA LAST FOREVER.

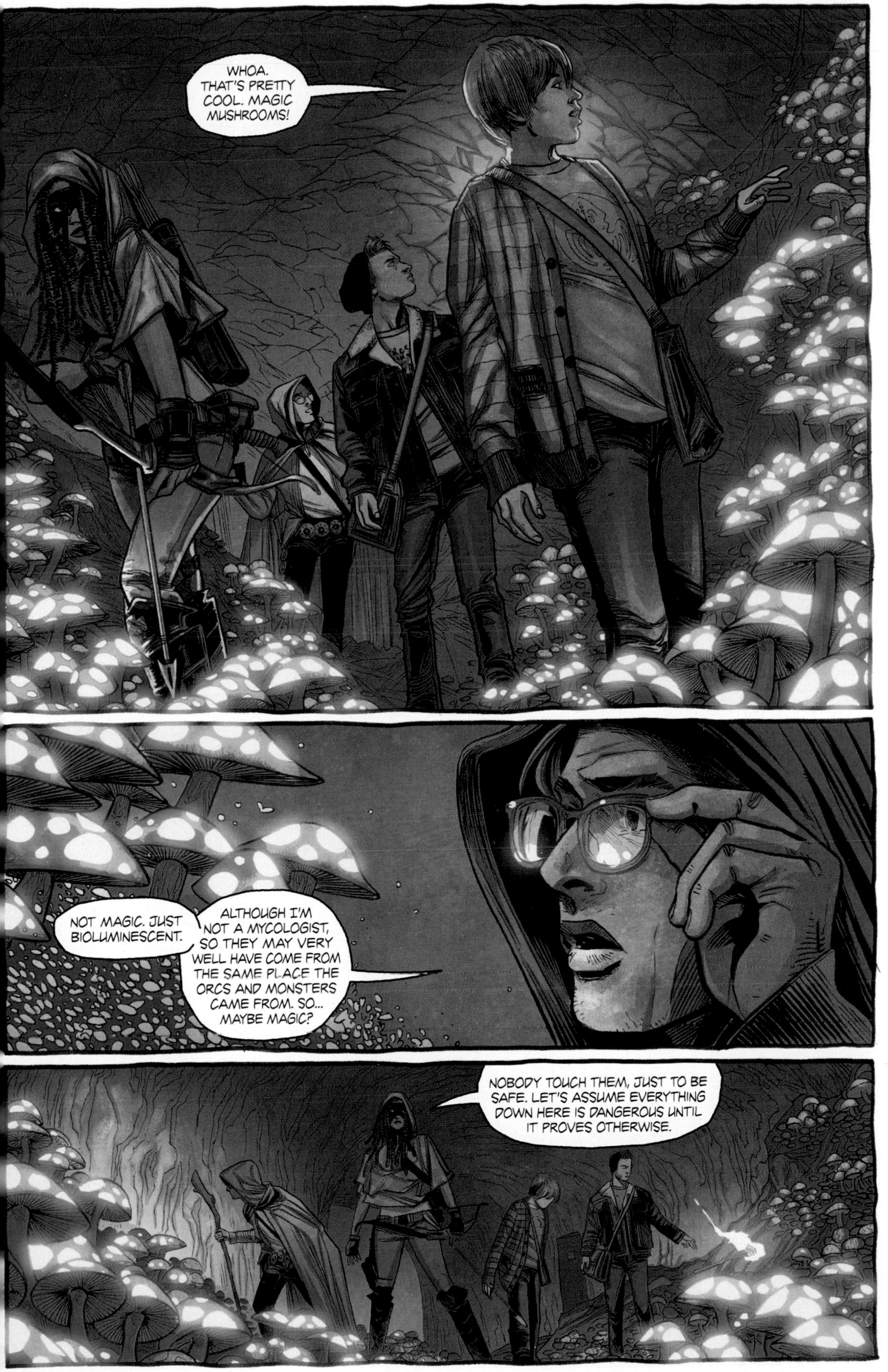
WHOA. THAT'S PRETTY COOL. MAGIC MUSHROOMS!
NOT MAGIC. JUST BIOLUMINESCENT.
ALTHOUGH I'M NOT A MYCOLOGIST, SO THEY MAY VERY WELL HAVE COME FROM THE SAME PLACE THE ORCS AND MONSTERS CAME FROM. SO... MAYBE MAGIC?
NOBODY TOUCH THEM, JUST TO BE SAFE. LET'S ASSUME EVERYTHING DOWN HERE IS DANGEROUS UNTIL IT PROVES OTHERWISE.

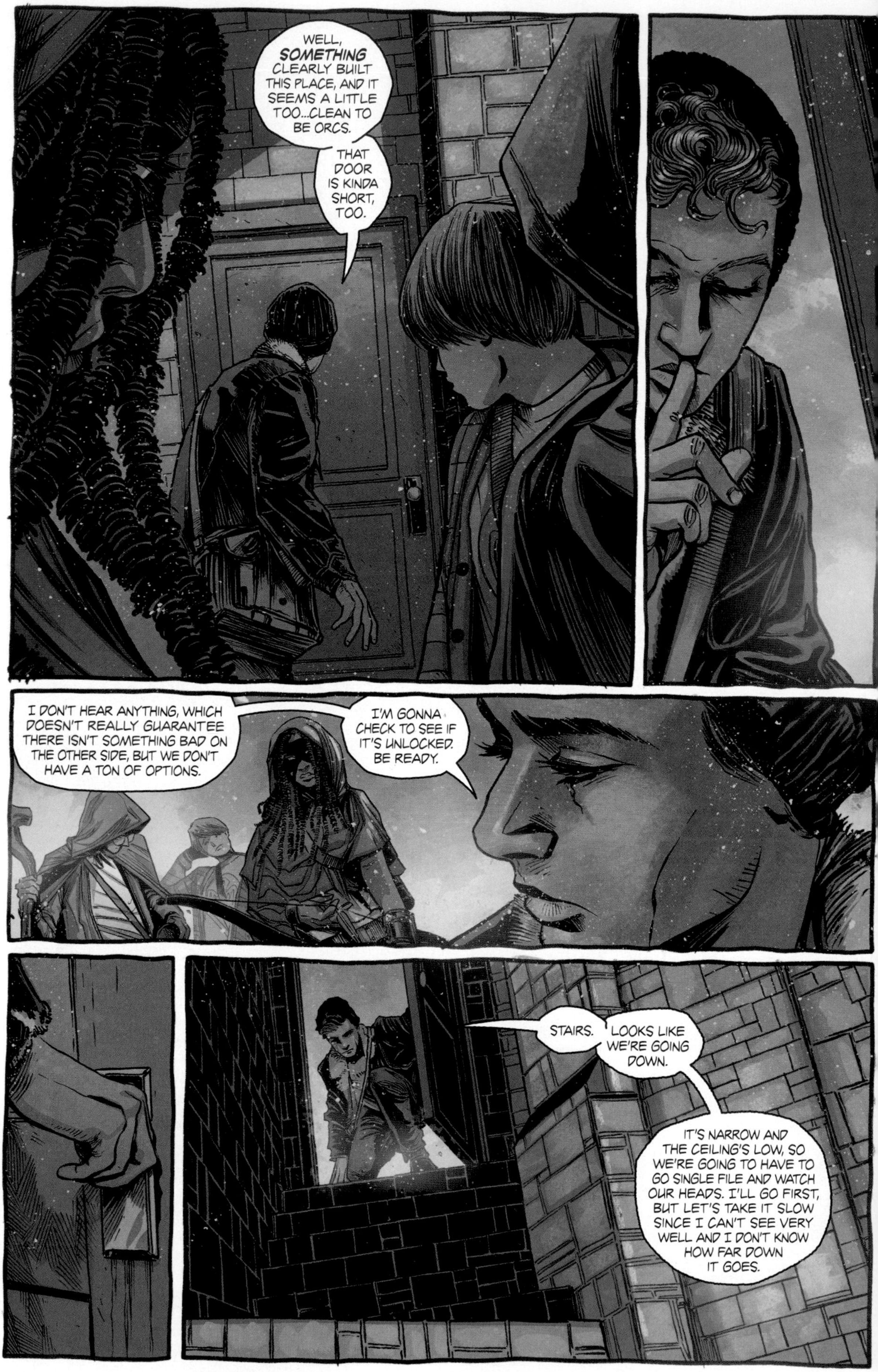
WELL, **SOMETHING** CLEARLY BUILT THIS PLACE, AND IT SEEMS A LITTLE TOO...CLEAN TO BE ORCS.
THAT DOOR IS KINDA SHORT, TOO.
I DON'T HEAR ANYTHING, WHICH DOESN'T REALLY GUARANTEE THERE ISN'T SOMETHING BAD ON THE OTHER SIDE, BUT WE DON'T HAVE A TON OF OPTIONS.
I'M GONNA CHECK TO SEE IF IT'S UNLOCKED. BE READY.
STAIRS.
LOOKS LIKE WE'RE GOING DOWN.
IT'S NARROW AND THE CEILING'S LOW, SO WE'RE GOING TO HAVE TO GO SINGLE FILE AND WATCH OUR HEADS. I'LL GO FIRST, BUT LET'S TAKE IT SLOW SINCE I CAN'T SEE VERY WELL AND I DON'T KNOW HOW FAR DOWN IT GOES.

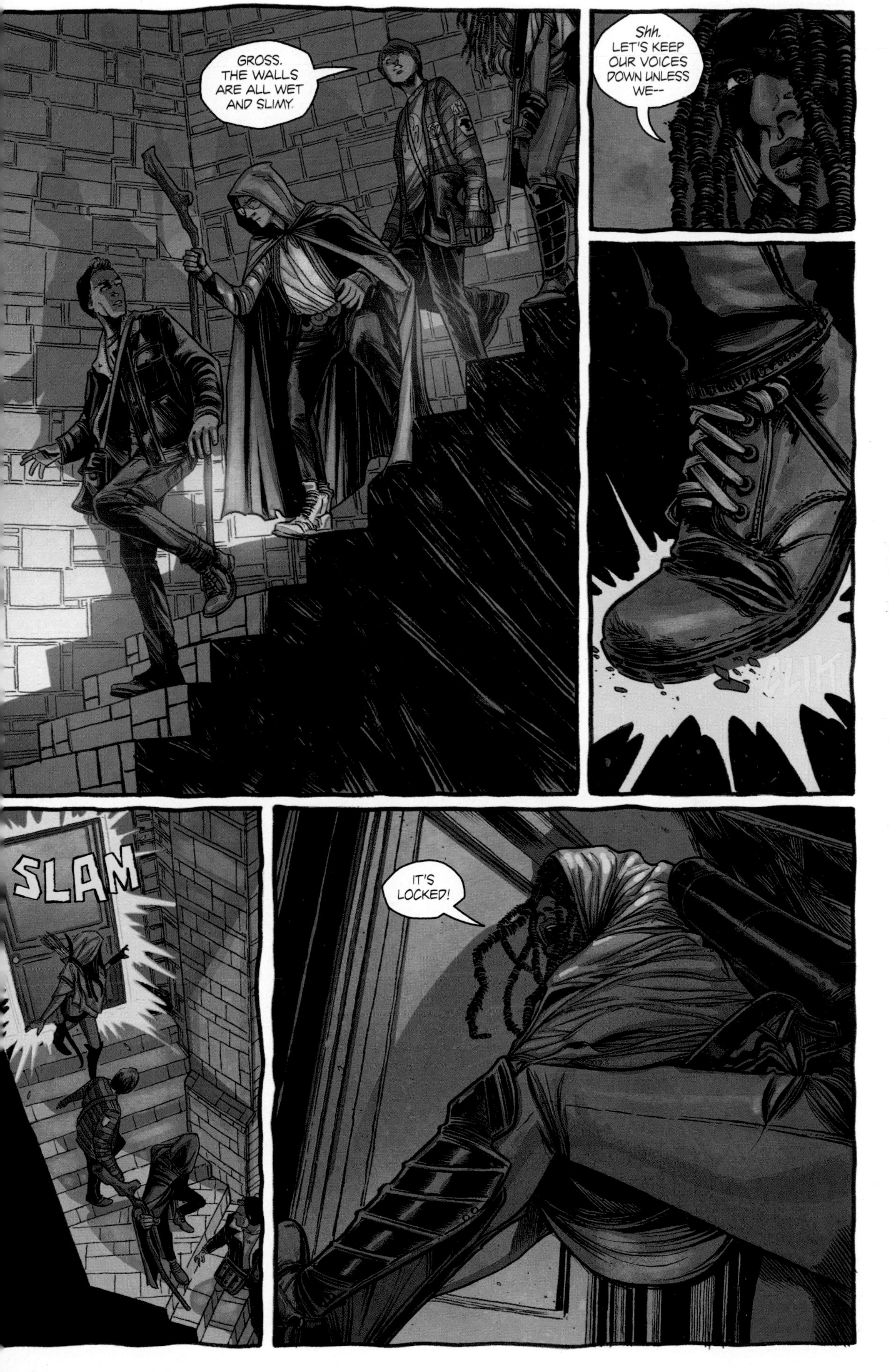
GROSS. THE WALLS ARE ALL WET AND SLIMY.
Shh. LET'S KEEP OUR VOICES DOWN UNLESS WE--
CLIK
SLAM
IT'S LOCKED!

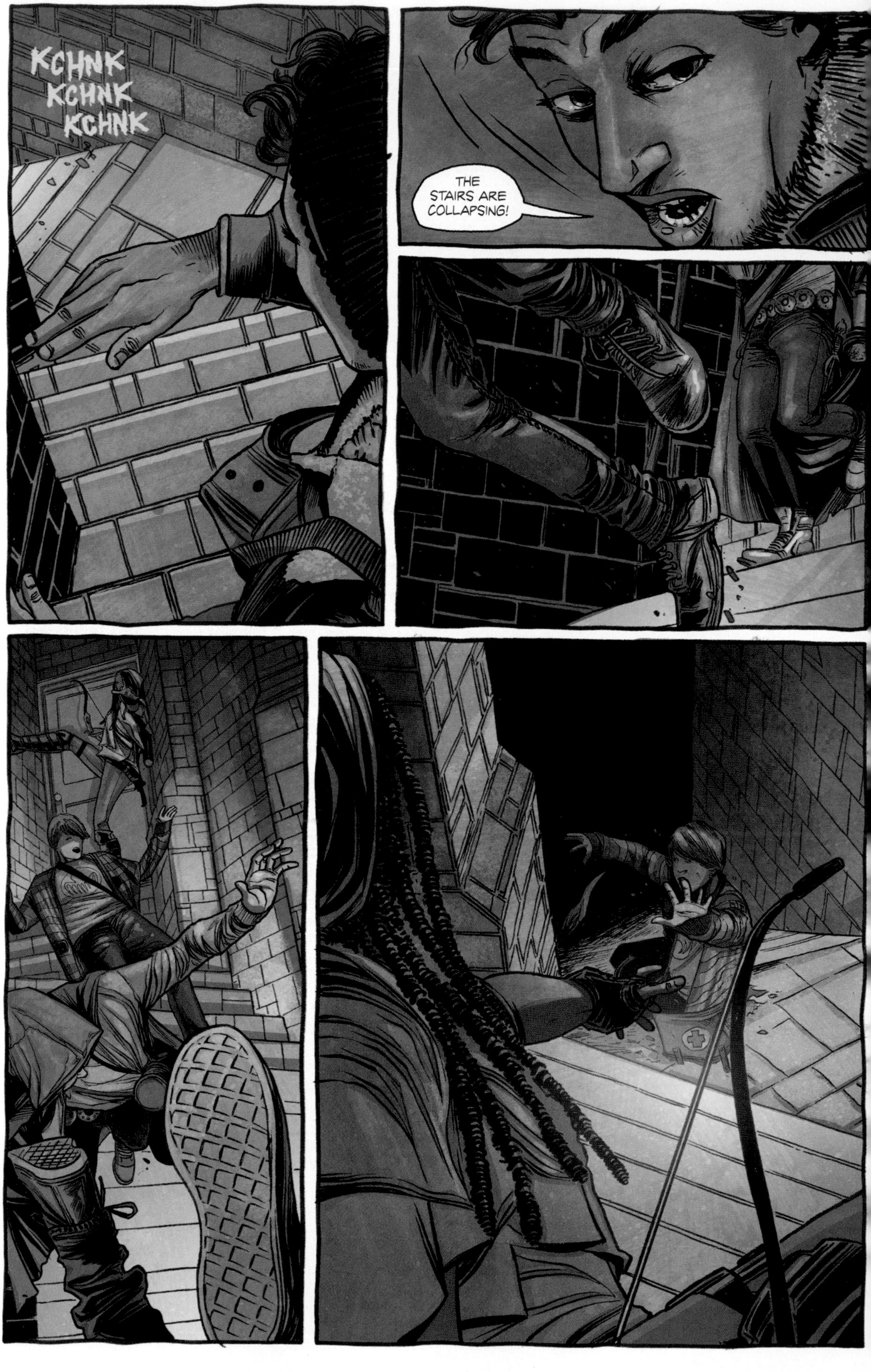
KCHNK
KCHNK
KCHNK
THE STAIRS ARE COLLAPSING!

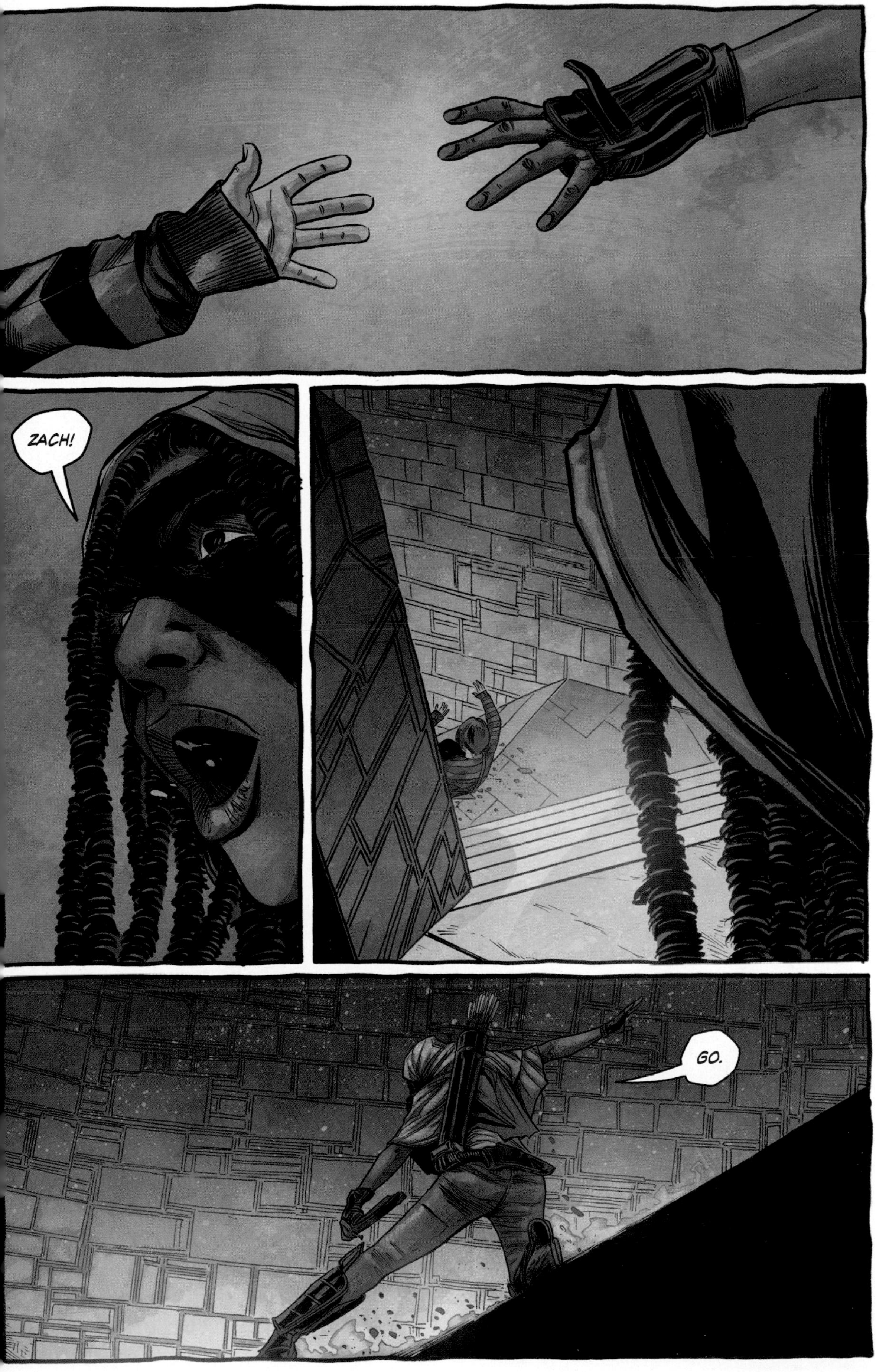
ZACH!
GO.

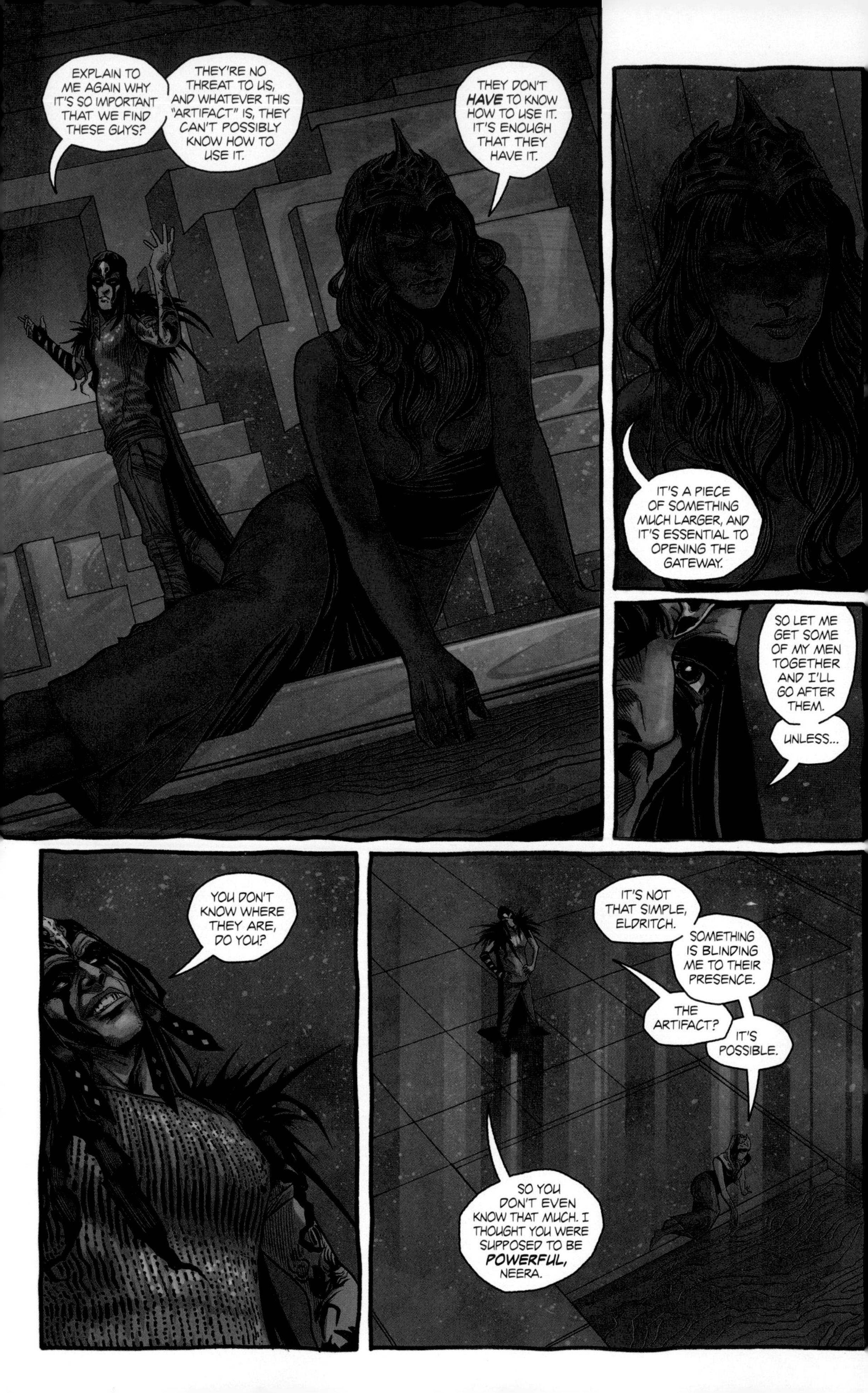
EXPLAIN TO ME AGAIN WHY IT'S SO IMPORTANT THAT WE FIND THESE GUYS?
THEY'RE NO THREAT TO US, AND WHATEVER THIS "ARTIFACT" IS, THEY CAN'T POSSIBLY KNOW HOW TO USE IT.
THEY DON'T **HAVE** TO KNOW HOW TO USE IT. IT'S ENOUGH THAT THEY HAVE IT.
IT'S A PIECE OF SOMETHING MUCH LARGER, AND IT'S ESSENTIAL TO OPENING THE GATEWAY.
SO LET ME GET SOME OF MY MEN TOGETHER AND I'LL GO AFTER THEM.
UNLESS...
YOU DON'T KNOW WHERE THEY ARE, DO YOU?
IT'S NOT THAT SIMPLE, ELDRITCH.
SOMETHING IS BLINDING ME TO THEIR PRESENCE.
THE ARTIFACT?
IT'S POSSIBLE.
SO YOU DON'T EVEN KNOW THAT MUCH. I THOUGHT YOU WERE SUPPOSED TO BE **POWERFUL,** NEERA.

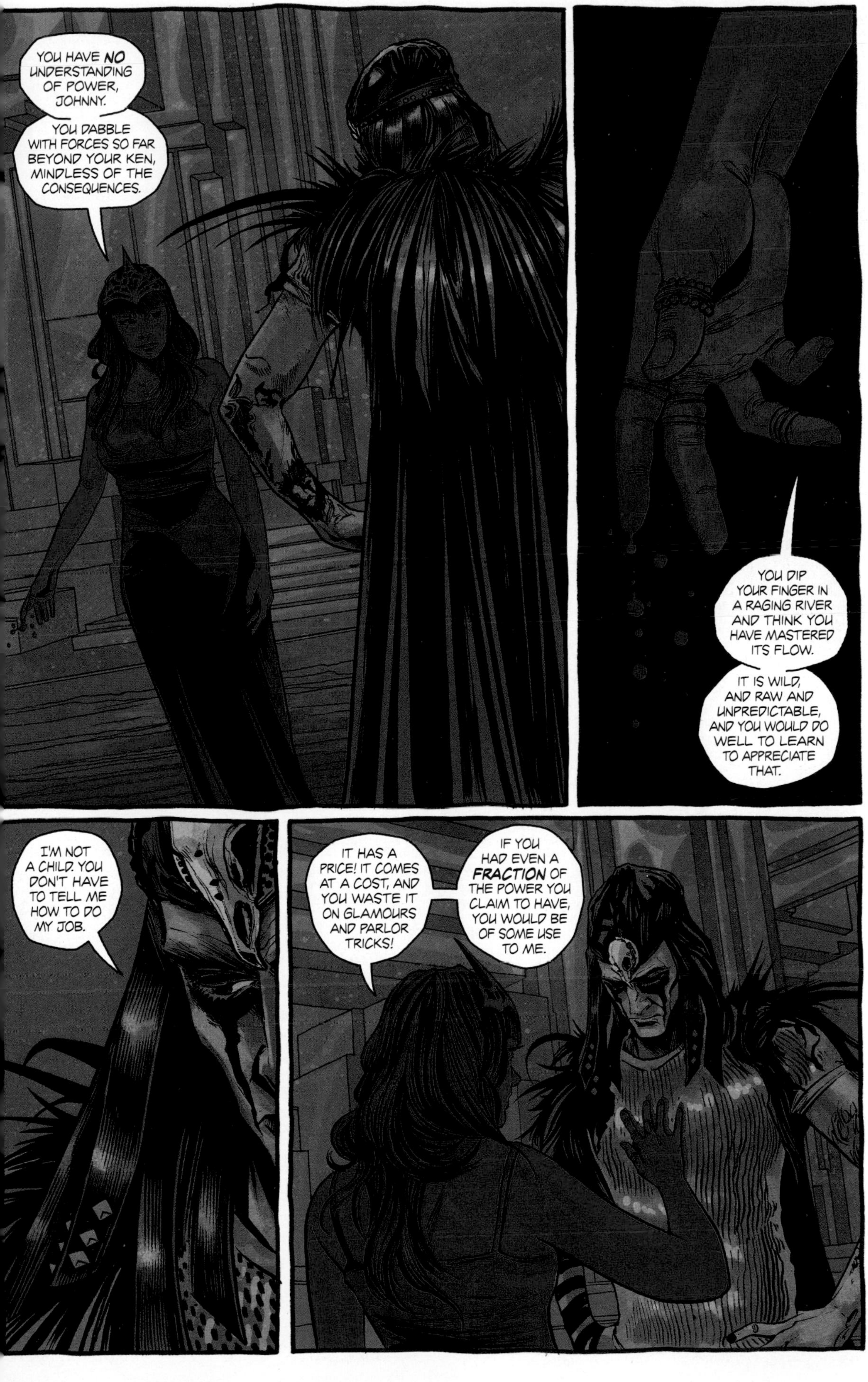
YOU HAVE NO UNDERSTANDING OF POWER, JOHNNY.
YOU DABBLE WITH FORCES SO FAR BEYOND YOUR KEN, MINDLESS OF THE CONSEQUENCES.
YOU DIP YOUR FINGER IN A RAGING RIVER AND THINK YOU HAVE MASTERED ITS FLOW.
IT IS WILD, AND RAW AND UNPREDICTABLE, AND YOU WOULD DO WELL TO LEARN TO APPRECIATE THAT.
I'M NOT A CHILD. YOU DON'T HAVE TO TELL ME HOW TO DO MY JOB.
IT HAS A PRICE! IT COMES AT A COST, AND YOU WASTE IT ON GLAMOURS AND PARLOR TRICKS!
IF YOU HAD EVEN A FRACTION OF THE POWER YOU CLAIM TO HAVE, YOU WOULD BE OF SOME USE TO ME.

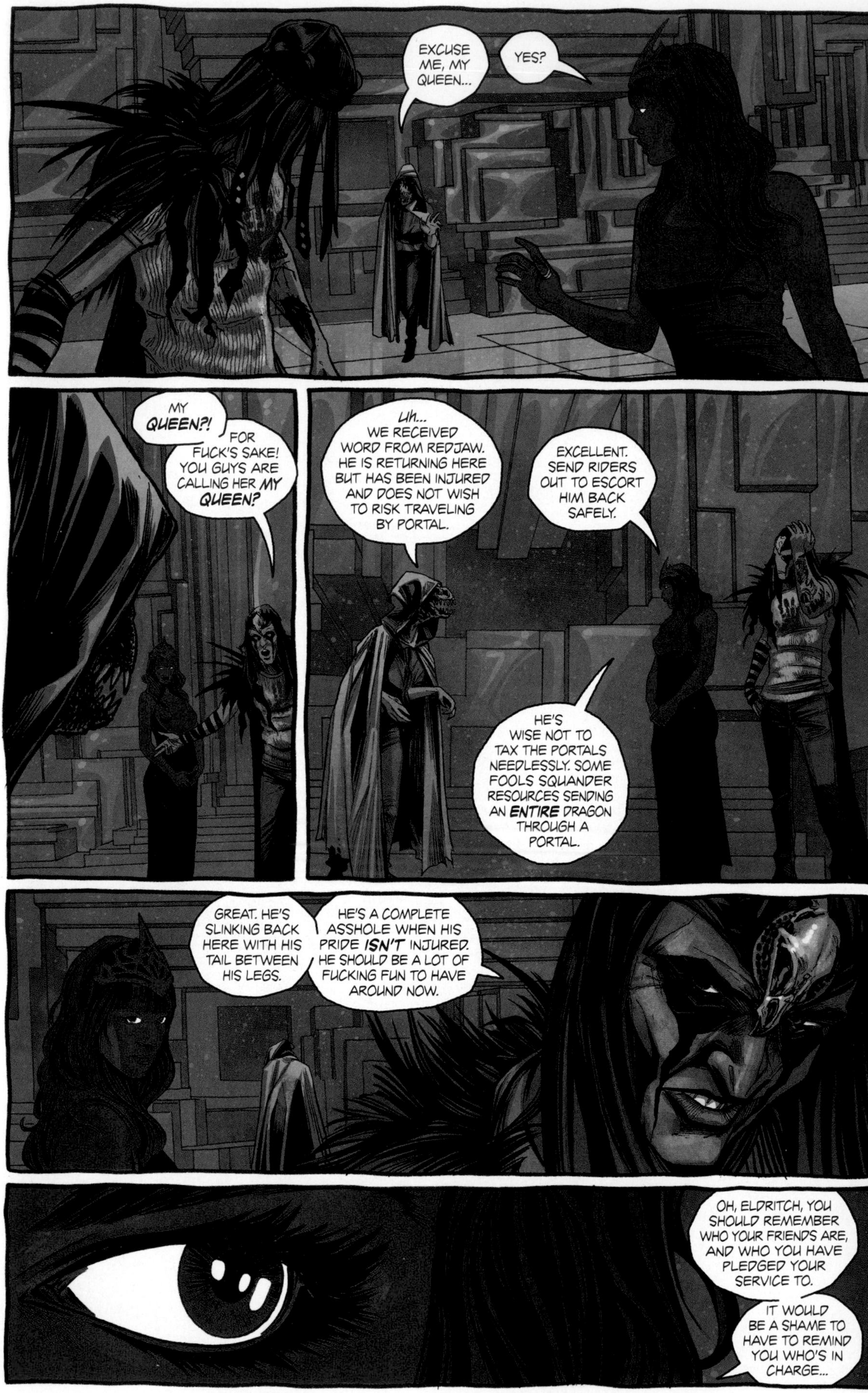

EXCUSE ME, MY QUEEN...
YES?
MY QUEEN?!
FOR FUCK'S SAKE! YOU GUYS ARE CALLING HER MY QUEEN?
UH... WE RECEIVED WORD FROM REDJAW. HE IS RETURNING HERE BUT HAS BEEN INJURED AND DOES NOT WISH TO RISK TRAVELING BY PORTAL.
EXCELLENT. SEND RIDERS OUT TO ESCORT HIM BACK SAFELY.
HE'S WISE NOT TO TAX THE PORTALS NEEDLESSLY. SOME FOOLS SQUANDER RESOURCES SENDING AN ENTIRE DRAGON THROUGH A PORTAL.
GREAT. HE'S SLINKING BACK HERE WITH HIS TAIL BETWEEN HIS LEGS.
HE'S A COMPLETE ASSHOLE WHEN HIS PRIDE ISN'T INJURED. HE SHOULD BE A LOT OF FUCKING FUN TO HAVE AROUND NOW.
OH, ELDRITCH, YOU SHOULD REMEMBER WHO YOUR FRIENDS ARE, AND WHO YOU HAVE PLEDGED YOUR SERVICE TO.
IT WOULD BE A SHAME TO HAVE TO REMIND YOU WHO'S IN CHARGE...

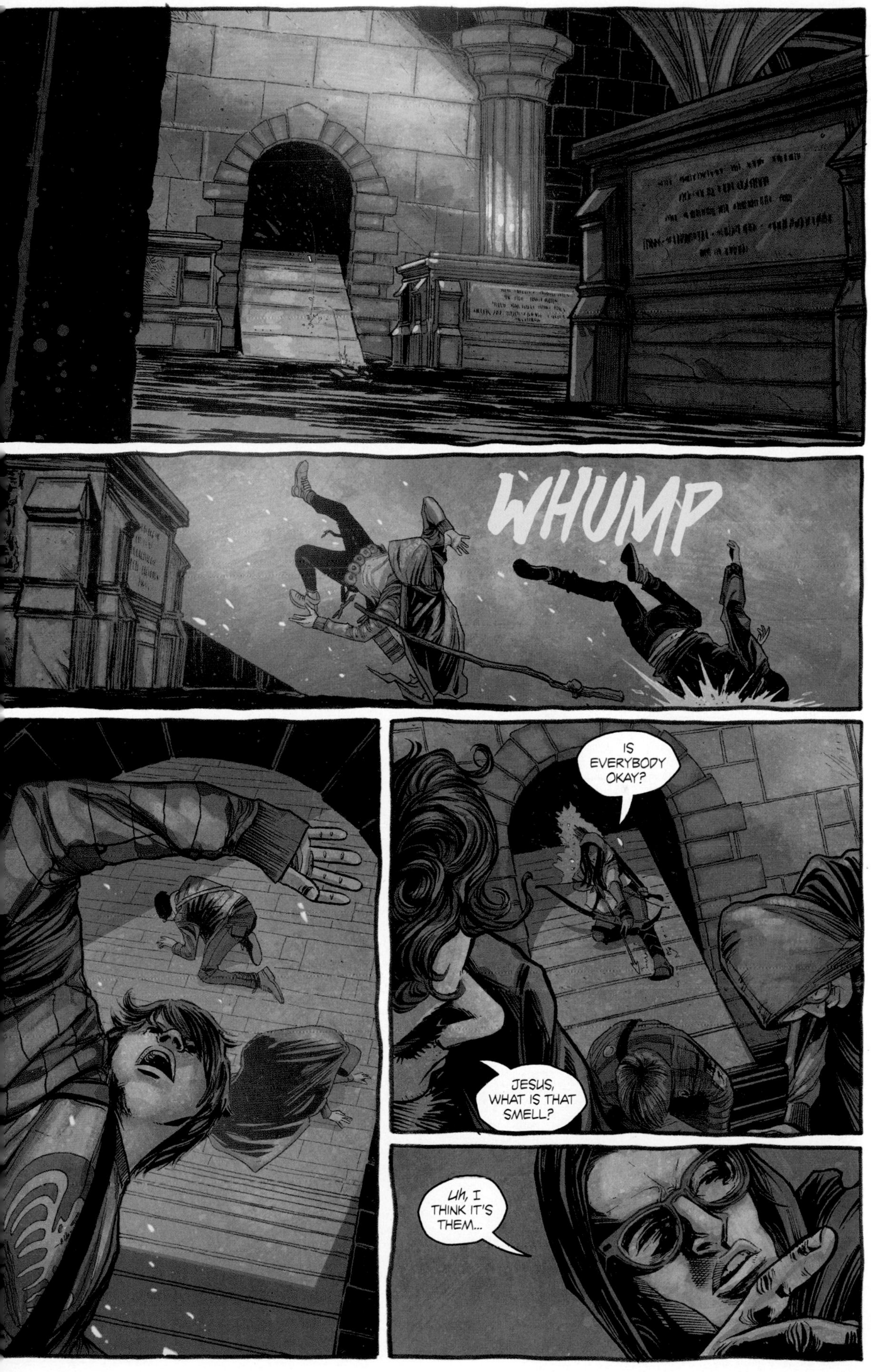
WHUMP
IS EVERYBODY OKAY?
JESUS, WHAT IS THAT SMELL?
UH, I THINK IT'S THEM...

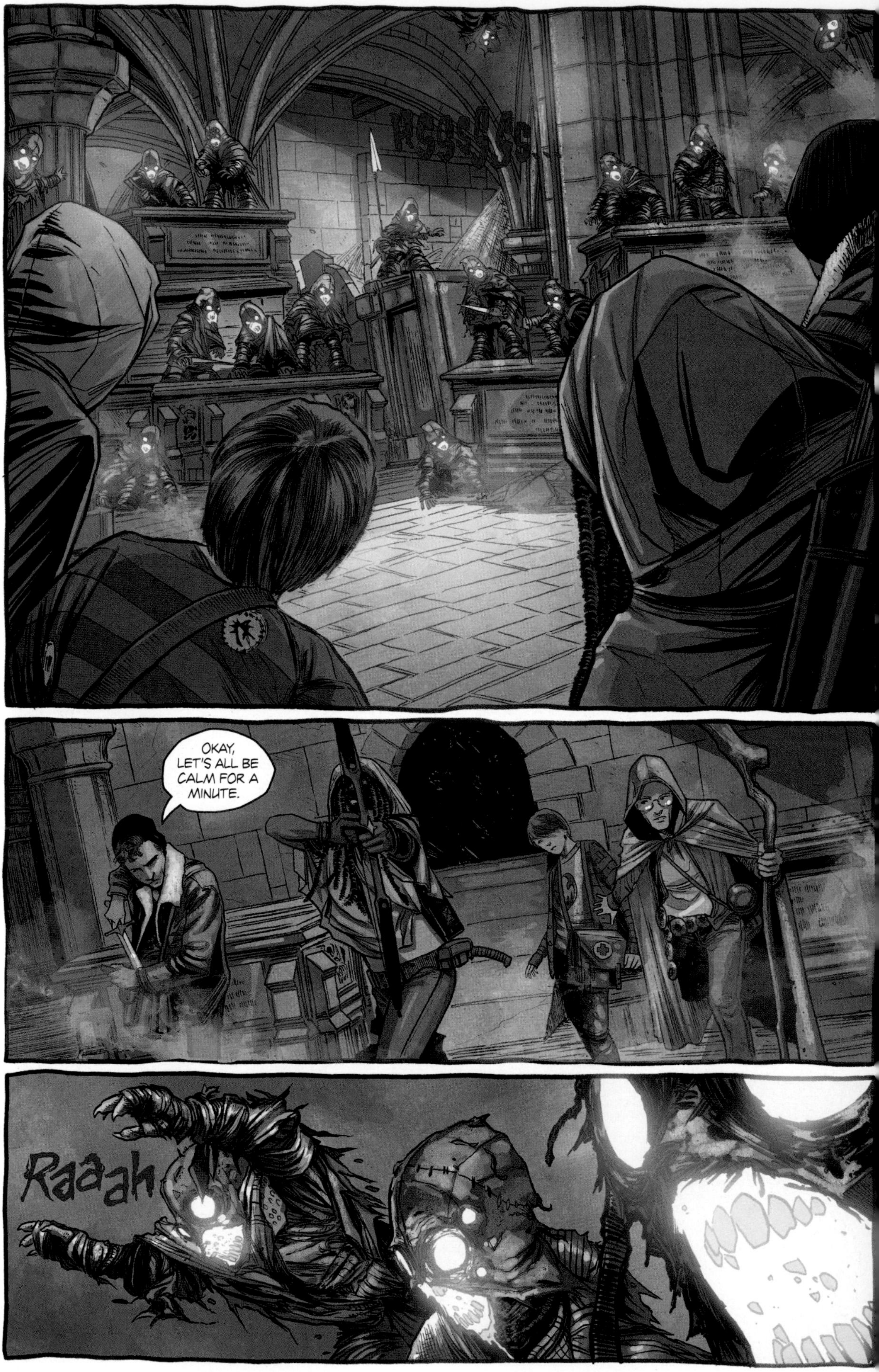
OKAY, LET'S ALL BE CALM FOR A MINUTE.
Raaah

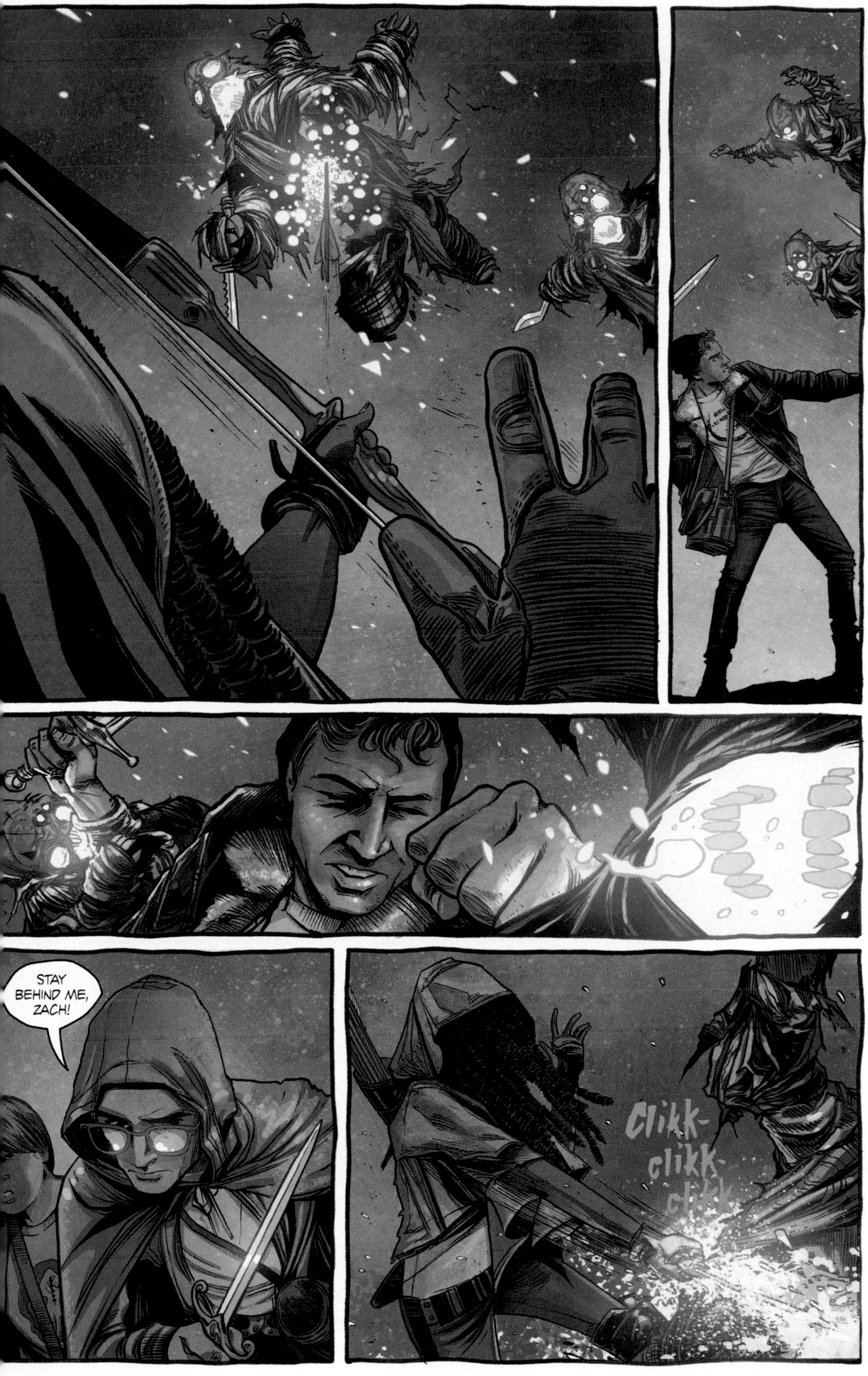
STAY BEHIND ME, ZACH!
Clikk-
clikk-
clikk

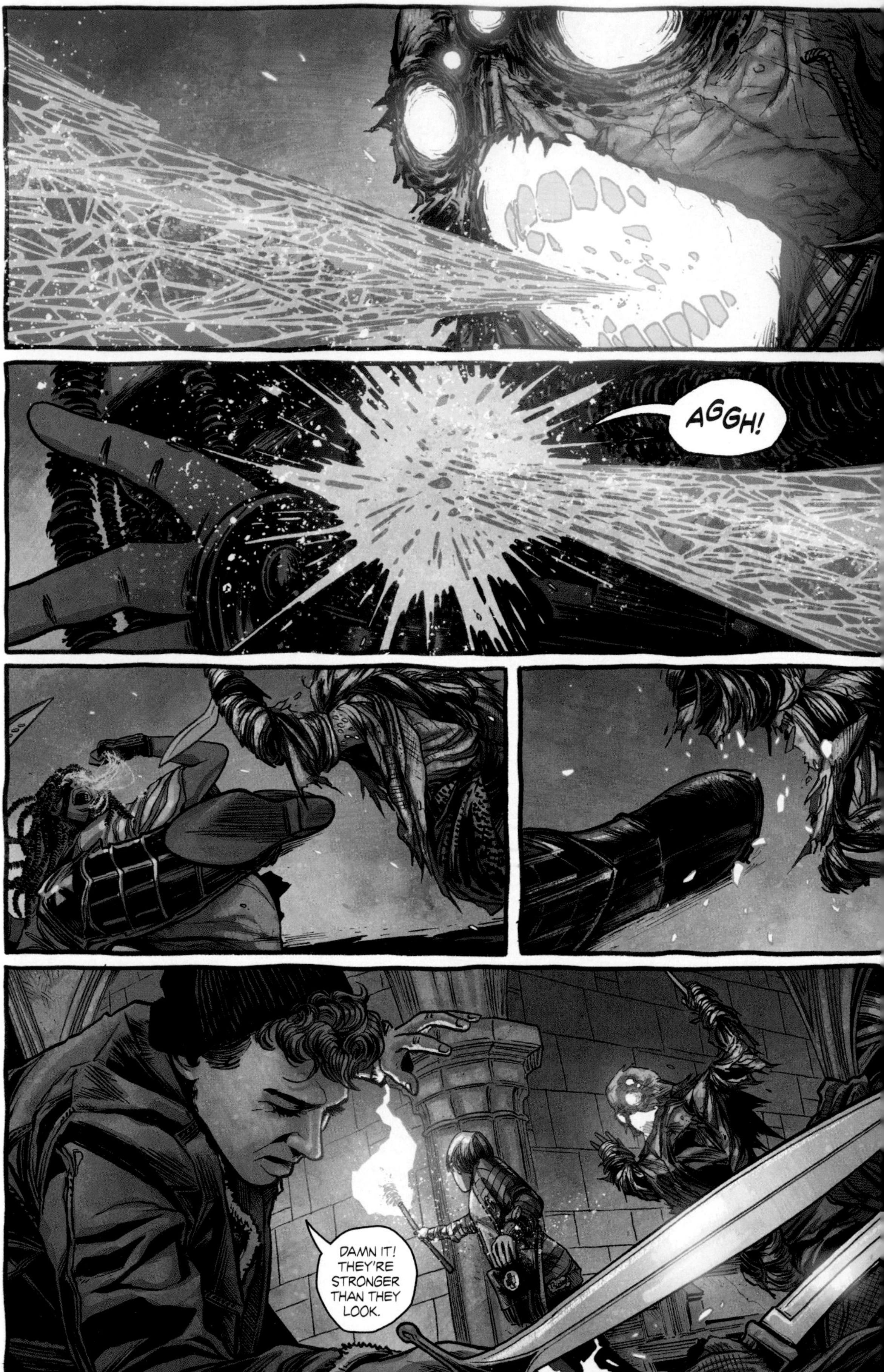
AGGH!
DAMN IT! THEY'RE STRONGER THAN THEY LOOK.

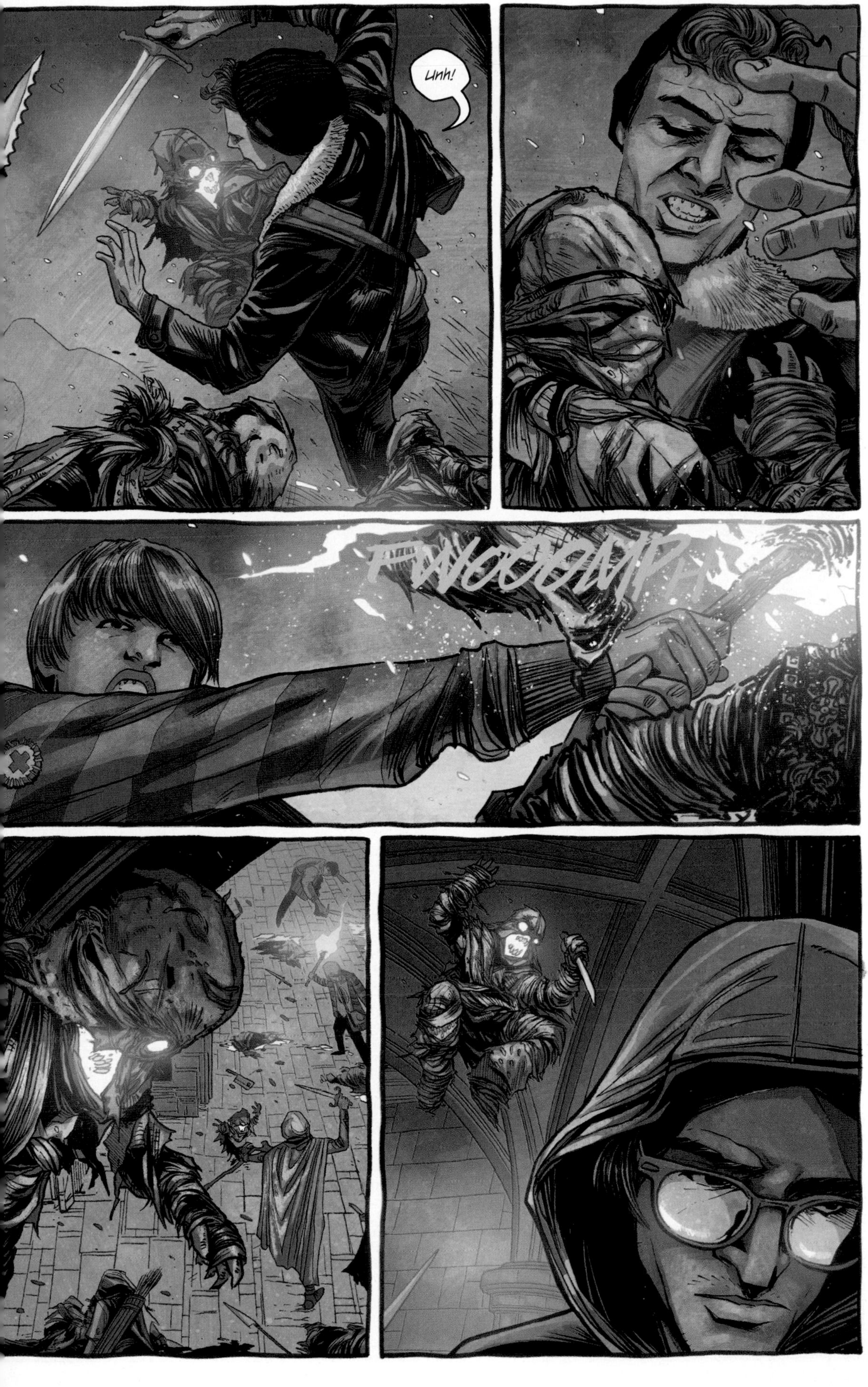
Unh!
FWOOOMPH

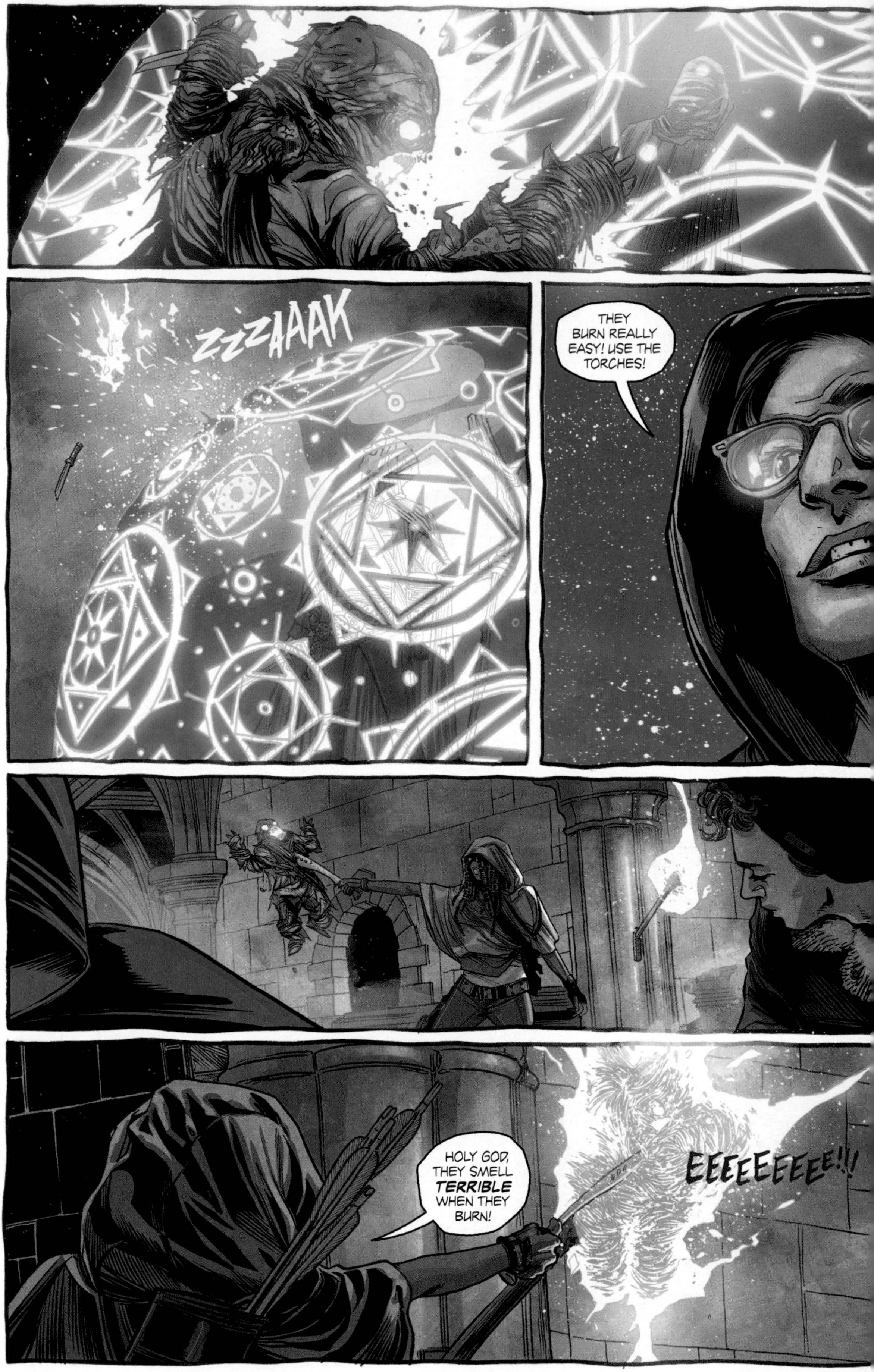
ZZZAAAK
THEY BURN REALLY EASY! USE THE TORCHES!
HOLY GOD, THEY SMELL TERRIBLE WHEN THEY BURN!
EEEEEEEEE!!!

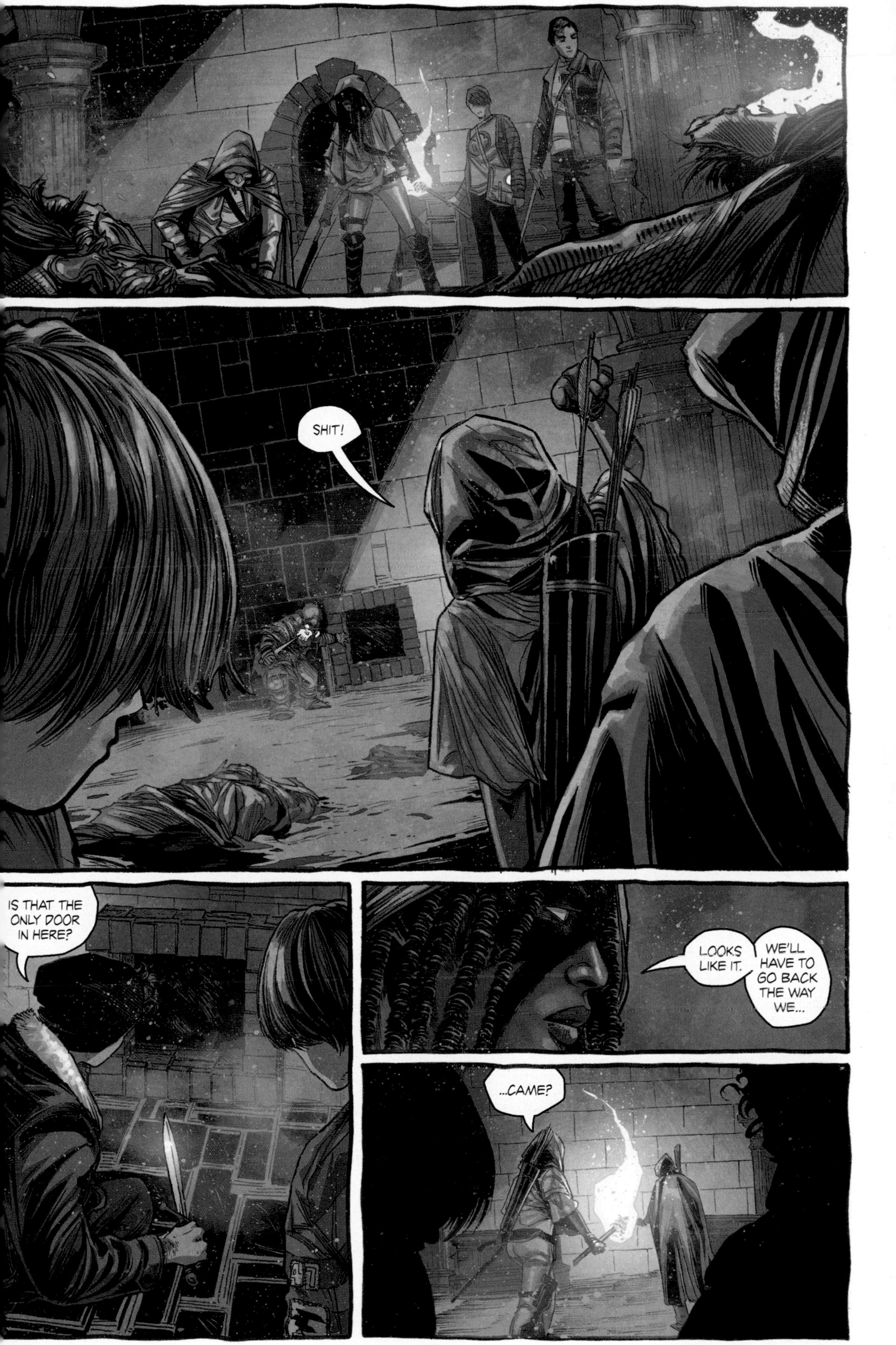
SHIT!
IS THAT THE ONLY DOOR IN HERE?
LOOKS LIKE IT.
WE'LL HAVE TO GO BACK THE WAY WE...
...CAME?

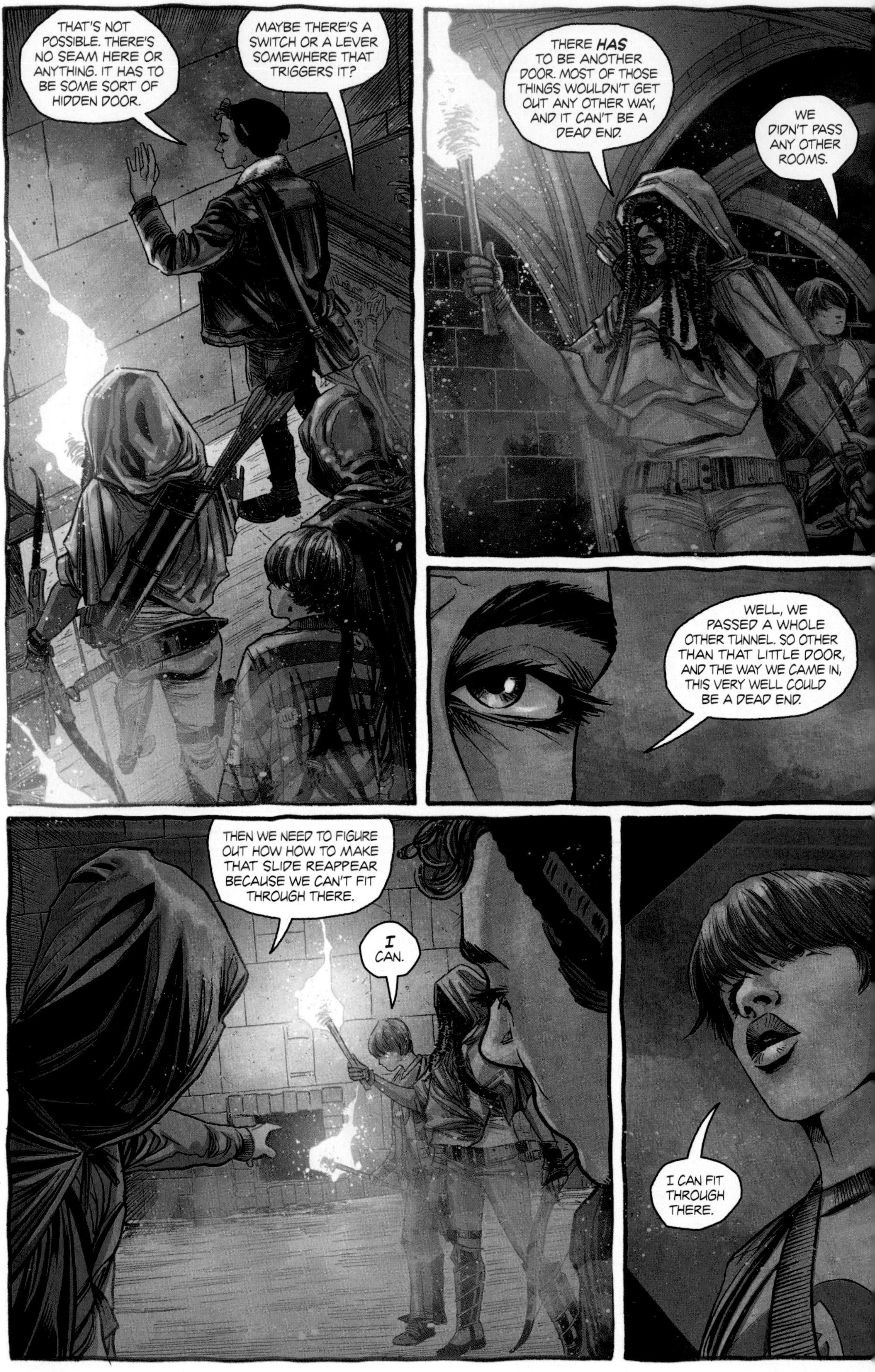
THAT'S NOT POSSIBLE. THERE'S NO SEAM HERE OR ANYTHING. IT HAS TO BE SOME SORT OF HIDDEN DOOR.
MAYBE THERE'S A SWITCH OR A LEVER SOMEWHERE THAT TRIGGERS IT?
THERE HAS TO BE ANOTHER DOOR. MOST OF THOSE THINGS WOULDN'T GET OUT ANY OTHER WAY, AND IT CAN'T BE A DEAD END.
WE DIDN'T PASS ANY OTHER ROOMS.
WELL, WE PASSED A WHOLE OTHER TUNNEL. SO OTHER THAN THAT LITTLE DOOR, AND THE WAY WE CAME IN, THIS VERY WELL COULD BE A DEAD END.
THEN WE NEED TO FIGURE OUT HOW HOW TO MAKE THAT SLIDE REAPPEAR BECAUSE WE CAN'T FIT THROUGH THERE.
I CAN.
I CAN FIT THROUGH THERE.

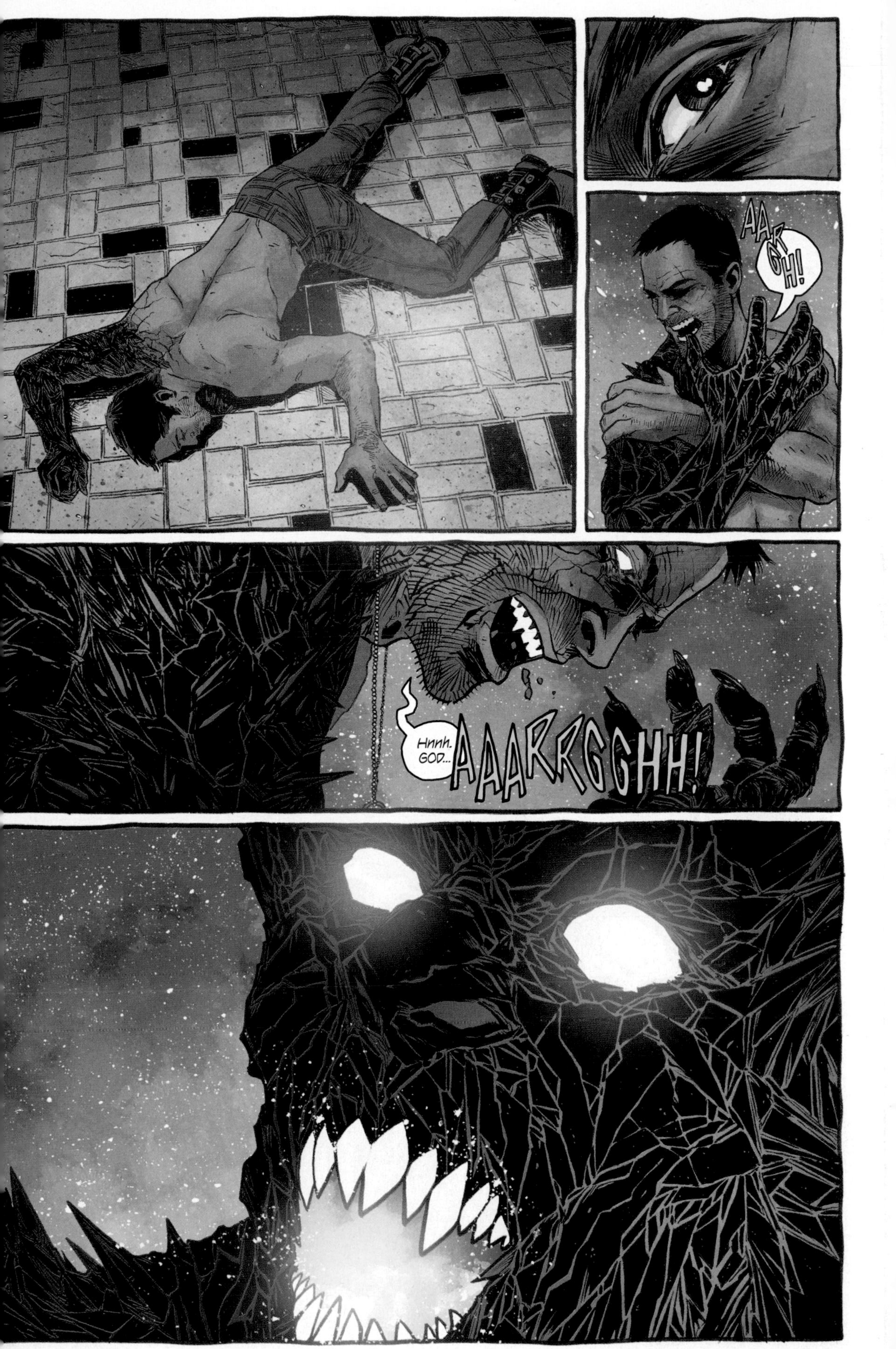
AARGH!
Hnnh. GOD...
AAARRGGHH!

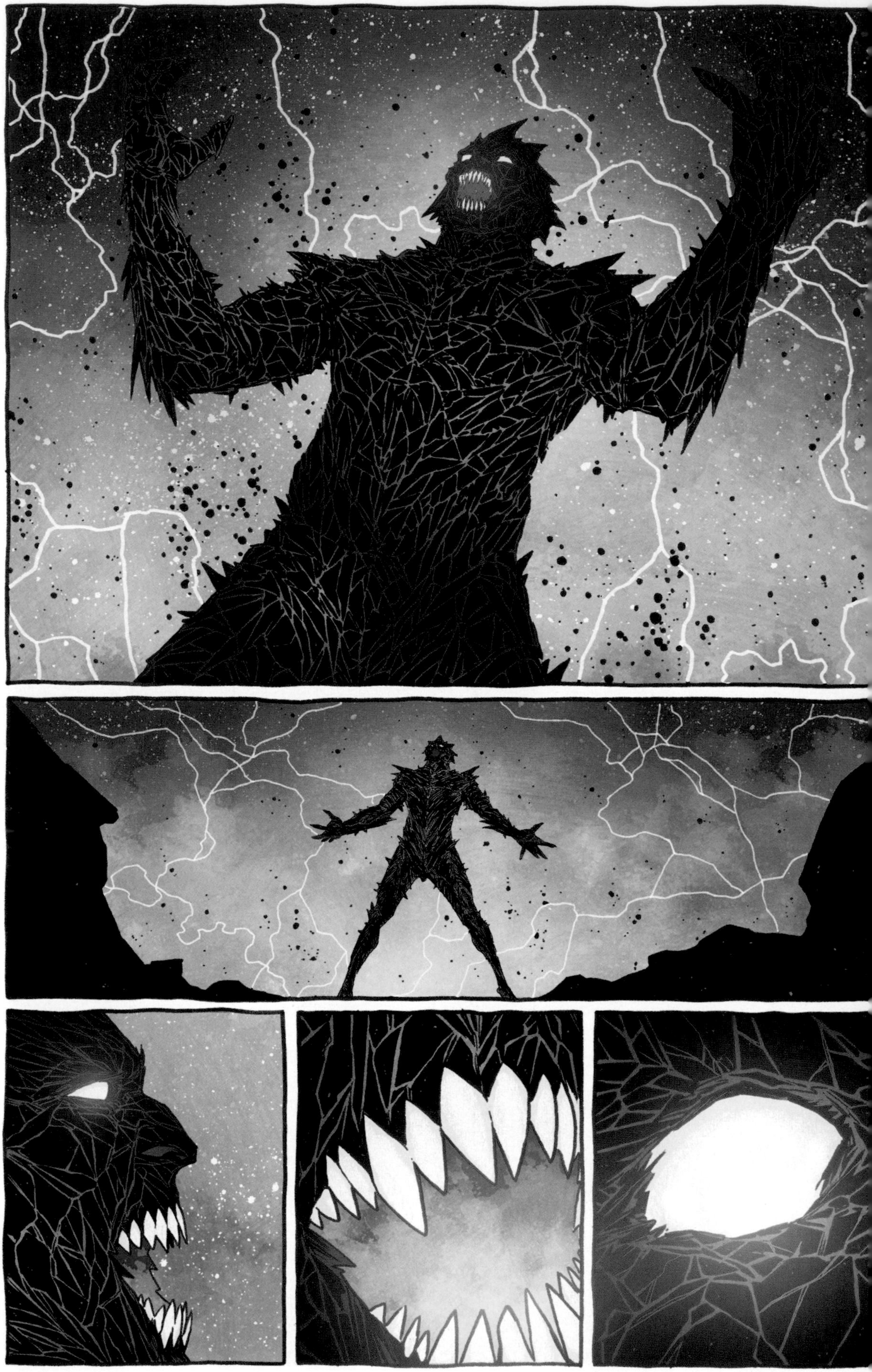

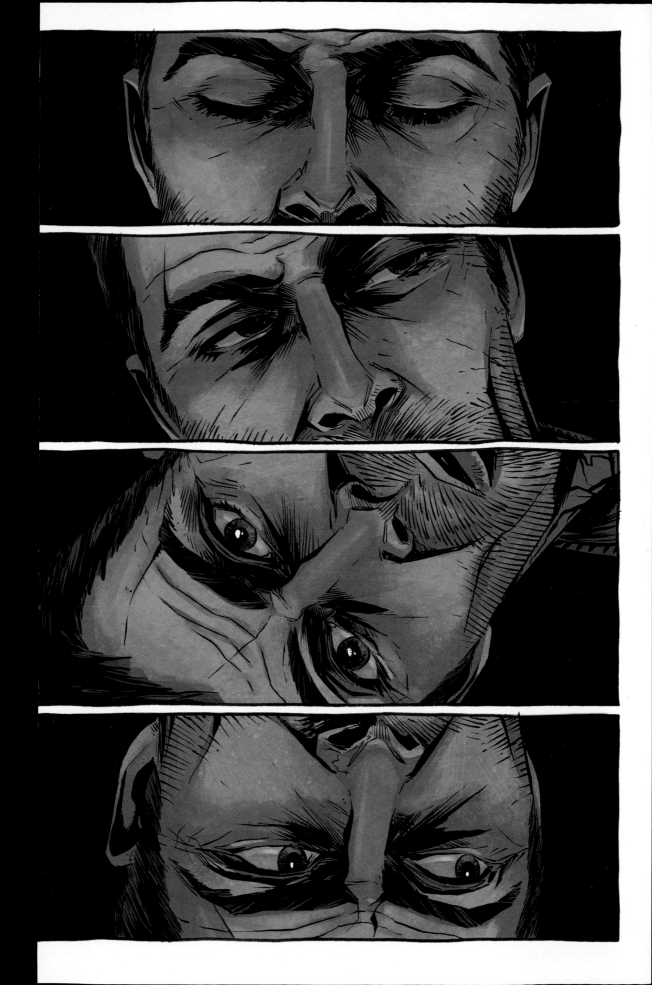

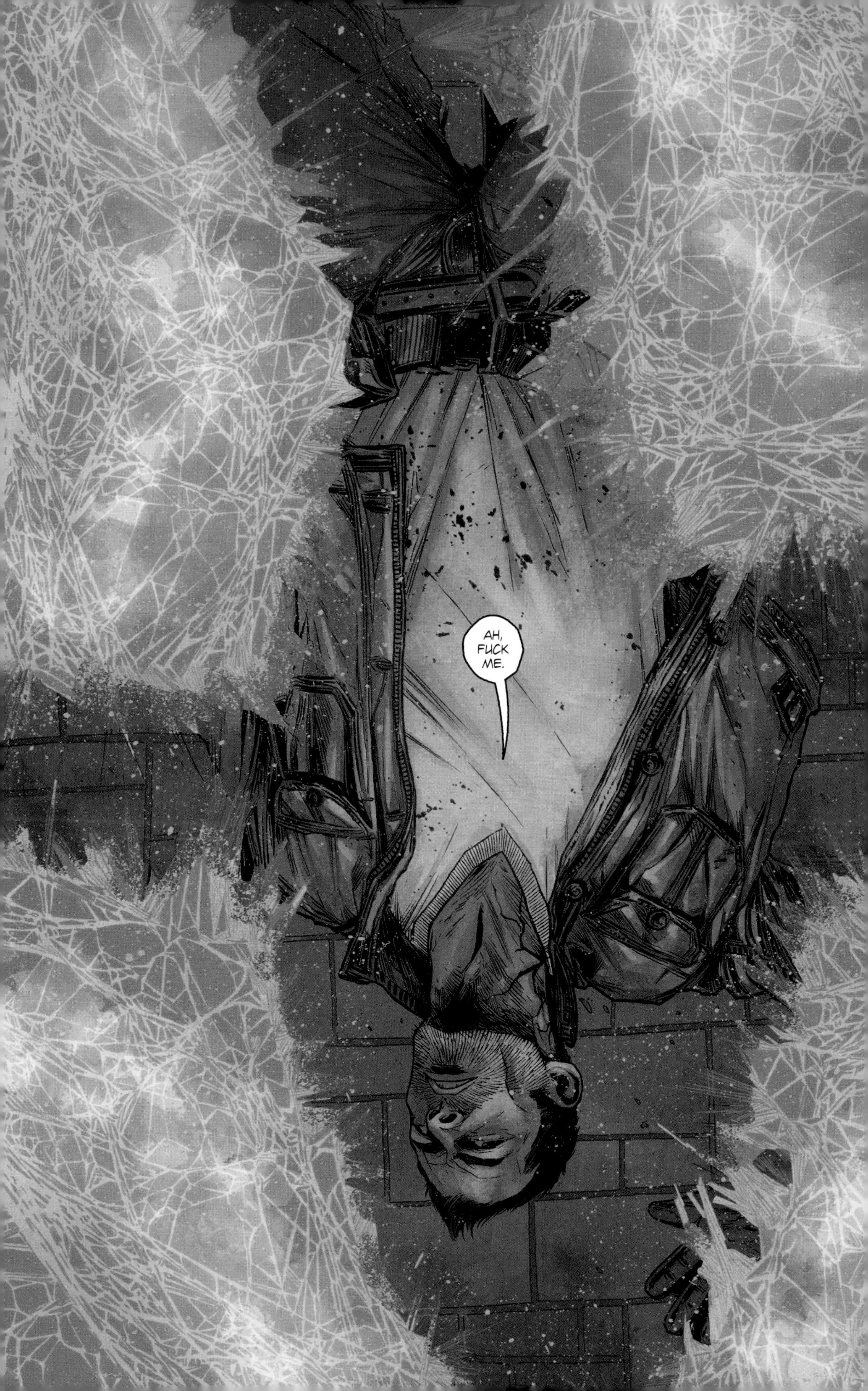
AH, FUCK ME.

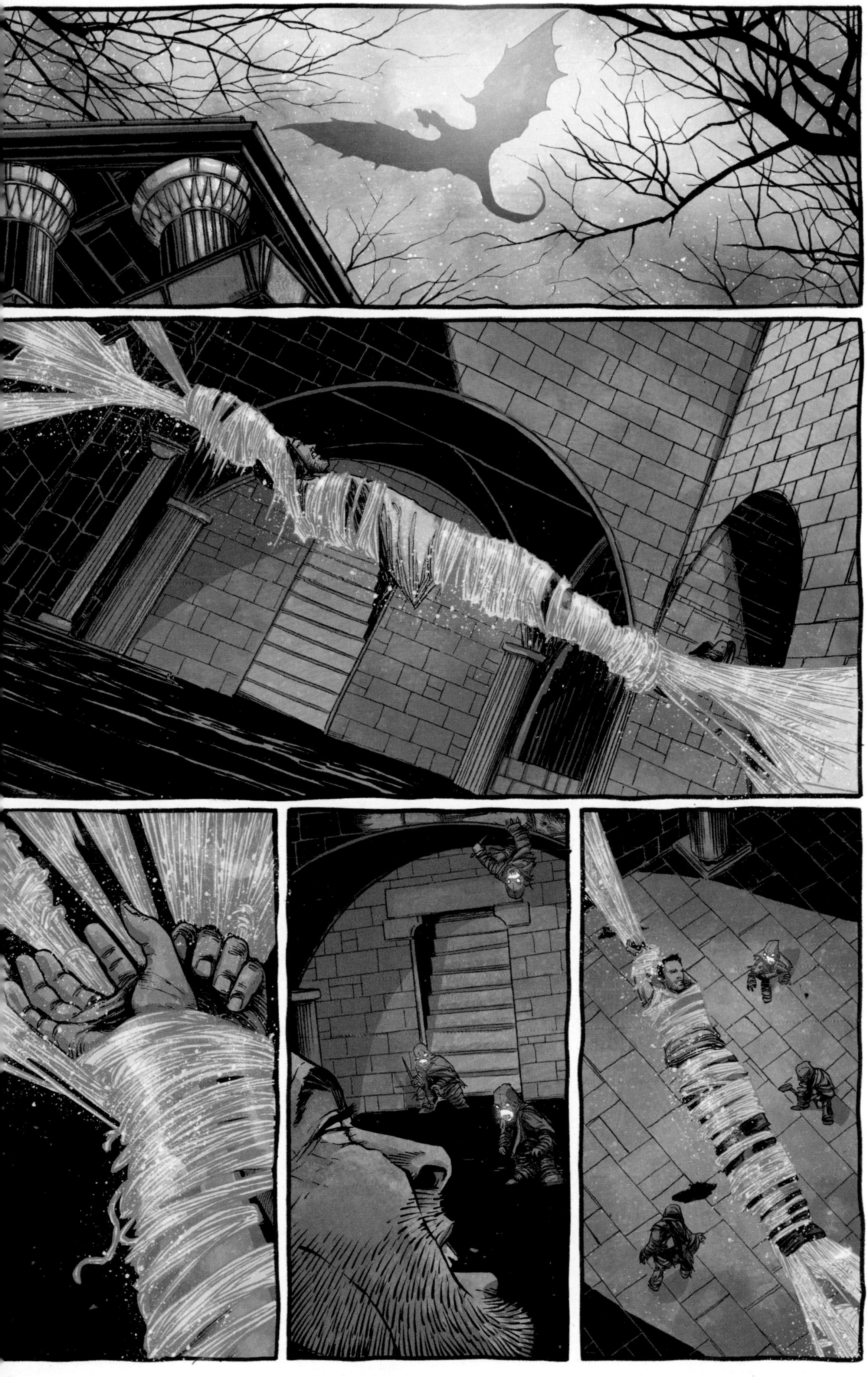

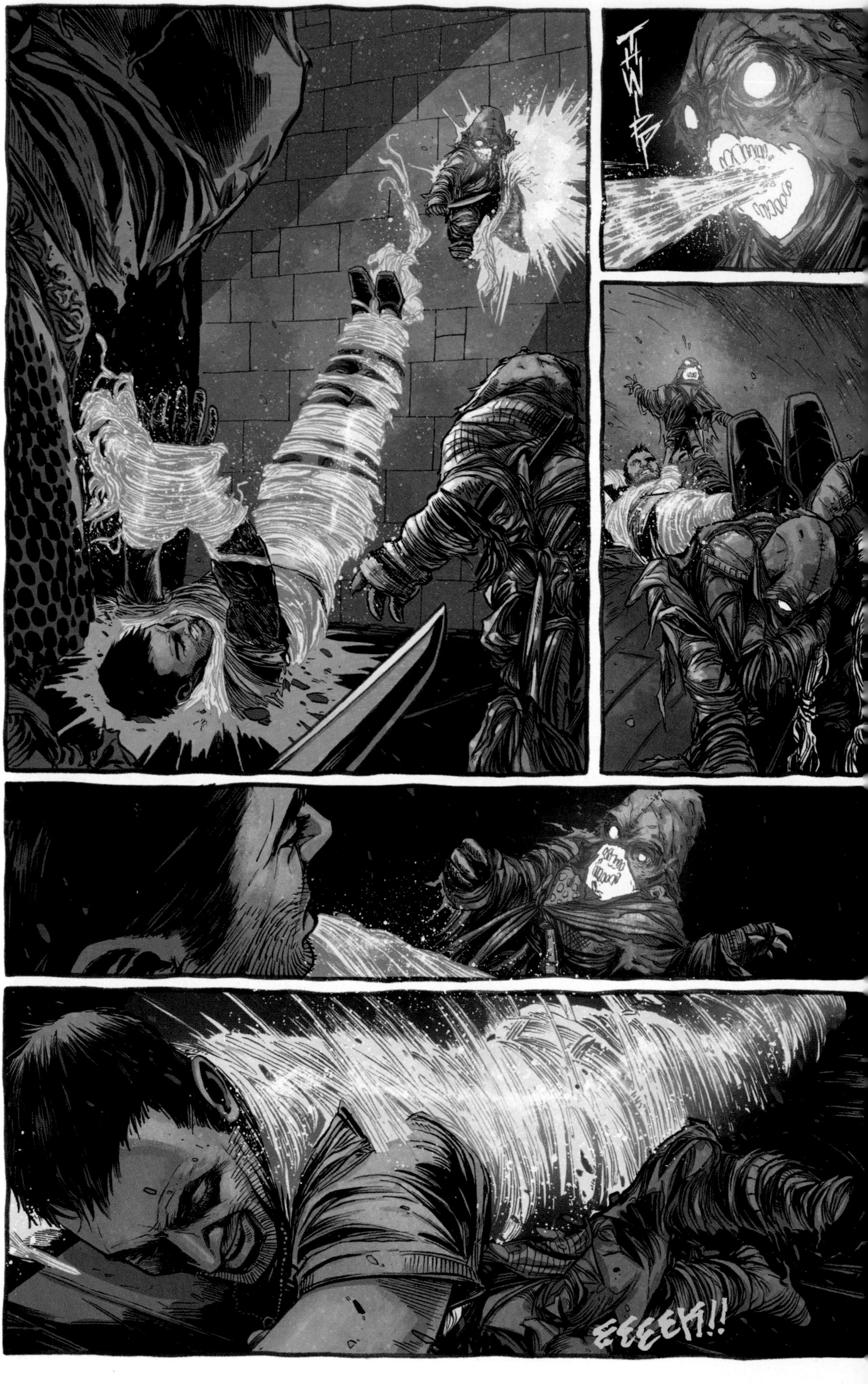
THWIPP
EEEEK!!

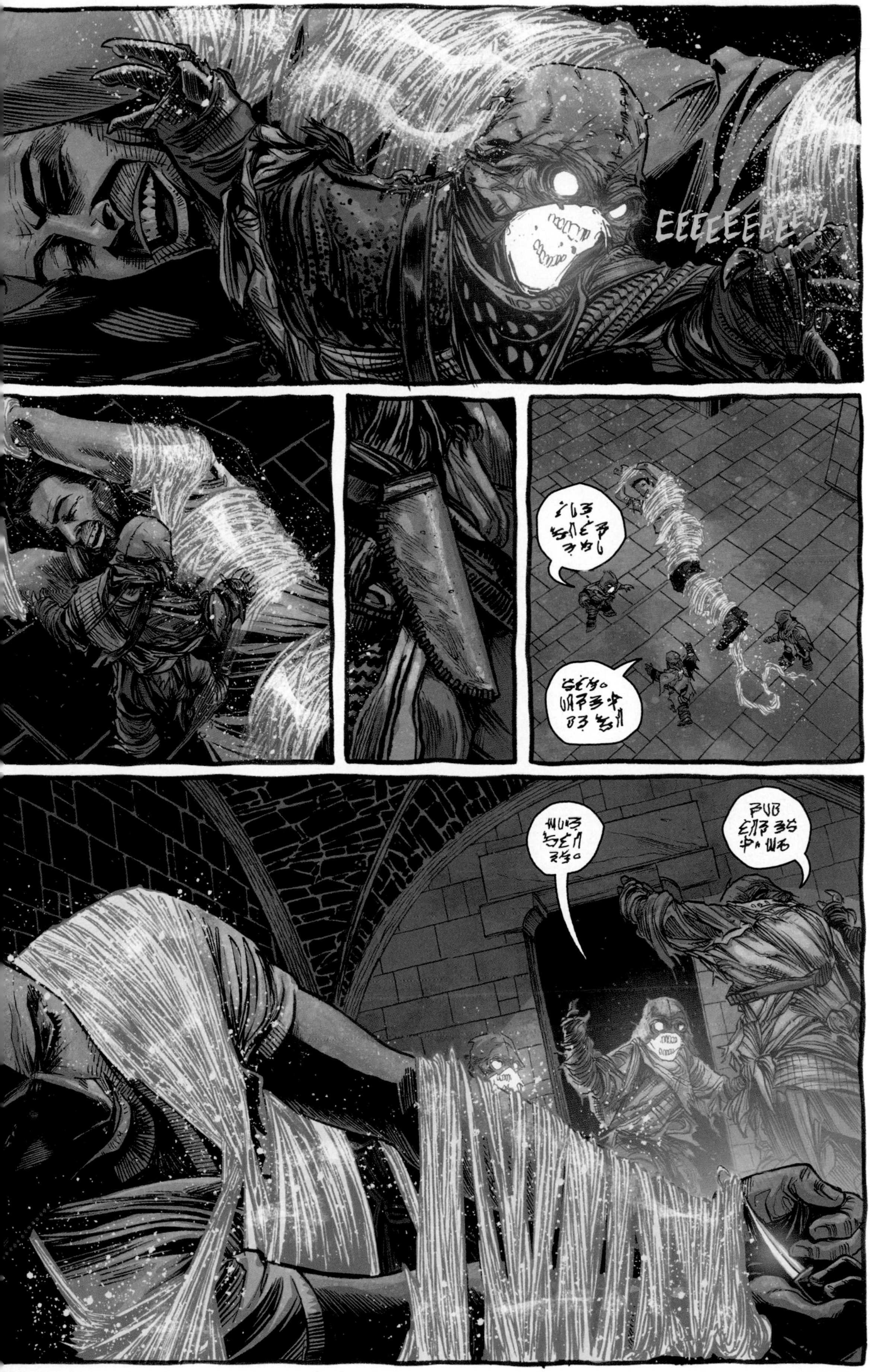
EEEEEEEEE!!

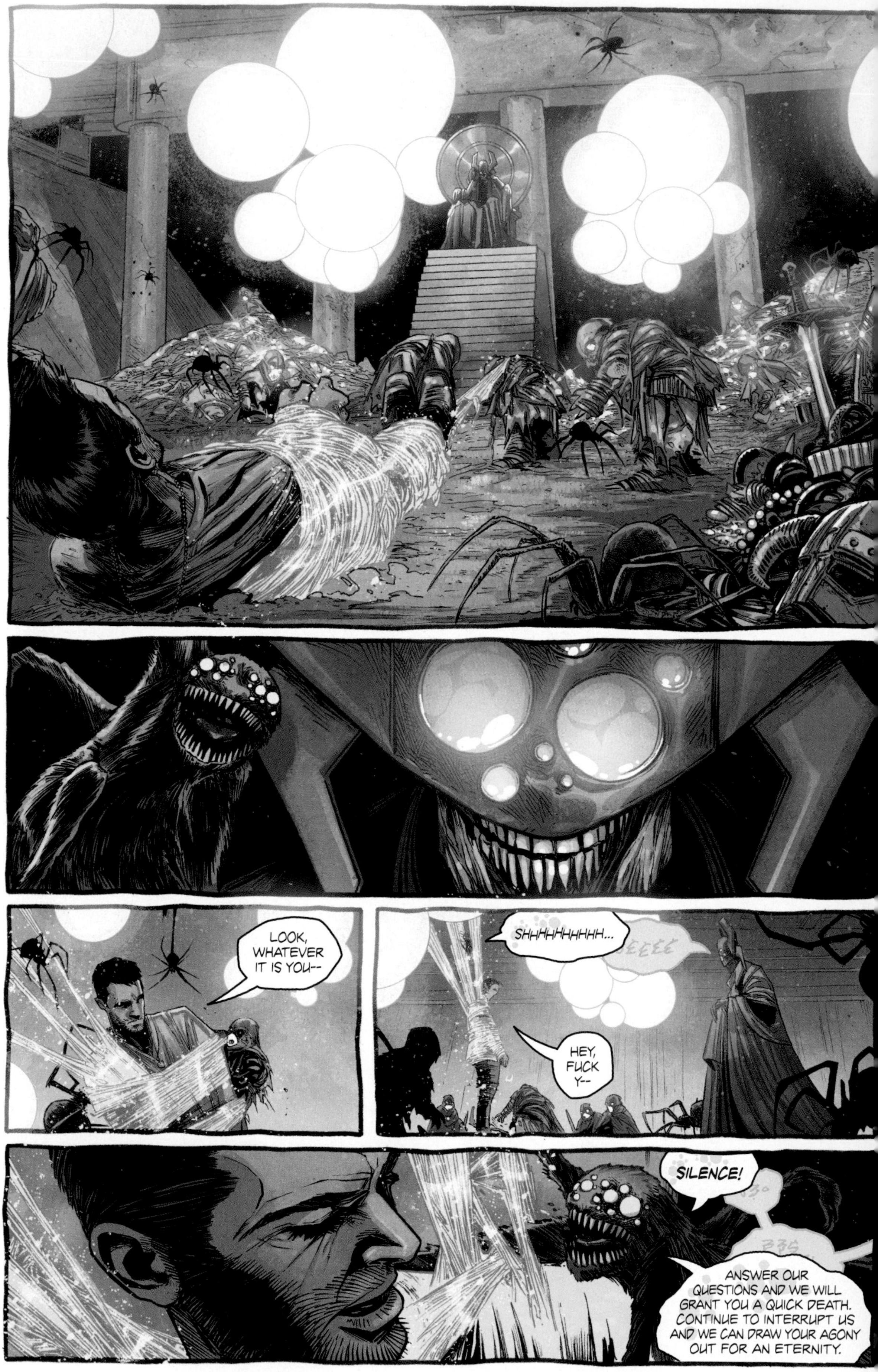
LOOK, WHATEVER IT IS YOU--
SHHHHHHHHHH...
HEY, FUCK Y--
SILENCE!
ANSWER OUR QUESTIONS AND WE WILL GRANT YOU A QUICK DEATH. CONTINUE TO INTERRUPT US AND WE CAN DRAW YOUR AGONY OUT FOR AN ETERNITY.

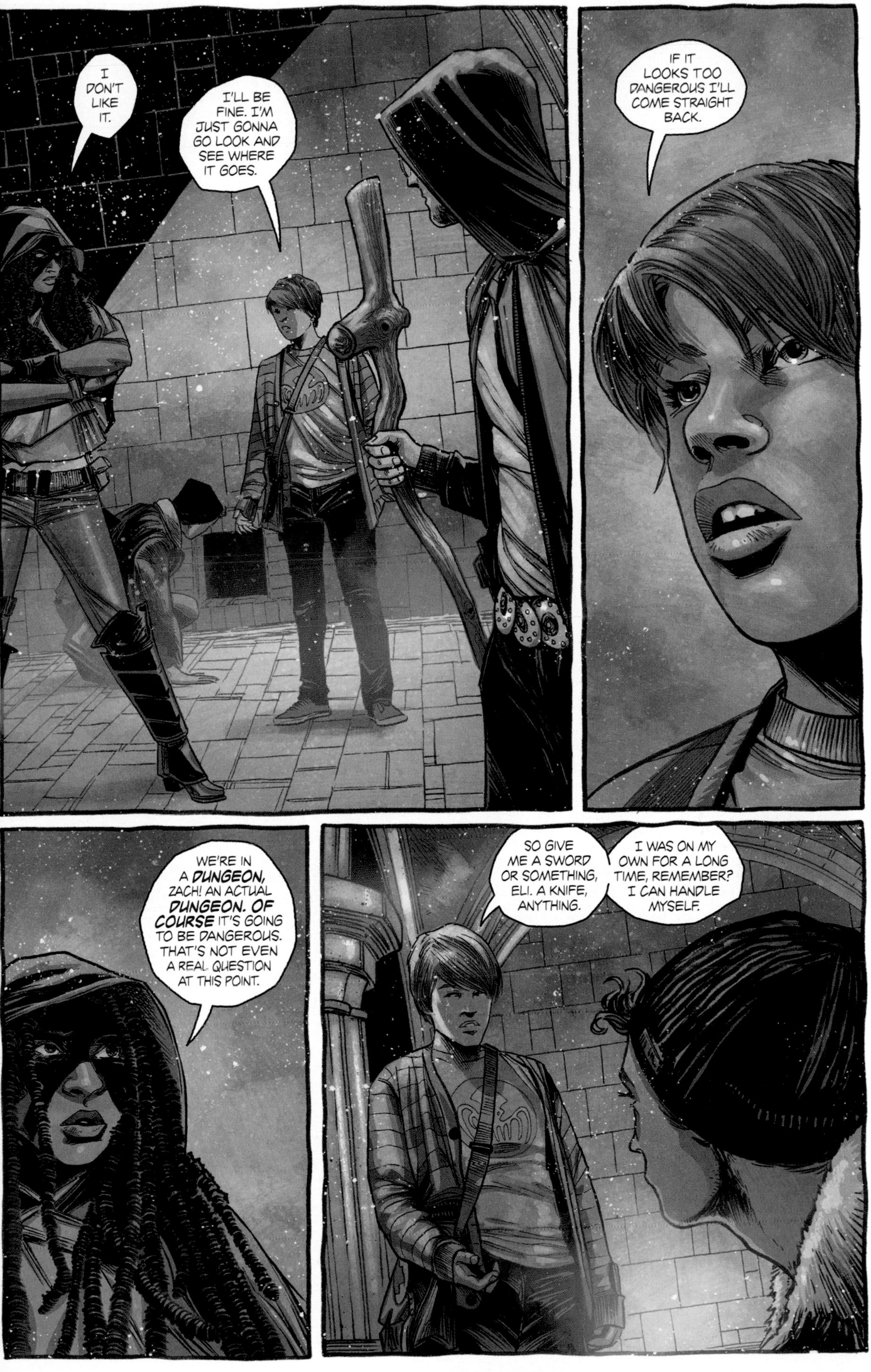
I DON'T LIKE IT.
I'LL BE FINE. I'M JUST GONNA GO LOOK AND SEE WHERE IT GOES.
IF IT LOOKS TOO DANGEROUS I'LL COME STRAIGHT BACK.
WE'RE IN A DUNGEON, ZACH! AN ACTUAL DUNGEON. OF COURSE IT'S GOING TO BE DANGEROUS. THAT'S NOT EVEN A REAL QUESTION AT THIS POINT.
SO GIVE ME A SWORD OR SOMETHING, ELI. A KNIFE, ANYTHING.
I WAS ON MY OWN FOR A LONG TIME, REMEMBER? I CAN HANDLE MYSELF.

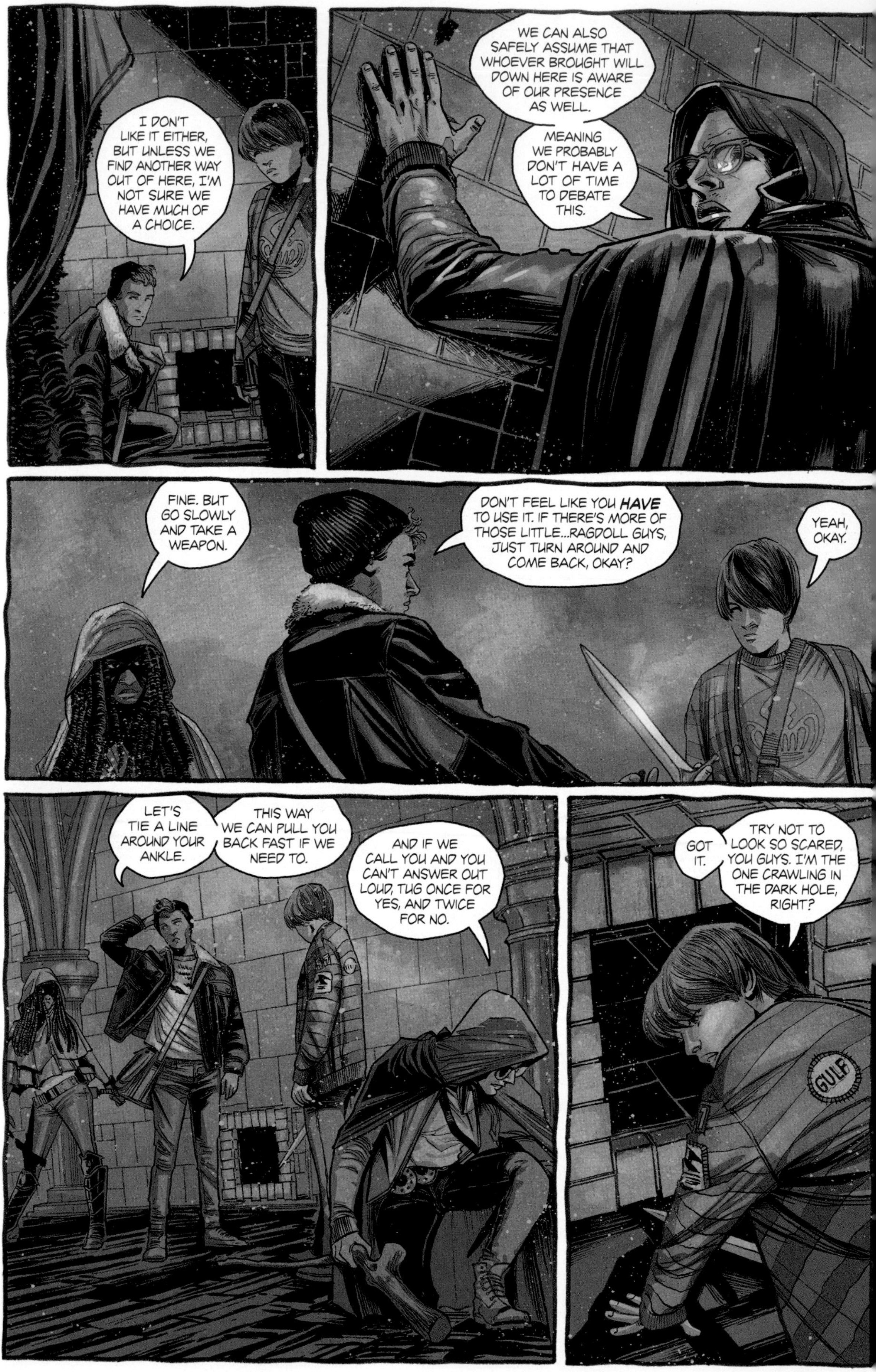
I DON'T LIKE IT EITHER, BUT UNLESS WE FIND ANOTHER WAY OUT OF HERE, I'M NOT SURE WE HAVE MUCH OF A CHOICE.
WE CAN ALSO SAFELY ASSUME THAT WHOEVER BROUGHT WILL DOWN HERE IS AWARE OF OUR PRESENCE AS WELL.
MEANING WE PROBABLY DON'T HAVE A LOT OF TIME TO DEBATE THIS.
FINE. BUT GO SLOWLY AND TAKE A WEAPON.
DON'T FEEL LIKE YOU **HAVE** TO USE IT. IF THERE'S MORE OF THOSE LITTLE...RAGDOLL GUYS, JUST TURN AROUND AND COME BACK, OKAY?
YEAH, OKAY.
LET'S TIE A LINE AROUND YOUR ANKLE.
THIS WAY WE CAN PULL YOU BACK FAST IF WE NEED TO.
AND IF WE CALL YOU AND YOU CAN'T ANSWER OUT LOUD, TUG ONCE FOR YES, AND TWICE FOR NO.
GOT IT.
TRY NOT TO LOOK SO SCARED, YOU GUYS. I'M THE ONE CRAWLING IN THE DARK HOLE, RIGHT?
GULF

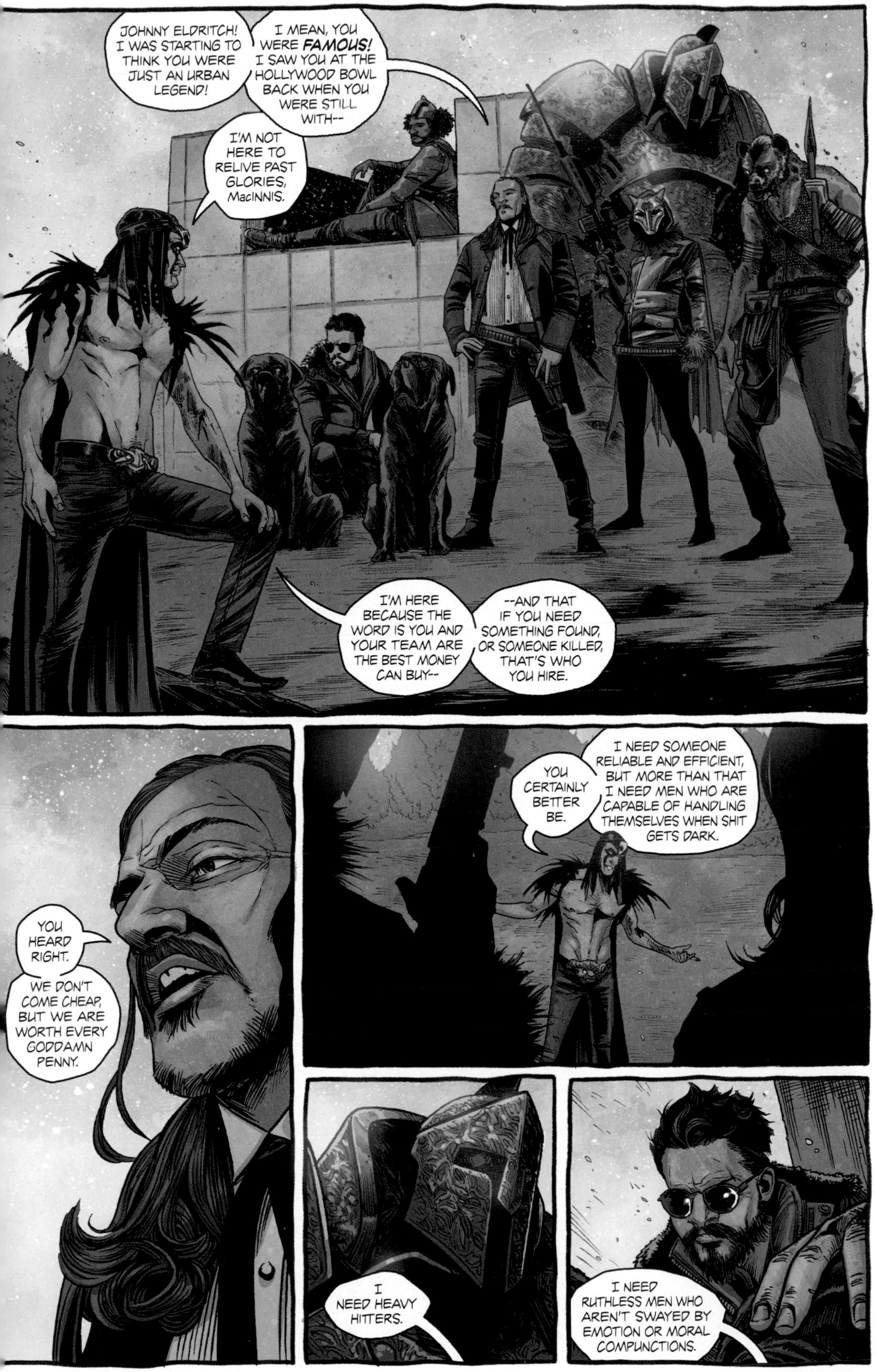
JOHNNY ELDRITCH! I WAS STARTING TO THINK YOU WERE JUST AN URBAN LEGEND!
I MEAN, YOU WERE FAMOUS! I SAW YOU AT THE HOLLYWOOD BOWL BACK WHEN YOU WERE STILL WITH--
I'M NOT HERE TO RELIVE PAST GLORIES, MacINNIS.
I'M HERE BECAUSE THE WORD IS YOU AND YOUR TEAM ARE THE BEST MONEY CAN BUY--
--AND THAT IF YOU NEED SOMETHING FOUND, OR SOMEONE KILLED, THAT'S WHO YOU HIRE.
YOU HEARD RIGHT.
WE DON'T COME CHEAP, BUT WE ARE WORTH EVERY GODDAMN PENNY.
YOU CERTAINLY BETTER BE.
I NEED SOMEONE RELIABLE AND EFFICIENT, BUT MORE THAN THAT I NEED MEN WHO ARE CAPABLE OF HANDLING THEMSELVES WHEN SHIT GETS DARK.
I NEED HEAVY HITTERS.
I NEED RUTHLESS MEN WHO AREN'T SWAYED BY EMOTION OR MORAL COMPUNCTIONS.

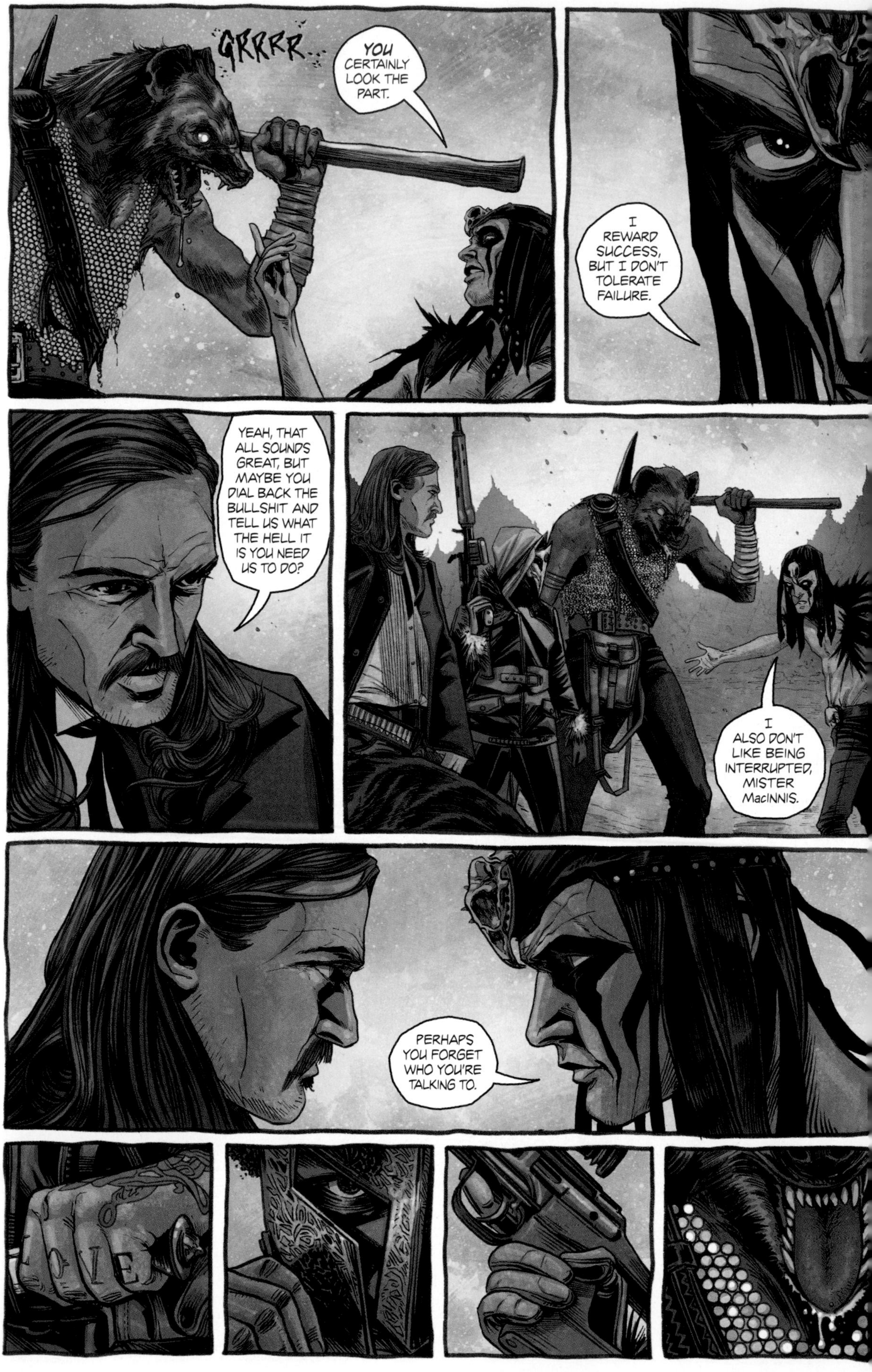
GRRRR...
YOU CERTAINLY LOOK THE PART.
I REWARD SUCCESS, BUT I DON'T TOLERATE FAILURE.
YEAH, THAT ALL SOUNDS GREAT, BUT MAYBE YOU DIAL BACK THE BULLSHIT AND TELL US WHAT THE HELL IT IS YOU NEED US TO DO?
I ALSO DON'T LIKE BEING INTERRUPTED, MISTER MacINNIS.
PERHAPS YOU FORGET WHO YOU'RE TALKING TO.
LOVE

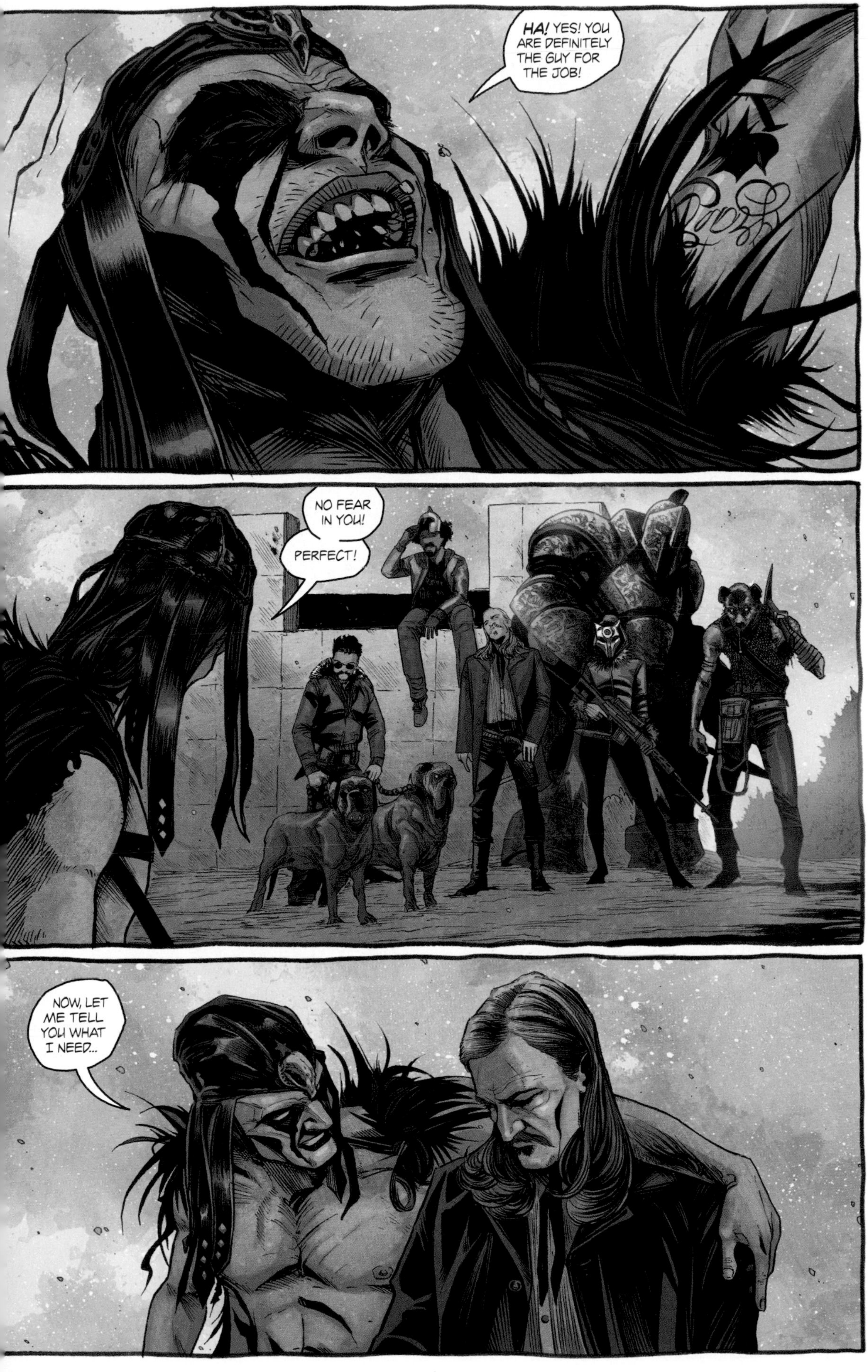
HA! YES! YOU ARE DEFINITELY THE GUY FOR THE JOB!
NO FEAR IN YOU!
PERFECT!
NOW, LET ME TELL YOU WHAT I NEED...

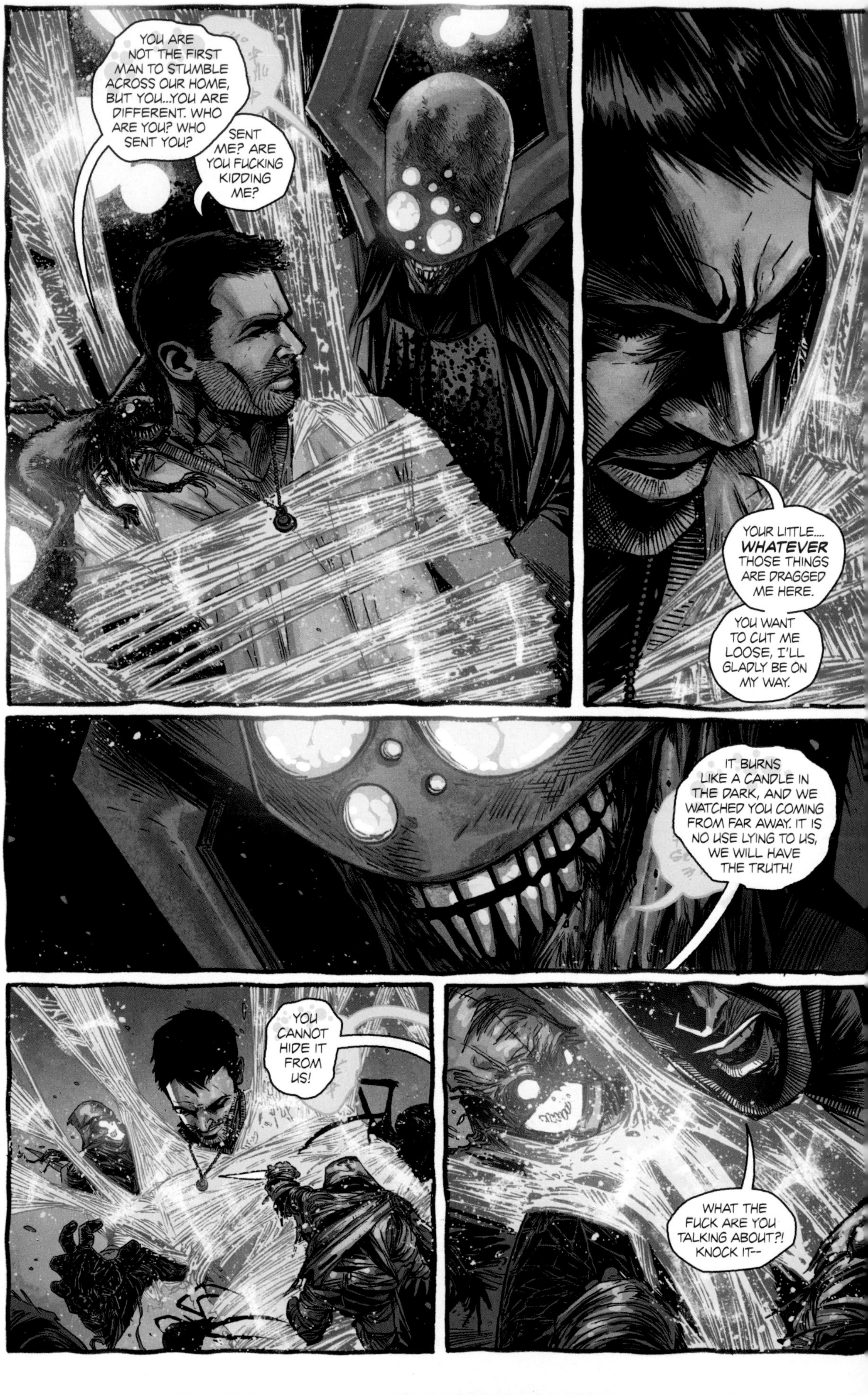
YOU ARE NOT THE FIRST MAN TO STUMBLE ACROSS OUR HOME, BUT YOU...YOU ARE DIFFERENT. WHO ARE YOU? WHO SENT YOU?
SENT ME? ARE YOU FUCKING KIDDING ME?
YOUR LITTLE.... **WHATEVER** THOSE THINGS ARE DRAGGED ME HERE.
YOU WANT TO CUT ME LOOSE, I'LL GLADLY BE ON MY WAY.
IT BURNS LIKE A CANDLE IN THE DARK, AND WE WATCHED YOU COMING FROM FAR AWAY. IT IS NO USE LYING TO US, WE WILL HAVE THE TRUTH!
YOU CANNOT HIDE IT FROM US!
WHAT THE FUCK ARE YOU TALKING ABOUT?! KNOCK IT--

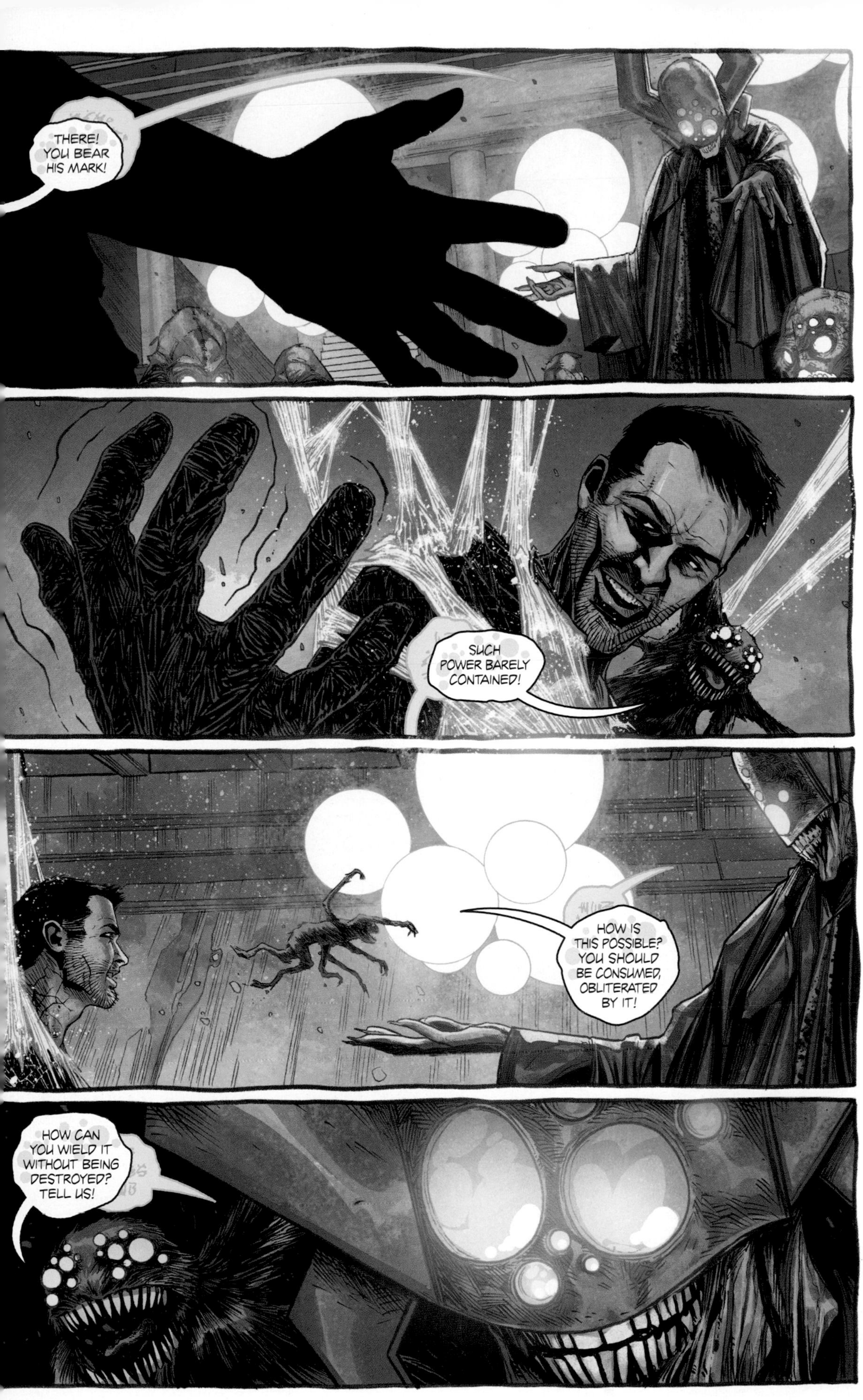
THERE! YOU BEAR HIS MARK!
SUCH POWER BARELY CONTAINED!
HOW IS THIS POSSIBLE? YOU SHOULD BE CONSUMED, OBLITERATED BY IT!
HOW CAN YOU WIELD IT WITHOUT BEING DESTROYED? TELL US!

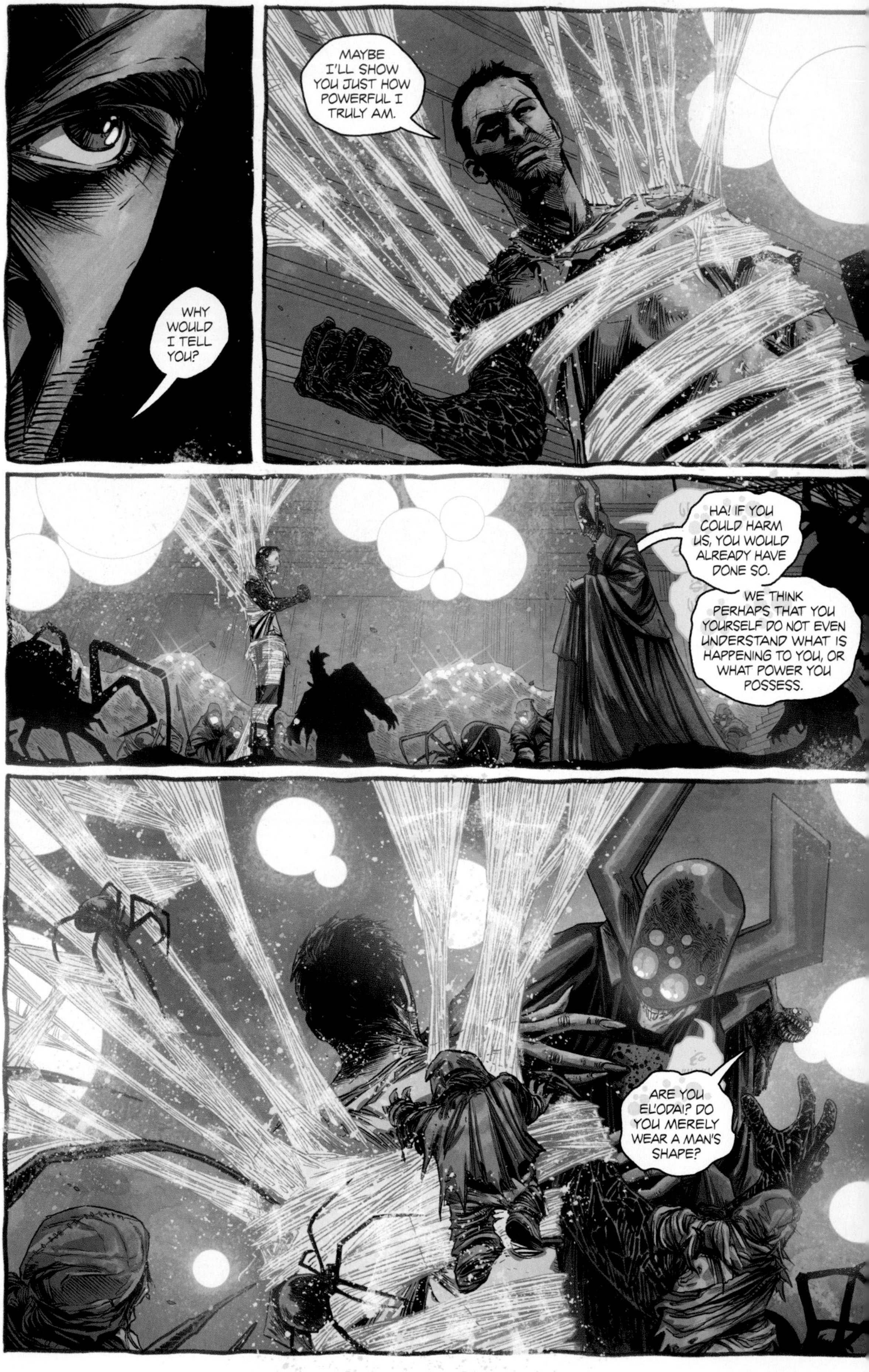
WHY WOULD I TELL YOU?
MAYBE I'LL SHOW YOU JUST HOW POWERFUL I TRULY AM.
HA! IF YOU COULD HARM US, YOU WOULD ALREADY HAVE DONE SO.
WE THINK PERHAPS THAT YOU YOURSELF DO NOT EVEN UNDERSTAND WHAT IS HAPPENING TO YOU, OR WHAT POWER YOU POSSESS.
ARE YOU EL'ODAI? DO YOU MERELY WEAR A MAN'S SHAPE?

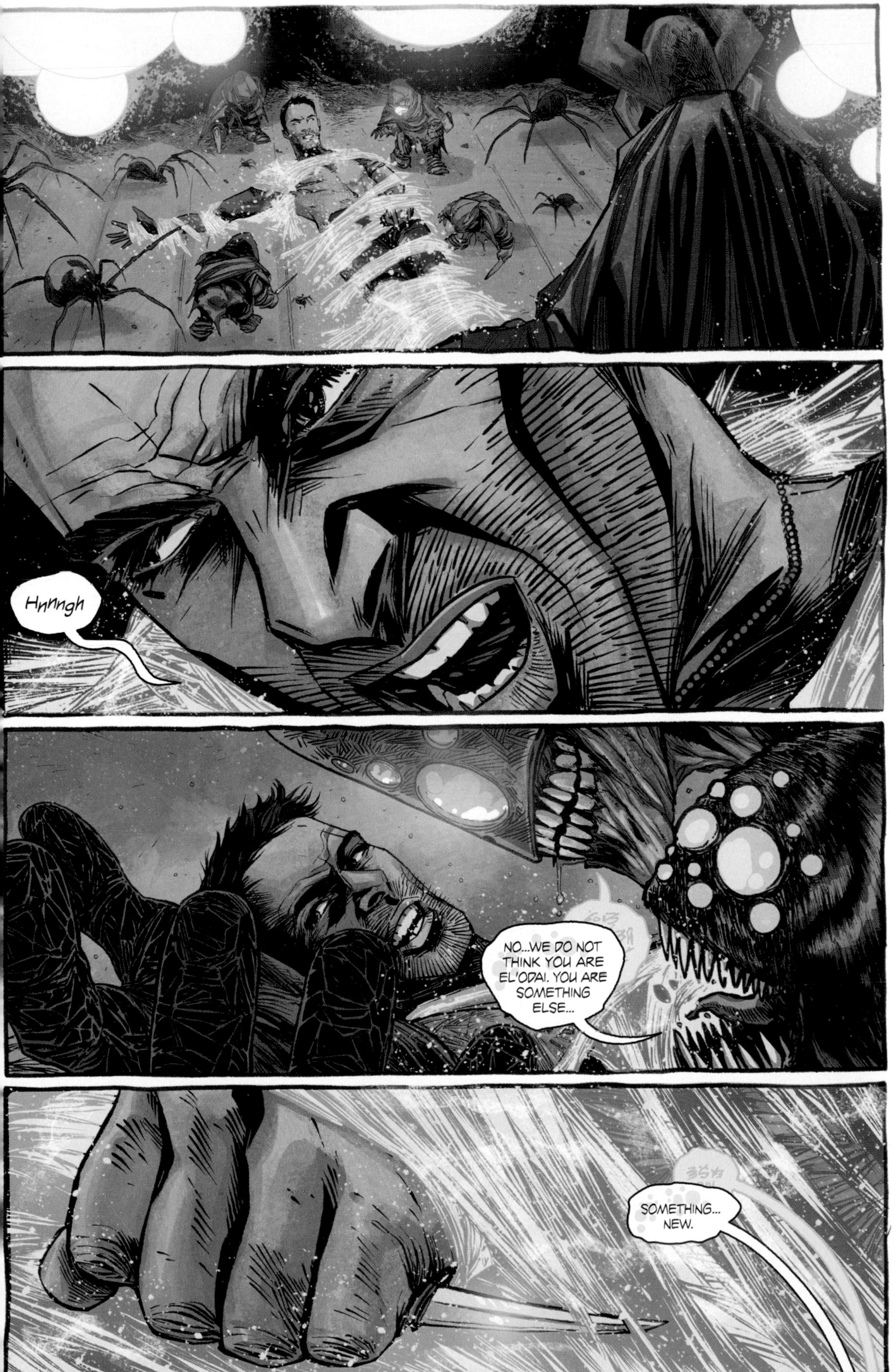
Hnnngh
NO...WE DO NOT THINK YOU ARE EL'ODAI. YOU ARE SOMETHING ELSE...
SOMETHING... NEW.

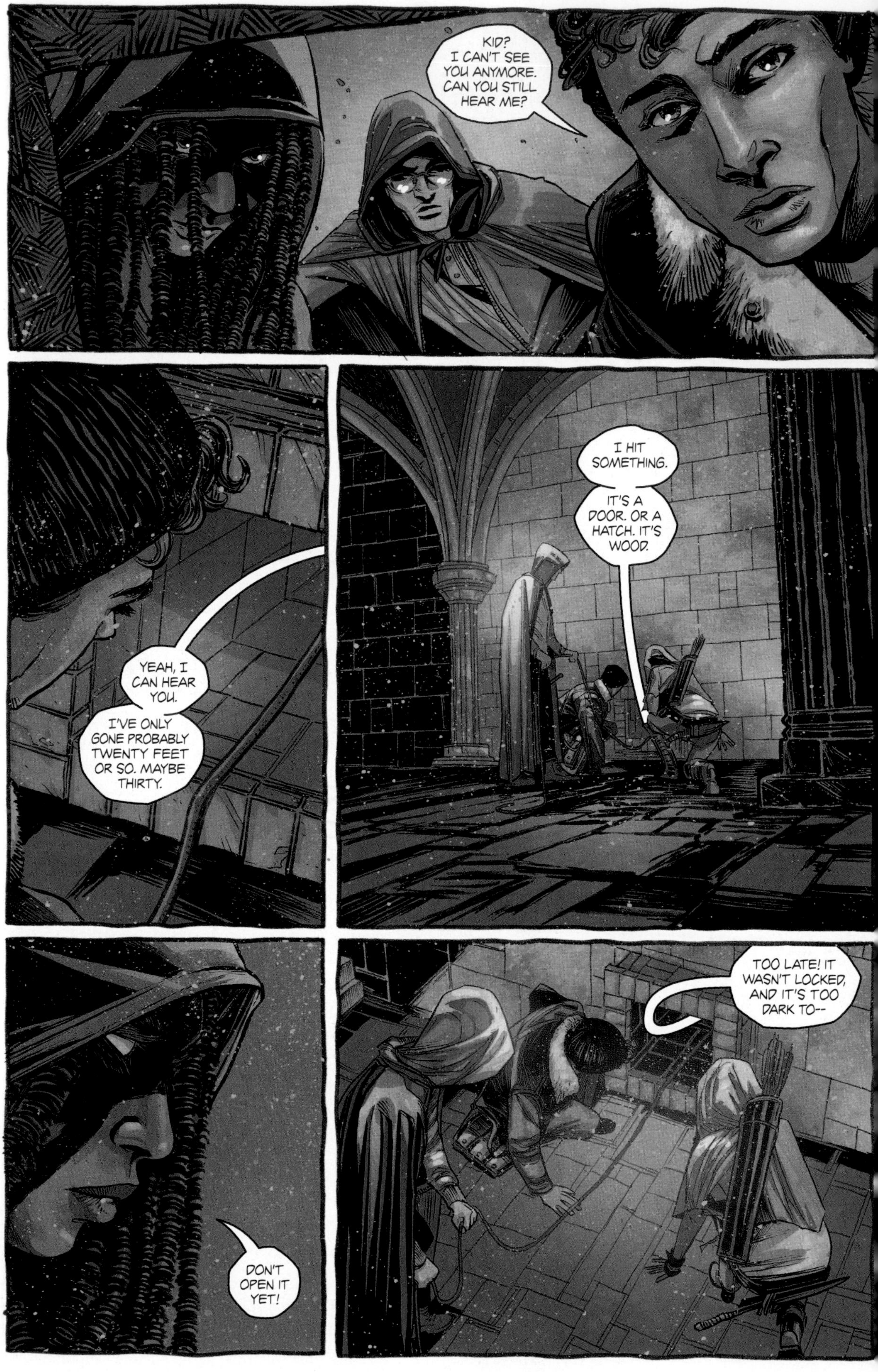
KID? I CAN'T SEE YOU ANYMORE. CAN YOU STILL HEAR ME?
YEAH, I CAN HEAR YOU.
I'VE ONLY GONE PROBABLY TWENTY FEET OR SO. MAYBE THIRTY.
I HIT SOMETHING.
IT'S A DOOR. OR A HATCH. IT'S WOOD.
DON'T OPEN IT YET!
TOO LATE! IT WASN'T LOCKED, AND IT'S TOO DARK TO--

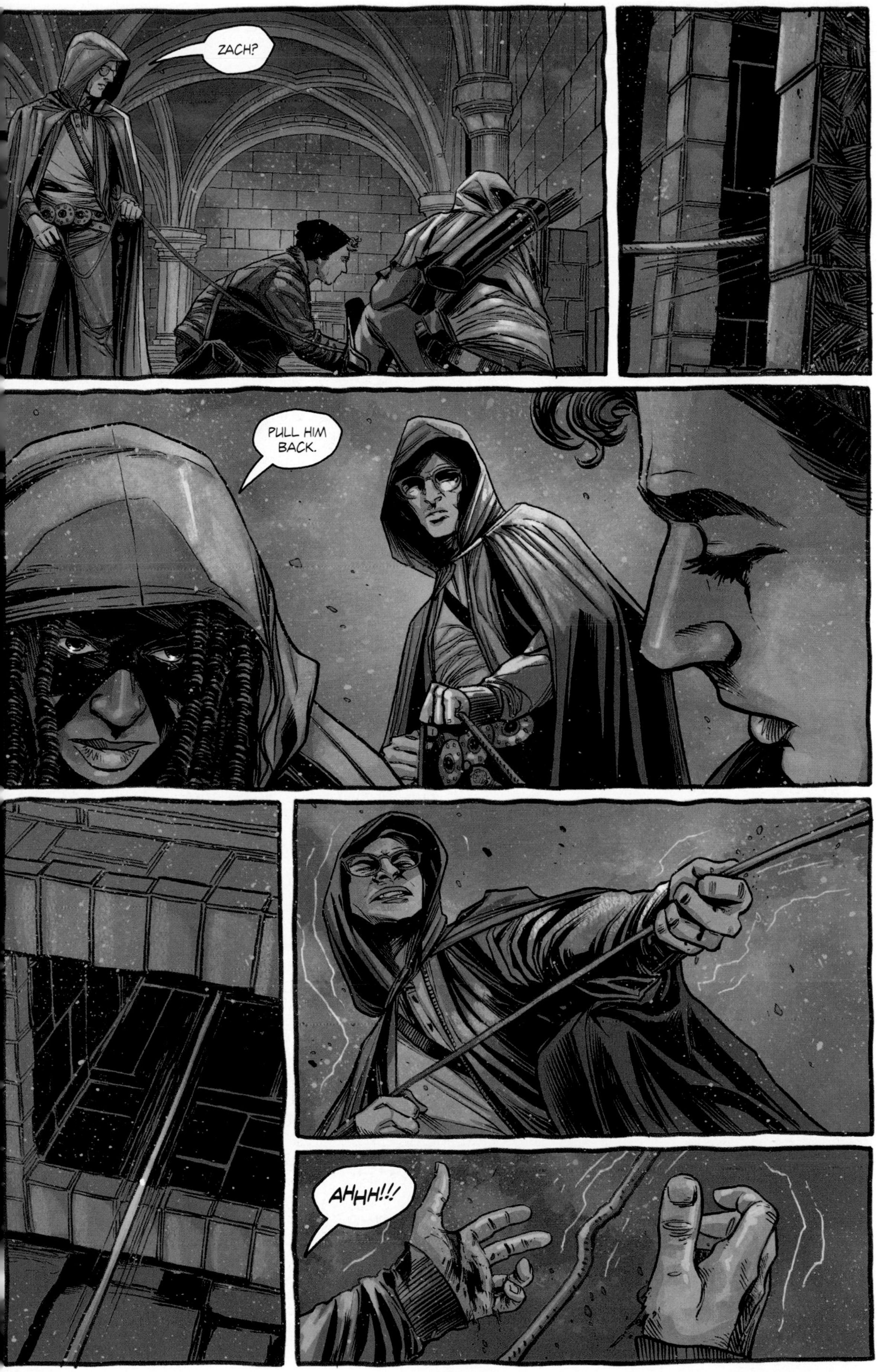
ZACH?
PULL HIM BACK.
AHHH!!!

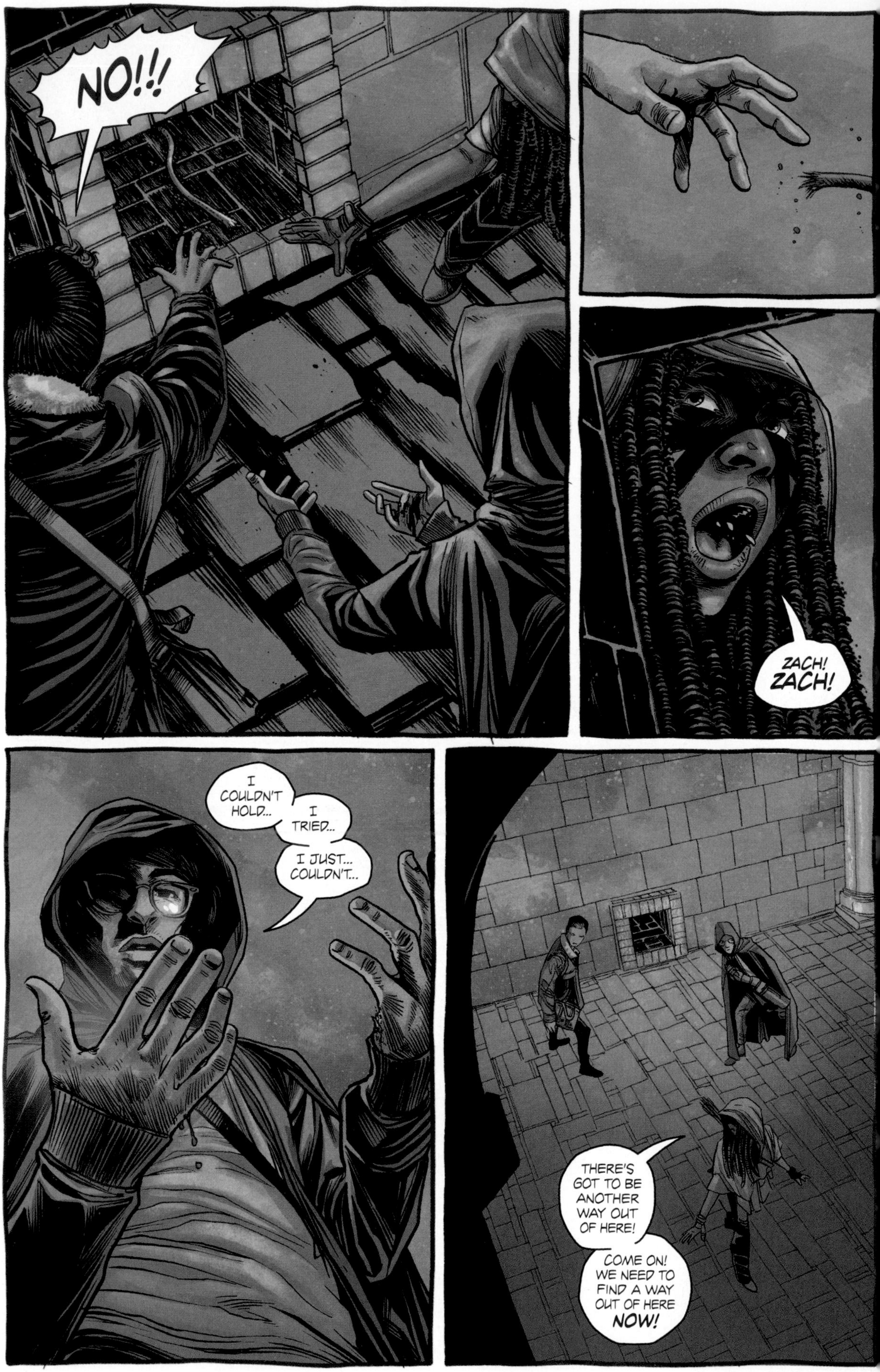
NO!!!
ZACH! ZACH!
I COULDN'T HOLD...
I TRIED...
I JUST... COULDN'T...
THERE'S GOT TO BE ANOTHER WAY OUT OF HERE!
COME ON! WE NEED TO FIND A WAY OUT OF HERE NOW!

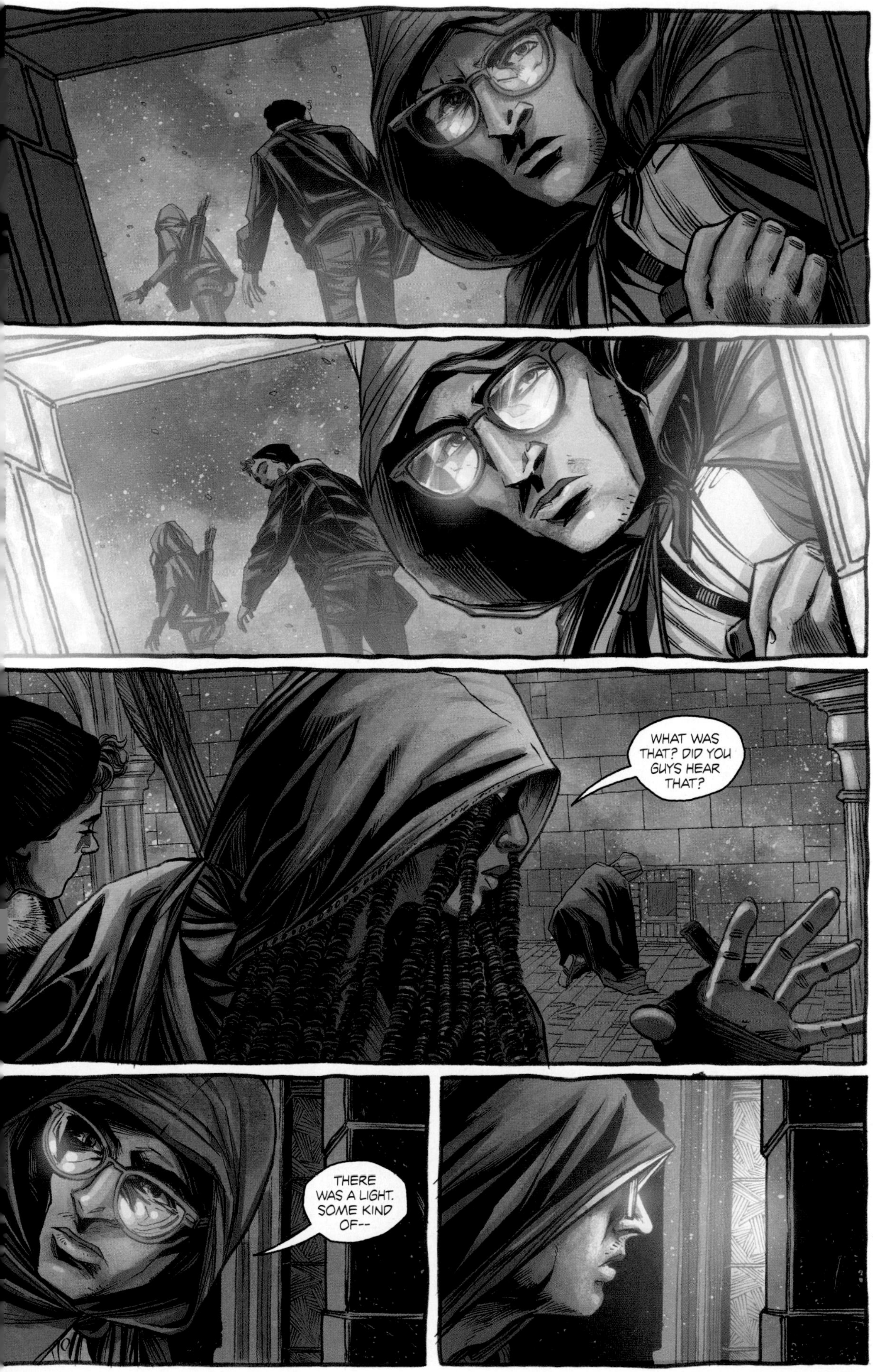
WHAT WAS THAT? DID YOU GUYS HEAR THAT?
THERE WAS A LIGHT. SOME KIND OF--

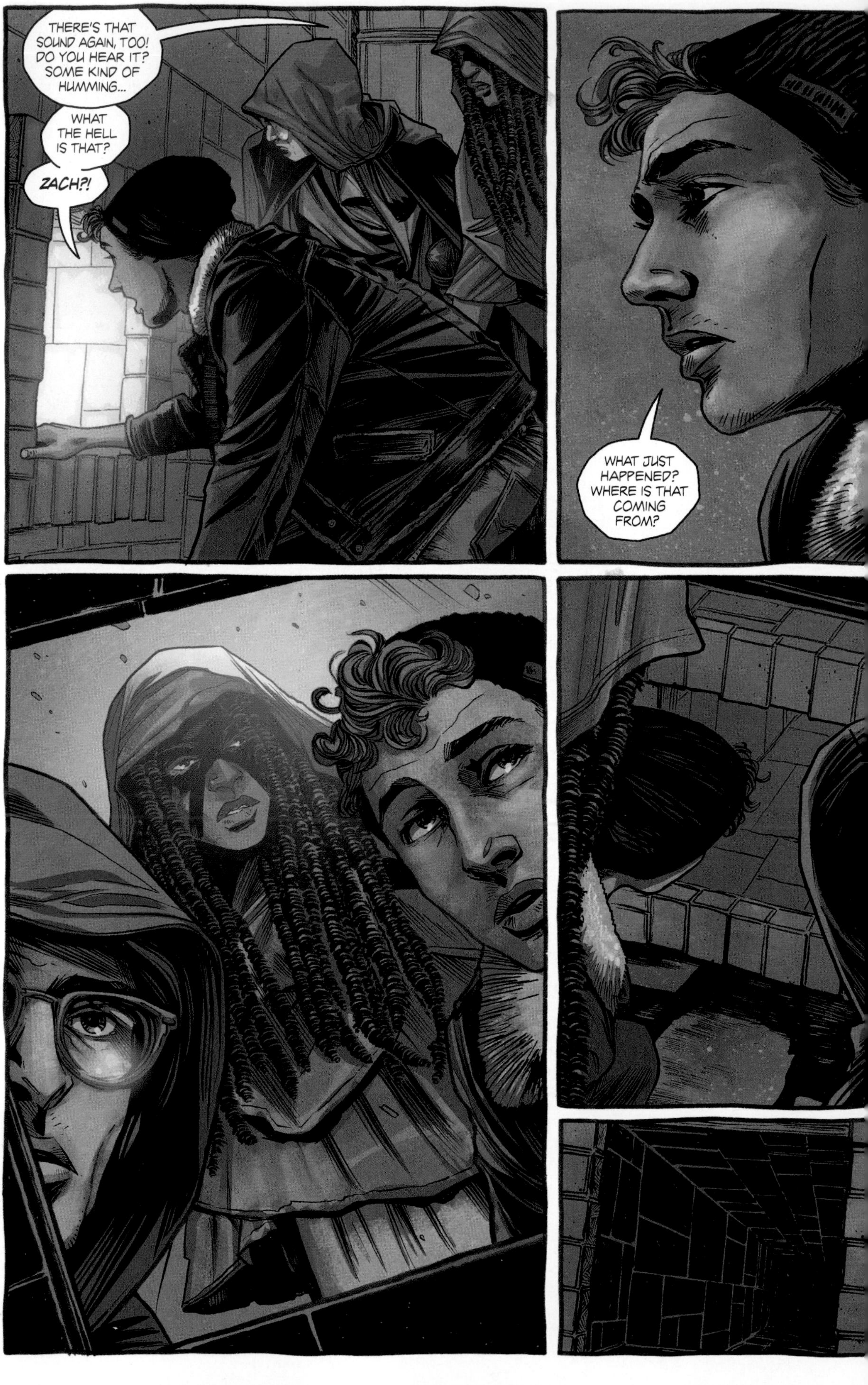
THERE'S THAT SOUND AGAIN, TOO! DO YOU HEAR IT? SOME KIND OF HUMMING...
WHAT THE HELL IS THAT?
ZACH?!
WHAT JUST HAPPENED? WHERE IS THAT COMING FROM?

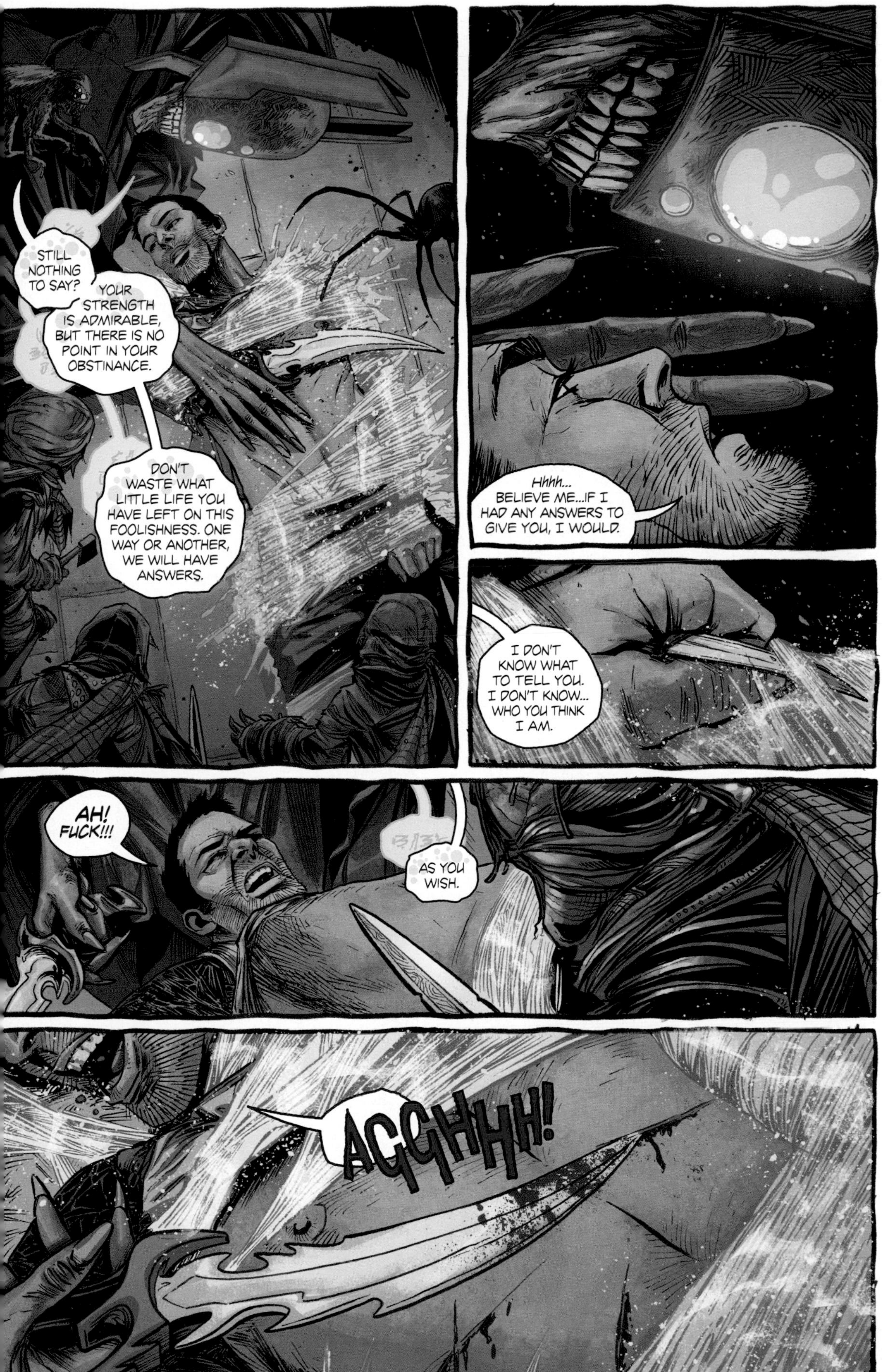
STILL NOTHING TO SAY?
YOUR STRENGTH IS ADMIRABLE, BUT THERE IS NO POINT IN YOUR OBSTINANCE.
DON'T WASTE WHAT LITTLE LIFE YOU HAVE LEFT ON THIS FOOLISHNESS. ONE WAY OR ANOTHER, WE WILL HAVE ANSWERS.
Hhhh... BELIEVE ME...IF I HAD ANY ANSWERS TO GIVE YOU, I WOULD.
I DON'T KNOW WHAT TO TELL YOU. I DON'T KNOW... WHO YOU THINK I AM.
AH! FUCK!!!
AS YOU WISH.
AGGHHH!

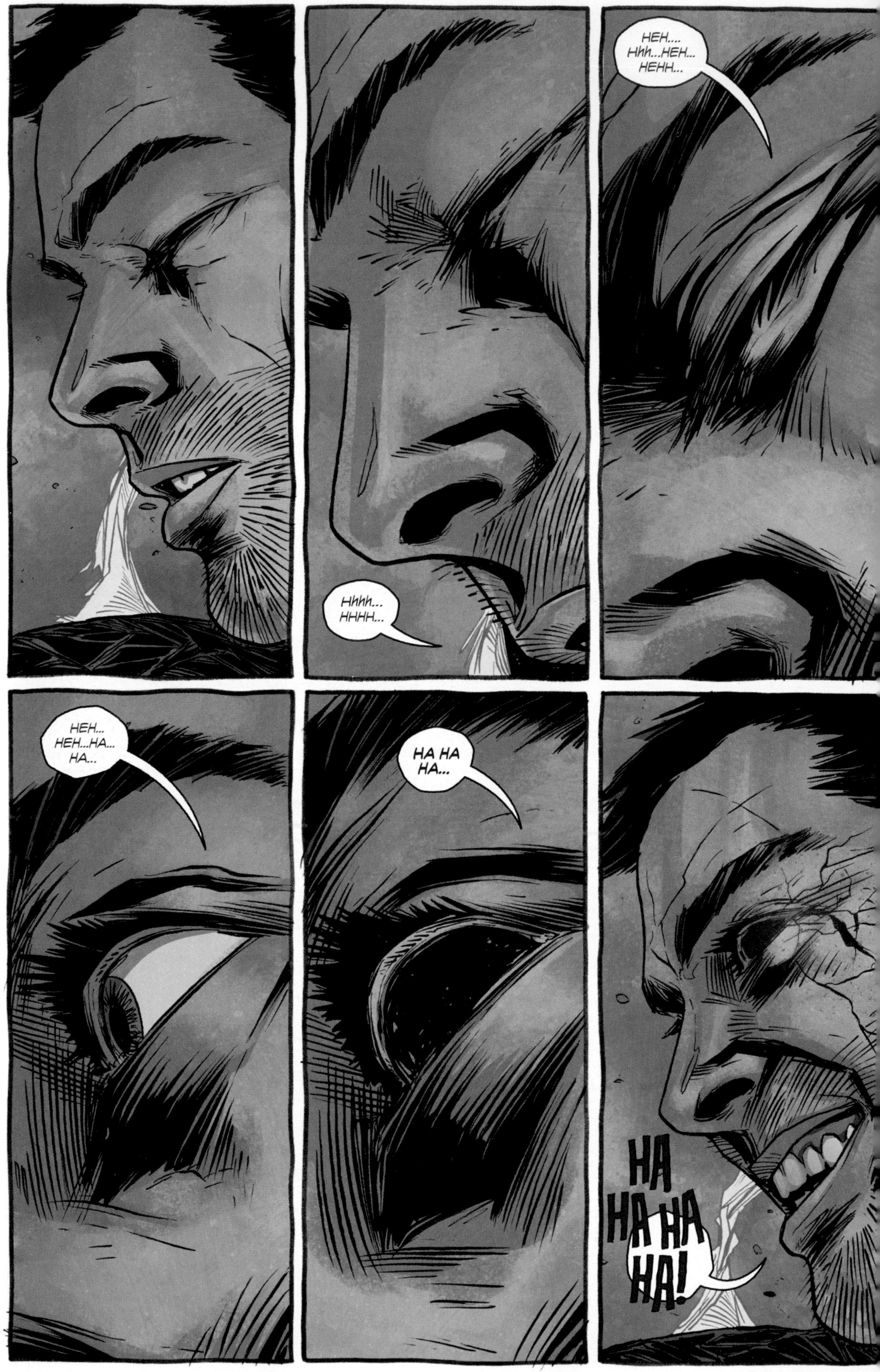
Hhhh... HHHH...
HEH.... Hhh...HEH... HEHH...
HEH... HEH...HA... HA...
HA HA HA...
HA HA HA HA HA!

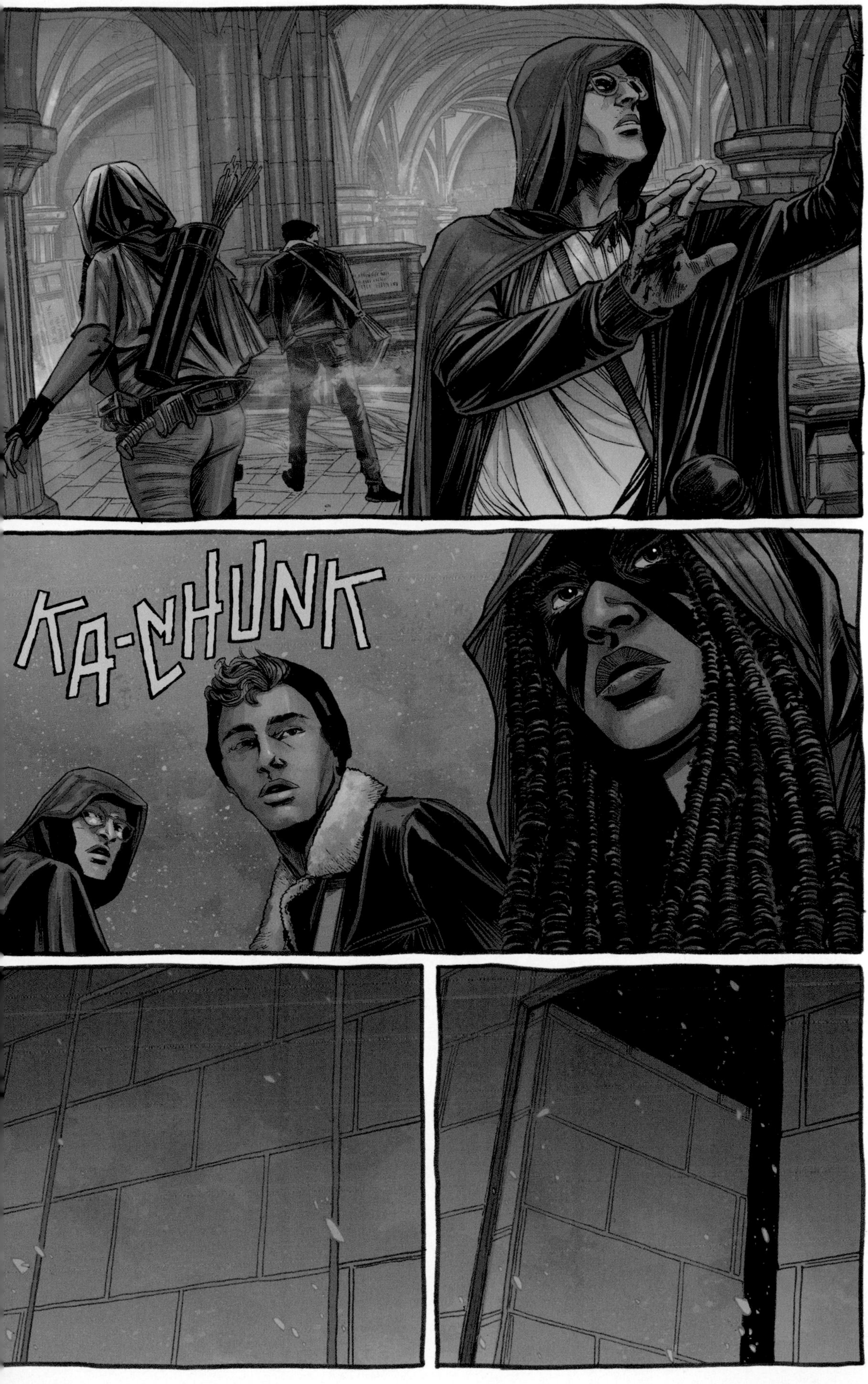
KA-CHUNK

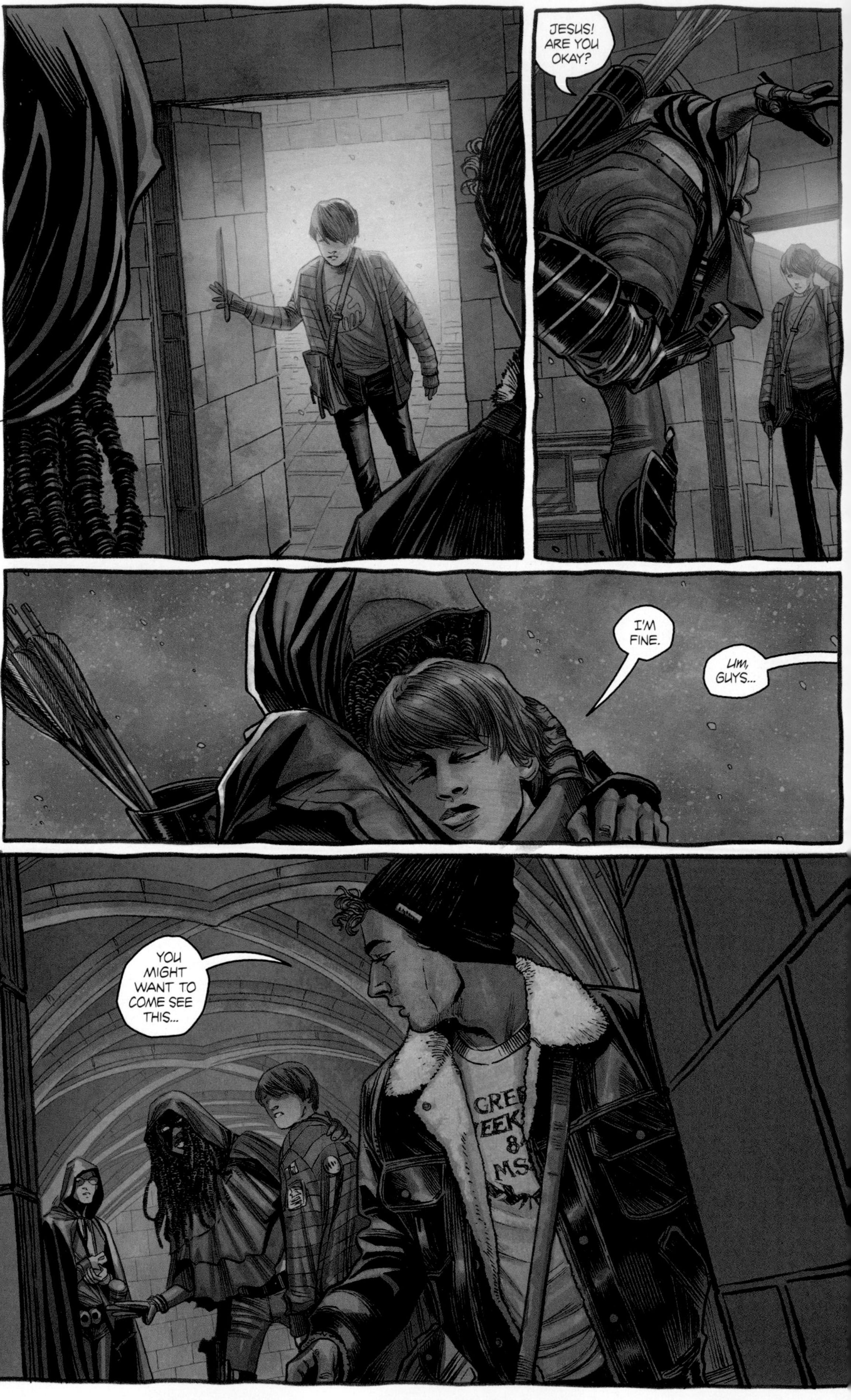
JESUS! ARE YOU OKAY?
I'M FINE.
UM, GUYS...
YOU MIGHT WANT TO COME SEE THIS...

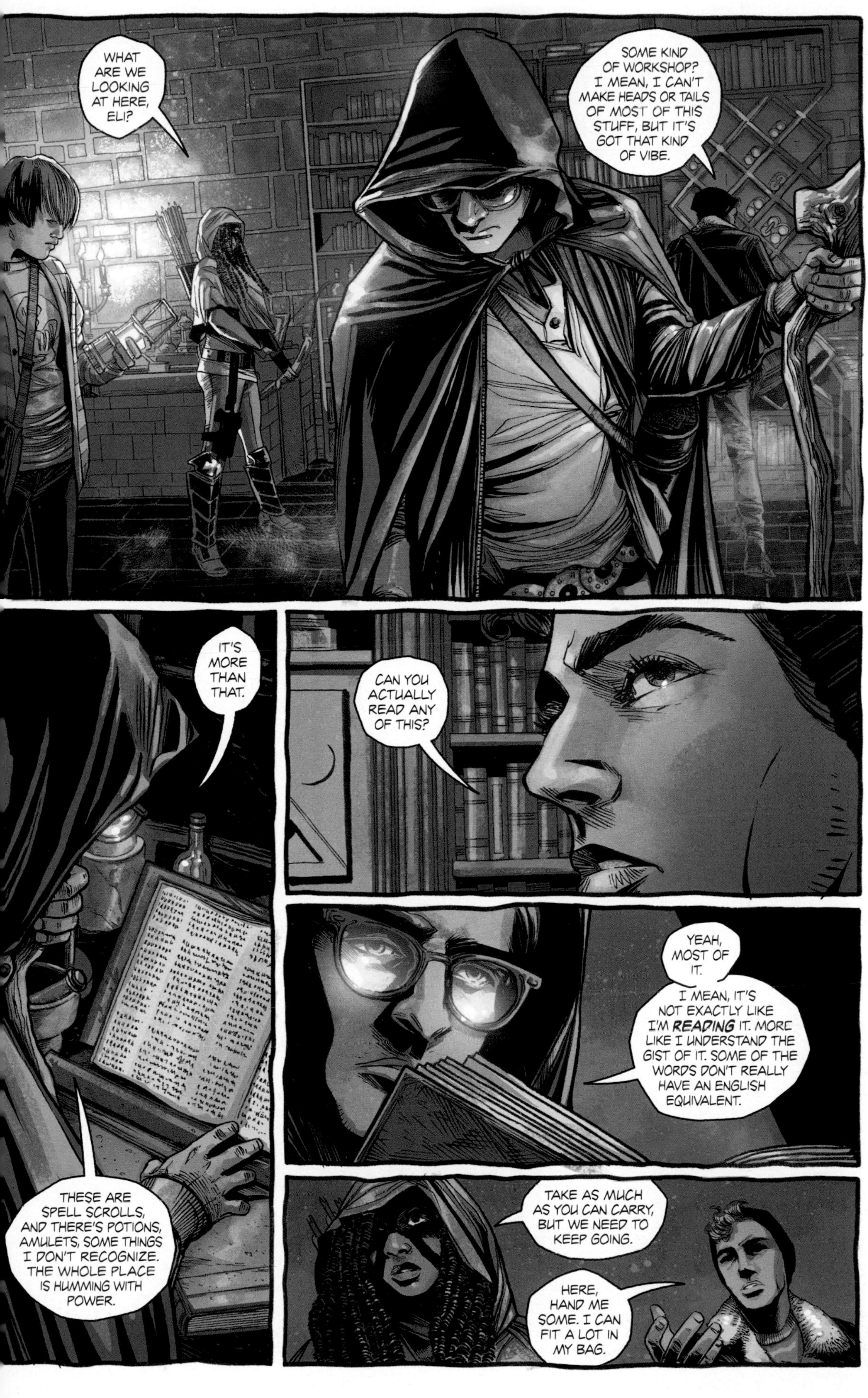

WHAT ARE WE LOOKING AT HERE, ELI?
SOME KIND OF WORKSHOP? I MEAN, I CAN'T MAKE HEADS OR TAILS OF MOST OF THIS STUFF, BUT IT'S GOT THAT KIND OF VIBE.
IT'S MORE THAN THAT.
THESE ARE SPELL SCROLLS, AND THERE'S POTIONS, AMULETS, SOME THINGS I DON'T RECOGNIZE. THE WHOLE PLACE IS HUMMING WITH POWER.
CAN YOU ACTUALLY READ ANY OF THIS?
YEAH, MOST OF IT.
I MEAN, IT'S NOT EXACTLY LIKE I'M **READING** IT. MORE LIKE I UNDERSTAND THE GIST OF IT. SOME OF THE WORDS DON'T REALLY HAVE AN ENGLISH EQUIVALENT.
TAKE AS MUCH AS YOU CAN CARRY, BUT WE NEED TO KEEP GOING.
HERE, HAND ME SOME. I CAN FIT A LOT IN MY BAG.

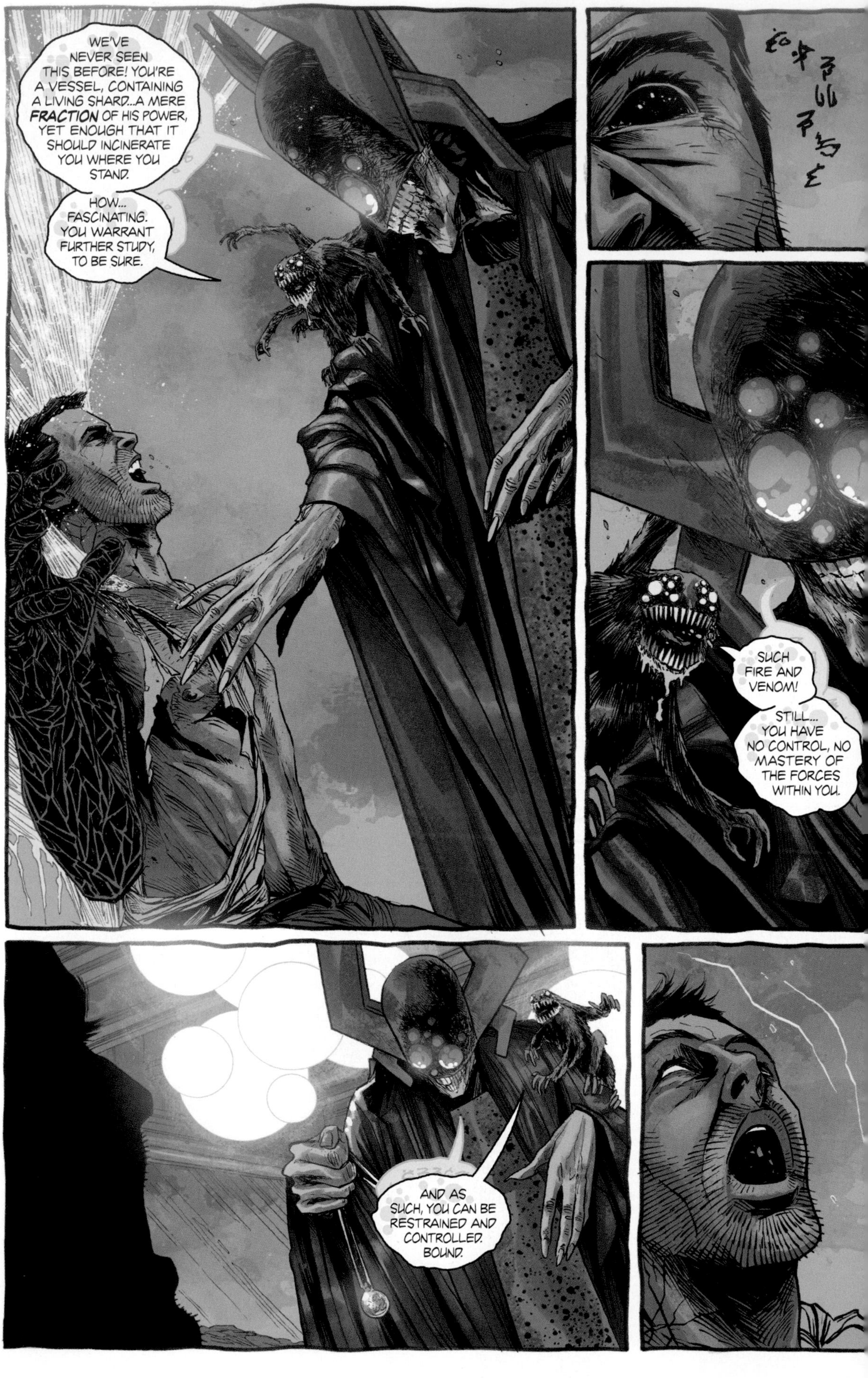
WE'VE NEVER SEEN THIS BEFORE! YOU'RE A VESSEL, CONTAINING A LIVING SHARD...A MERE **FRACTION** OF HIS POWER, YET ENOUGH THAT IT SHOULD INCINERATE YOU WHERE YOU STAND.
HOW... FASCINATING. YOU WARRANT FURTHER STUDY, TO BE SURE.
SUCH FIRE AND VENOM!
STILL... YOU HAVE NO CONTROL, NO MASTERY OF THE FORCES WITHIN YOU.
AND AS SUCH, YOU CAN BE RESTRAINED AND CONTROLLED. BOUND.

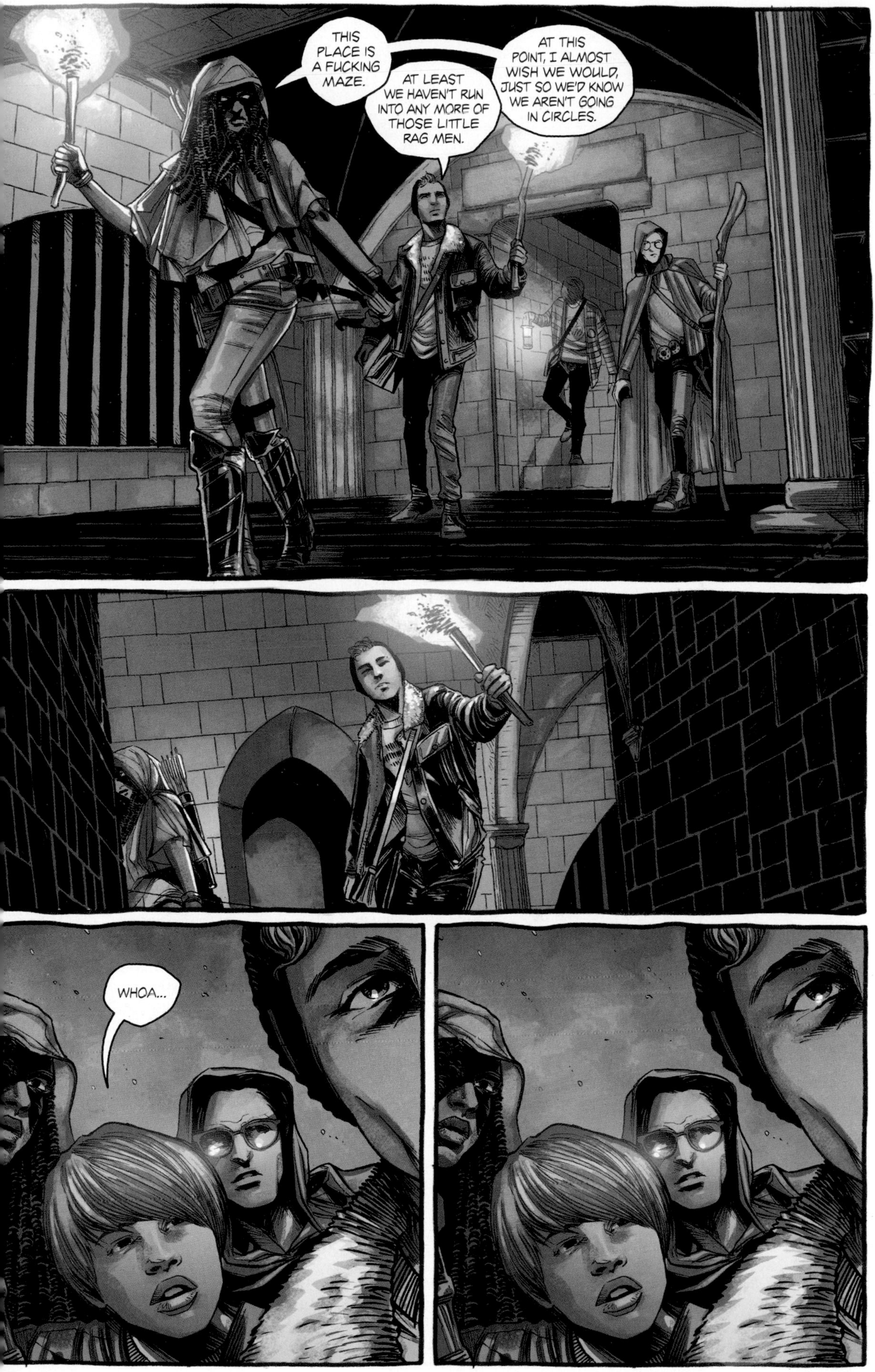
THIS PLACE IS A FUCKING MAZE.
AT LEAST WE HAVEN'T RUN INTO ANY MORE OF THOSE LITTLE RAG MEN.
AT THIS POINT, I ALMOST WISH WE WOULD, JUST SO WE'D KNOW WE AREN'T GOING IN CIRCLES.
WHOA...

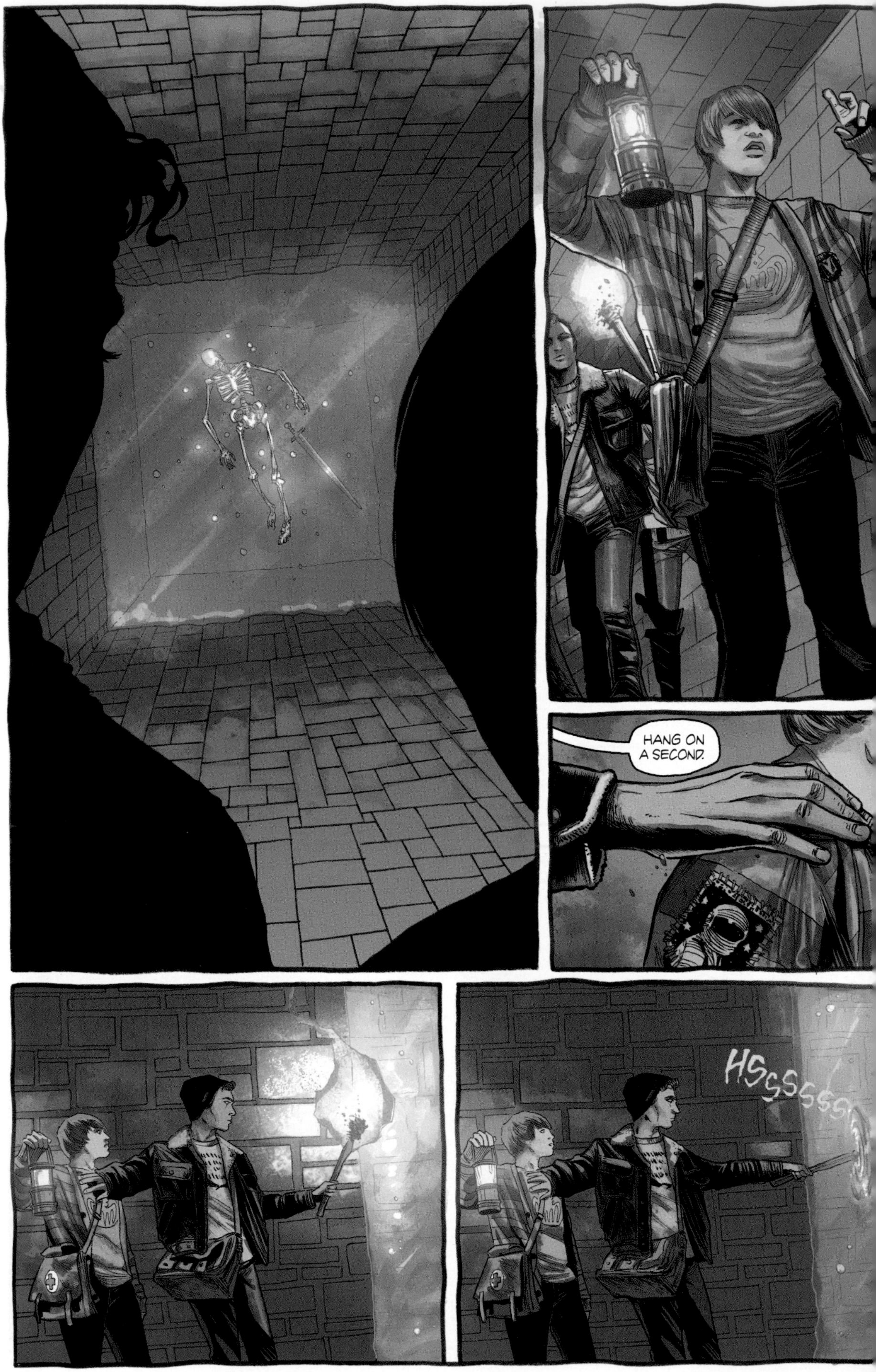
HANG ON A SECOND.
HSSSSSSS

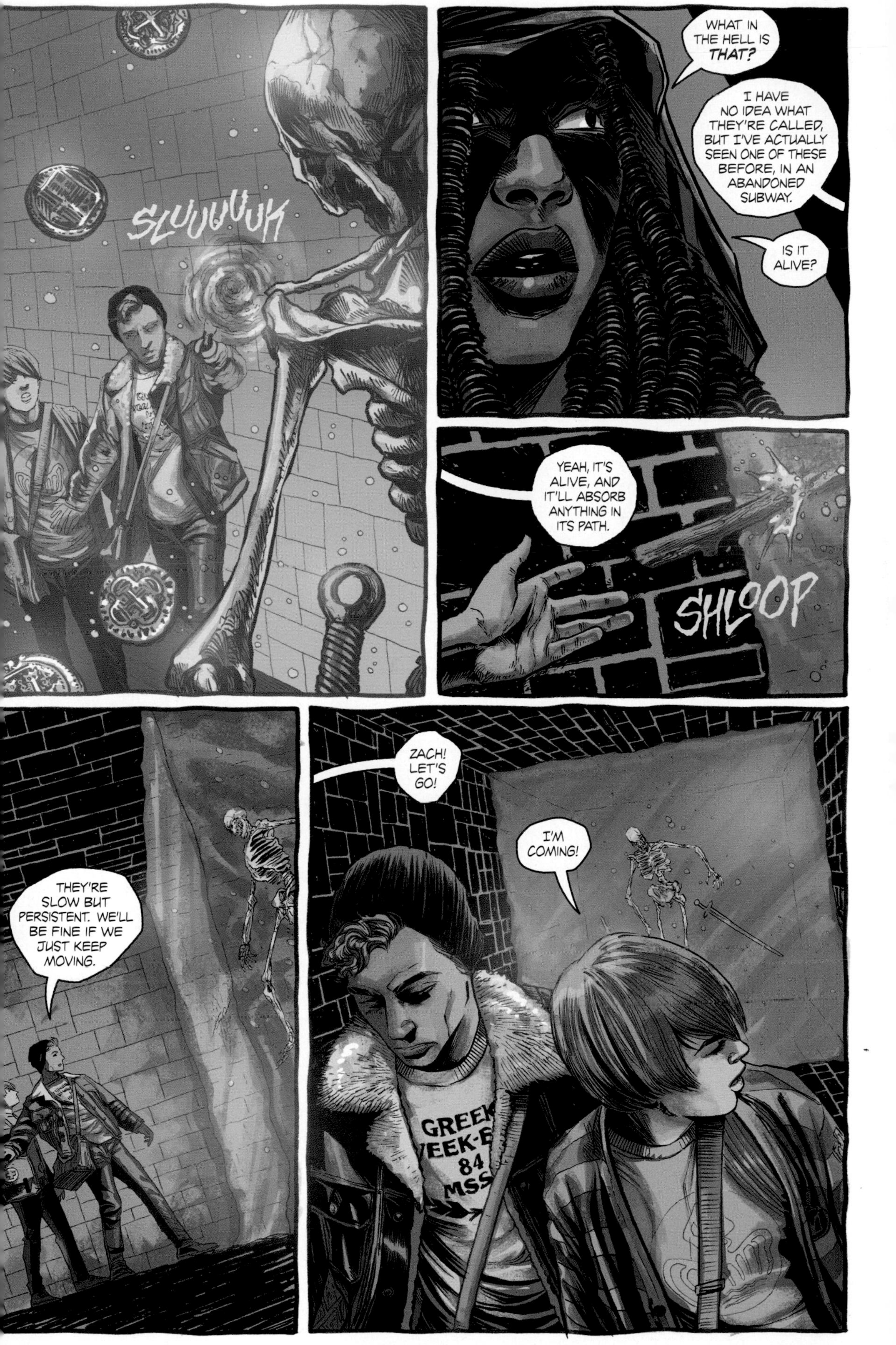
SLUUUUUK
WHAT IN THE HELL IS THAT?
I HAVE NO IDEA WHAT THEY'RE CALLED, BUT I'VE ACTUALLY SEEN ONE OF THESE BEFORE, IN AN ABANDONED SUBWAY.
IS IT ALIVE?
YEAH, IT'S ALIVE, AND IT'LL ABSORB ANYTHING IN ITS PATH.
SHLOOP
THEY'RE SLOW BUT PERSISTENT. WE'LL BE FINE IF WE JUST KEEP MOVING.
ZACH! LET'S GO!
I'M COMING!
GREEK
VEEK-E
84
MSS

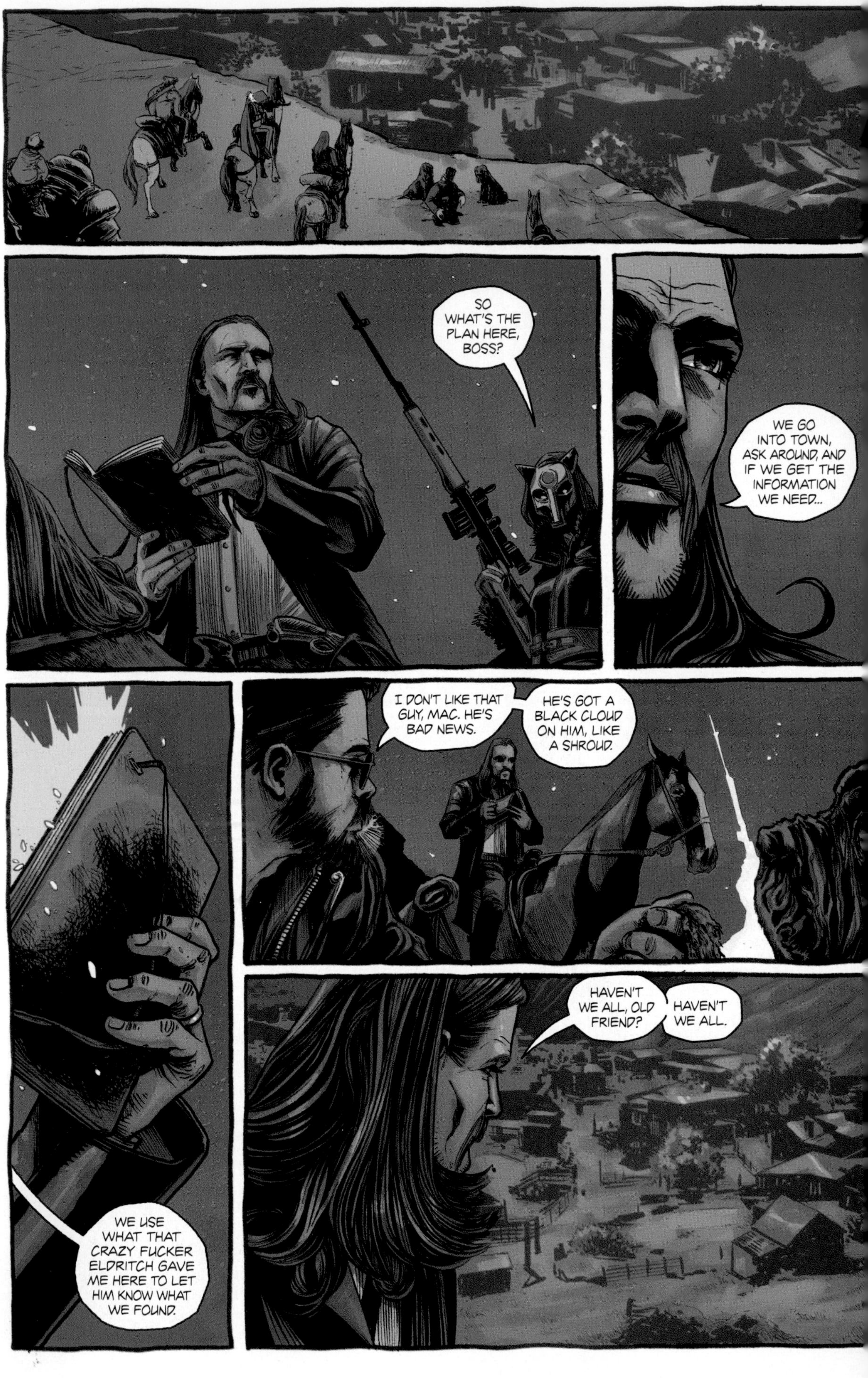
SO WHAT'S THE PLAN HERE, BOSS?
WE GO INTO TOWN, ASK AROUND, AND IF WE GET THE INFORMATION WE NEED...
WE USE WHAT THAT CRAZY FUCKER ELDRITCH GAVE ME HERE TO LET HIM KNOW WHAT WE FOUND.
I DON'T LIKE THAT GUY, MAC. HE'S BAD NEWS.
HE'S GOT A BLACK CLOUD ON HIM, LIKE A SHROUD.
HAVEN'T WE ALL, OLD FRIEND?
HAVEN'T WE ALL.

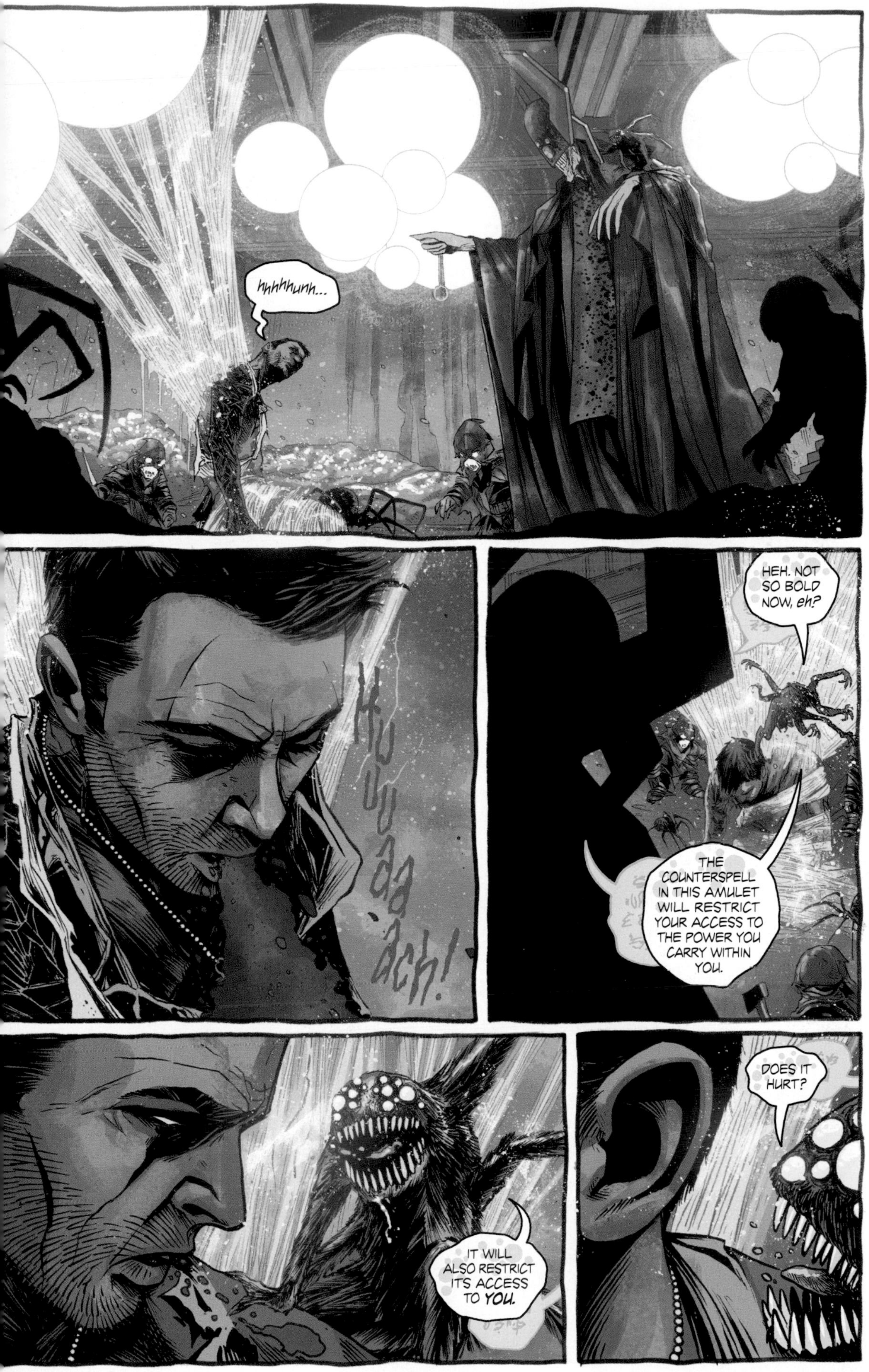
hhhhhunh...
Huuuaaaach!
HEH. NOT SO BOLD NOW, eh?
THE COUNTERSPELL IN THIS AMULET WILL RESTRICT YOUR ACCESS TO THE POWER YOU CARRY WITHIN YOU.
IT WILL ALSO RESTRICT ITS ACCESS TO YOU.
DOES IT HURT?

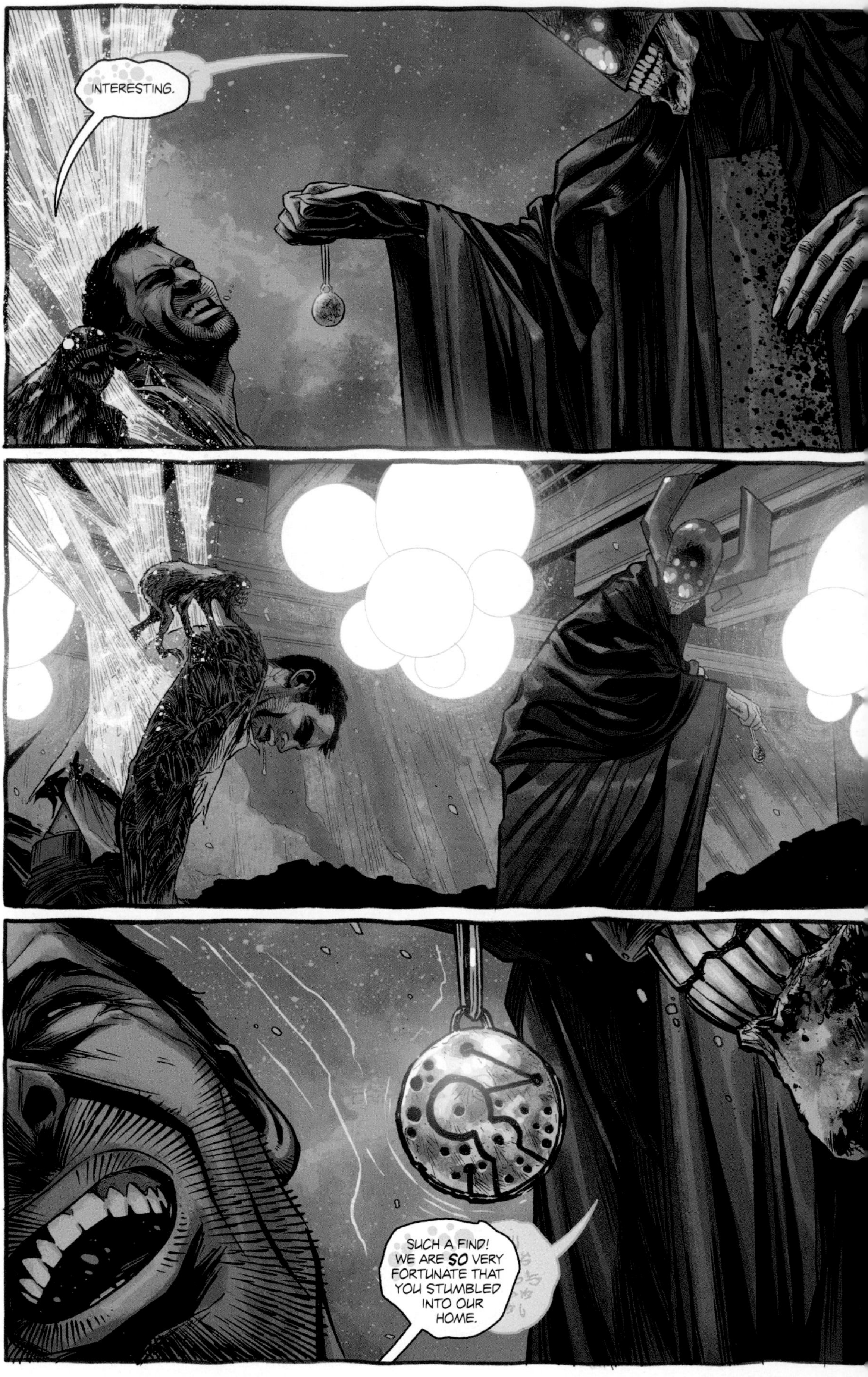
INTERESTING.
SUCH A FIND! WE ARE SO VERY FORTUNATE THAT YOU STUMBLED INTO OUR HOME.

AH, ADMIRING YOUR LOYAL SUBJECTS... **LORD** ELDRITCH?

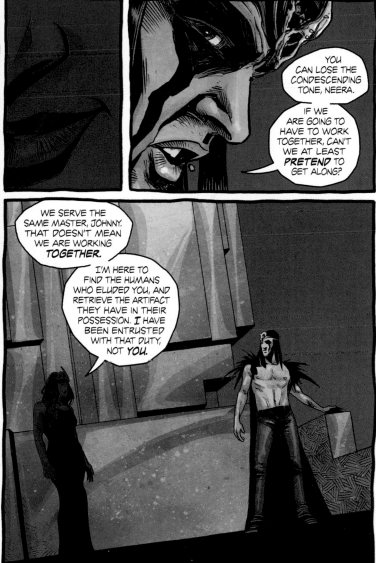

YOU CAN LOSE THE CONDESCENDING TONE, NEERA.

IF WE ARE GOING TO HAVE TO WORK TOGETHER, CAN'T WE AT LEAST **PRETEND** TO GET ALONG?

WE SERVE THE SAME MASTER, JOHNNY. THAT DOESN'T MEAN WE ARE WORKING **TOGETHER.**

I'M HERE TO FIND THE HUMANS WHO ELUDED YOU, AND RETRIEVE THE ARTIFACT THEY HAVE IN THEIR POSSESSION. I HAVE BEEN ENTRUSTED WITH THAT DUTY, NOT **YOU.**

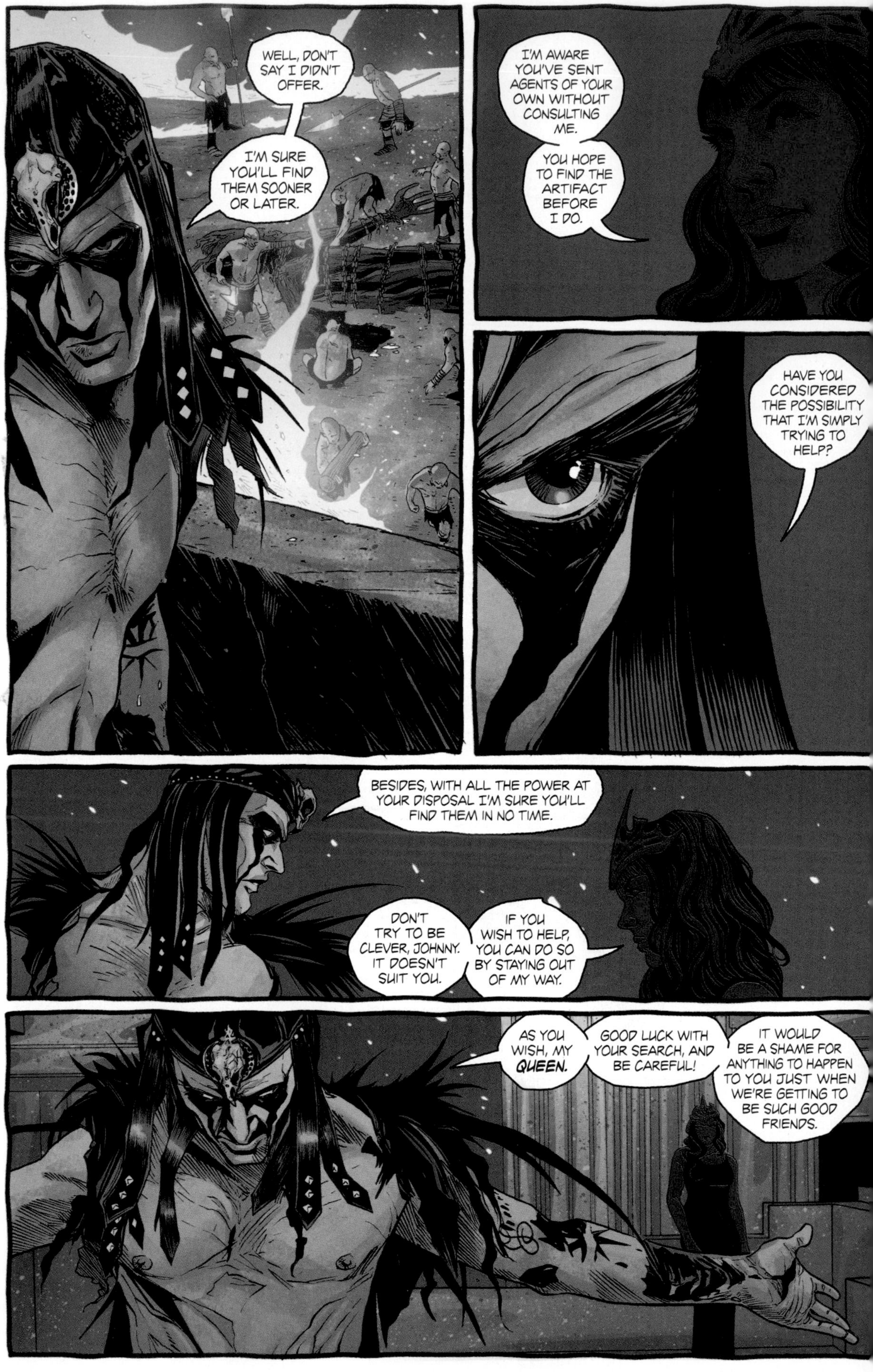
WELL, DON'T SAY I DIDN'T OFFER.
I'M SURE YOU'LL FIND THEM SOONER OR LATER.
I'M AWARE YOU'VE SENT AGENTS OF YOUR OWN WITHOUT CONSULTING ME.
YOU HOPE TO FIND THE ARTIFACT BEFORE I DO.
HAVE YOU CONSIDERED THE POSSIBILITY THAT I'M SIMPLY TRYING TO HELP?
BESIDES, WITH ALL THE POWER AT YOUR DISPOSAL I'M SURE YOU'LL FIND THEM IN NO TIME.
DON'T TRY TO BE CLEVER, JOHNNY. IT DOESN'T SUIT YOU.
IF YOU WISH TO HELP, YOU CAN DO SO BY STAYING OUT OF MY WAY.
AS YOU WISH, MY **QUEEN.**
GOOD LUCK WITH YOUR SEARCH, AND BE CAREFUL!
IT WOULD BE A SHAME FOR ANYTHING TO HAPPEN TO YOU JUST WHEN WE'RE GETTING TO BE SUCH GOOD FRIENDS.

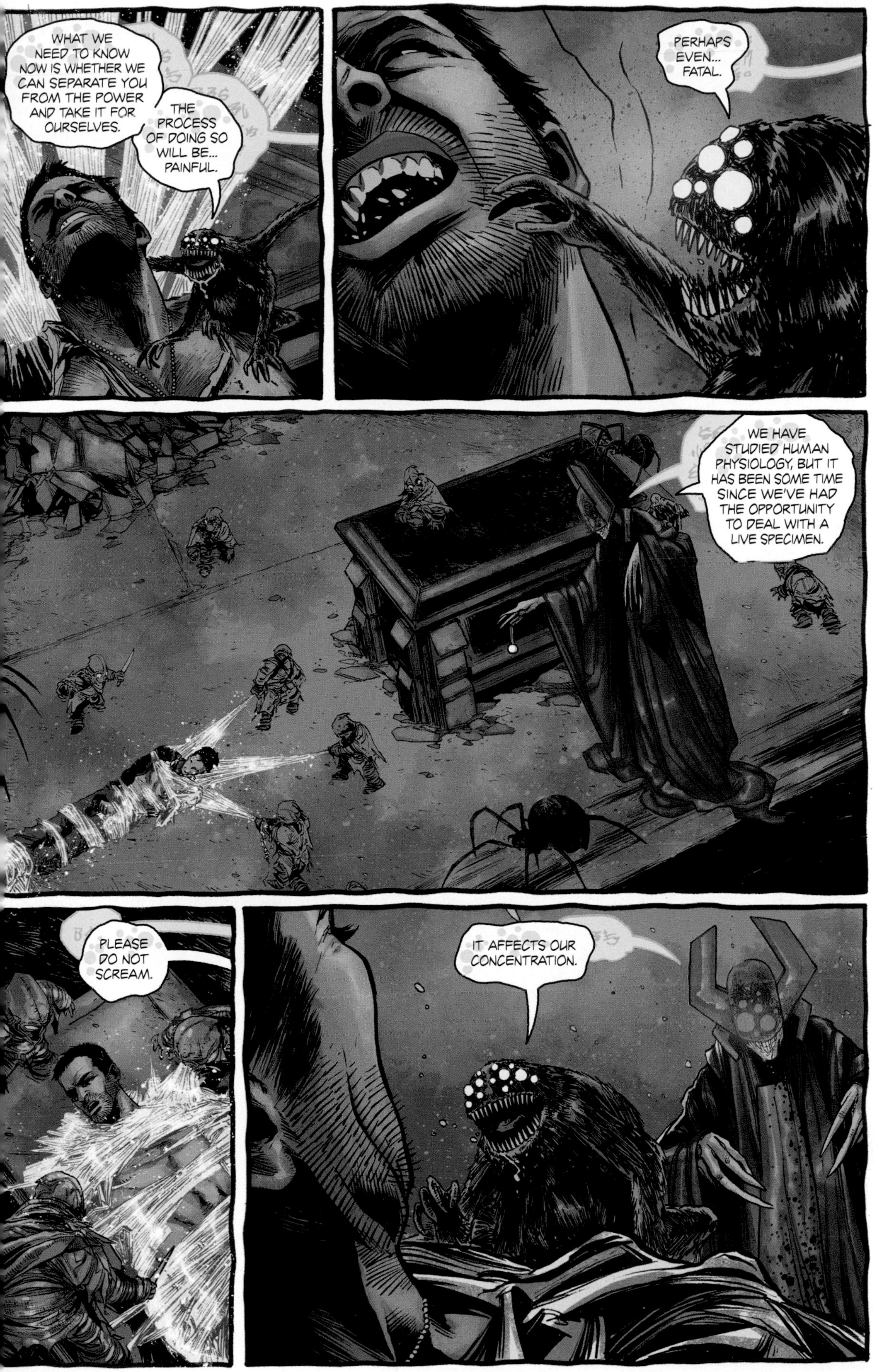
WHAT WE NEED TO KNOW NOW IS WHETHER WE CAN SEPARATE YOU FROM THE POWER AND TAKE IT FOR OURSELVES.
THE PROCESS OF DOING SO WILL BE... PAINFUL.
PERHAPS EVEN... FATAL.
WE HAVE STUDIED HUMAN PHYSIOLOGY, BUT IT HAS BEEN SOME TIME SINCE WE'VE HAD THE OPPORTUNITY TO DEAL WITH A LIVE SPECIMEN.
PLEASE DO NOT SCREAM.
IT AFFECTS OUR CONCENTRATION.

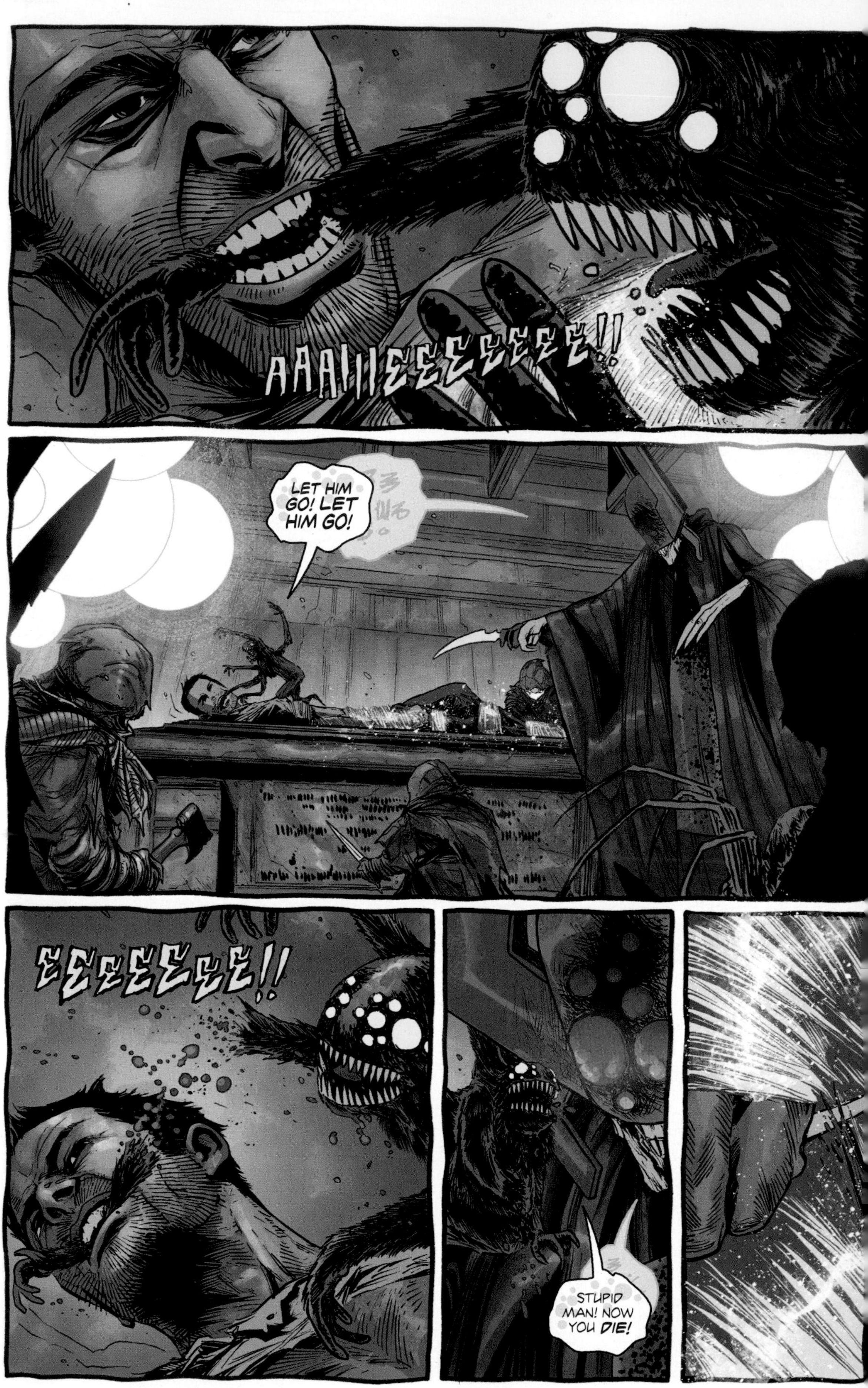
AAAIIIEEEEEEEE!!
LET HIM GO! LET HIM GO!
EEEEEEEE!!
STUPID MAN! NOW YOU *DIE!*

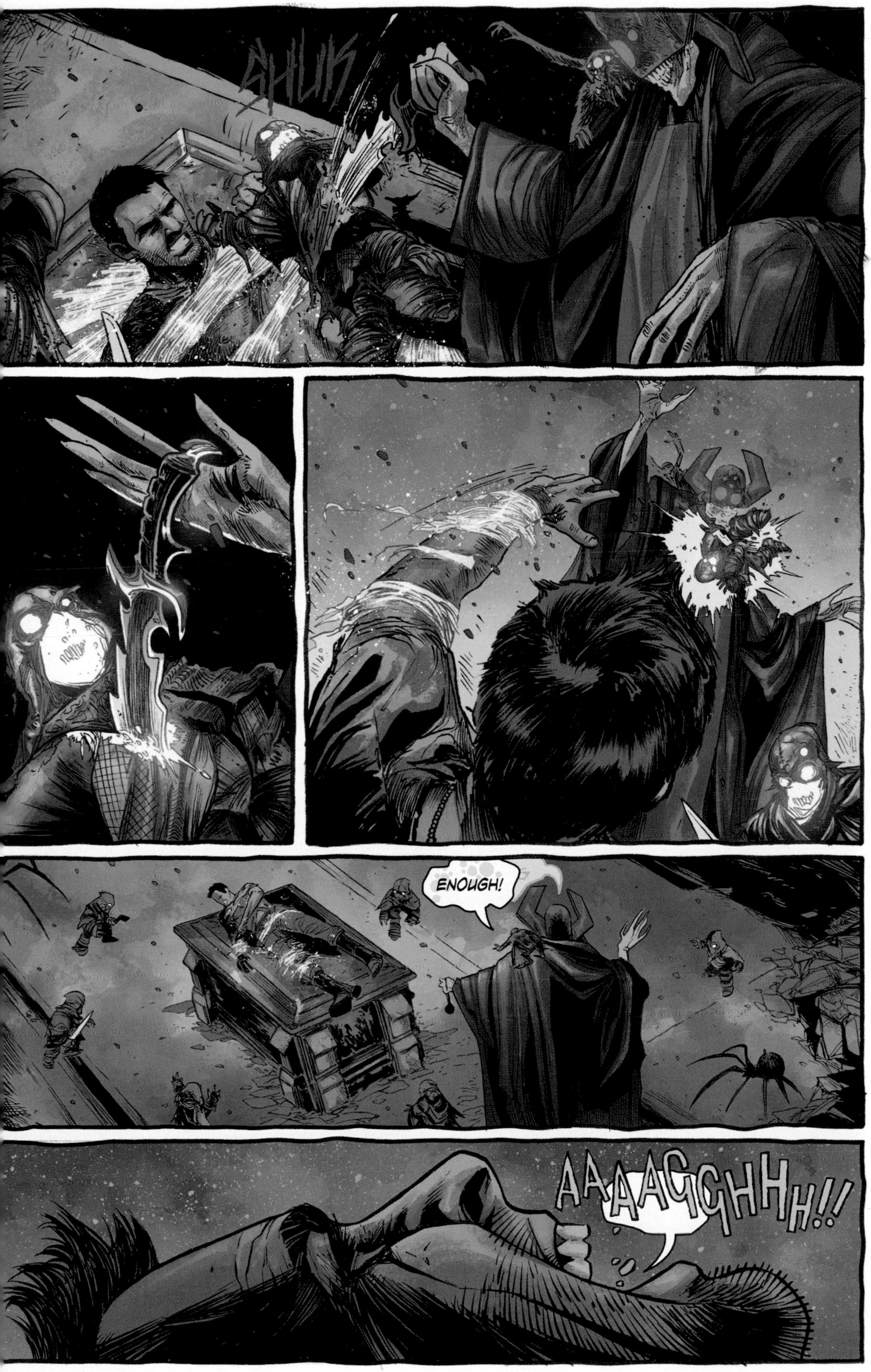
SHUK
ENOUGH!
AAAAAGGHHHH!!

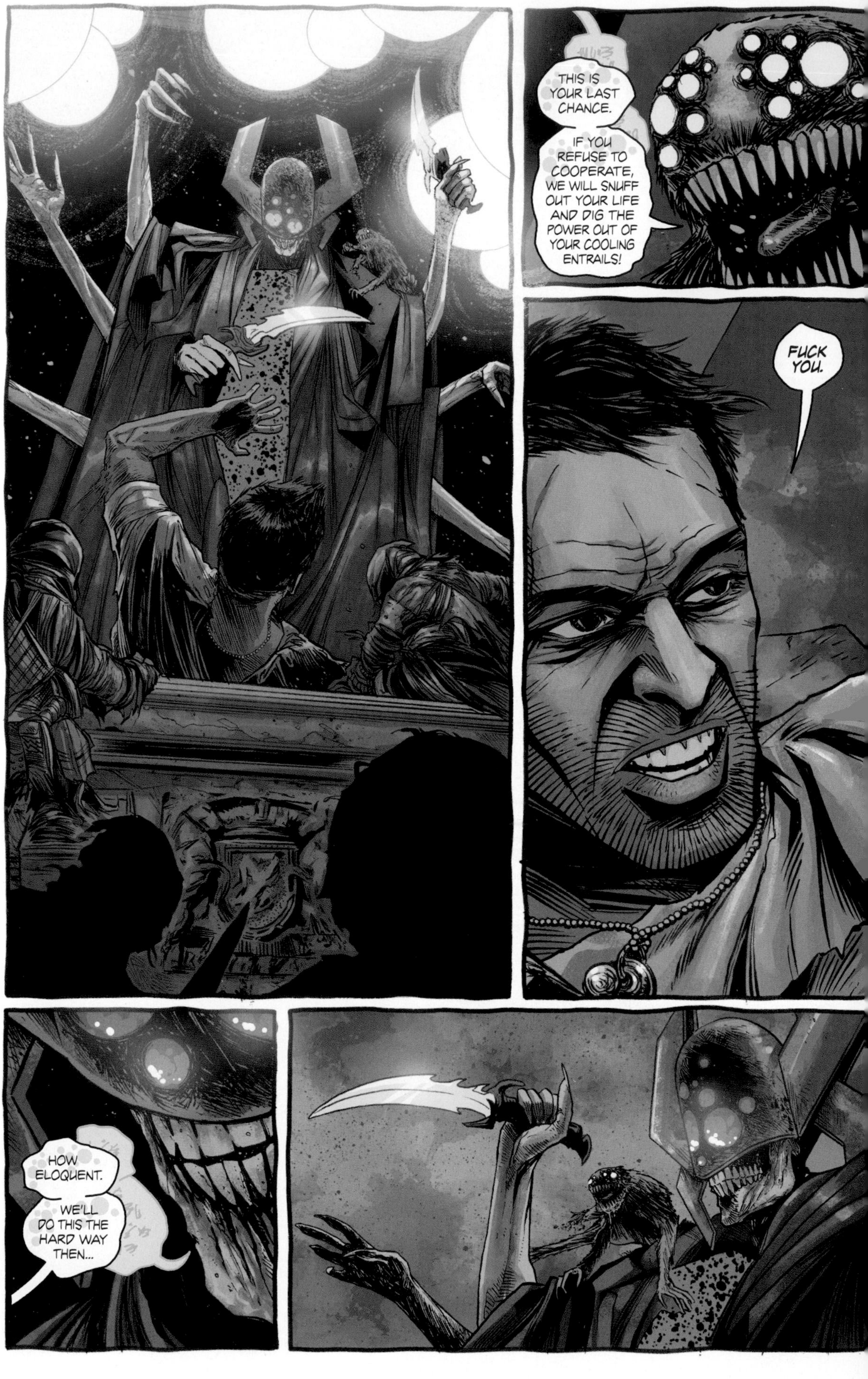
THIS IS YOUR LAST CHANCE.
IF YOU REFUSE TO COOPERATE, WE WILL SNUFF OUT YOUR LIFE AND DIG THE POWER OUT OF YOUR COOLING ENTRAILS!
FUCK YOU.
HOW ELOQUENT.
WE'LL DO THIS THE HARD WAY THEN...

SHUNK

WE INTERRUPTING ANYTHING?

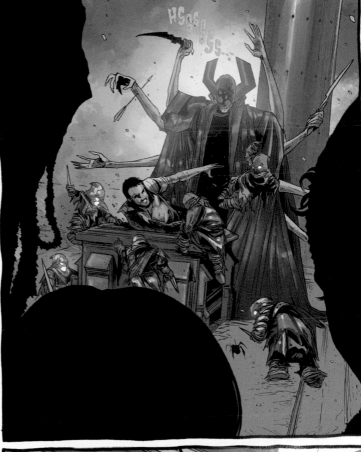

HSSSSSS...

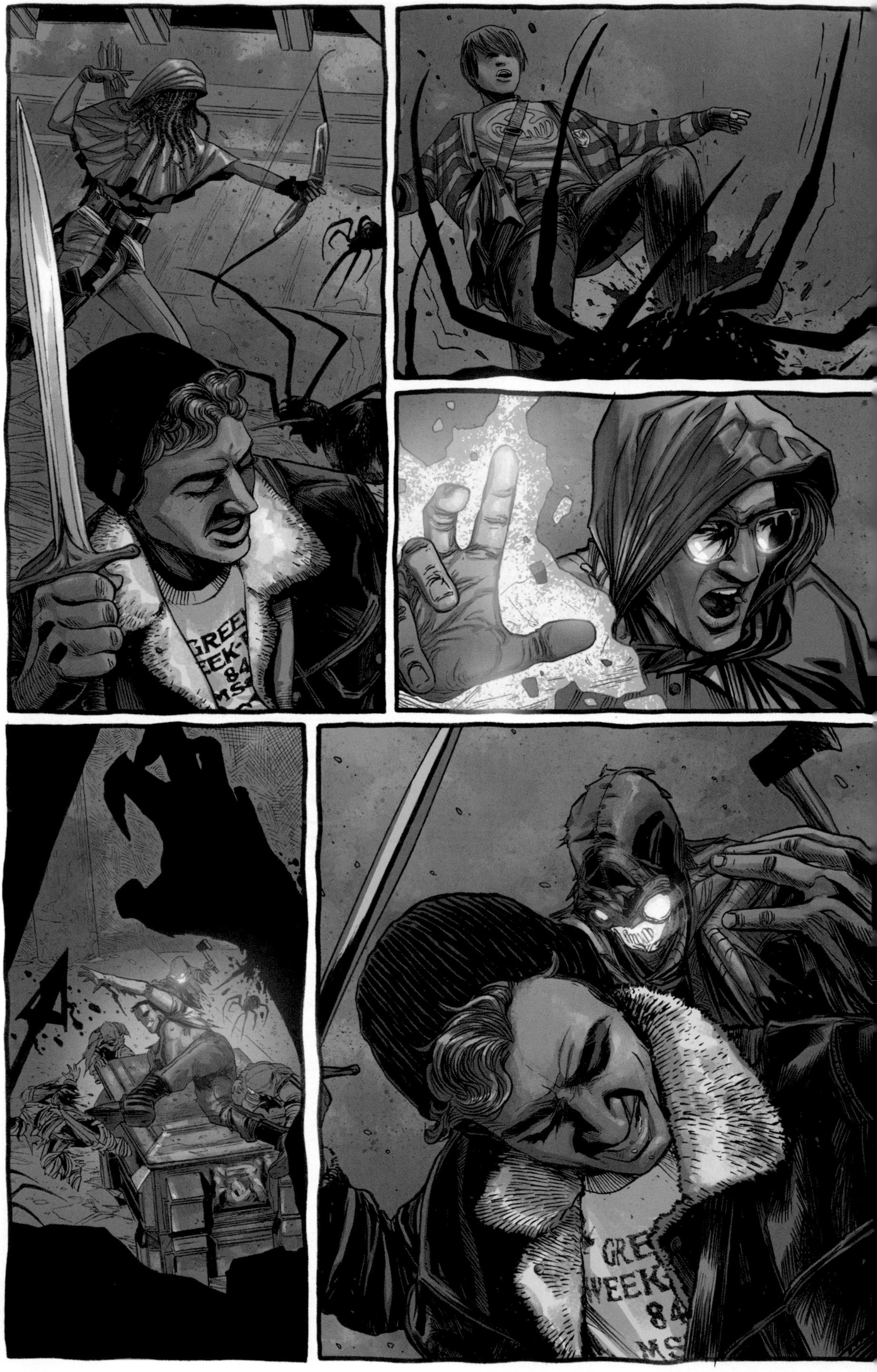

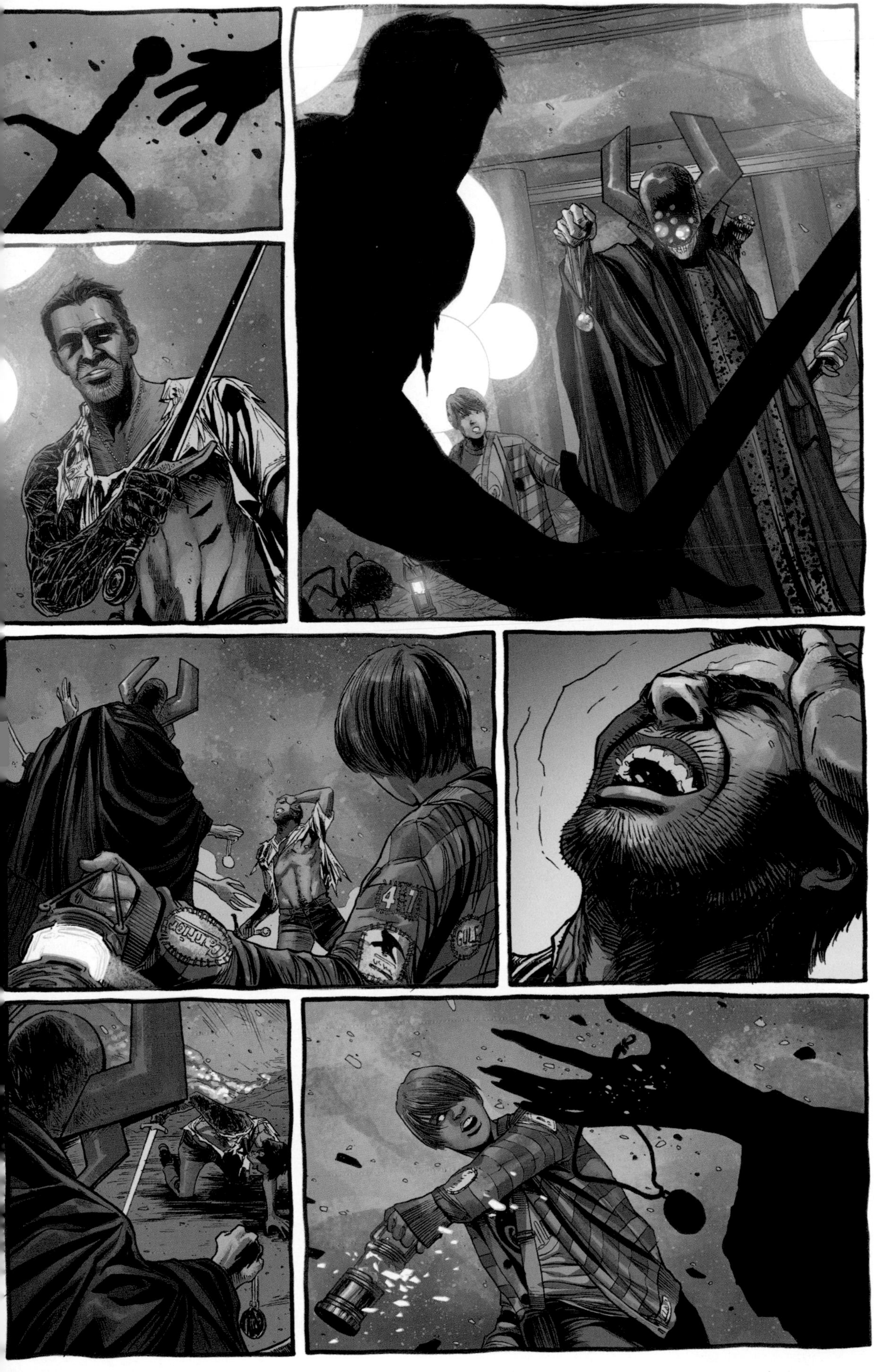
GULF

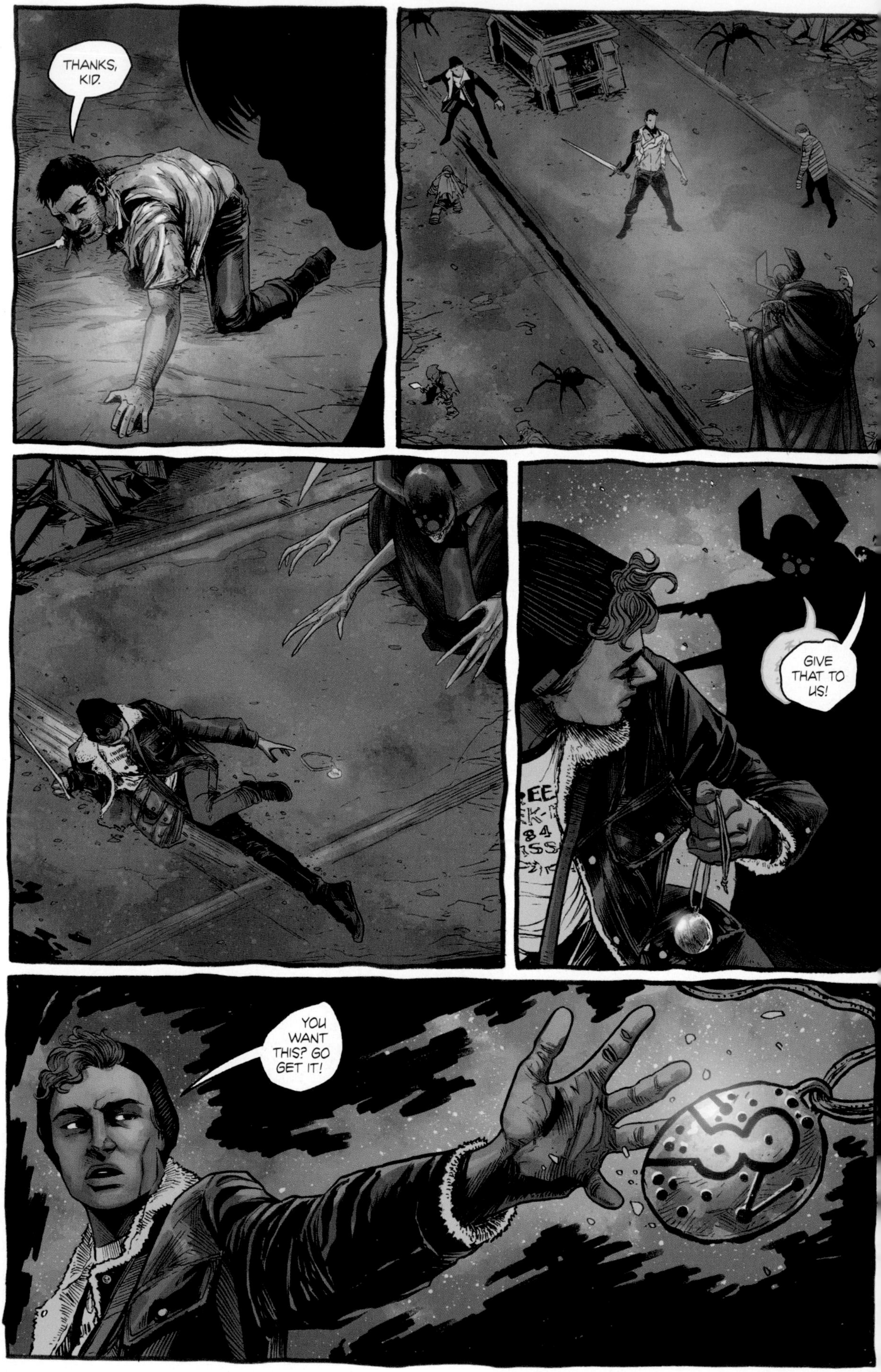
THANKS, KID.
GIVE THAT TO US!
YOU WANT THIS? GO GET IT!

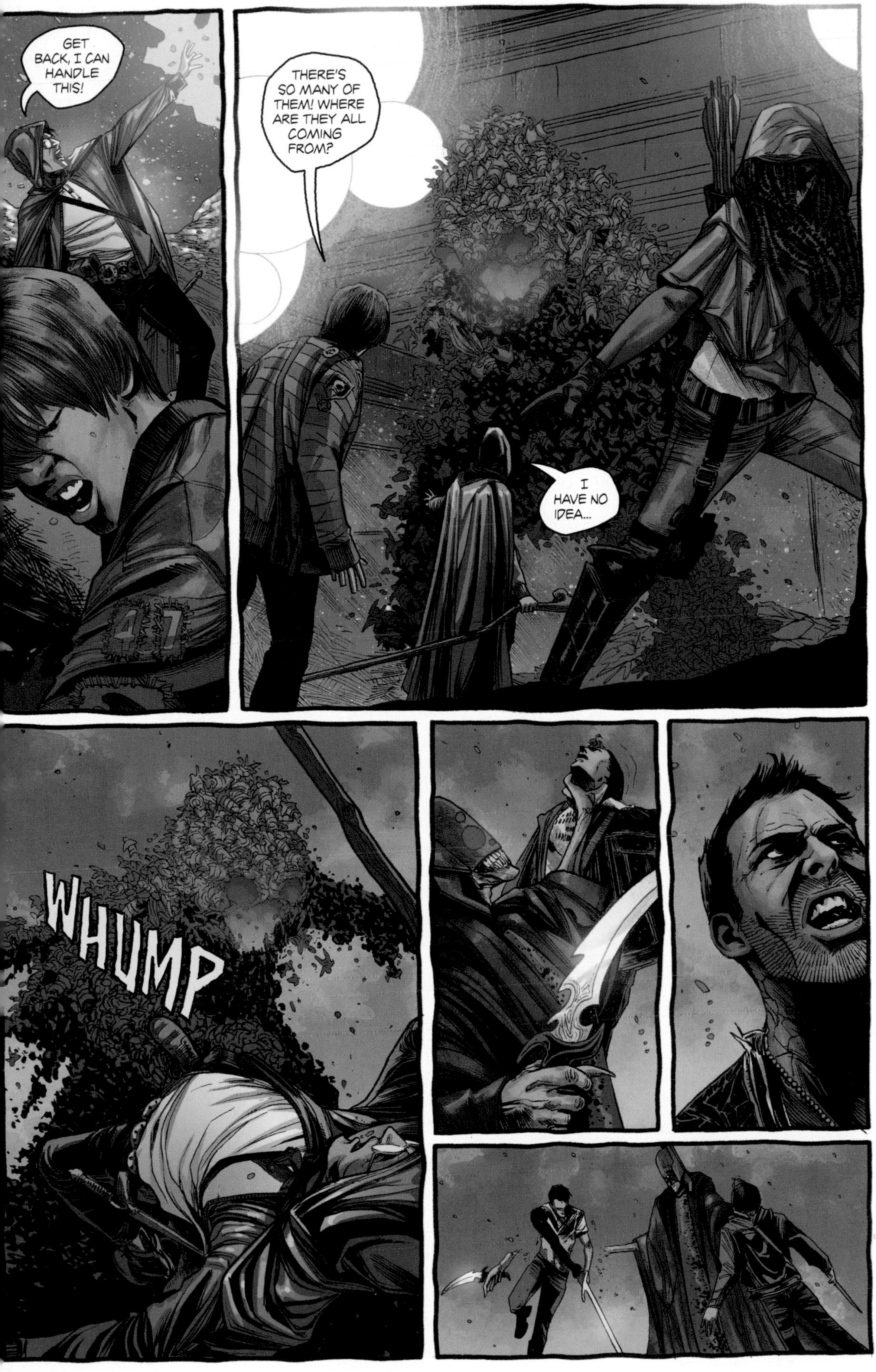
GET BACK, I CAN HANDLE THIS!
THERE'S SO MANY OF THEM! WHERE ARE THEY ALL COMING FROM?
I HAVE NO IDEA...
WHUMP

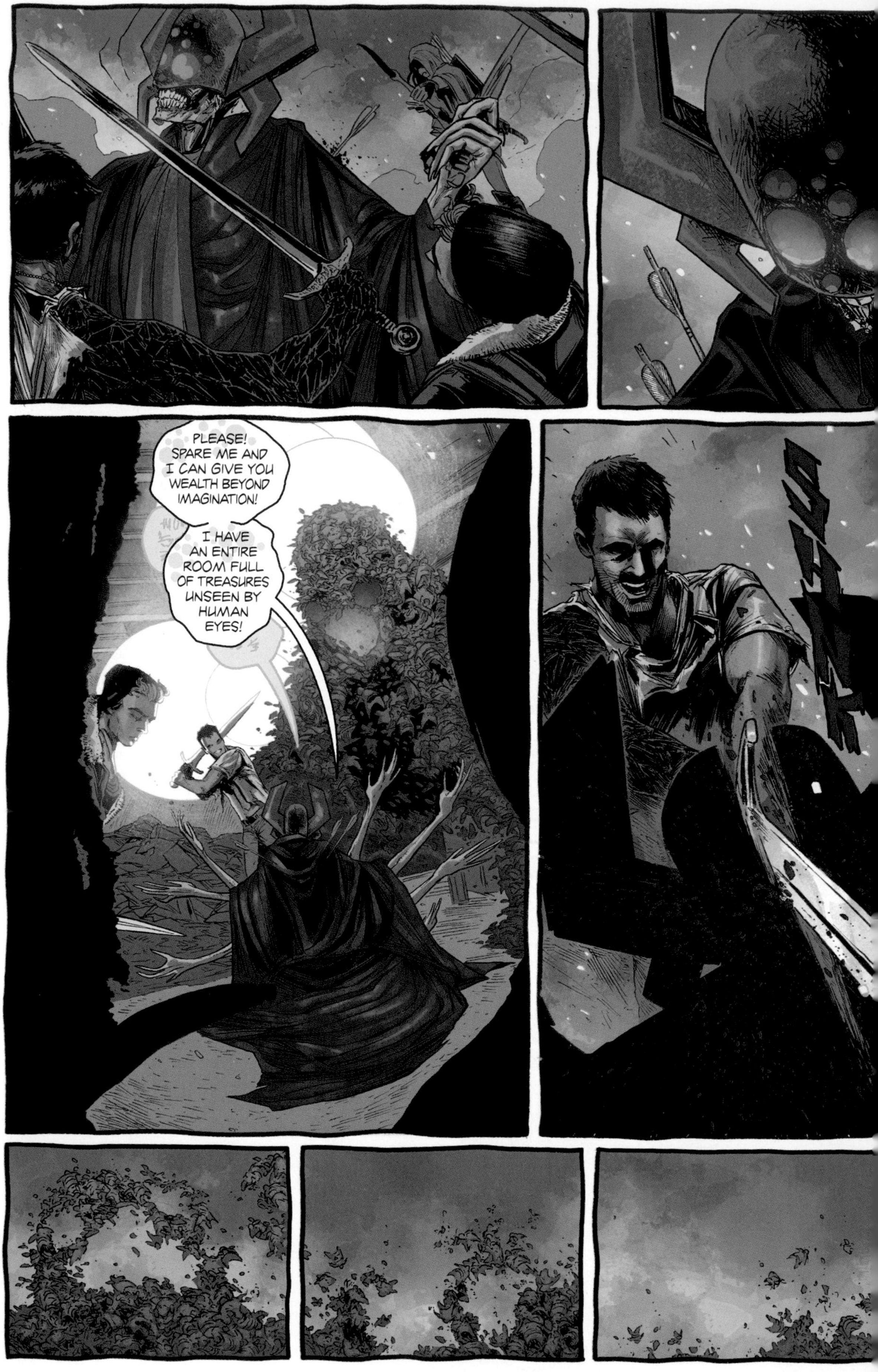
PLEASE! SPARE ME AND I CAN GIVE YOU WEALTH BEYOND IMAGINATION!
I HAVE AN ENTIRE ROOM FULL OF TREASURES UNSEEN BY HUMAN EYES!

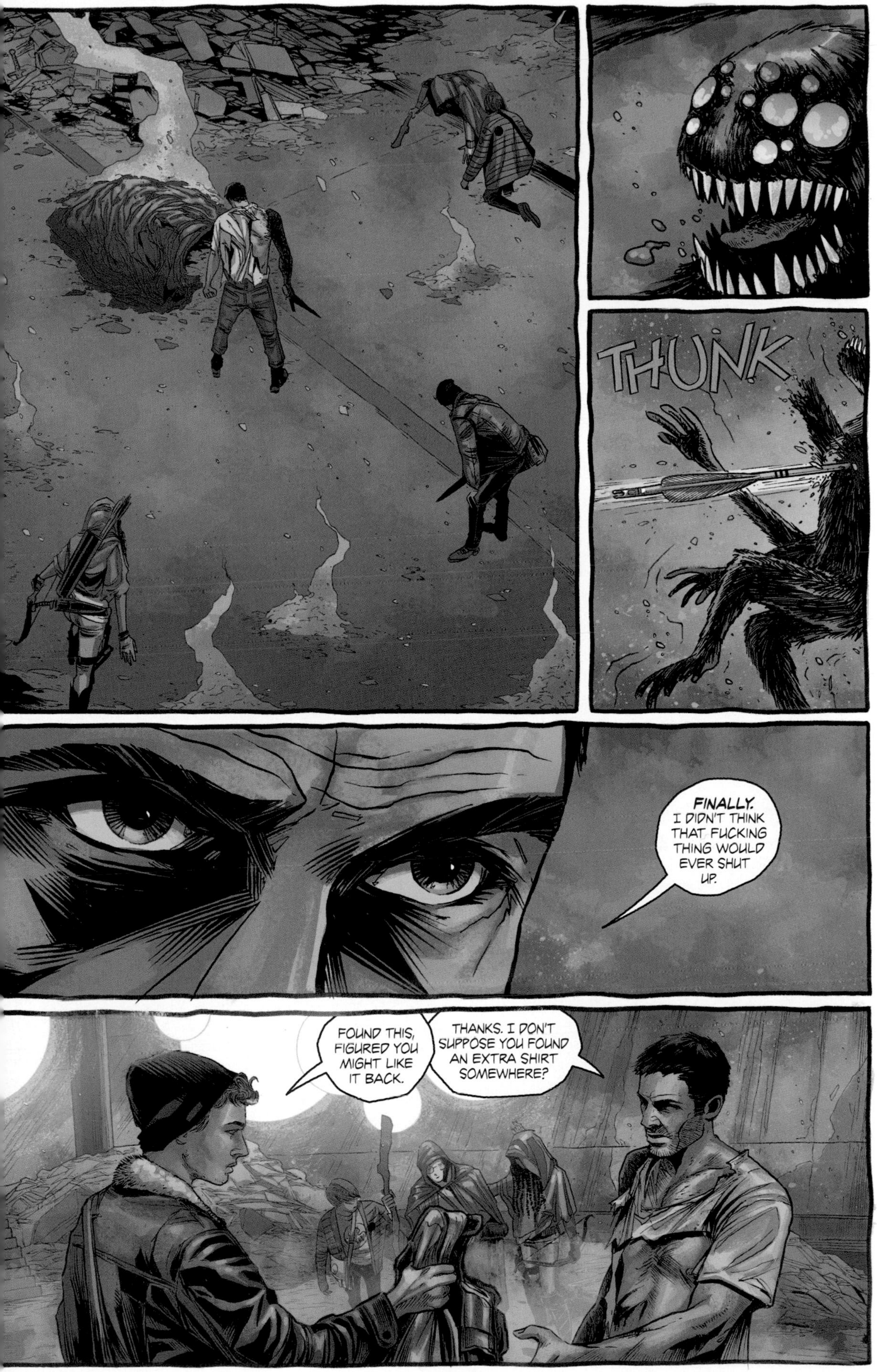
THUNK
FINALLY. I DIDN'T THINK THAT FUCKING THING WOULD EVER SHUT UP.
FOUND THIS, FIGURED YOU MIGHT LIKE IT BACK.
THANKS. I DON'T SUPPOSE YOU FOUND AN EXTRA SHIRT SOMEWHERE?

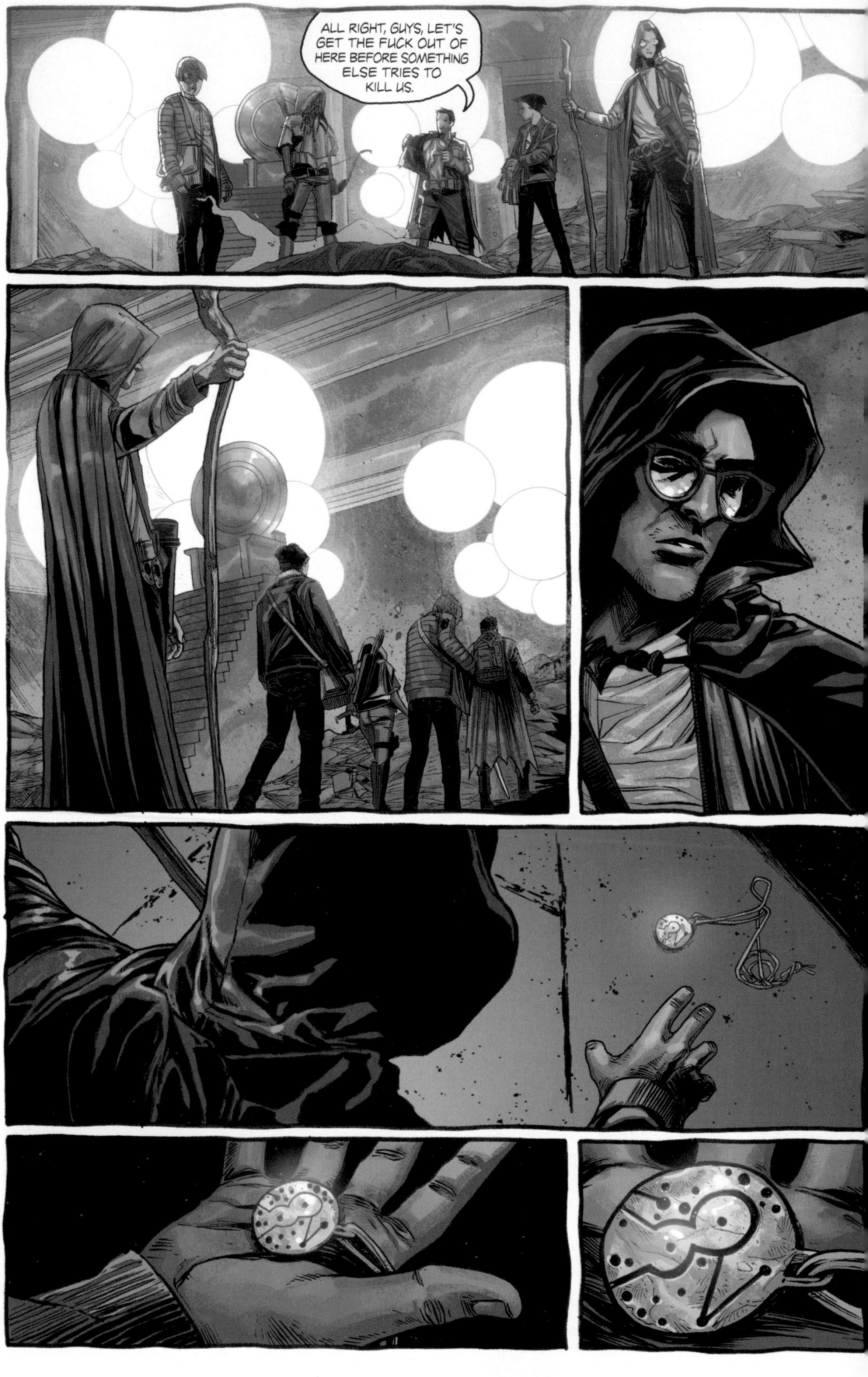
ALL RIGHT, GUYS, LET'S GET THE FUCK OUT OF HERE BEFORE SOMETHING ELSE TRIES TO KILL US.

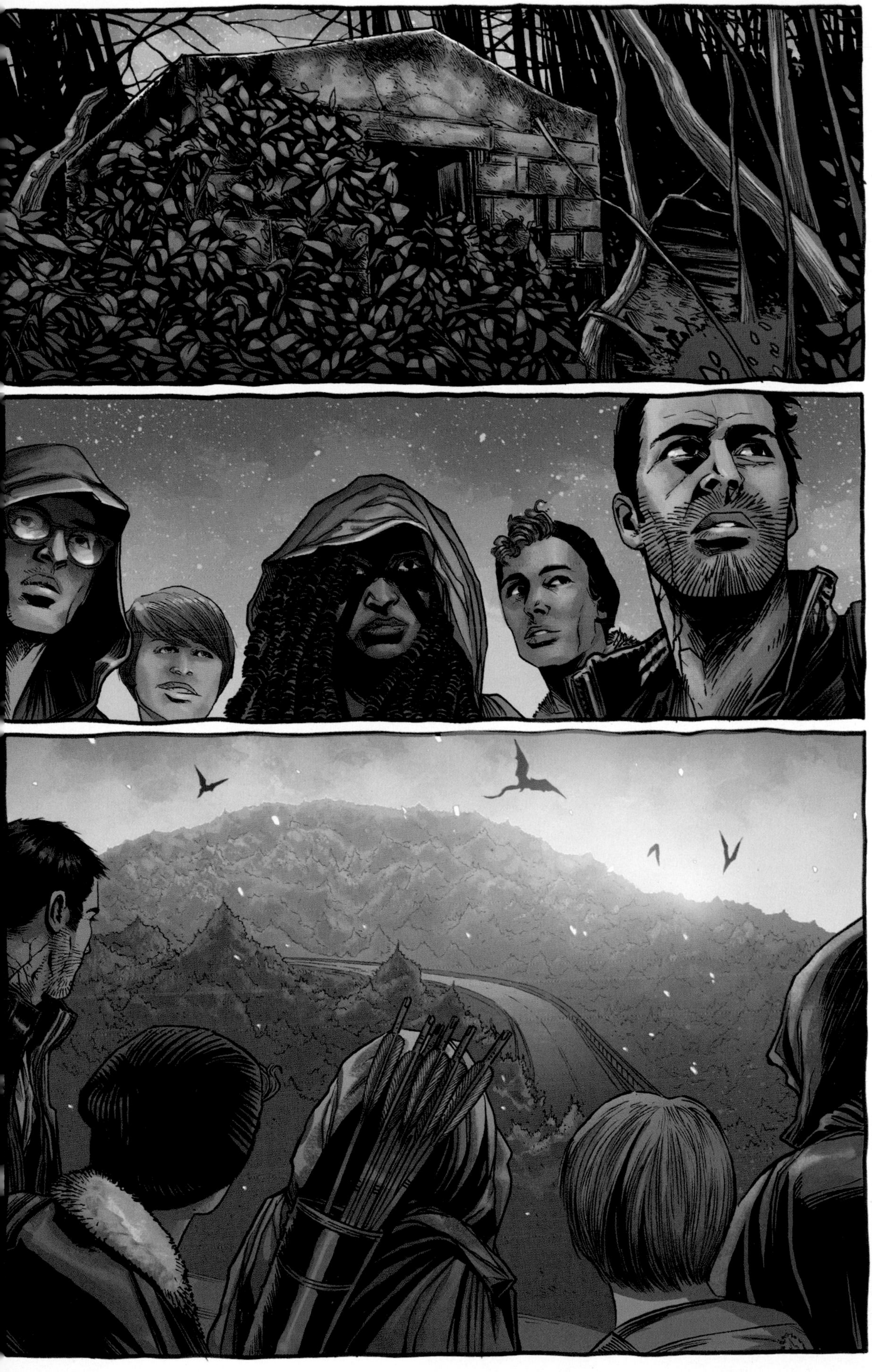

BONUS CONTENT

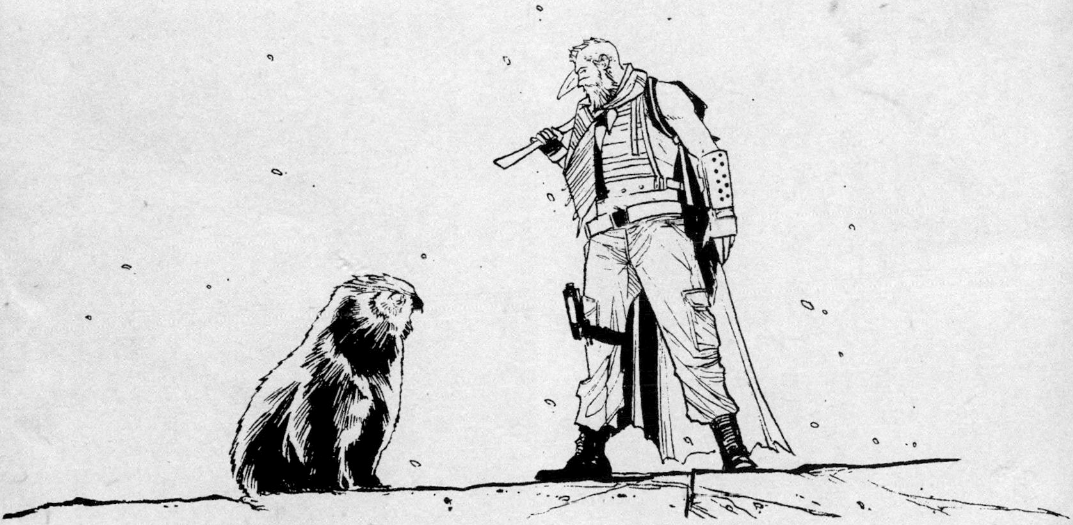

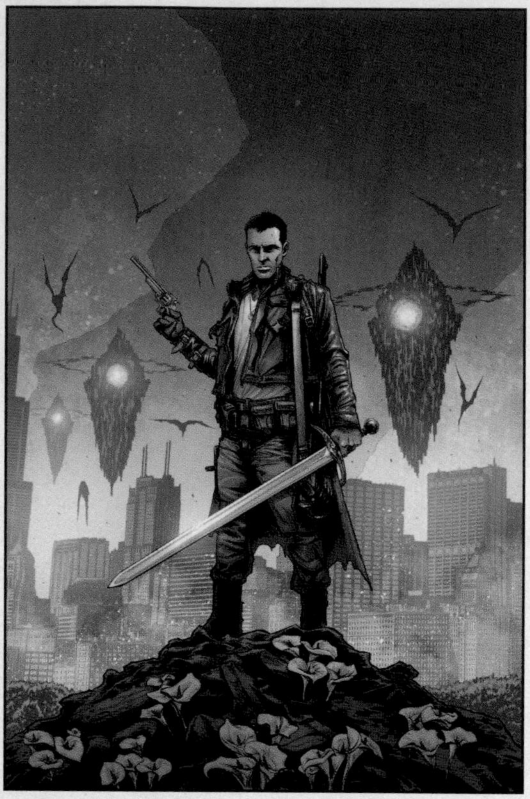

ISSUE 1 COVER A
JEREMY HAUN & NICK FILARDI

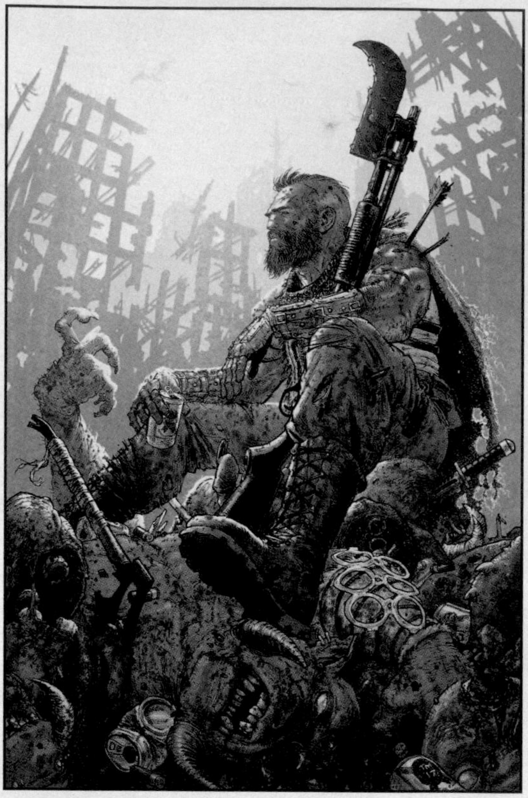

ISSUE 1 COVER B
TONY MOORE

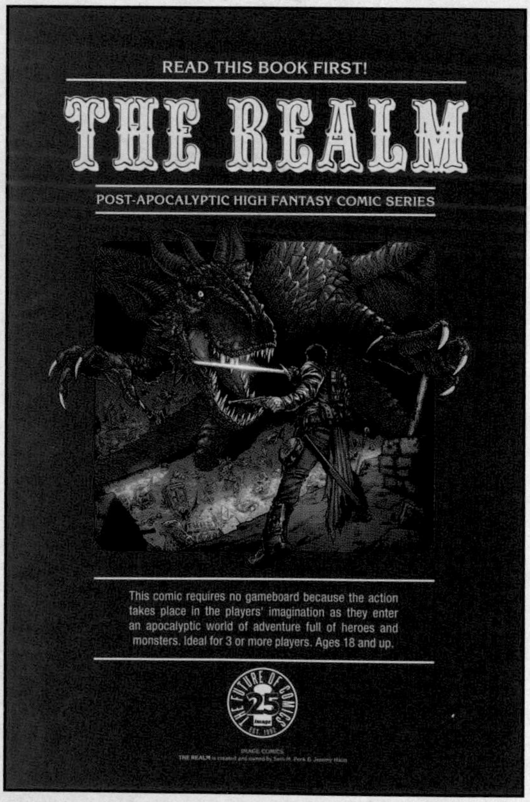
READ THIS BOOK FIRST!
THE REALM
POST-APOCALYPTIC HIGH FANTASY COMIC SERIES
This comic requires no gameboard because the action takes place in the players' imagination as they enter an apocalyptic world of adventure full of heroes and monsters. Ideal for 3 or more players. Ages 18 and up.
THE FUTURE OF COMICS 25 EST. 1992

ISSUE 1 *SECRET VARIANT*
JEREMY HAUN & NICK FILARDI
& THOMAS MAUER

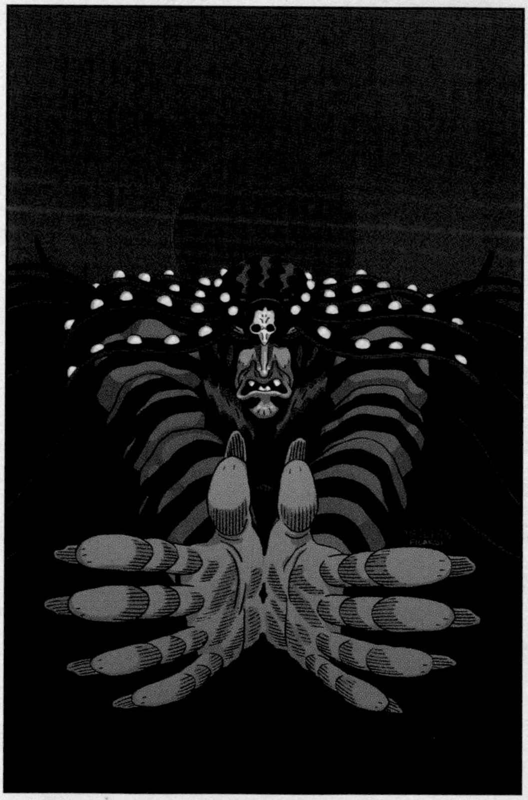

ISSUE 1 *NYCC 2017 EXCLUSIVE*
ANDREW MACLEAN
& NICK FILARDI

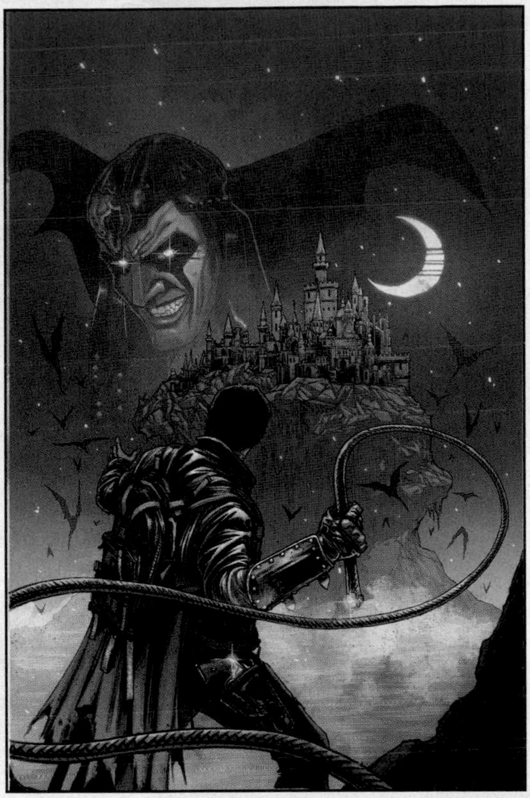

ISSUE 1 *STORE EXCLUSIVE*
HAUN & FILARDI & MAUER
COMIC QUEST

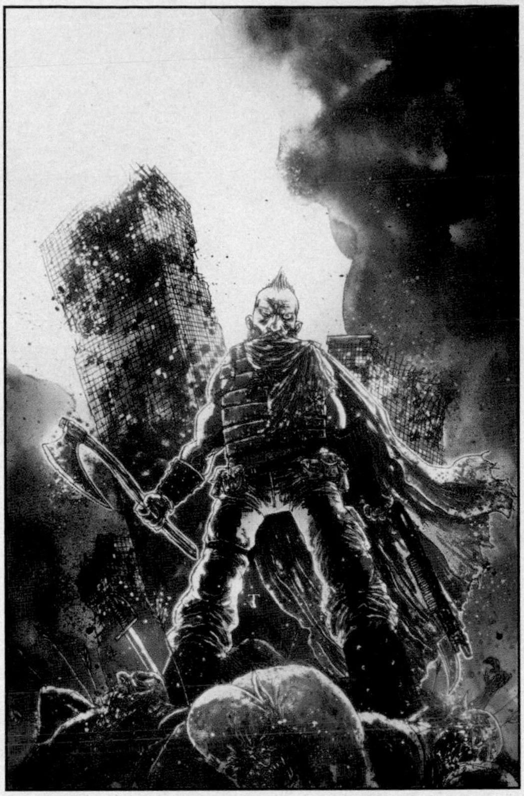

ISSUE 1 *STORE EXCLUSIVE*
BEN TEMPLESMITH
PULP NOUVEAUX COMIX

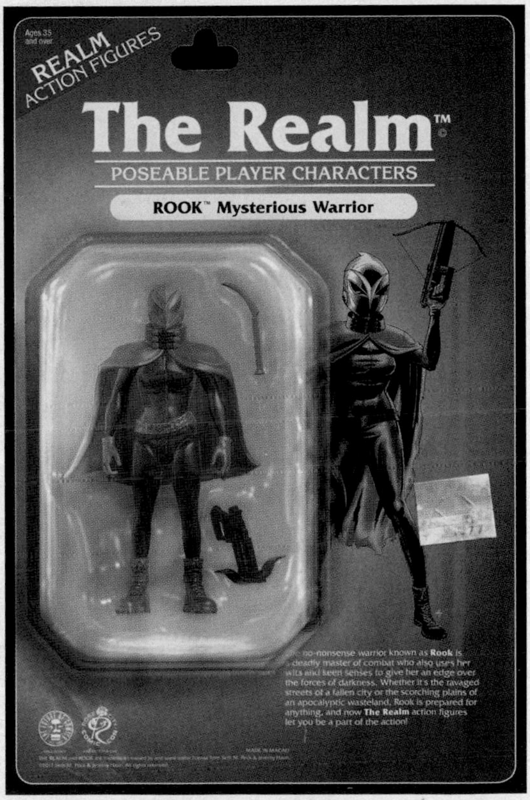
Ages 35 and over
REALM ACTION FIGURES
The Realm™ ©
POSEABLE PLAYER CHARACTERS
ROOK™ Mysterious Warrior
no-nonsense warrior known as Rook is
deadly master of combat who also uses her
wits and keen senses to give her an edge over
the forces of darkness. Whether it's the ravaged
streets of a fallen city or the scorching plains of
an apocalyptic wasteland, Rook is prepared for
anything, and now The Realm action figures
let you be a part of the action!
MADE IN MACAO

ISSUE 1 *RCCC 2017 EXCLUSIVE*
MICHAEL ADAMS & NICK FILARDI & THOMAS MAUER & SHANE WHITE

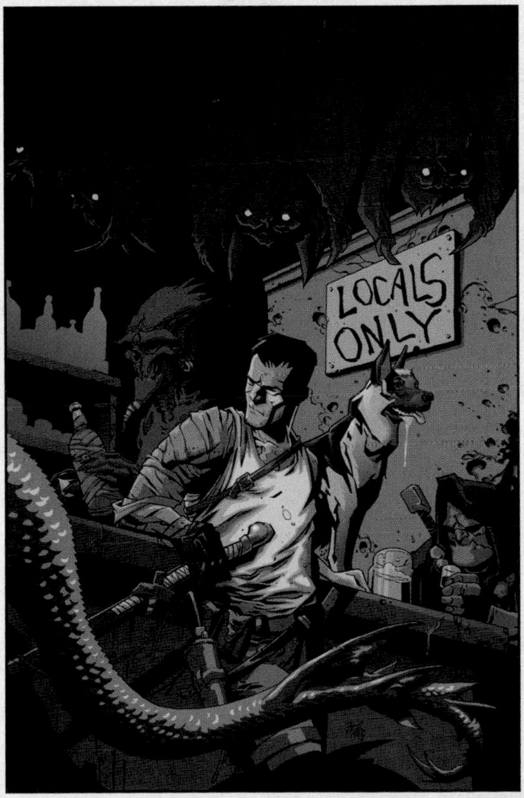
LOCALS ONLY

ISSUE 1 *HOMETOWN VARIANT*
PHIL HESTER & ANDE PARKS & MEGAN LEVENS

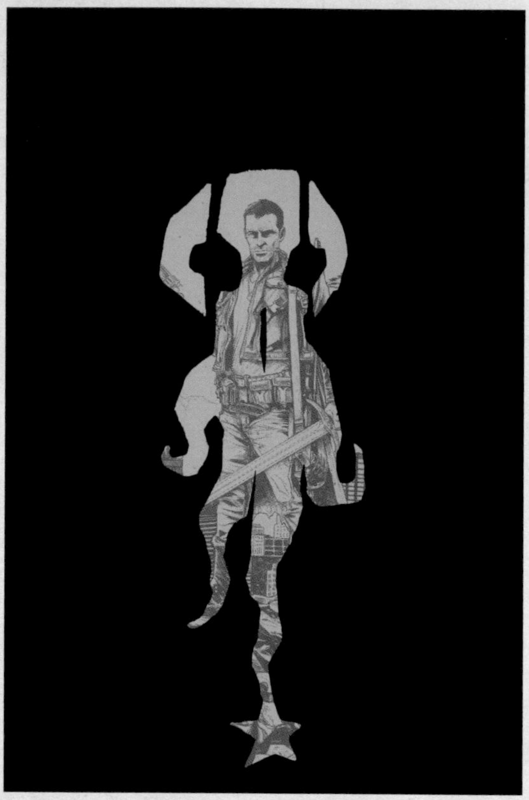

ISSUE 1 *TOUR 2017 VARIANT*
JEREMY HAUN & THOMAS MAUER

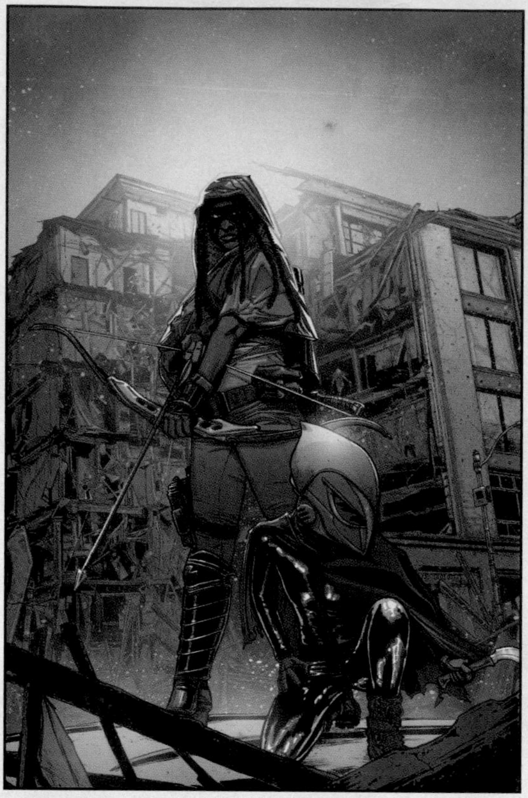

ISSUE 2 COVER A
JEREMY HAUN & NICK FILARDI

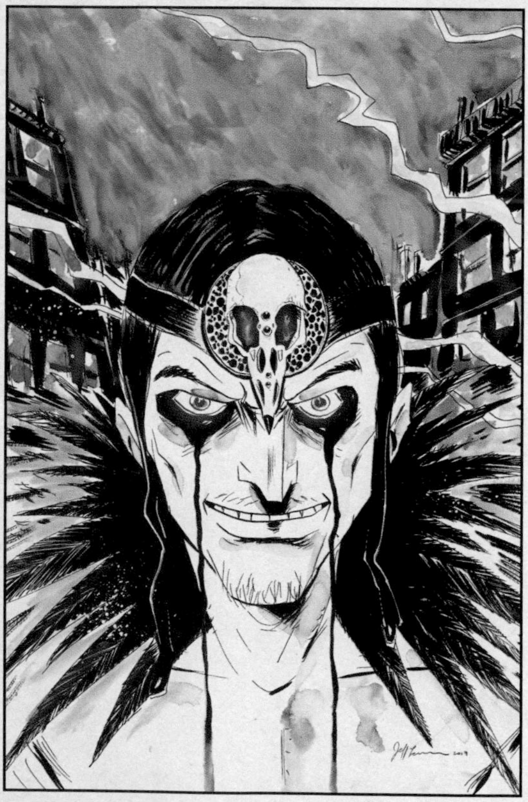

ISSUE 2 COVER B
JEFF LEMIRE

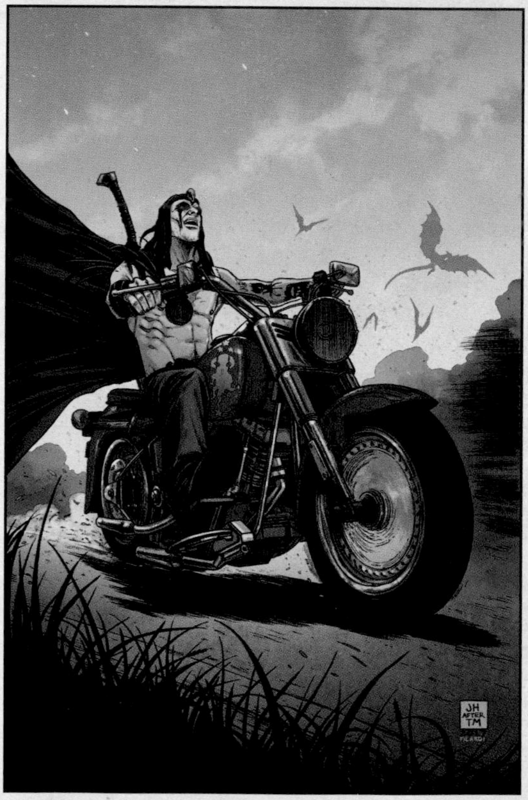
JH AFTER TM
FILARDI

ISSUE 2 *THE WALKING DEAD TRIBUTE*
JEREMY HAUN & NICK FILARDI

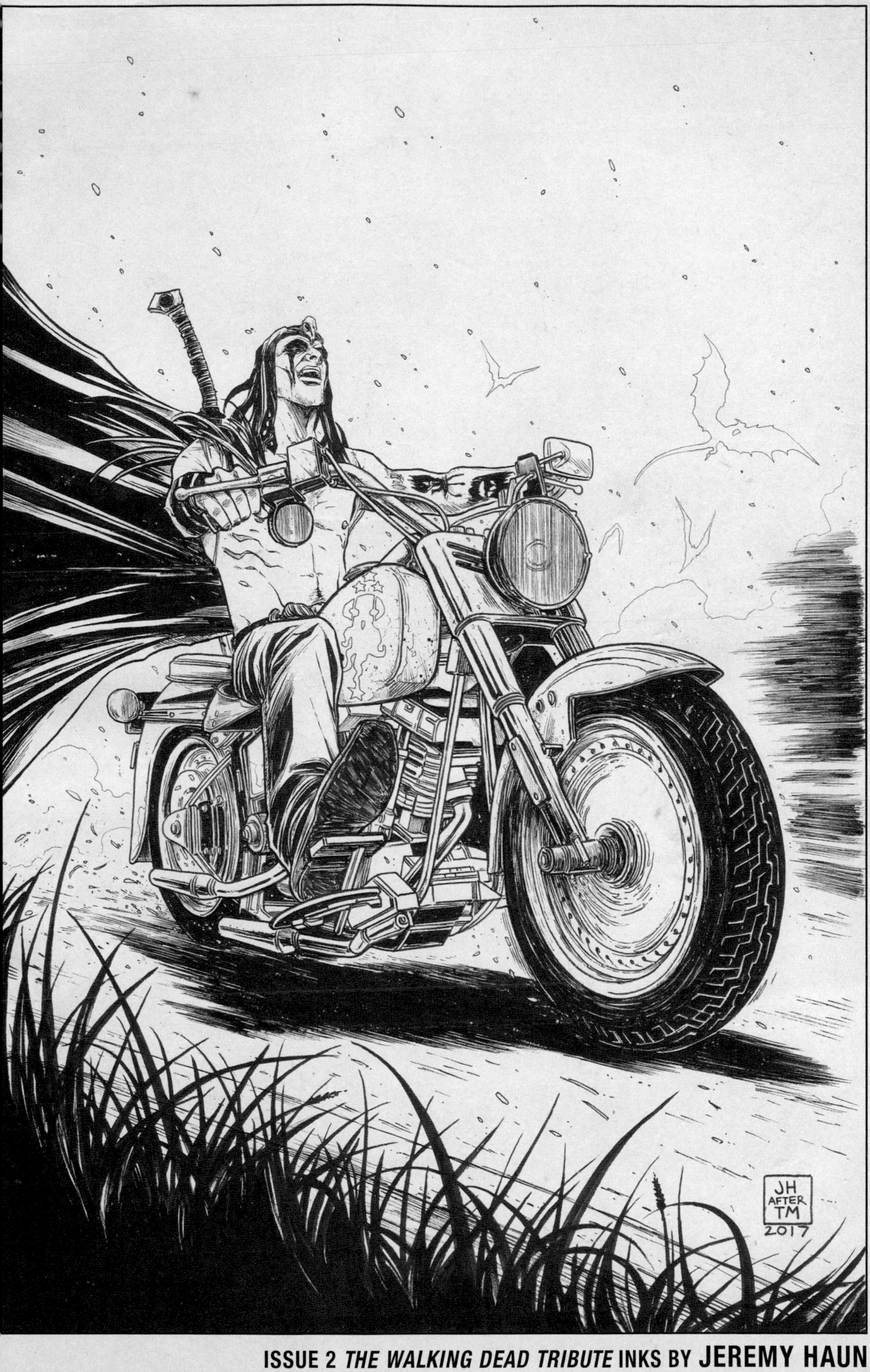
JH
AFTER
TM
2017

ISSUE 2 *THE WALKING DEAD TRIBUTE* INKS BY **JEREMY HAUN**

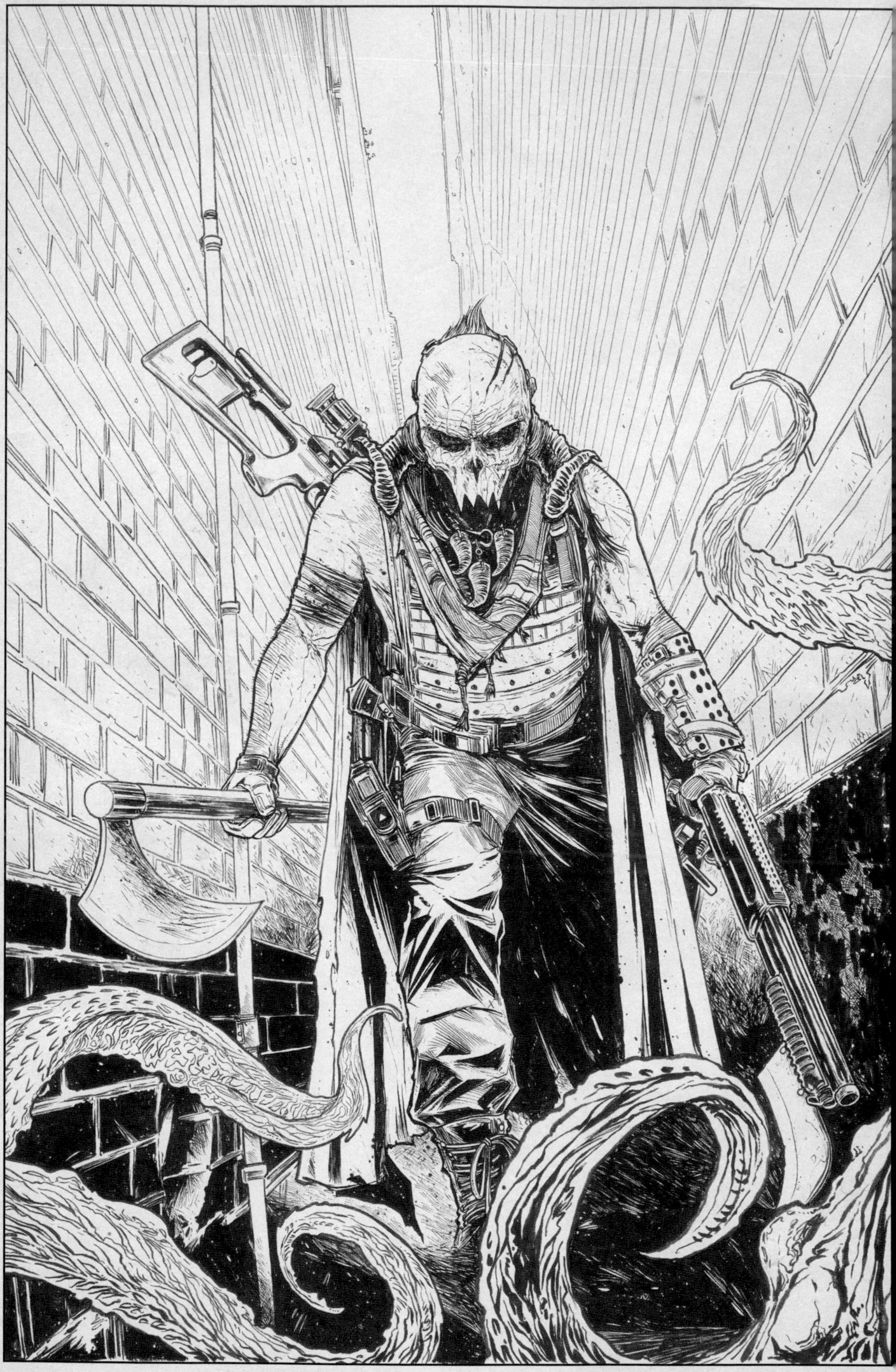

ISSUE 3 COVER INKS BY **JEREMY HAUN**

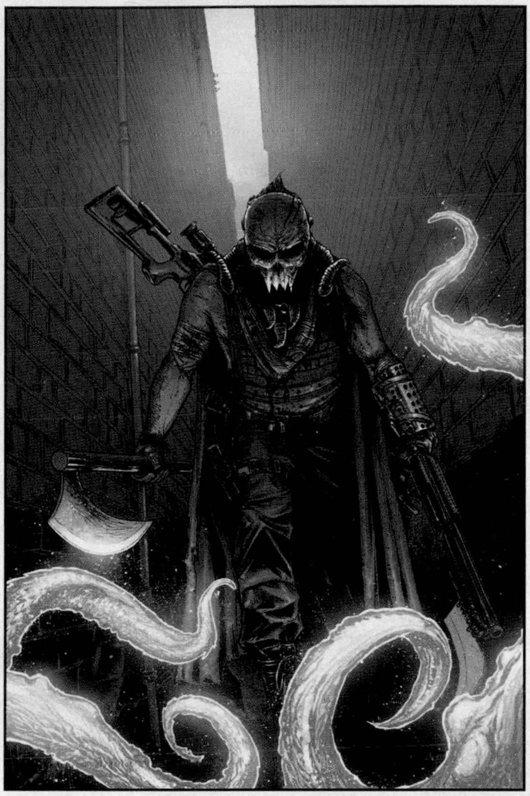

ISSUE 3 COVER A
JEREMY HAUN & NICK FILARDI

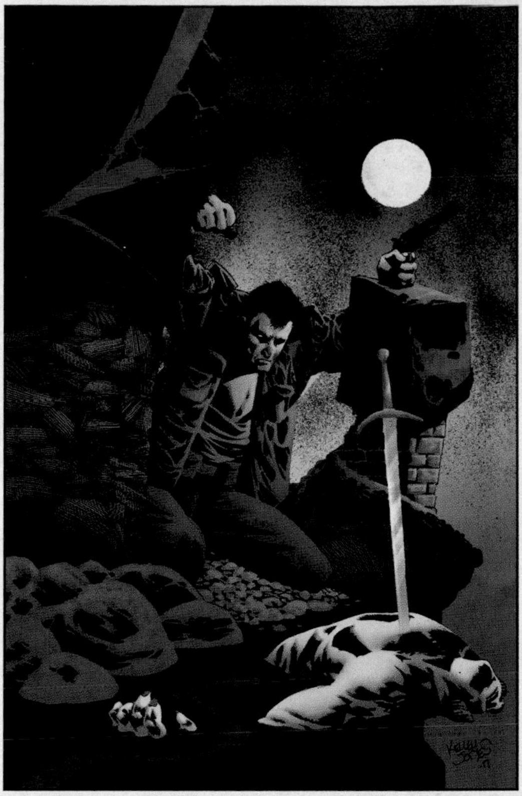

ISSUE 3 COVER B
KELLEY JONES & MICHELLE MADSEN

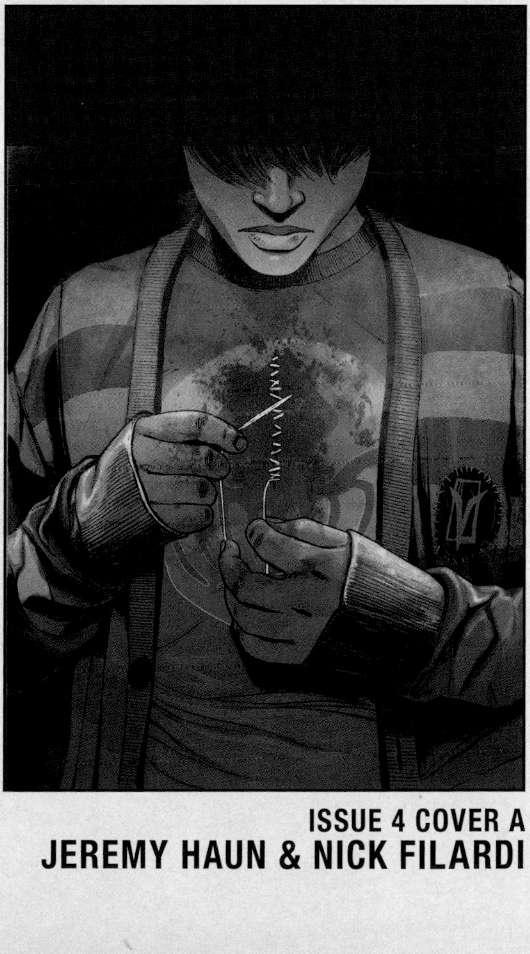

ISSUE 4 COVER A
JEREMY HAUN & NICK FILARDI

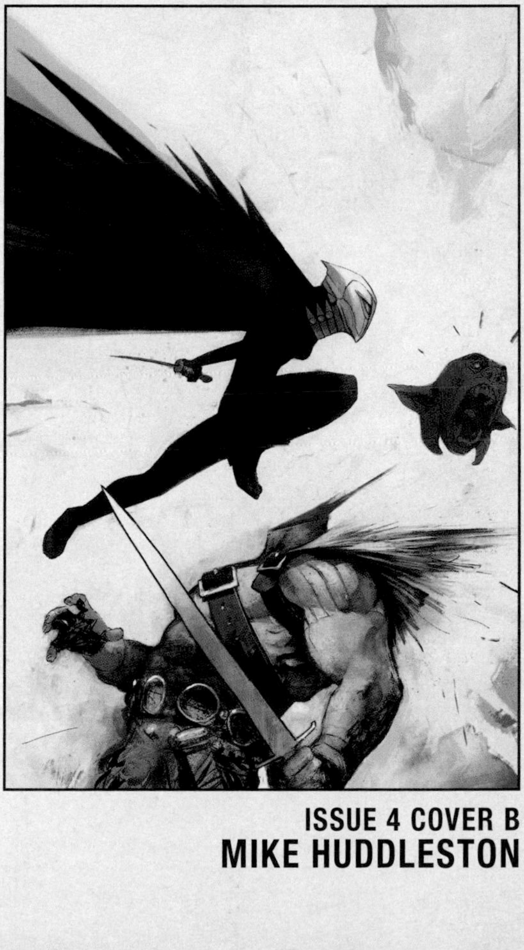

ISSUE 4 COVER B
MIKE HUDDLESTON

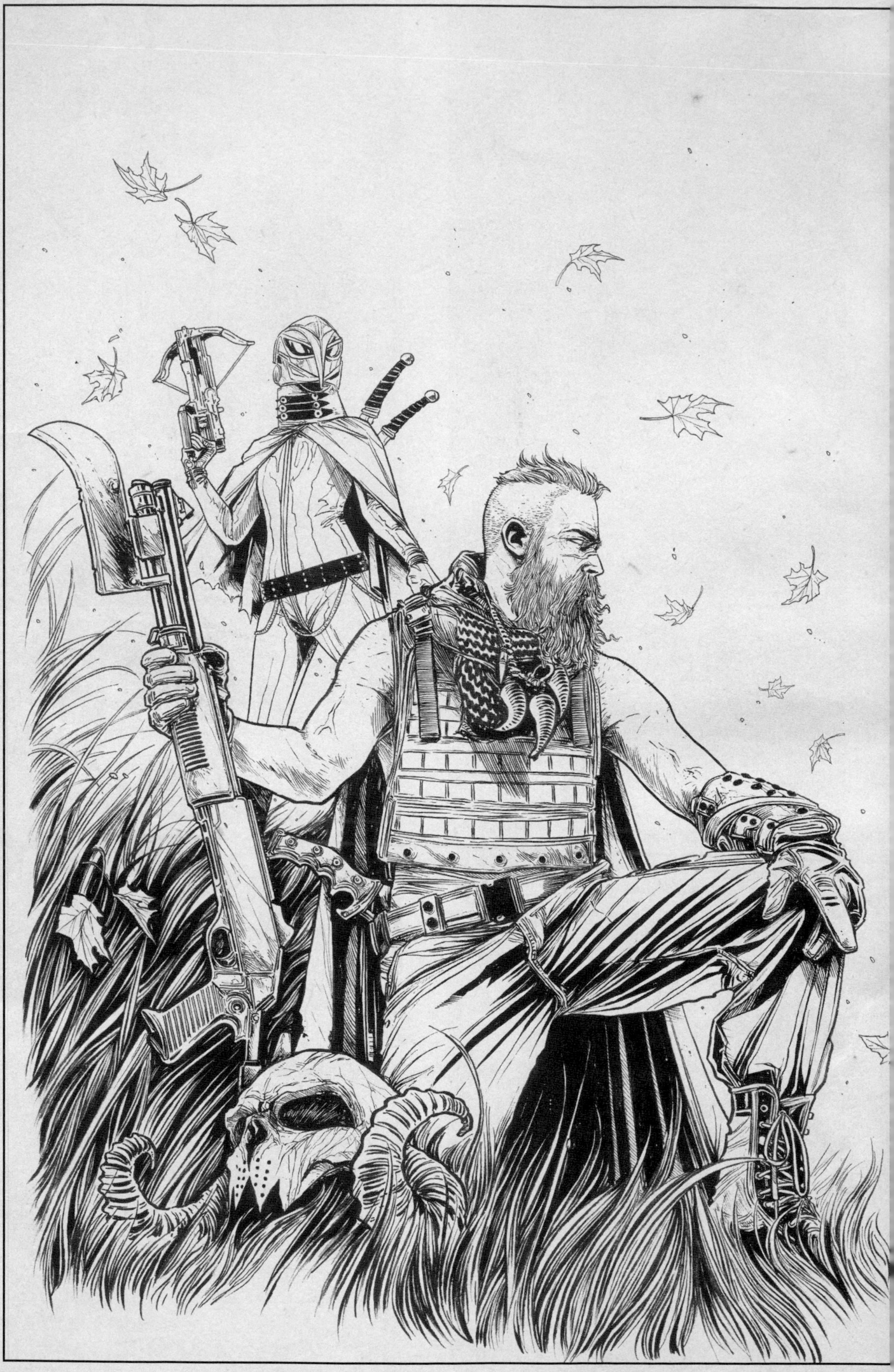

ISSUE 6 COVER INKS BY **JEREMY HAUN**

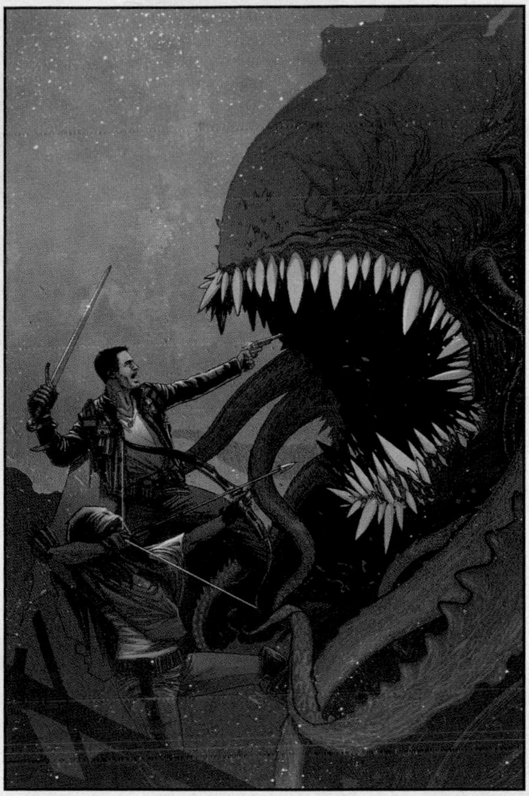

ISSUE 5 COVER A
JEREMY HAUN & NICK FILARDI

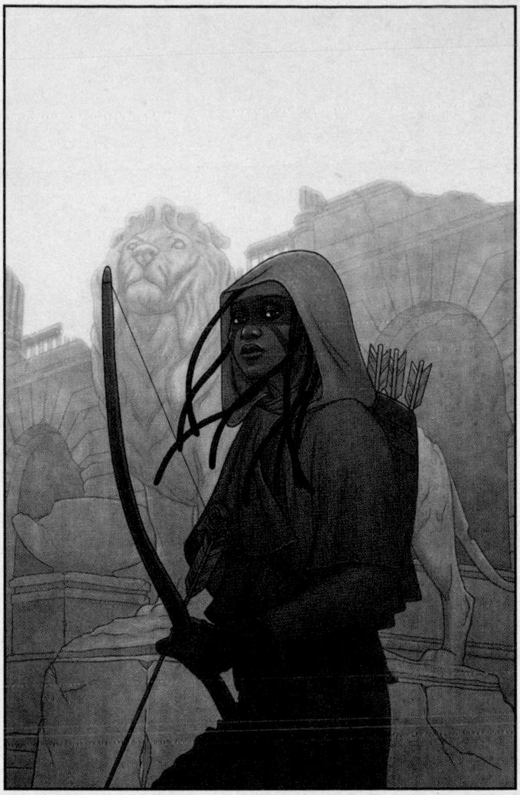

ISSUE 5 COVER B
JENNY FRISON

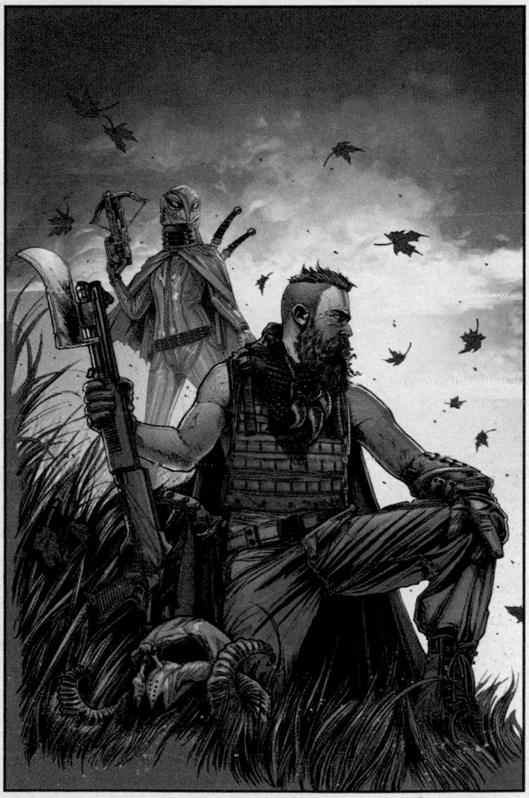

ISSUE 6 COVER A
JEREMY HAUN & NICK FILARDI

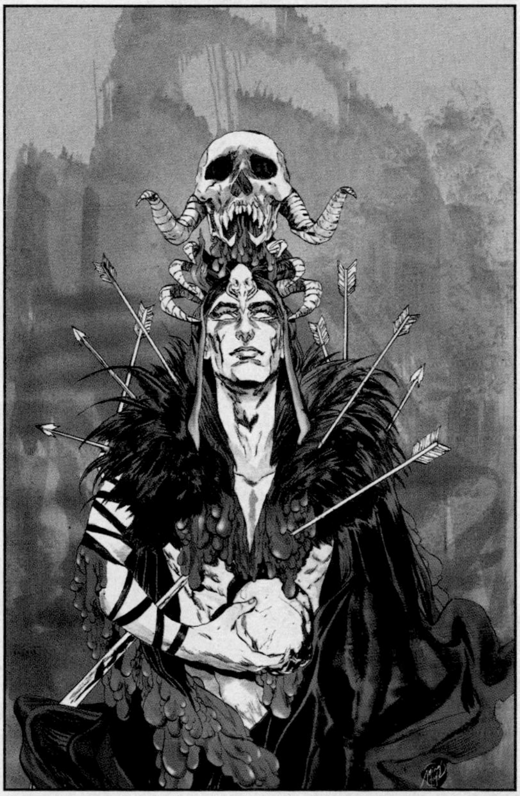

ISSUE 6 COVER B
MING DOYLE

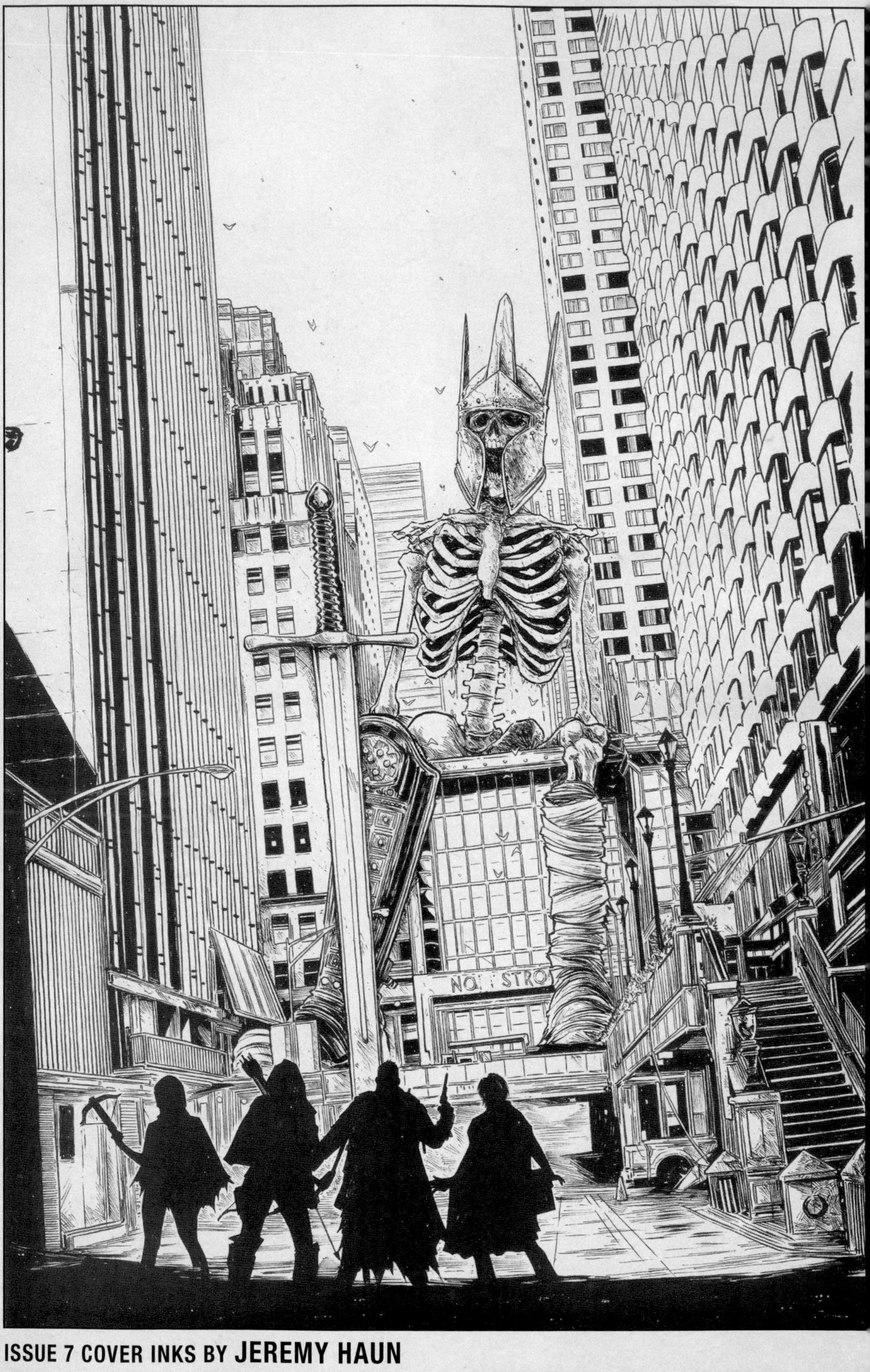
NO STRO
ISSUE 7 COVER INKS BY **JEREMY HAUN**

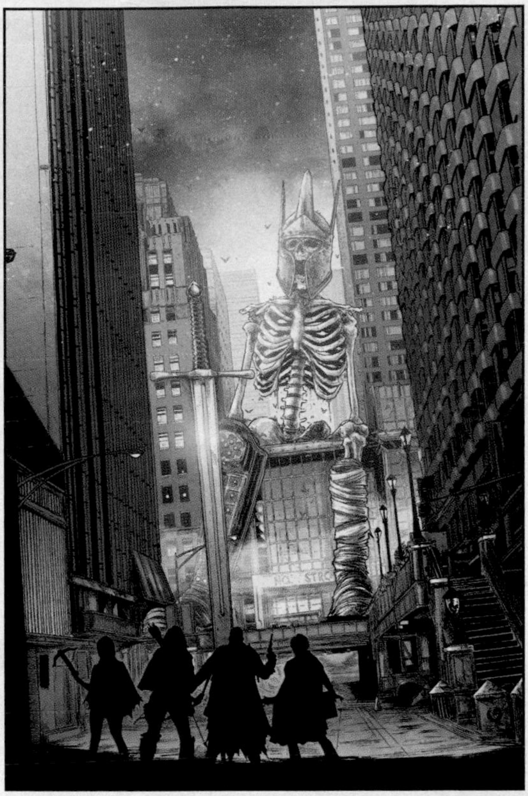

ISSUE 7 COVER A
JEREMY HAUN & NICK FILARDI

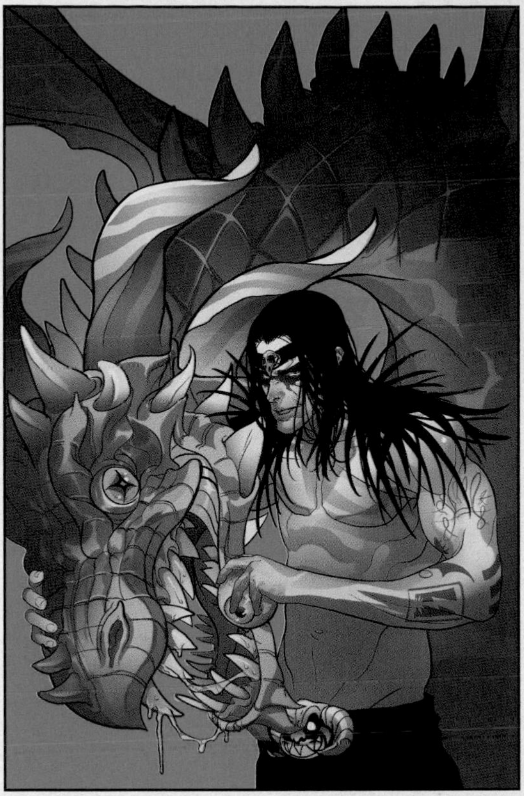

ISSUE 7 COVER B
BALDEMAR RIVAS

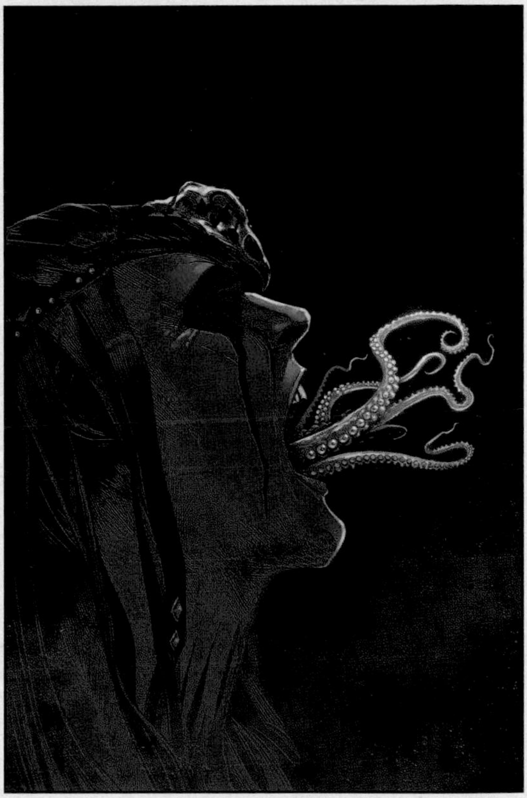

ISSUE 8 COVER A
JEREMY HAUN & NICK FILARDI

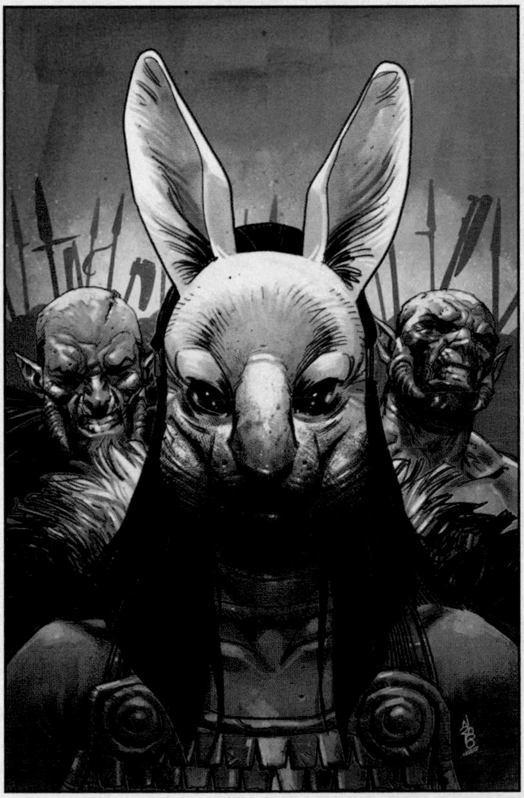

ISSUE 8 COVER B
NIC KLEIN

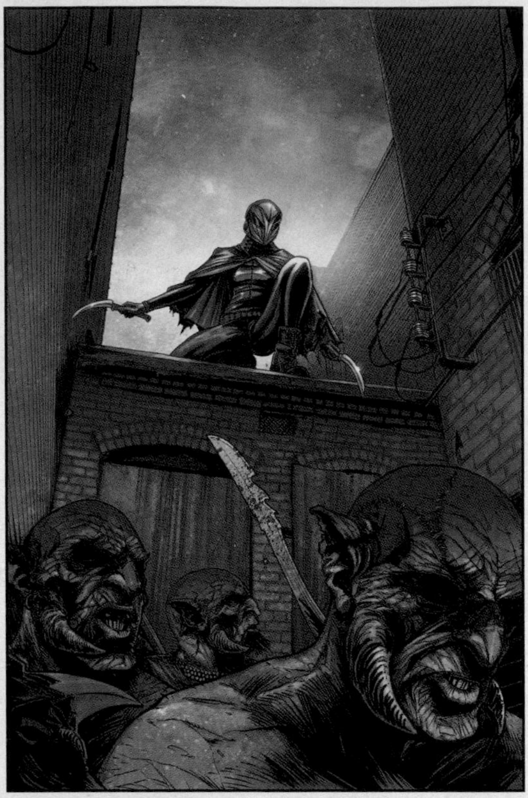

ISSUE 9 COVER A
JEREMY HAUN & NICK FILARDI

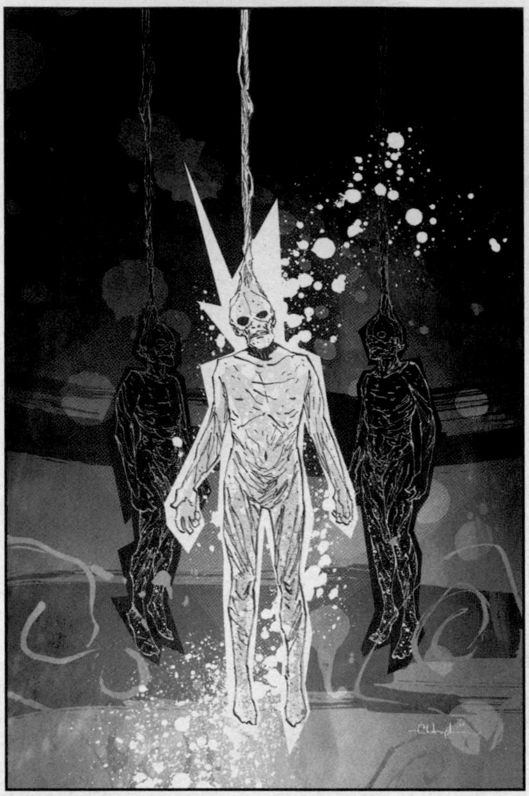

ISSUE 9 COVER B
CHRISTOPHER MITTEN

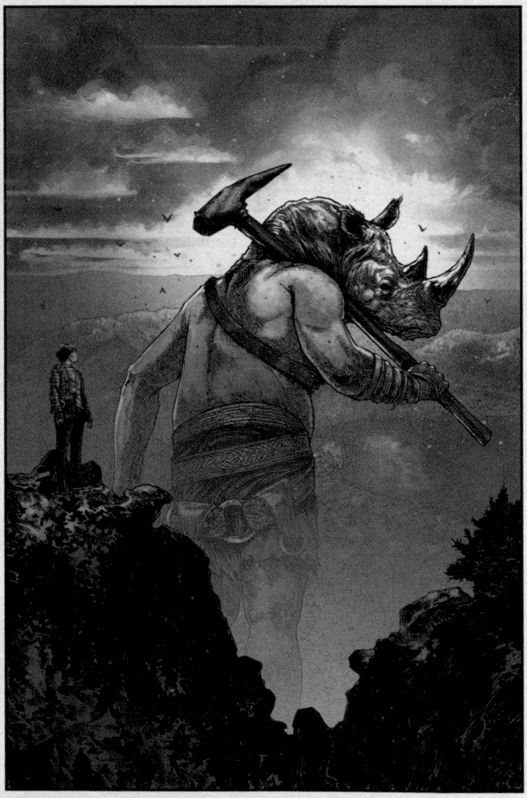

ISSUE 10 COVER A
JEREMY HAUN & NICK FILARDI

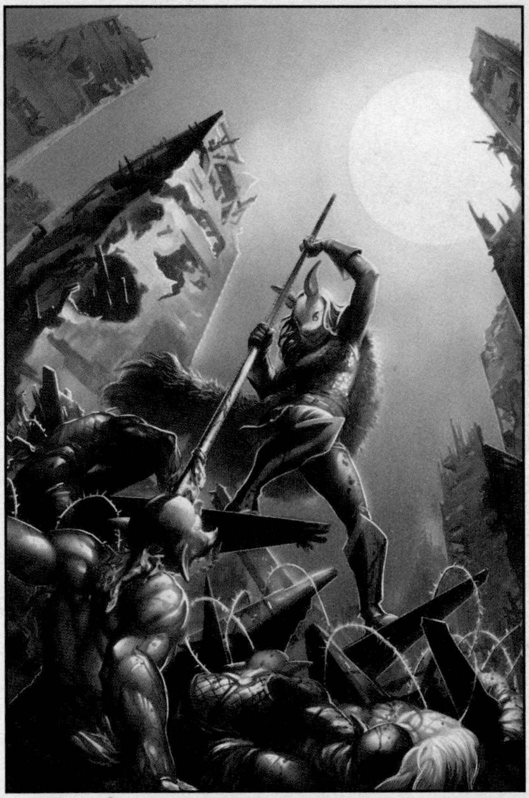

ISSUE 10 COVER B
MEGHAN HETRICK

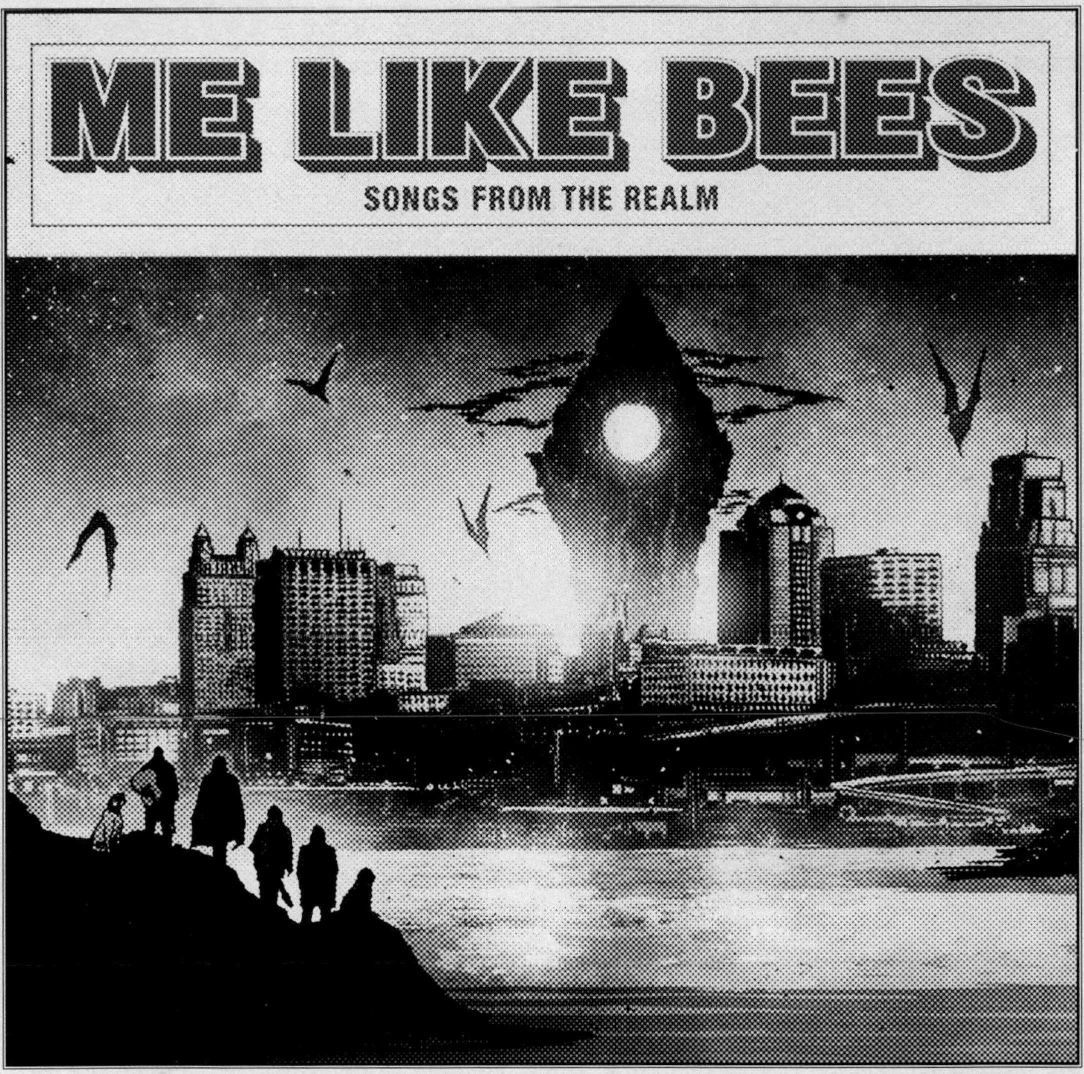
ME LIKE BEES
SONGS FROM THE REALM

NOTES ON YOUR GUIDES

SETH PECK was born in St. Louis and raised on a steady diet of books and hockey. He likes dogs more than people and plans to die on the moon.

JEREMY HAUN, co-writer, co-creator, and artist of THE REALM, has also worked on *Constantine* and *Batwoman* from DC. Over the past decade plus, along with wearing calluses on his fingers doing work for DC, Marvel, Image, and others, he has created and written several projects. Some you might know are the graphic novel *Narcoleptic Sunday, The Leading Man, Dino Day,* and THE BEAUTY. He is a part of the Bad Karma Creative group, whose *Bad Karma Volume One* debuted at NYCC 2013, thanks to Kickstarter funding.

Jeremy resides in a crumbling mansion in Joplin, Missouri, with his wife and two superheroes-in-training.

NICK FILARDI has colored for just about every major comic book publisher including DC, Marvel, Oni Press, and Dark Horse. He's currently also coloring covers for THE BEAUTY. When he isn't buried in pages, you can find his digital likeness pulling up other colorists with tips and tricks at twitch.tv/nickfil, making dad jokes at twitter.com/nickfil, and just spreading dope art at instagram.com/nick_filardi. He lives in Florida with his 3-legged dog and fiancée.

THOMAS MAUER has lent his lettering and design talent to numerous critically acclaimed and award-winning projects. Among his recent work are COPPERHEAD, CRUDE, ELSEWHERE, and THE BEAUTY, as well as *Dead Kings, Lark's Killer,* and the World Food Programme's *Living Level-3* educational comics.

JOEL ENOS is a writer and editor of comics and stories and is currently editing the series THE REALM, THE BEAUTY, and REGRESSION, all three published by Image Comics.

NEW TOURS AVAILABLE SOON.